BEAST

OF THE HEARTLAND

AND OTHER STORIES

BY

LUCIUS SHEPARD

FOUR WALLS EIGHT WINDOWS

NEW YORK

© 1997, 1999 LUCIUS SHEPARD

PUBLISHED IN THE UNITED STATES BY:

FOUR WALLS EIGHT WINDOWS
39 WEST 14TH STREET, ROOM 503
NEW YORK, N.Y., 10011

VISIT OUR WEBSITE AT
HTTP://WWW.FOURWALLSEIGHTWINDOWS.COM

FIRST U.S. PRINTING MARCH 1999.

LIBRARY OF CONGRESS
CATALOGING-IN-PUBLICATION DATA:

SHEPARD, LUCIUS.
(BARNACLE BILL THE SPACER AND OTHER STORIES)
BEAST OF THE HEARTLAND AND OTHER STORIES/
BY LUCIUS SHEPARD.
P. CM.
ISBN 1-56858-126-2
I. SCIENCE FICTION, AMERICAN. I. TITLE.
PS3569.H3939B3   1999
813´.54--DC21   99-12109
CIP

10 9 8 7 6 5 4 3 2 1

PRINTED IN CANADA

CONTENTS

Barnacle Bill The Spacer   1

A Little Night Music   79

Human History   95

Sports in America   179

The Sun Spider   205

All the Perfumes of Araby   239

Beast of the Heartland   265

BARNACLE BILL THE SPACER

The way things happen, not the great movements of time but the ordinary things that make us what we are, the savage accidents of our births, the simple lusts that because of whimsy or a challenge to one's pride become transformed into complex tragedies of love, the heartless operations of change, the wild sweetness of other souls that intersect the orbits of our lives, travel along the same course for a while, then angle off into oblivion, leaving no formal shape for us to consider, no easily comprehensible pattern from which we may derive enlightenment . . . I often wonder why it is when stories are contrived from such materials as these, the storyteller is generally persuaded to perfume the raw stink of life, to replace bloody loss with talk of noble sacrifice, to reduce the grievous to the wistfully sad. Most people, I suppose, want their truth served with a side of sentiment; the perilous uncertainty of the world dismays them, and they wish to avoid being brought hard against it. Yet by this act of avoidance they neglect the profound sadness that can arise from a contemplation of the human spirit *in extremis* and blind themselves to beauty. That beauty, I mean, which is the iron of our existence. The beauty that enters through a wound, that whispers a black word in our ears at funerals, a word that causes us to shrug off our griever's weakness and say, No more, never again. The beauty that inspires anger, not regret, and provokes struggle, not the idle aesthetic of a beholder. That, to my mind, lies at the core of the only stories worth telling. And that is the fundamental purpose of the storyteller's art, to illumine such beauty, to declare its central importance and make it shine forth from the inevitable wreckage of our hopes and the sorry matter of our decline.

1

This, then, is the most beautiful story I know.

It all happened not so along ago on Solitaire Station, out beyond the orbit of Mars, where the lightships are assembled and launched, vanishing in thousand-mile-long shatterings, and it happened to a man by the name of William Stamey, otherwise known as Barnacle Bill.

Wait now, many of you are saying, I've heard that story. It's been told and retold and told again. What use could there be in repeating it?

But what have you heard, really?

That Bill was a sweet, balmy lad, I would imagine. That he was a carefree sort with a special golden spark of the Creator in his breast and the fey look of the hereafter in his eye, a friend to all who knew him. That he was touched not retarded, moon-struck and not sick at heart, ill-fated rather than violated, tormented, sinned against.

If that's the case, then you would do well to give a listen, for there were both man and boy in Bill, neither of them in the least carefree, and the things he did and how he did them are ultimately of less consequence than why he was so moved and how this reflects upon the spiritual paucity and desperation of our age.

Of all that, I would suspect, you have heard next to nothing.

Bill was thirty-two years old at the time of my story, a shambling, sour-smelling unkempt fellow with a receding hairline and a daft, moony face whose features – weak-looking blue eyes and Cupid's bow mouth and snub nose – were much too small for it, leaving the better part of a vast round area unexploited. His hands were always dirty, his station jumpsuit mapped with stains, and he was rarely without a little cloth bag in which he carried, among other items, a trove of candy and pornographic VR crystals. It was his taste for candy and pornography that frequently brought us together – the woman with whom I lived, Arlie Quires, operated the commissary outlet where Bill would go to replenish his supplies, and on occasion, when my duties with Security Section permitted, I would help Arlie out at the counter. Whenever Bill came in he would prefer to have me wait on him; he was, you understand, intimidated by everyone he encountered, but by pretty women most of all. And Arlie, lithe and brown and clever of feature, was not only pretty but had a sharp mouth that put him off even more.

There was one instance in particular that should both serve to illustrate Bill's basic circumstance and provide a background for all that later transpired. It happened one day about six months before the return of the lightship *Perseverance*. The shift had just changed over on the assembly platforms, and the commissary bar was filled with workers. Arlie had run off somewhere, leaving me in charge, and from my vantage behind the counter, located in an ante-room whose walls were covered by a holographic photomural of a blue-sky day in the now-defunct Alaskan wilderness, and furnished with metal tables and chairs, all empty at that juncture, I could see coloured lights playing back and forth within the bar, and hear the insistent rhythms of a pulse group. Bill, as was his habit, peeked in from the corridor to make sure none of his enemies were about, then shuffled on in, glancing left and right, ducking his head, hunching his shoulders, the very image of a guilty party. He shoved his money-maker at me, three green telltales winking on the slim metal cylinder, signifying the amount of credit he was releasing to the commissary, and demanded in that grating, adenoidal voice of his that I give him 'new stuff', meaning by this new VR crystals.

'I've nothing new for you,' I told him.

'A ship came in.' He gave me a look of fierce suspicion. 'I saw it. I was outside, and I saw it!'

Arile and I had been quarrelling that morning, a petty difference concerning whose turn it was to use the priority lines to speak with relatives in London that had subsequently built into a major battle; I was in no mood for this sort of exchange. 'Don't be an ass,' I said. 'You know they won't have unloaded the cargo yet.'

His suspicious look flickered, but did not fade. 'They unloaded already,' he said. 'Sleds were going back and forth.' His eyes went a bit dreamy and his head wobbled, as if he were imagining himself back out on the skin of the station, watching the sleds drifting in and out of the cargo bays; but he was, I realized, fixed upon a section of the holographic mural in which a brown bear had just ambled out of the woods and was sniffing

3

about a pile of branches and sapling trunks at the edge of a stream that might have been a beaver dam. Though he had never seen a real one, the notion of animals fascinated Bill, and when unable to think of anything salient to say, he would recite facts about giraffes and elephants, kangaroos and whales, and beasts even more exotic, all now receded into legend.

'Bloody hell!' I said. 'Even if they've unloaded, with processing and inventory, it'll be a week or more before we see anything from it. If you want something, give me a specific order. Don't just stroll in here and say' – I tried to imitate his delivery – ' "Gimme some new stuff." '

Two men and a woman stepped in from the corridor as I was speaking; they fell into line, keeping a good distance between themselves and Bill, and on hearing me berating him, they established eye contact with me, letting me know by their complicitors' grins that they supported my harsh response. That made me ashamed of having yelled at him.

'Look here,' I said, knowing that he would never be able to manage the specific. 'Shall I pick you out something? I can probably find one or two you haven't done.'

He hung his great head and nodded, bulled into submissiveness. I could tell by his body language that he wanted to turn and see whether the people behind him had witnessed his humiliation, but he could not bring himself to do so. He twitched and quivered as if their stares were pricking him, and his hands gripped the edge of the counter, fingers kneading the slick surface.

By the time I returned from the stockroom several more people had filtered in from the corridor, and half a dozen men and women were lounging about the entrance to the bar, laughing and talking, among them Braulio Menzies, perhaps the most dedicated of Bill's tormentors, a big, balding, sallow man with sleek black hair and thick shoulders and immense forearms and a Mephistophelean salt-and-pepper goatee that lent his generous features a thoroughly menacing aspect. He had left seven children, a wife and a mother behind in São Paolo to take a position as foreman in charge of a metalworkers' unit, and the better part of his wages were sent directly to his family, leaving him little to spend on entertainment; if he was drinking, and it

4

was apparent he had been, I could think of nothing that would have moved him to this end other than news from home. As he did not look to be in a cheerful mood, chances were the news had not been good.

Hostility was thick as cheap perfume in the room. Bill was still standing with his head hung down, hands gripping the counter, but he was no longer passively maintaining that attitude – he had gone rigid, his neck was corded, his fingers squeezed the plastic, recognizing himself to be the target of every disparaging whisper and snide laugh. He seemed about to explode, he was so tightly held. Braulio stared at him with undisguised loathing, and as I set Bill's goods down on the counter, the skinny blonde girl who was clinging to Braulio's arm sang, 'He can't get no woman, least not one that's human, he's Barnacle Bill the Spacer.'

There was a general outburst of laughter, and Bill's face grew flushed; an ugly, broken noise issued from his throat. The girl, her smallish breasts half-spilling out from a skimpy dress of bright blue plastic, began to sing more of her cruel song.

'Oh, that's brilliant, that is!' I said. 'The creative mind never ceases to amaze!' But my sarcasm had no effect upon her.

I pushed three VR crystals and a double handful of hard candy, Bill's favourite, across to him. 'There you are,' I said, doing my best to speak in a kindly tone, yet at the same time hoping to convey the urgency of the situation. 'Don't be hanging about, now.'

He gave a start. His eyelids fluttered open, and he lifted his gaze to meet mine. Anger crept into his expression, hardening the simple terrain of his face. He needed anger, I suppose, to maintain some fleeting sense of dignity, to hide from the terror growing inside him, and there was no one else whom he dared confront.

'No!' he said, swatting at the candy, scattering much of it on to the floor. 'You cheated! I want more!'

'Gon' mek you a pathway, boog man!' said a gangly black man, leaning in over Bill's shoulder. 'Den you best travel!' Others echoed him, and one gave Bill a push toward the corridor.

Bill's eyes were locked on mine. 'You cheated me, you give me some more! You owe me more!'

'Right!' I said, my temper fraying. 'I'm a thoroughly dishonest human being. I live to swindle gits like yourself.' I added a few pieces of candy to his pile and made to shoo him away. Braulio came forward, swaying, his eyes none too clear.

'Let the son'beetch stay, man,' he said, his voice burred with rage. 'I wan' talk to heem.'

I came out from behind the counter and took a stand between Braulio and Bill. My actions were not due to any affection for Bill – though I did not wish him ill, neither did I wish him well; I suppose, I perceived him as less a person than an unwholesome problem. In part, I was still motivated by the residue of anger from my argument with Arlie, and of course it was my duty as an officer in the Security Section to maintain order. But I think the actual reason I came to his defence was that I was bored. We were all of us bored on Solitaire. Bored and bad-tempered and despairing, afflicted with the sort of feverish malaise that springs from a sense of futility.

'That's it,' I said wearily to Braulio. 'That's enough from all of you. Bugger off.'

'I don't wan' hort you, John,' said Braulio, weaving a bit as he tried to focus on me. 'Joos' you step aside.'

A couple of his co-workers came to stand beside him. Jammers with silver nubs protruding from their crewcut scalps, the tips of receivers that channelled radio waves, solar energy, any type of signal, into their various brain centres, producing a euphoric kinaesthesia. I had a philosophical bias against jamming, no doubt partially the result of some vestigial Christian reflex. The sight of them refined my annoyance.

'You poor sods are tuned to a dark channel,' I said. 'No saved by the bell. Not today. No happy endings.'

The jammers smiled at one another. God only knows what insane jangle was responsible for their sense of well-being. I smiled, too. Then I kicked the nearer one in the head, aiming at but missing his silver stub; I did for his friend with a smartly delivered backfist. They lay motionless, their smiles still in place. Perhaps, I thought, the jamming had turned the beating into a stroll through the park. Braulio faded a step and adopted a defensive posture. The onlookers edged away. The throb of music from the bar seemed to be giving a readout of the tension in the room.

There remained a need in me for violent release, but I was not eager to mix it with Braulio; even drunk, he would be formidable, and in any case, no matter how compelling my urge to do injury, I was required by duty to make a show of restraint.

'Violence,' I said, affecting a comical lower-class accent, hoping to defuse the situation. 'The wine of the fucking underclass. It's like me father used to say, son, 'e'd say, when you're bereft of reason and the wife's sucked up all the cooking sherry, just amble on down to the pub and have a piss in somebody's face. There's nothing so sweetly logical as an elbow to the throat, no argument so poignant as that made by grinding somebody's teeth beneath your heel. The very cracking of bones is in itself a philosophical language. And when you've captioned someone's beezer with a nice scar, it provides them a pleasant 'omily to read each time they look in the mirror. Aristotle, Plato, Einstein. All the great minds got their start brawling in the pubs. Groin punches. Elbows to the throat. These are often a first step toward the expression of the most subtle mathematical concepts. It's a fantastic intellectual experience we're embarking upon 'ere, and I for one, ladies and gents, am exhilarated by the challenge.'

Among the onlookers there was a general slackening of expression and a few titters. Braulio, however, remained focused, his eyes pinned on Bill.

'This is ridiculous,' I said to him. 'Come on, friend. Do me the favour and shut it down.'

He shook his head, slowly, awkwardly, like a bear bothered by a bee.

'What's the point of it all, man?' I nodded at Bill. 'He only wants to vanish. Why don't you let him?'

The blonde girl shrilled, 'Way you huffin' this bombo's shit, you two gotta be flatbackin', man!'

'I didn't catch your name, darling,' I said. 'Tarantula, was it? You'd do well to feed her more often, Braulio. Couple of extra flies a day ought to make her more docile.'

I ignored her curses, watching Braulio's shoulders; when the right one dropped a fraction, I tried a round kick; but he ducked under it and rolled away, coming up into the fluid, swaying stance of a *capoeirista*. We circled one another, looking for an opening. The crowd cleared a space around us. Then someone – Bill, I think – brushed against me. Braulio started what appeared to be a cartwheel, but as he braced on one hand at the mid-point of the move, his long left leg whipped out and caught me a glancing blow on the temple. Dazed, I reeled backward, took a harder blow on the side of my neck and slammed into the counter. If he had been sober, that would have done for me; but he was slow to follow, and as he moved in, I kicked him in the liver. He doubled over, and I drove a knee into his face, then swept his legs from under him. He fell heavily, and I was on him, no longer using my techniques, but punching in a frenzy like a streetfighter, venting all my ulcerated emotions. Some-body was clawing at my neck, my face. The blonde girl. She was screaming, sobbing, saying, 'No, no, stop it, you're killin' him.' Then somebody else grabbed me from behind, pinned my arms, and I saw what I had wrought. Braulio's cheekbone was crushed, one eye was swollen shut, his upper lip had been smashed into a pulp.

'He's grievin', man!' The blonde girl dropped to her knees beside him. 'That's all he be doin'! Grievin' his little ones!' Her hands fluttered about his face. Most of the others stood expressionless, mute, as if the sight of violence had mollified their resentments.

I wrenched free of the man holding me.

'Fuckin' Security bitch!' said the blonde. 'All he's doin's grievin'.'

'I don't give a fat damn what he was doing. There's no law says' – I laboured for breath – 'says he can exorcise it this way. Is there now?'

This last I addressed to those who had been watching, and though some refused to meet my eyes, from many I received nods and a grumbling assent. They cared nothing about my fate or Braulio's; they had been willing to witness whatever end we might have reached. But now I understood that something had happened to Braulio's children, and I understood too why he had chosen Bill to stand in for those who were truly culpable, and I felt sore in my heart for what I had done.

'Take him to the infirmary,' I said, and then gestured at the jammers, who were still down, eyes closed, their smiles in place. 'Them, too.' I put a hand to my neck; a lump had materialized underneath my right ear and was throbbing away nicely.

Bill moved up beside me, clutching his little cloth sack. His smell and his softness and his witling ways, every facet of his being annoyed me. I think he was about to say something, but I had no wish to hear it; I saw in him then what Braulio must have seen: a pudgy monstrosity, a uselessness with two legs.

'Get out of here!' I said, disgusted with myself for having interceded on his behalf. 'Go back to your goddamn crawl and stay there.'

His shoulders hitched as if he were expecting a blow, and he started pushing his way through the press at the door. Just before he went off along the corridor, he turned back. I believe he may have still wanted to say something, perhaps to offer thanks or – just as likely – to drive home the point that he was dissatisfied with the quantity of his goods. In his face was a mixture of petulant defiance and fear, but that gave me no clue to his intent. It was his usual expression, one that had been thirty-two years in the making, for due to his peculiar history, he had every cause to be defiant and afraid.

Bill's mother had been a medical technician assigned to the station by the Seguin Corporation, which owned the development contract for the lightship programme, and so, when his pre-natal scan displayed evidence of severe retardation, she was able to use her position to alter computer records in order to disguise his condition; otherwise, by station law – in effect, the law of the corporation – the foetus would have been aborted. Why she did this, and why she then committed suicide seventeen months after Bill's birth, remains a mystery, though it is assumed that her irrational actions revolved around the probability that Bill's father, a colonist aboard the lightship *Perseverance*, would never more be returning.

The discovery that Bill was retarded incited a fierce controversy. A considerable plurality of the station's workforce insisted that the infant be executed, claiming that since living space was at a premium, to allow this worthless creature to survive would be an affront to all those who had made great personal sacrifices in order to come to Solitaire. This group consisted in the main of those whose lives had been shaped by or whose duty it was to uphold the quota system: childless women and administrators and – the largest element of the plurality and of the population in general – people who, like Braulio, had won a job aboard the station and thus succeeded in escaping the crushing poverty and pollution of Earth, but who had not been sufficiently important to have their families sent along, and so had been forced to abandon them. In opposition stood a vocal minority comprised of those whose religious or philosophical bias would not permit such a callous act of violence; but this was, I believe, a stance founded almost entirely on principle, and I doubt that many of those involved were enthusiastic about Bill in the specific. Standing apart from the fray was a sizeable group who, for various social and political reasons, maintained neutrality; yet I imagine that at least half of them would, if asked, have expressed their distaste for the prospect of Bill's continued existence. Fistfights and shouting matches soon became the order of the day. Meetings were held; demands made; ultimatums presented. Finally, though, it was not politics or threats of force or calls to reason that settled the issue, but rather a corporate decision.

Among Seguin's enormous holdings was a company that supplied evolved animals to various industries and government agencies, where they were utilized in environments that had been deemed too stressful or physically challenging for human workers. The difficulty with such animals lay in maintaining control over them – the new nanotechnologies were considered untrustworthy and too expensive, and computer implants, though serviceable, inevitably failed. There were a number of ongoing research programmes whose aim it was to perfect the implants, and thus Seguin, seeing an opportunity for a rigorous test, not to mention a minor public-relations coup that would speak to the deeply humane concerns of the corporation, decided – in a reversal of traditional scientific methodology – to test on Bill a new implant that would eventually be used to govern the behaviour of chimpanzees and dogs and the like.

The implant, a disc of black alloy about the size of a soy wafer, contained a personality designed to entertain and jolly and converse with its host; it was embedded just beneath the skin behind the ear, and it monitored emotional levels, stimulating appropriate activity by means of electrical charges capable of bestowing both pleasure and pain. According to Bill, his implant was named Mister C, and it was – also according to Bill – his best friend, this despite the fact that it would hurt him whenever he was slow to obey its commands. I could always tell when Mister C was talking to him. His face would empty, and his eyes dart about as if trying to see the person who was speaking, and his hands would clench and unclench. Not a pleasant thing to watch. Still I suppose that Mister C was, indeed, the closest thing Bill had to a friend. Certainly it was attentive to him and was never too busy to hold a conversation; more importantly, it enabled him to perform the menial chores that had been set him: janitorial duties, fetch and carry, and, once he had reached the age of fifteen, the job that eventually earned him the name Barnacle Bill. But none of this assuaged the ill feeling toward him that prevailed throughout the station, a sentiment that grew more pronounced following the incident with Braulio. Two of Braulio's sons had been killed by a death squad who had mistaken them for members of a gang, and this tragedy caused people to begin talking about what an injustice it was that Bill should have so privileged an existence while others more worthy should be condemned to hell on Earth. Before long, the question of Bill's status was raised once again, and the issue was seized upon by Menckyn Samuelson, one of Solitaire's leading lights and – to my shame, because he was such a germ – a fellow Londoner. Samuelson had emigrated to the station as a low-temperature physicist and since had insinuated himself into a position of importance in the administration. I did not understand what he stood to gain from hounding Bill – he had, I assumed, some hidden political agenda – but he flogged the matter at every opportunity to whomever would listen and succeeded in stirring up a fiercely negative reaction toward Bill.

Opinion came to be almost equally divided between the options of executing him, officially or otherwise, and shipping him back to an asylum on Earth, which – as everyone knew – was only a slower and more expensive form of the first option.

There was a second development resulting from my fight with Braulio, one that had a poignant effect on my personal life, this being that Bill and I began spending a good deal of time together.

It seemed the old Chinese proverb had come into play, the one that states if you save somebody's life you become responsible for them. I had not saved his life, perhaps, but I had certainly spared him grievous injury; thus he came to view me as his protector, and I . . . well, initially I had no desire to be either his protector or his apologist, but I was forced to adopt both these roles. Bill was terrified. Everywhere he went he was cursed or cuffed or ill-treated in some fashion, a drastic escalation of the abuse he had always suffered. And then there was the blonde girl's song: 'Barnacle Bill the Spacer'. Scarcely a day passed when I did not hear a new verse or two. Everyone was writing them. Whenever Bill passed in a corridor or entered a room people would start to sing. It harrowed him from place to place, that song. He woke to it and fell asleep to it, and whatever self-esteem he had possessed was soon reduced to ashes.

When he first began hanging about me, dogging me on my rounds, I tried to put him off, but I could not manage it. I held myself partly to blame for the escalation of feeling against him; if I had not been so vicious in my handling of Braulio, I thought, Bill might not have come to this pass. But there was another, more significant reason behind my tolerance. I had, it appeared, developed a conscience. Or at least so I chose to interpret my growing concern for him. I have had cause to wonder if those protective feelings that emerged from some corner of my spirit were not merely a form of perversity, if I were using my relationship with Bill to demonstrate to the rest of the station that I had more power than most, that I could walk a contrary path without fear of retribution; but I remain convinced that the compassion I came to feel toward him was the product of a renewal of the ideals I had learned in the safe harbour of my family's home back in Chelsea, conceptions of personal honour and trust and responsibility that I had long believed to be as extinct as the tiger and the dove. It may be there was a premonitory force at work in me, for it occurs to me now that the rebirth of my personal hopes was the harbinger of a more general rebirth; and yet because of all that has happened, because of how my hopes were served, I have also had reason to doubt the validity of every hope, every renewal, and to consider whether the rebirth of hope is truly possible for such diffuse, heartless, and unruly creatures as ourselves.

One day, returning from my rounds with Bill shuffling along at my shoulder, I found a black crescent moon with a red star tipping its lower horn painted on the door of Bill's quarters: the symbol used by the Strange Magnificence, the most prominent of the gang religions flourishing back on Earth, to mark their intended victims. I doubt that Bill was aware of its significance. Yet he seemed to know instinctively the symbol was a threat, and no ordinary one at that. He clung to my arm, begging me to stay with him, and when I told him I had to leave, he threw a tantrum, rolling about on the floor, whimpering, leaking tears, wailing that bad things were going to happen. I assured him that I would have no trouble in determining who had painted the symbol; I could not believe that there were more than a handful of people on Solitaire with ties to the Magnificence. But this did nothing to soothe him. Finally, though I realized it might be a mistake, I told him he could spend the night in my quarters.

'Just this once,' I said. 'And you'd better keep damn quiet, or you'll be out on your bum.'

He nodded, beaming at me, shifting his feet, atremble with eagerness. Had he a tail he would have wagged it. But by the time we reached my quarters, his mood had been disrupted by the dozens of stares and curses directed his way. He sat on a cushion, rocking back and forth, making a keening noise, completely unmindful of the decor, which had knocked me back a pace on opening the door. Arlie was apparently in a less than sunny mood herself, for she had slotted in a holographic interior of dark greens and browns, with heavy chairs and a sofa and tables whose wood had been worked into dragons' heads and clawed feet and such; the walls were adorned with brass light fixtures shaped like bestial masks with glowing eyes, and the rear of the room had been tranformed into a receding perspective of sequentially smaller, square segments of black delineated by white lines, like a geometric tunnel into nowhere, still leading, I trusted, to something resembling a bedroom. The overall atmosphere was one of derangement, of a cramped magical lair through whose rear wall a hole had been punched into some negative dimension. Given this, I doubted that she would look kindly upon Bill's presence, but when she appeared in the far reaches of the tunnel – her chestnut hair done up, wearing a white Grecian-style robe, walking through an infinite black depth, looking minute at first, then growing larger by half with each successive segment she entered – she favoured him with a cursory nod and turned her attention to me.

' 'Ave you eaten?' she asked, and before I could answer she told me she wasn't hungry, there were some sandwiches, or I could do for myself, whatever I wanted, all in the most dispirited of tones. She was, as I have said, a pretty woman, with a feline cast of feature and sleek, muscular limbs; having too many interesting lines in her face, perhaps, to suit the prevailing standards of beauty, but sensual to a fault. Ordinarily, sexual potential surrounded her like an aura. That day, however, her face had settled into a dolorous mask, her shoulders had slumped and she seemed altogether drab.

'What's the matter?' I asked.

She shook her head. 'Nuffin'.'

'Nothing?' I said. 'Right! You look like the Queen just died, and the place is fixed up like the death of philosophy. But everything's just bloody marvellous, right?'

'Do you mind?' she snapped. 'It's personal!'

'Personal, is it? Well, excuse me. I certainly wouldn't want to be getting *personal* with you. What the hell's the matter? You been struck by the monthlies?'

She pinned me with a venomous stare. 'God, you're disgustin'! What is it? You 'aven't broken any 'eads today, so you've decided to bash me around a bit?'

'All right, all right,' I said. 'I'm sorry.'

'Nao,' she said. 'G'wan with it. Oi fuckin' love it when you're masterful. Really, Oi do!' She turned and started back along the tunnel. 'Oi'll just await your pleasure, shall Oi?' she called over her shoulder. 'Oi mean, you will let me know what more Oi can do to serve?'

'Christ!' I said, watching her ass twitching beneath the white cloth, thinking that I would have to make a heartfelt act of contrition before I laid hands on it again. I knew, of course, why I had baited her. It was for the same reason that had brought on her depression, that provoked the vast majority of our aberrant behaviours. Frustration, anger, despair, all feelings that – no matter their immediate causes – in some way arose from the fact that Solitaire had proved to be an abject failure. Of the twenty-seven ships assembled and launched, three had thus far returned. Two of the ships had reported no hospitable environments found. The crew of the third ship had been unable to report anything, being every one of them dead, apparently by each other's hands.

We had gotten a late start on the colonization of space, far too late to save the home planet, and it was unclear whether the piddling colonies on Mars and Europa and in the asteroids would allow us to survive. Perhaps it should have been clear, perhaps we should have realized that despite the horror and chaos of Earth, the brush wars, the almost weekly collapse of governments, our flimsy grasp of the new technologies, despite the failure of Solitaire and everything else . . . perhaps it should have been more than clear that our species possessed a root stubbornness capable of withstanding all but the most dire of cataclysms, and that eventually our colonies would thrive. But they would never be able to absorb the desperate population of Earth, and the knowledge that our brothers and sisters and parents were doomed to a life of diminishing expectations, to famines and wars and accidents of industry that would ulti-mately kill off millions, it caused those of us fortunate enough to have escaped to become dazed and badly weighted in our heads, too heavy with a sense of responsibility to comprehend the true moral requisites of our good fortune. Even if successful the lightship programme would only bleed off a tiny percentage of Earth's population, and most, I assumed, would be personnel attached to the Seguin Corporation and those whom the corporation or else some corrupt government agency deemed worthy; yet we came to perceive ourselves as the common people's last, best hope, and each successive failure struck at our hearts and left us so crucially dismayed, we developed astonishing talents for self-destruction. Like neurotic Prometheans, we gnawed at our own livers and sought to despoil every happy thing that fell to us. And when we grew too enervated to practise active self-destruction, we sank into clinical depression, as Arlie was doing now.

I sat thinking of these things for a long while, watching Bill rock back and forth, now and then popping a piece of hard candy into his mouth, muttering, and I reached no new conclusions, unless an evolution of distaste for the corporation and the world and the universe could be considered new and conclusive. At length, weary of the repetitive circuit of my thoughts, I decided it was time I tried to make my peace with Arlie. I doubted I had the energy for prolonged apology, but I hoped that intensity would do the trick.

'You can sleep on the couch,' I said to Bill, getting to my feet. 'The bathroom' – I pointed off along the corridor – 'is down there somewhere.'

He bobbed his head, but as he kept his eyes on the floor, I could not tell if it had been a response or simply a random movement.

'Did you hear me?' I asked.

'I gotta do somethin',' he said.

'Down there.' I pointed again. 'The bathroom.'

'They gonna kill me 'less I do somethin'.'

He was not, I realized, referring to his bodily functions.

'What do you mean?'

His eyes flicked up to me, then away. ' 'Less I do somethin' good, *really* good, they gonna kill me.'

'Who's going to kill you?'

'The men,' he said.

The men, I thought, sweet Jesus! I felt unutterably sad for him.

'I gotta find somethin',' he said with increased emphasis. 'Somethin' good, somethin' makes 'em like me.'

I had it now – he had seized on the notion that by some good deed or valuable service he could change people's opinion of him.

'You can't do anything, Bill. You just have to keep doing your job, and this will all wash away, I promise you.'

'Mmn-mn.' He shook his head vehemently like a child in denial. 'I gotta find somethin' good to do.'

'Look,' I said. 'Anything you try is very likely to backfire. Do you understand me? If you do something and you bugger it, people are going to be more angry at you than ever.'

He tucked his lower lip beneath the upper and narrowed his eyes and maintained a stubborn silence.

'What does Mister C say about this?' I asked.

That was, apparently, a new thought. He blinked; the tightness left his face. 'I don't know.'

'Well, ask him. That's what he's there for . . . to help you with your problems.'

'He doesn't always help. Sometimes he doesn't know stuff.'

'Try, will you? Just give it a try.'

He did not seem sure of this tactic, but after a moment he pawed at his head, running his palm along the crewcut stubble, then squeezed his eyes shut and began to mumble, long, pattering phrases interrupted by pauses for breath, like a child saying his prayers as fast as he can. I guessed that he was outlining the entire situation for Mister C. After a minute his face went blank, the tip of his tongue pushed out between his lips, and I imagined the cartoonish voice – thus I had been told the implant's voice would manifest – speaking to him in rhymes, in silly patter. Then, after another few seconds, his eyes snapped open and he beamed at me.

'Mister C says good deeds are always good,' he announced proudly, obviously satisfied that he had been proven right, and popped another piece of candy into his mouth.

I cursed the simplicity of the implant's programming, sat back down, and for the next half-hour or so I attempted to persuade Bill that his best course lay in doing absolutely nothing, in keeping a low profile. If he did, I told him, eventually the dust would settle and things would return to normal. He nodded and said, yes, yes, uh-huh, yet I could not be certain that my words were having an effect. I knew how resistant he could be to logic, and it was quite possible that he was only humouring me. But as I stood to take my leave of him, he did something that went

17

some way toward convincing me that I had made an impression: he reached out and caught my hand, held it for a second, only a second, but one during which I thought I felt the sorry hits of his life, the dim vibrations of all those sour, loveless nights and lonely ejaculations. When he released my hand he turned away, appearing to be embarrassed. I was embarrassed myself. Embarrassed and, I must admit, a bit repelled at having this ungainly lump display affection toward me. Yet I was also moved, and trapped between those two poles of feeling, I hovered above him, not sure what to do or say. There was, however, no need for me to deliberate the matter. Before I could summon speech he began mumbling once again, lost in a chat with Mister C.

'Good night, Bill,' I said.

He gave no response, as still as a Buddha on his cushion.

I stood beside him for a while, less observing him than cataloguing my emotions, then, puzzling more than a little over their complexity, I left him to his candy and his terror and his inner voices.

Apology was not so prickly a chore as I had feared. Arlie knew as well as I the demons that possessed us, and once I had submitted to a token humiliation, she relented and we made love. She was demanding in the act, wild and noisy, her teeth marked my shoulder, my neck; but as we lay together afterward in the dark, some trivial, gentle music trickling in from the speakers above us, she was tender and calm and seemed genuinely interested in the concerns of my day.

'God 'elp us!' she said. 'You don't actually fink the Magnificence is at work 'ere, do you?'

'Christ, no!' I said. 'Some miserable dwight's actin' on mad impulse, that's all. Probably done it 'cause his nanny wiped his bum too hard when he's a babe.'

'Oi 'ope not,' she said. 'Oi've seen their work back 'ome too many toimes to ever want to see it again.'

'You never told me you'd had dealings with the Magnificence.'

'Oi never 'ad what you'd call dealin's with 'em, but they was all over our piece of 'eaven, they were. 'Alf the bloody houses sported some kind of daft mark. It was a bleedin' fertile field for 'em, with nobody 'avin' a job and the lads just 'angin' about on the corners and smokin' gannie. 'Twas a rare day the Bills didn't come 'round to scrape up some yobbo wearing his guts for a necktie and the mark of his crime carved into his fore'ead. Nights you'd hear 'em chantin' down by the stadium. 'Orrid stuff they was singin'. Wearin' that cheap black satin gear and those awful masks. But it 'ad its appeal. All the senile old 'ooligans were diggin' out their jackboots and razors, and wantin' to go marchin' again. And in the pubs the soaks would be sayin', yes, they do the odd bad thing, the Magnificence, but they've got the public good to 'eart. The odd bad thing! Jesus! Oi've seen messages written on the pavement in 'uman bones. Coloured girls with their 'ips broken and their legs lashed back behind their necks. Still breathin' and starin' at you with them 'ollow eyes, loike they were mad to die. You were lucky, John, to be living up in Chelsea.'

'Lucky enough, I suppose,' I said stiffly, leery of drawing such distinctions; the old British class wars, though somewhat muted on Solitaire, were far from dormant, and even between lovers, class could be a dicey subject. 'Chelsea's not exactly the Elysian Fields.'

'Oi don't mean nuffin' by it, luv. You don't have to tell me the 'ole damn world's gone rotten long ago. Oi remember how just a black scrap of a life looked loike a brilliant career when Oi was livin' there. Now Oi don't know how Oi stood it.'

I pulled her close against me and we lay without speaking for a long while. Finally Arlie said, 'You know, it's 'alf nice 'avin' 'im 'ere.'

'Bill, you mean?'

'Yeah, Bill.'

'I hope you'll still feel that way if he can't find the loo,' I said.

Arlie giggled. 'Nao, I'm serious. It's loike 'avin' family again. The feel of somebody snorin' away in the next room. That's the thing we miss 'avin' here. We're all so bloody isolated. Two's a crowd and all that. We're missin' the warmth.'

'I suppose you're right.'

I touched her breasts, smoothed my hand along the swell of her hip, and soon we were involved again, more gently than before, more giving to the other, as if what Arlie had said about family had created a resonance in our bodies. Afterward I was so fatigued, the darkness seemed to be slowly circulating around us, pricked by tiny bursts of actinic light, the way a djinn must circulate within its prison bottle, a murky cloud of genius and magic. I was at peace lying there, yet I felt strangely excited to be so peaceful and my thoughts, too, were strange, soft, almost formless, the kind of thoughts I recalled having had as a child when it had not yet dawned on me that all my dreams would eventually be hammered flat and cut into steely dies so they could withstand the dreadful pressures of a dreamless world.

Arlie snuggled closer to me, her hand sought mine, clasped it tightly. 'Ah, Johnny,' she said. 'Toimes loike this, Oi fink Oi was born to forget it all.'

The next day I was able to track down the villain who had painted the menacing symbol on Bill's door. The cameras in the corridor outside his door had malfunctioned, permitting the act of vandalism to go unobserved; but this was hardly surprising – the damned things were always failing, and should they not fail on their own, it was no great feat to knock them out by using an electromagnet. Lacking a video record, I focused my attention on the personnel files. Only nine people on Solitaire proved to have had even minimal ties with the Strange Magnificence; by process of elimination I was able to reduce the number of possible culprits to three. The first of them I interviewed, Roger Thirwell, a pale, rabbity polymath in his mid-twenties who had emigrated from Manchester just the year before, admitted his guilt before I had scarcely begun his interrogation.

'I was only tryin' to do the wise and righteous,' he said, squaring his shoulders and puffing out his meagre chest. 'Samuelson's been tellin' us we shouldn't sit back and allow things to just happen. We should let our voices be heard. Solitaire's our home. We should be the ones who decide how it's run.'

'And so, naturally,' I said, 'when it came time to let your majestic voice resound, the most compelling topic you could find upon which to make a statement was the fate of a halfwit.'

'It's not that simple and you know it. His case speaks to a larger issue. Samuelson says . . .'

'Fuck you,' I said. 'And fuck Samuelson.' I was sick of him, sick of his Midlands accent, sick especially of his references to Samuelson. What possible service, I wondered, could a dwight such as he have provided for the Magnificence? Something to do with logistics, probably. Anticipating police strategies or solving computer defences. Yet from what I knew of the Magnificence, it was hard to imagine them putting up with this nit for very long. They would find a hard use for him and then let him fall off the edge of the world.

'Why in hell's name did you paint that thing on his door?' I asked. 'And don't tell me Samuelson ordered you to do it.'

The light of hope came into his face, and I would have sworn he was about to create some fantasy concerning Samuelson and himself in order to shift the guilt to broader shoulders. But all he said was, 'I wanted to scare him.'

'You could have achieved that with a bloody stick figure,' I said.

'Yeah, but no one else would have understood it. Samuelson says we ought to try to influence as many people as possible whenever we state our cause, no matter how limited our aims. That way we enlist others in our dialogue.'

I was starting to have some idea of what Samuelson's agenda might be, but I did not believe Thirwell could further enlighten me on the subject. 'All you've succeeded in doing,' I told him, 'is to frighten other people. Or is it your opinion that there are those here who would welcome a chapter of the Magnificence?'

He ducked his eyes and made no reply.

'If you're homesick for them, I can easily arrange for you to take a trip back to Manchester,' I said.

This elicited from Thirwell a babble of pleas and promises. I saw that I would get no more out of him, and I cautioned him that if he were ever to trouble Bill again I would not hesitate to make good on my threat. I then sent him on his way and headed off to pay a call on Menckyn Samuelson.

Samuelson's apartment, like those belonging to most corporate regals, was situated in a large module adjoining the even larger module that housed the station's propulsion controls, and was furnished with antiques and pictures that would have fetched a dear price back on Earth, but here were absolutely priceless, less evidence of wealth than emblems of faith . . . the faith we were all taught to embrace, that one day life would be as once it had been, a vista of endless potential and possibility. The problem with Samuelson's digs, however, was that his taste was abysmally bad: he had assembled a motley collection of items, Guilford chests and blond Finnish chairs, a Jefferson corner cabinet and freeform video sculptures, Victorian sideboard and fibre-optic chandelier, that altogether created the impression one had stumbled into a pawn shop catering to millionaires. It may be that my amusement at this appalling display showed in my face, for though he presented a smile and an outstretched hand, I sensed a certain stiffness in his manner. Nevertheless the politician in him brought him through that awkward moment. Soon he was nattering away, pouring me a glass of whisky, ushering me to an easy chair, plopping himself down into another, giving out with an expansive sigh, and saying, 'I'm so awfully glad you've come, John. I've been meaning to have you in for a cup of reminiscence, you know. Two old Londoners like ourselves, we can probably find a few choice topics to bang around.'

He lifted his chin, beaming blandly, eyes half-lidded, as if expecting something pleasant to be dashed into his face. It was such a thespian pose, such a clichéd take on upper-class manners, so redolent of someone trying to put on airs, I had to restrain a laugh. Everything about him struck me as being just the slightest bit off. He was a lean, middle-aged man, dressed in a loose cotton shirt and moleskin trousers, alert in manner, almost handsome, but the nose was a tad sharp, the eyes set a fraction too close together, the cheekbones not sufficiently prominent, the chin a touch insubstantial, too much forehead and not enough hair. He had the essential features of good breeding, yet none of the charming detail, like the runt of a pedigree litter.

'Yes,' I said, 'we must do that sometime. However, today I've come on station business.'

'I see.' He leaned back, crossed his legs, cradled his whisky in his lap. 'Then p'rhaps after we've concluded your business, there'll be time for a chat, eh?'

'Perhaps.' I had a swallow of whisky, savoured the smoky flavour. 'I'd like to talk with you about William Stamey.'

'Ah, yes. Old Barnacle Bill.' Samuelson's brow was creased by a single furrow, the sort of line a cartoonist would use to indicate a gently rolling sea. 'A bothersome matter.'

'It might be considerably less bothersome if you left it alone.'

Not a crack in the veneer. He smiled, shook his head. 'I should dearly love to, old fellow. But I'm afraid you've rather a short-sighted view of the situation. The question we must settle is not the question of Bill *per se*, but of general policy. We must develop clear guide . . .'

'Come on! Give it up!' I said. 'I'm not one of your damned pint and kidney pies boy who get all narky and start to drool at the thought of their rights being abused. Their rights! Jesus Christ! The poor scuts have been buggered more times than a Sydney whore, and they still think it feels good. You wouldn't waste a second on this if it were merely a question of policy. I want to know what you're really after.'

'Oh my God,' Samuelson said, bemused. 'You're not going to be an easy lay, are you?'

'Not for you, darling. I'm saving myself for the one I love.'

'And just who is that, I wonder.' He swirled the whisky in his glass, watched it settle. 'What do you think I'm after?'

'Power. What else is it makes your toby stiffen?'

He made a dry noise. 'A simplistic answer. Not inaccurate, I'll admit. But simplistic all the same.'

'I'm here for an education,' I told him, 'not to give a lecture.'

'And I may enlighten you,' Samuelson said. 'I very well may. But let me ask you something first. What's your interest in all this?'

'I'm looking after Bill's interests.'

He arched his eyebrow. 'Surely there's more to it than that.'

'That's the sum of it. Aside from the odd deep-seated psychological motive, of course.'

'Of course.' His smile could have sliced an onion; when it vanished, his cheeks hollowed. 'I should imagine there's an element of *noblesse oblige* involved.'

'Call it what you like. The fact remains, I'm on the case.'

'For now,' he said. 'These things have a way of changing.'

'Is that a threat? Don't waste your time. I'm the oldest slut on the station, Samuelson. I know where all the big balls have been dragging, and I've made certain I'm protected. Should anything happen to me or mine, it's your superiors who're going to start squealing. They'll be most perturbed with you.'

'You've nothing on me.' This said with, I thought, forced confidence.

'True enough,' I said. 'But I'm working on it, don't you worry.'

Samuelson drained his glass, got to his feet, went to the sideboard and poured himself a fresh whisky. He held up the bottle, gave me an enquiring look.

'Why not?' I let him fill my glass, which I then lifted in a toast. 'To England. May the seas wash over her and make her clean.'

He gave an amused snort. 'England,' he said, and drank. He sat back down, adjusted his bottom. 'You're an amazing fellow, John. I've been told as much, but now, having had some firsthand experience, I believe my informants may have underestimated you.' He pinched the crease of one trouserleg. 'Let me put something to you. Not as a threat, but as an item for discussion. You do understand, don't you, that the sort of protection you've developed is not proof against every circumstance?'

'Absolutely. In the end it all comes down to a question of who's got the biggest guns and the will to use them. Naturally I'm prepared along those lines.'

'I don't doubt it. But you're not seeking a war, are you?'

I knocked back half my whisky, rested the glass on my lap. 'Look here, I'm quite willing to live as one with you, no matter. Until lately, you've done nothing to interfere with my agenda. But this dust-up over Bill, and now this bit with your man Thirwell and his paint gun, I won't have it. Too many people here, Brits and Yanks alike, have a tendency to soil their nappy when they catch a scent of the Magnificence. I've no quarrel with you making a power play. And that's what you're doing, old boy. You're stirring up the groundlings, throwing a few scraps to the hounds so they'll be eager for the sound of your voice. You're after taking over the administrative end of things, and you've decided to give climbing the ladder of success a pass in favour of scaling the castle walls. A bloodless coup, perhaps. Or maybe a spot of blood thrown in to slake the fiercest appetites. Well, that's fine. I don't give a fuck who's sitting in the big chair, and I don't much care how they get there, so long as we maintain the status quo. But one thing I won't have is you frightening people.'

'People are forever being frightened,' he said. 'Whether there's a cause for fear or not. But that's not my intent.'

'Perhaps not. But you've frightened the bejesus out of Bill, and now you've frightened a good many others by bringing the Magnificence into the picture.'

'Thirwell's not my responsibility.'

'The hell he's not! He's the walking Book of Samuelson. Every other sentence begins, "Samuelson says . . ." Give him a pretty smile, and he'll be your leg-humper for life.'

'Leg-humper?' Samuelson looked bewildered.

'A little dog,' I said impatiently. 'You know the kind. Randy all the time. Jumps up on you and goes to having his honeymoon with your calf.'

'I've never heard the term. Not British, is it?'

'American, I think. I heard it somewhere. I don't know.'

'Marvellous expression. I'll have to remember it.'

'Remember this, too,' I said, trying to pick up the beat of my tirade. 'I'm holding you responsible for any whisper I hear of the Magnificence. Before we had this heart-to-heart I was inclined to believe you had no part in what Thirwell did. Now I'm not altogether sure. I think you're quite capable of using fear to manipulate the public. I think you may have known something of Thirwell's history and given him a nudge.'

'Even if that were true,' he said, 'I don't understand the depth of your reaction. We're a long way from the Magnificence here. A daub of paint or two can't have much effect.'

My jaw dropped a fraction on hearing that. 'You're not from London. You couldn't be and still say that.'

'Oh, I'm from London all right,' he said coldly. 'And I'm no virgin where the Magnificence is concerned. They left my brother stretched on King's Road one morning with the Equation of Undying Love scrawled in his own blood on the sidewalk beneath him. They mailed his private parts to his wife in a plastic container. But I've come a very long way from those days and those places. I'd be terrified of the Magnificence if they were here. But they're not here, and I'll be damned if I'll treat them like the bogeyman just because some sad little twit with too much brain and the social skills of a ferret paints the Magelantic Exorcism on somebody's door.'

His statement rang true, but nevertheless I made a mental note to check on his brother. 'Wonderful,' I said. 'It's good you've come to terms with all that. But not everyone here has managed to put as much distance between themselves and their old fears as you seem to have done.'

'That may be, but I'm . . .' He broke off, clicked his tongue against his teeth. 'All right. I see your point.' He tapped his fingers on the arm of his chair. 'Let's see if we can't reach an accord. It's not in my interests at the moment to break off my campaign against Bill, but' – he held up a hand to stop me from interrupting – 'but I will acknowledge that I've no real axe to grind where he's concerned. He's serving a strictly utilitarian purpose. So here's what I'll do. I will not allow him to be shipped back to Earth. At a certain juncture, I'll defuse the campaign. Perhaps I'll even make a public apology. That should help return him to grace. In addition, I'll do what I can to prevent further incidents involving the Magnificence. Frankly I very much doubt there'll be further problems. If there are, it won't be because I'm encouraging them.'

'All well and good,' I said. 'Very magnanimous, I'm sure. But nothing you've promised guarantees Bill's safety during the interim.'

'You'll have to be his guarantee. I'll try to maintain the temper of the station at a simmer. The rest is up to you.'

'Up to me? No, you're not going to avoid responsibility that way. I'll do my best to keep him from harm, but if he gets hurt, I'll hurt you. That much I can guarantee.'

'Then let's hope that nothing happens to him, shall we? For both our sakes.' His smile was so thin, such a sideways stretching of the lip muscles, I thought it must be making his gums ache. 'Funny. I can't decide whether we've established a working relationship or declared war.'

'I don't think it matters,' I said.

'No, probably not.' He stood, straightened the fall of his trousers, and again gave me that bland, beaming, expectant look. 'Well, I won't keep you any longer. Do drop around once the dust has settled. We'll have that chat.'

'About London.'

'Right.' He moved to the door.

'I don't know as I'd have very much to say about London,' I told him. 'Nothing fit for reminiscence, at any rate.'

'Really?' he said, ushering me out into the corridor. 'The old girl's petticoats have gotten a trifle bloody, I'll admit. Terrible, the things that go on nowadays. The hunting parties, hive systems, knife dances. And of course, the Magnificence. But here, you know' – he patted his chest – 'in her heart, I firmly believe there's still a bit of all right. Or maybe it's just I'm the sentimental sort. Like the song says, "call 'er a satan, call 'er a whore, she'll always be Mother to me".'

Unlike Samuelson, I no longer thought of London as mother or home, or in any framework that smacked of the wholesome. Even 'satan' would have been a euphemism. London for me was a flurry of night visions: a silhouetted figure standing in the window of a burning building, not waving its arms, not leaning out, but calm, waiting to be taken by the flames; men and women in tight black satin, white silk masks all stamped with the same feral, exultant expression, running through the streets, singing; moonlight painting the eddies of the Thames into silk, water lapping at a stone pier, and floating just beyond the shadow of the pier, the enormous bulk of a man I had shot only a minute before, nearly four hundred pounds of strangler, rapist, cannibal, brought down by a bullet weighing no more than one of his teeth; the flash of a shotgun from around a dark corner, like the flash of heat lightning; the charge of poisonous light flowing along the blade of a bloody macro-knife just removed from the body of a fellow detective; a garbage bag resting on a steel table that contained the neatly butchered remains of seven infants; the façade of St Paul's dyed into a grooved chaos of vermilion, green, and purple by stone-destroying bacteria released by the artist, Miralda Hate; the wardrobe of clothing sewn of human skin and embroidered in gilt and glitter with verses from William Blake that we found in a vacant Brixton flat; the blind man who begged each evening on St Martin's Lane, spiders crawling in the hollow globes of his glass eyes; the plague of saints, young men and women afflicted by a drug that bred in them the artificial personalities of Biblical characters and inspired them to martyr themselves during certain phases of the moon; the eyes of wild dogs in Hyde Park gleaming in the beam of my torch like the flat discs of highway reflectors; those and a thousand equally blighted memories, that was my London. Nightmare, grief, and endless fever.

It was Solitaire that was home and mother to me, and I treated it with the appropriate respect. Though I was an investigative officer, not a section guard, I spent a portion of nearly every day patrolling various areas, searching less for crime than for symptoms of London, incidences of infection that might produce London-like effects. The station was not one place, but many: one hundred and forty-three modules, several of which were larger than any of the Earth orbit stations, connected by corridors encased in pressure shells that could be disengaged by means of the Central Propulsion Control and – as each module was outfitted with engines – moved to a new position in the complex, or even to a new orbit; should the Central Propulsion Control (CPC) be destroyed or severely damaged, disengagement was automatic, and the modules would boost into pre-programmed orbits. I hardly ever bothered to include places such as the labs, tank farms, infirmaries, data management centres, fusion modules, and such on my unofficial rounds; nor did I include the surface of the station, the electronic and solar arrays, radiator panels, communications and tracking equipment; those areas were well maintained and had no need of a watchman. I generally limited myself to entertainment and dwelling modules like East Louie, where Bill's quarters and mine were located, idiosyncratic environments decorated with holographic scenarios so ancient that they had blanked out in patches and you would often see a coded designation or a stretch of metal wall interrupting the pattern of, say, a hieroglyphic mural; and from time to time I also inspected those sections of the station that were rarely visited and were only monitored via recordings several times a day – storage bays and transport hangars and the CPC (the cameras in those areas were supposed to transmit automatic alarms whenever anyone entered, but the alarm system was on the fritz at least half the time, and due to depleted staff and lack of materials, repairs such as that were not a high priority).

The CPC was an immense, white, portless room situated, as I've said, in the module adjoining that which housed Samuelson's digs and the rest of the corporate dwelling units. The room was segmented by plastic panels into work stations, contained banks of terminals and control panels, and was of little interest to me; but Bill, once he learned its function, was fascinated by the notion that his world could separate into dozens of smaller worlds and arrow off into the nothing, and each time we visited it, he would sit at the main panel and ask questions about its operation. There was never anyone else about, and I saw no harm in answering the questions. Bill did not have sufficient mental capacity to understand the concept of launch codes, let alone to program a computer so it would accept them. Solitaire was the only world he would ever know, and he was eager to accumulate as much knowledge about it as possible. Thus I encouraged his curiosity and showed him how to call up pertinent information on his own computer.

Due to Arlie's sympathetic response, Bill took to sleeping in our front room nearly every night, this in addition to tagging along on my rounds, and therefore it was inevitable that we became closer; however, closeness is not a term I happily apply to the relationship. Suffice it to say that he grew less defiant and petulant, somewhat more open and, as a consequence, more demanding of attention. Because his behaviour had been modified to some degree, I found his demands more tolerable. He continued to cling to the notion that in order to save himself he would have to perform some valuable service to the community, but he never insisted that I help him in this; he appeared satisfied merely to hang about and do things with me. And to my surprise I found there were some things I actually enjoyed doing with him. I took especial pleasure in going outside with him, in accompanying him on *his* rounds and watching as he cleared barnacles away from communications equipment and other delicate mechanisms.

Sauter's Barnacle was, of course, not a true barnacle, yet it possessed certain similarities to its namesake, the most observable of which was a supporting structure that consisted of a hard exoskeleton divided into plates so as to allow movement. They bore a passing resemblance to unopened buds, the largest about the size of a man's fist, and they were variously coloured, some streaked with metallic shades of red, green, gold, and silver (their coloration depended to a great extent on the nature of the substrate and their nutrient sources), so that when you saw a colony of them from a distance, spreading over the surface of a module – and all the modules were covered by hundreds of thousands of them – they had the look of glittering beds of moss or lichen. I knew almost nothing about them, only that they fed on dust, that they were sensitive to changes in light, that they were not found within the orbit of Mars, and that wherever there was a space station, they were, as my immediate superior, the Chief of Security, Gerald Sessions, put it, 'thick as flies on shit'. Once it had been learned that they did no harm, that, indeed, their excretions served to strengthen the outer shells of the modules, interest in them had fallen off sharply. There was, I believe, some ongoing research into their physical characteristics, but it was not of high priority.

Except with Bill.

To Bill the barnacles were purpose, a reason for being. They were, apart from Mister C, the most important creatures in the universe, and he was obsessive in his attentiveness toward them. Watching him stump about over the skin of the station, huge and clumsy in his pressure suit, a monstrous figure made to appear even more monstrous by the light spraying up around him from this or that port, hosing offending clumps of barnacles with bursts of oxygen from the tank that floated alongside him, sending them drifting up from their perches, I had the impression not of someone performing a menial task, but of a gardener tending his prize roses or – more aptly – a shepherd his flock. And though according to the best information, the barnacles were mindless things, incapable of any activity more sophisticated than obeying the basic urges of feeding and reproduction, it seemed they responded to him; even after he had chased them away they would wobble about him like strange pets, bumping against his faceplate and sometimes settling on him briefly, vivid against the white material of the pressure suit, making it appear that he was wearing jewelled rosettes on his back and shoulders. (I did not understand at the time that these were females which, unable to affect true mobility, had been stimulated to detach from the station by the oxygen and now were unable to reattach to the colony.)

With Bill's example before me, I was no longer able to take the barnacles for granted, and I began reading about them whenever I had a spare moment. I discovered that the exoskeleton was an organic-inorganic matrix composed of carbon compounds and silicate minerals, primarily olivine, pyroxene, and magnetite, substances commonly found in meteorites. Changes in light intensity were registered by iridescent photophores that dotted the plates; even the finest spray of dust passing between the barnacle and a light source would trigger neurological activity and stimulate the opening of aperture plates, permitting the egress of what Jacob Sauter (the barnacles' Linnaeus, an amateur at biology) had called the 'tongue', an organ utilized both in feeding and in the transmission of seminal material from the male to the female. I learned that only the males could move about the colony, and that they did so by first attaching to the substrate with their tongues, which were coated with adhesive material, then detaching at one of their upper plate segments, and finally re-attaching to the colony with the stubby segmented stalks that depended from their bottom plates. 'In effect,' Sauter had written, 'they are doing cartwheels.'

The most profound thing I discovered, however, had nothing to do with the barnacles, or rather had only peripherally to do with them, and was essentially a rediscovery, a rewakening of my wonderment at the bleak majesty surrounding us. The cold diamond chaos of the stars, shining so brightly they might have just been finished that day; the sun, an old god grown small and tolerable to the naked eye; the surreal brilliance and solidity that even the most mundane object acquired against the backdrop of that black, unvarying distance; that blackness itself, somehow managing to seem both ominous and serene, absence and

31

presence, metal-hard and soft as illusion, like a fold in God's magisterial robe; the station with its spidery complexes of interconnecting corridors and modules, all coated with the rainbow swirls and streaks of the barnacles' glittering colours, and beams of light spearing out from it at every angle, like some mad, gay, rickety toy, the sight of which made me expect to hear calliope music; the Earth transport vessels, grey and bulky as whales, berthed in the geometric webs of their docks; the remote white islands of the assembly platforms, and still more remote, made visible by setting one's faceplate for maximum visual enhancement, the tiny silver needle we were soon to hurl into the haystack of the unknown. It was glorious, that vista. It made a comprehensible map of our endeavours and led me to understand that we had not botched it completely. Not yet. I had seen it all before, but Bill's devotion to the barnacles had rekindled the embers of my soul, my cognizance of the scope of our adventure, and looking out over the station, I would think I could feel the entire blast and spin of creation inside my head, the flood of particles from a trillion suns, the crackling conversations of electric clouds to whom the frozen seas of ammonia above which they drifted were repositories of nostalgia, the endless fall of matter through the less-than-nothing of a pure anomaly, the white face of Christ blurred and streaming within the frost-coloured fire of a comet's head, the quasars not yet congealed into dragons and their centuries, the unerring persistence of meteors that travel for uncounted millennia through the zero dark to scoot and burn across the skies onto the exposure plates of mild astronomers and populate the legends of a summer night and tumble into cinders over the ghosted peaks of the Karakorum and then are blown onto the back porches of men who have never turned their faces to the sky and into the dreams of children. I would have a plunderous sense of my own destiny, and would imagine myself hurling through the plenum at the speed of thought, of wish, accumulating a momentum that was in itself a charge to go, to witness, to take, and I was so enlivened I would believe for an instant that, like a hero returning from war, I could lift my hand and let shine a blessing down upon everyone around me, enabling them to see and feel all I had seen and felt, to know as I knew that despite everything we were closer to heaven than we had ever been before.

It was difficult for me to regain my ordinary take on life following these excursions, but after the departure of the lightship *Sojourner*, an event that Bill and I observed together from a catwalk atop the solar array in East Louie, it was thrust hard upon me that I had best set a limit on my woolgathering and concentrate on the matters at hand, for it was coming more and more to look as if the Strange Magnificence had gained a foothold on Solitaire. Scraps of black satin had been found tied to several crates in one of the storage bays, one of them containing drugs; copies of *The Book of Inexhaustible Delirium* began turning up; and while I was on rounds with Bill one day, I discovered a cache of packet charges in the magnetism lab, each about half the size of a flattened soccer ball, any one of which would have been sufficient to destroy a module. Gerald Sessions and I divided them up and stored them in our apartments, not trusting our staff with the knowledge of their existence. Perhaps the most troubling thing of all, the basic question of whether or not the Magnificence had the common good to heart was being debated in every quarter of the station, an argument inspired by fear and fear alone, and leading to bloody fights and an increase in racial tension and perversion of every sort. The power of the Strange Magnificence, you see, lay in the subversive nihilism of their doctrine, which put forward the idea that it was man's duty to express all his urges, no matter how dark or violent, and that from the universal exorcism of these black secrets would ultimately derive a pure consensus, a vast averaging of all possible behaviours that would in turn reveal the true character of God and the manifest destiny of the race. Thus the leaders of the Magnificence saw nothing contradictory in funding a group in York, say, devoted to the expulsion of Pakistanis from Britain by whatever means necessary while simultaneously supporting a Sufi cult. They had no moral or philosophical problem with anything because according to them the ultimate morality was a work-in-progress. Their tracts were utter tripe, quasi-intellectual homilies dressed up in the kind of adjective-heavy, gothic prose once used to give weight to stories of ghosts and ancient evil; their anthems were even less artful, but the style suited the product, and the product was an easy sell to the disenfranchised, the desperate and the mad, categories into one of which almost everyone alive would fit to some extent, and definitely were one or another descriptive of everyone on Solitaire. As I had promised him, once these symptoms started to manifest, I approached Samuelson again, but he gave every evidence of being as concerned about the Magnificence as was I, and though I was not certain I believed his pose, I was too busy with my official duties and my unofficial one – protecting Bill, who had become the target of increased abuse – to devote much time to him. Then came the day of the launch.

It was beautiful, of course. First a tiny stream of fire, like a scratch made on a wall painted black, revealing a white undercoat. This grew smaller and smaller, and eventually disappeared; but mere seconds after its disappearance, what looked to be an iridescent crack began to spread across the blackness, reaching from the place where *Sojourner* had gone superluminal to its point of departure, widening to a finger's breadth, then a hand's, and more, like an all-coloured piece of lightning hardened into a great jagged sword that was sundering the void, and as it swung toward us, widening still, I thought I saw in it intimations of faces and forms and things written, as one sees the images of circuitry and patterns such as might be found on the skin of animals when staring at the grain of a varnished board, and the sight of these half-glimpsed faces and the rest, not quite decipherable yet familiar in the way a vast and complex sky with beams of sunlight shafting down through dark clouds appears to express a familiar glory . . . those sights were accompanied by a feeling of instability, a shivery apprehension of my own insubstantiality which, although it shook me to my soul, disabling any attempt to reject it, was also curiously exalting, and I yearned for that sword to swing through me, to bear me away into a thundering genesis where I would achieve completion, and afterward, after it had faded, leaving me bereft and confused, my focus upon it had been so intent, I felt I had witnessed not an exercise of intricate technology but a simple magical act of the sort used to summon demons from the ready rooms of Hell or to wake a white spirit in the depths of an underground lake. I turned to Bill. His faceplate was awash in reflected light, and what I could make out of his face was coloured an eerie green by the read-outs inside his helmet. His mouth was opened, his eyes wide. I spoke to him, saying I can't recall what, but wanting him to second my amazement at the wonderful thing we had seen.

'Somethin's wrong,' he said.

I realized then that he was gazing in another direction; he might have seen *Sojourner*'s departure, but only out of the corner of his eye. His attention was fixed upon one of the modules – the avionics lab, I believe – from which a large number of barnacles had detached and were drifting off into space.

'Why're they doin' that?' he asked. 'Why're they leavin'?'

'They're probably sick of it here,' I said, disgruntled by his lack of sensitivity. 'Like the rest of us.'

'No,' he said. 'No, must be somethin' wrong. They wouldn't leave 'less somethin's wrong.'

'Fine,' I said. 'Something's wrong. Let's go back in.'

He followed me reluctantly into the airlock, and once we had shucked off our suits, he talked about the barnacles all the way back to my quarters, insisting that they would not have vacated the station if there had been nothing wrong.

'They like it here,' he said. 'There's lots of dust, and nobody bothers 'em much. And they . . .'

'Christ!' I said. 'If something's wrong, figure it out and tell me! Don't just blither on!'

'I can't.' He ducked his eyes, swung his arms in exaggerated fashion, as if he were getting ready to skip. 'I don't know how to figure it out.'

'Ask Mister C.' We had reached my door, and I punched out the entry code.

'He doesn't care.' Bill pushed out his lower lip to cover the upper, and he shook his head back and forth, actually not shaking it so much as swinging it in great slow arcs. 'He thinks it's stupid.'

'What?' The door cycled open, the front room was pitch-dark.

'The barnacles,' Bill said. 'He thinks everything I like is stupid. The barnacles and the CPC and . . .'

Just then I heard Arlie scream, and somebody came hurtling out of the dark, knocking me into a chair and down onto the floor. In the spill of light from the corridor, I saw Arlie getting to her feet, covering her breasts with her arms. Her blouse was hanging in tatters about her waist; her jeans were pushed down past her hips; her mouth was bloody. She tried to speak, but only managed a sob.

Sickened and terrified at the sight of her, I scrambled out into the corridor. A man dressed all in black was sprinting away, just turning off into one of the common rooms. I ran after him. Each step spiked the boil of my emotions with rage, and by the time I entered the common room, done up as the VR version of a pub, with dart boards and dusty, dark wood, and a few fraudulent old red-cheeked men slumped at corner tables, there was murder in my heart. I yelled at people taking their ease to call Security, then raced into the next corridor.

Not a sign of the man in black.

The corridor was ranged by about twenty doors, the panel of light above most showing blue, signalling that no one was within. I was about to try one of the occupied apartments when I noticed that the telltale beside the airlock hatch was winking red. I went over to the hatch, switched on the closed-circuit camera. On the screen above the control panel appeared a grainy black-and-white picture of the airlock's interior; the man I had been chasing was pacing back and forth, making an erratic humming noise. A pale, twitchy young man with a malnourished look and bones that seemed as frail as a bird's, the product of some row-house madonna and her pimply king, of not enough veggies and too many cigarettes, of centuries of a type of ignorance as peculiarly British as the hand-rolled lawns of family estates. I recognized him at once. Roger Thirwell. I also recognized his clothes. The tight black satin trousers and shirt of the Strange Magnificence, dotted with badges proclaiming levels of spiritual attainment and attendance at this or that function.

'Hello, Roger,' I said into the intercom. 'Lovely day for a rape, isn't it, you filthy bastard?'

He glanced around, then up to the monitor. Fear came into his face, then was washed away by hostility, which in turn was replaced by a sort of sneering happiness. 'Send me to Manchester, will you?' he said. 'Send me down the tube to bloody Manchester! I think not! Perhaps you realize now I'm not the sort to take threats lying down.'

'Yeah, you're a fucking hero! Why don't you come out and show me how much of a man you are.'

He appeared distracted, as if he had not heard me. I began to suspect that he was drugged, but drugged or not, I hated him.

'Come on out of there!' I said. 'I swear to God, I'll be gentle.'

'I'll show you,' he said. 'You want to see the man I am, I'll show you.'

But he made no move.

'I had her in the mouth,' he said quietly. 'She's got a lovely, lovely mouth.'

I didn't believe him, but the words afflicted me nevertheless. I pounded on the hatch. 'You beady-eyed piece of shit! Come out, damn you!'

Voices talking excitedly behind me, then somebody put an arm on my shoulder and said in a carefully enunciated baritone, 'Let me handle this one, John.'

It was Gerald Sessions, my superior, a spindly black man with a handsome, open face and freckly light complexion and spidery arms that possessed inordinate strength. He was a quiet, private sort, not given to displays of emotion, understated in all ways, possessed of the glum manner of someone who continually feels themselves put upon; yet because of our years together, he was a man for whom I had developed some affection, and though I trusted no one completely, he was one of the few people whom I was willing to let watch my back. Standing beside him were four guards, among them his bodyguard and lover, Ernesto Carbajal, a little fume of a fellow with thick, oily yet well-tended black hair and a prissy cast to his features; and behind them, at a remove, was a grave-looking Menckyn Samuelson, nattily attired in dinner jacket and white trousers. Apparently he had been called away from a social occasion.

'No, thank you,' I told Gerald. 'I plan to hurt the son of a bitch. Send someone round to check on Arlie, will you?'

'It's been taken care of.' He studied me a moment. 'All right. Just don't kill him.'

I turned back to the screen just as Thirwell, who had moved to the outer hatch and was gazing at the control panel, burst into song.

> 'Night, my brother, gather round me,
> Breed the reign of violence,
> And with temptations of the spi-i-rit
> Blight the curse of innocence.
> Oh, supple daughters of the twilight,
> Will we have all our pleasures spent,
> When God emerges from the shadows,
> Blinding in his Strange Magni-i-fi-i-cence . . .'

He broke off and let out a weak chuckle. I was so astounded by this behaviour that my anger was muted and my investigative sensibilities engaged.

'Who're your contacts on Solitaire?' I asked. 'Talk to me, and maybe things will go easier for you.'

Thirwell continued staring at the panel, seemingly transfixed by it.

'Give it up, Roger,' I said. 'Tell us about the Magnificence. You help us, and we'll do right by you, I swear.'

He lifted his face to the ceiling and, in a shattered tone, verging on tears, said, 'Oh, God!'

'I may be wrong,' I said, 'but I don't believe he's going to answer you. You'd best brace it up in there, get your head clear.'

'I don't know,' he said.

'Sure you do. You know. It was your brains got you here. Now use them. Think. You have to make the best of this you can.' It was hard to make promises of leniency to this little grout who'd had his hands on Arlie, but the rectitude of the job provided me a framework in which I was able to function. 'Look here, I can't predict what's going to happen, but I can give you this much. You tell us what you know, chapter and verse, and I'll speak up for you. There could be mitigating circumstances. Drugs. Coercion. Blackmail. That strike a chord, Roger? Hasn't someone been pushing you into this? Yeah, yeah, I thought so. Mitigating circumstances. That being the case, it's likely the corporation will go lightly with you. And one thing I can promise for certain sure. We'll keep you safe from the Magnificence.'

Thirwell turned to the monitor. From the working of his mouth and the darting of his eyes, I could see he was close to falling apart.

'That's it, there's the lad. Come along home.'

'The Magnificence.' He glanced about, as if concerned that someone might be eavesdropping. 'They told me . . . uh . . . I . . .' He swallowed hard and peered at the camera as if trying to see through to the other side of the lens. 'I'm frightened,' he said in a whispery, conspiratorial tone.

'We're all frightened, Roger. It's shit like the Magnificence keeps us frightened. Time to stop being afraid, don't you think? Maybe that's the only way to stop. Just to do it, I mean. Just to say, the hell with this! I'm . . .'

'P'rhaps if I had a word with him,' said Samuelson, leaning in over my shoulder. 'You said I had some influence with the boy. P'rhaps . . .'

I shoved him against the wall; Gerald caught him on the rebound and slung him along the corridor, holding a finger up to his lips, indicating that Samuelson should keep very quiet. But the damage was done. Thirwell had turned back to the control panel and was punching in the code that would break the seal on the outer hatch.

'Don't be an ass!' I said. 'That way's no good for anyone.'

He finished punching in the code and stood staring at the stud that would cycle the lock open. The Danger lights above the inner hatch were winking, and a computer voice had begun repeating, Warning, Warning. The outer hatch has been unsealed, the airlock has not been depressurized. Warning, Warning . . .

'Don't do it, Roger!'

'I have to', he said. 'I realize that now. I was confused, but now it's okay. I can do it.'

'Nobody wants this to happen, Roger.'

'I do, I want it.'

'Listen to me!'

Thirwell's hand went falteringly toward the stud. 'Lord of the alley mouths,' he said, 'Lord of the rifles, Lord of the inflamed, Thou who hath committed every vileness . . .'

'For Christ's sake, man!' I said. 'Nobody's going to hurt you. Not the Magnificence, not anyone. I'll guarantee your safety.'

'. . every sin, every violence, stand with me now, help me shape this dying into an undying love . . .' His voice dropped in volume, becoming too low to hear.

'Goddamn it, Thirwell! You silly bastard. Will you stop jabbering that nonsense! Don't give in to it! Don't listen to what they've taught you. It's all utter rot!'

Thirwell looked up at the camera, at me. Terror warped his features for a moment, but then the lines of tension softened and he giggled. 'He's right,' he said. 'The man's dead on right. You'll never understand.'

'Who's right? What won't I understand?'

'Watch,' said Thirwelll gleefully. 'Watch my face.'

I kept silent, trying to think of the perfect thing to say, something to foil his demented impulse.

'Are you watching?'

'I want to understand,' I said. 'I want you to help me understand. Will you help me, Roger? Will you tell me about the Magnificence?'

'I can't. I can't explain it.' He drew a deep breath, let it out slowly. 'But I'll show you.'

He smiled blissfully at the camera as he pushed the stud.

Explosive decompression, even when viewed on a black-and-white monitor, is not a good thing to see. I looked away. Inadvertently, my eyes went to Samuelson. He was standing about fifteen feet away, hands behind his back, expressionless, like a minister composing himself before delivering his sermon; but there was something else evident in that lean, blank face, something happening beneath the surface, some slight engorgement, and I knew, *knew*, that he was not distressed in the least by the death, that he was pleased by it. No one of his position, I thought, would be so ingenuous as to interrupt a security man trying to talk in a potential suicide. And if what he had done to Thirwell had been intentional, a poorly disguised threat, if he had that much power and menace at his command, then he might well be responsible for what Thirwell had done to Arlie.

I strolled over to him. His eyes tracked my movements. I stopped about four feet away and studied him, searching for signs of guilt, for hints of a black satin past, of torchlight and blood and group sing-alongs. There was weakness in his face, but was it a weakness bred by perversion and brutality, or was it simply a product of fear? I decided that for Arlie's sake, for Thirwell's, I should assume the worst. 'Guess what I'm going to do next?' I asked him. Before he could answer I kicked him in the pit of the stomach, and as he crumpled, I struck him a chopping left to the jaw that twisted his head a quarter-turn. Two of the guards started toward me, but I warned them back. Carbajal fixed me with a look of prim disapproval.

'That was a stupid damn thing to do,' said Gerald, ambling over and gazing down at Samuelson, who was moaning, stirring.

'He deserves worse,' I said. 'Thirwell was coming out. I'm certain of it. And then this bastard opened his mouth.'

'Yeah.' Gerald leaned against the wall, crossed his legs. 'So how come you figure he did it?'

'Why don't you ask him? Be interesting to see how he responds.'

Gerald let out a sardonic laugh. 'Man's an altruist. He was trying to help.' He picked at a rough place on one of his knuckles. 'The real question I got is how deep he's in it. Whether he's involved with the Magnificence, or if he's just trying to convince everyone he is, I need to know so I can make an informed decision.'

I did not much care for the edge of coldness in his voice. 'And what decision is that, pray?'

Carbajal, staring at me over his shoulder, flashed me a knowing smile.

'He already don't like you, John,' said Gerald. 'Man told me so. Now he's gonna want your ass on a plaque. And I have to decide whether or not I should let him have you.'

'Oh, really?'

'This is some serious crap, man. I defy Samuelson, we're gonna have us one helluva situation. Security lined up against Administration.'

Samuelson was trying to sit up; his jaw was swollen and discoloured. I hoped it was broken.

'We could be talkin' about a war,' Gerald said.

'I think you're exaggerating,' I said. 'Even so, a civil war wouldn't be the worst thing that could happen, not so long as the right side won. There are a number of assholes on station who would make splendid casualties.'

Gerald said, 'No comment.'

Samuelson had managed to prop himself up on an elbow. 'I want you to arrest him,' he said to Gerald.

I looked at Gerald. 'Might I have a few words with him before you decide?'

He met my eyes for a few beats, then shook his head in dismay. 'Aw, fuck it,' he said.

'Thanks, friend,' I said.

'Fuck you, too,' he said; he walked a couple of paces away and stood gazing off along the corridor; Carbajal went with him, whispered in his ear and rubbed his shoulders.

'Did you hear what I told you?' Samuelson heaved himself up into a sitting position, cupping his jaw. 'Arrest him. Now!'

'Here, let me help you up.' I grabbed a fistful of Samuelson's jacket, hauled him to his feet, and slammed him into the wall. 'There. All better, are we?'

Samuelson's eyes darted left to right, hoping for allies. I bashed his head against the wall to get his attention, and he struggled against my hold.

'Such a tragedy,' I said in my best upper-crust accent. 'The death of young Thirwell, what?'

The fight went out of him; his eyes held on mine.

'That was as calculated a bit of murder as I've seen in many a year,' I told him.

'I haven't the foggiest notion what you're talking about!'

'Oh, yes you do! I had him walking the tightrope back. Then you popped in and reminded him of the consequences he'd be facing should he betray the Magnificence. God only knows what he thought you had in store for him.'

'I did no such thing! I was . . .'

I dug the fingers of my left hand in behind his windpipe; I would have liked to squeeze until thumb and fingers touched, but I only applied enough force to make him squeak. 'Shut your gob! I'm not finished.' I adjusted my grip to give him more air.

'You're dirty, Samuelson. You're the germ that's causing all the pale looks around here. I don't know how you got past the screens, but that's not important. Sooner or later I'm going to have your balls for breakfast. And when I've cleaned my plate, I'll send what's left of you to the same place you chased Thirwell. Of course you could tell me the names of everyone on Solitaire who's involved with the Magnificence. That might weaken my resolve. But don't be too long about it, because I am fucking lusting for you. I can scarcely wait for you to thwart me. My saliva gets all thick and ropy when I think of the times we could have together.' I gave him a shake, listened to him gurgle. 'I know what you are, and I know what you want. You've got a dream, don't you? A vast, spendid dream of men in black satin populating the stars. New planets to befoul. Well, it's just not going to happen. If it ever comes to pass that a ship returns with good news, you won't be on it, son. Nor will any of your tribe. You'll be floating out there in the black grip of Jesus, with your blood all frozen in sprays around you and your hearts stuffed in your fucking mouths.' I released him, gave him a cheerful wink. 'All right. Go ahead. Your innings.'

Samuelson scooted away along the wall, holding his throat. 'You're mad!' He glanced over at Gerald. 'The both of you!'

Gerald shrugged, spread his hands. 'It's part of the job description.'

'May we take it,' I said to Samuelson, 'that you're not intending to confess at this time?'

Samuelson noticed, as had I, that a number of people had come out of the common room and were watching the proceedings. 'I'll tell you what I intend,' he said, pulling himself erect in an attempt to look impressive. 'I intend to make a detailed report concerning your disregard for authority and your abuse of position.'

'Now, now,' Gerald said, walking toward him. 'Let's have no threats. Otherwise somebody' – his voice built into a shout – 'somebody might lose their temper!' He accompanied the shout by slapping his palm against the wall, and this sent Samuelson staggering back another dozen feet or so.

Several of the gathering laughed.

'Come clean, man,' I said to Samuelson. 'Do the right thing.

I'm told it's better than sex once those horrid secrets start spilling out.'

'If it'll make you feel any easier, you can dress up in your black satins first,' Gerald said. 'Having that smooth stuff next to your skin, that'll put a nice wiggle on things.'

'You know, Gerald,' I said. 'Maybe these poofs are onto something. Maybe the Magnificence has a great deal to offer.'

'I'm always interested in upgrading my pleasure potential,' he said. 'Why don't you give us the sales pitch, Samuelson?'

'Yeah,' I said. 'Let's hear about all the snarky quivers you get from twisting the arms off a virgin.'

The laughter swelled in volume, inspired by Samuelson's expression of foolish impotence.

'You don't understand who you're dealing with,' he said. 'But you will, I promise.'

There, I said to myself, there's his confession. Not enough to bring into court, but for a moment it was there in his face, all the sick hauteur and corrupted passion of his tribe.

'I bet you're a real important man with the Magnificence,' said Gerald. 'Bet you even got a title.'

'Minister of Scum and Delirium,' I suggested.

'I like it,' said Gerald. 'How 'bout Secretary of the Inferior?'

'Grand High Salamander,' said Carbajal, and tittered.

'Master of the Excremental.'

'Stop it,' said Samuelson, clenching his fists; he looked ready to stamp his foot and cry.

Several other titular suggestions came from the crowd of onlookers, and Gerald offered, 'Queen of the Shitlickers.'

'I'm warning you,' said Samuelson, then he shouted, 'I am warning you!' He was flushed, trembling. All the twitchy material of his inner core exposed. It had been fun bashing him about, but now I wanted to put my heel on him, feel him crunch underfoot.

'Go on,' Gerald said. 'Get along home. You've done all you can here.'

Samuelson shot him an unsteady look, as if not sure what Gerald was telling him.

Gerald waved him off. 'We'll talk soon.'

'Yes,' said Samuelson, straightening his jacket, trying to

muster a shred of dignity. 'Yes, indeed, we most certainly will.'
He delivered what I suppose he hoped was a withering stare and
stalked off along the corridor.

'There goes an asshole on a mission,' said Gerald, watching
him round the bend.

'Not a doubt in my mind,' I said.

'Trouble.' Gerald scuffed his heel against the steel floor,
glanced down as if expecting to see a mark. 'No shit, the man's
trouble.'

'So are we,' I said.

'Yeah, uh-huh.' He sounded unconvinced.

We exchanged a quick glance. We had been through a lot
together, Gerald and I, and I knew by the tilt of his head, the wry
set of his mouth, that he was very worried. I was about to make a
stab at boosting his spirits when I remembered something more
pressing.

'Oh, Christ!' I said. 'Arlie! I've got to get back.'

'Forgot about her, huh?' He nodded gloomily, as if my
forgetfulness were something he had long decried. 'You know
you're an asshole, don't you? You know you don't deserve the
love of woman or the friendship of man.'

'Yeah, yeah,' I said. 'Can you handle things here?'

He made a gesture of dismissal. Another morose nod. 'Just so
you know,' he said.

There were no seasons on Solitaire, no quick lapses into cold,
dark weather, no sudden transformations into flowers and
greenery; yet it seemed that in those days after Thirwell's suicide
the station passed through an autumnal dimming, one lacking
changes in foliage and temperature, but having in their stead a
flourishing of black satin ribbons and ugly rumours, a gradual
decaying of the spirit of the place into an oppressive atmosphere
of sullen wariness, and the slow occlusion of all the visible
brightness of our lives, a slump of patronage in the bars, the
common rooms standing empty, incidences of decline that
reminded me in sum of the stubborn resistance of the English
oaks to their inevitable change, their profuse and solemn green
surrendering bit by bit to the sparse imperatives of winter, like a
strong man's will gradually being eroded by grief.

War did not come immediately, as Gerald had predicted, but the sporadic violences continued, along with the arguments concerning the true intentions and nature of the Strange Magnificence, and few of us doubted that war, or something akin to it, was in the offing. Everyone went about their duties hurriedly, grimly – everyone, that is, except for Bill. He was so absorbed by his own difficulties, I doubted he noticed any of this, and though the focus of hostility had shifted away from him to an extent, becoming more diffuse and general, he grew increasingly agitated and continued to prattle on about having to 'do something' and – this a new chord in his simple symphony – that something must be terribly wrong because the barnacles were leaving.

That they were leaving was undeniable. Every hour saw the migration of thousands more, and large areas of the station's surface had been laid bare. Not completely bare, mind you. There remained a layer of the substrate laid down by the females, greenish silver in colour, but nonetheless it was a shock to see the station so denuded. I gave no real credence to Bill's contention that we were in danger, but neither did I totally disregard it, and so, partly to calm him, to reassure him that the matter was being investigated, I went back to Jacob Sauter's notes to learn if such migrations were to be expected.

According to the notes, pre-adult barnacles – Sauter called them 'larvae' – free-floated in space, each encapsulated in its own segment of a tube whose ends had been annealed so as to form a ring. Like the adult barnacle, the exterior of the ring was dotted with light-sensitive photophores, and when a suitable place for attachment was sensed, the ring colony was able to orient itself by means of excretions sprayed through pores in the skin of the tube, a method not dissimilar to that utilized by orbital vessels when aligning themselves for re-entry. The slightest change in forward momentum induced secretions to occur along the edge of the colony oriented for imminent attachment, and ultimately the colony stuck to its new home, whereupon the females excreted an acidic substrate that bonded with the metal. The barnacles were hermaphroditic, and the initial metamorphitosis always resulted in female barnacles alone. Once the female colony grew dense, some of the females would become male. When the colony reached a certain density it reproduced *en masse*. As the larval tubes were secreted, they sometimes intertwined, and this would result in braided ring-colonies, which helped insure variation in the gene pool. And that was all I could find on the subject of migration. If Sauter were to be believed, by giving up their purchase on the station, the barnacles were essentially placing their fate in the hands of God, taking the chance – and given the vastness of space, the absence of ring secretions, it was an extremely slim chance – that they would happen to bump into something and be able to cling long enough to attach themselves. If one were to judge their actions in human terms, it would appear that they must be terrified of something, otherwise they would stay where they were; but it would require an immense logical leap for me to judge them according to those standards and I had no idea what was responsible for their exodus.

Following my examination of Sauter's notes I persuaded Gerald to accompany me on an inspection tour of Solitaire's surface. I thought seeing the migration for himself might affect him more profoundly than had the camera views, and that he might then join me in entertaining the suspicion that – as unlikely a prospect as it was – Bill had stumbled onto something. But Gerald was not moved to agreement.

'Man, I don't know,' he said as we stood on the surface of East Louie, looking out toward the CPC and the administration module. There were a few sparse patches of barnacles around us, creatures that for whatever reason – impaired sensitivity, some form of silicate stubbornness – had not abandoned the station. Now and then one or several would drift up toward the glittering clouds of their fellows that shone against the blackness like outcroppings of mica in anthracite. 'What do I know about these damn things! They could be doing anything. Could be they ran out of food, and that's why they're moving. Shit! You giving the idiot way too much credit! He's got his own reasons for wanting this to mean something.'

I could not argue with him. It would be entirely consistent with Bill's character for him to view the migration as part of his personal apocalypse, and his growing agitation might stem from the fact that he saw his world being whittled down, his usefulness reduced, and thus his existence menaced all the more.

'Still,' I said, 'it seems odd.'

' "Odd" ain't enough. Weird, now, that might carry some weight. Crazy. Run amok. They qualify for my attention. But "odd" I can live with. You want to worry about this, I can't stop you. Me, I got more important things to do. And so do you.'

'I'm doing my job, don't you worry.'

'Okay. Tell me about it.'

Through the glaze of reflection on his faceplate, I could only make out his eyes and his forehead, and these gave no clue to his mood.

'There's not very much to tell. As far as I can determine Samuelson's pure through and through. There's a curious lack of depth to the background material, a few dead ends in the investigative reports. Deceased informants. Vanished employers. That sort of thing. It doesn't feel quite right to me, but it's nothing I could bring to the corporation. And it does appear that his elder brother was murdered by the Magnificence, which establishes at least one of his *bona fides*.'

'If Samuelson's part of the Magnificence, I . . .'

' "If", my ass!' I said. 'You know damned well he is.'

'I was going to say, his brother's murder is just the kind of tactic they like to use in order to draw suspicion away from one of their own. Hell, he may have hated his brother.'

'Or he may have loved him and wanted the pain.'

Gerald grunted.

'I've isolated fourteen files that have a sketchiness reminiscent of Samuelson's,' I said. 'Of course that doesn't prove anything. Most of them are administration and most are relatively new on Solitaire. But only a couple are his close associates.'

'That makes it more likely they're all dirty. They don't believe in bunching up. I'll check into it.' I heard a burst of static over my earphones, which meant that he had let out a heavy sigh. 'The damn thing is,' he went on, 'Samuelson might not be the lead dog. Whoever's running things might be keeping in the shadows for now.'

'No, not a chance,' I said. 'Samuelson's too lovely in the part.'

A construction sled, a boxy thing of silver struts powered by a man in a rocket pack, went arcing up from the zero physics lab and boosted toward one of the assembly platforms; all manner of objects were lashed to the struts, some of them – mostly tools, vacuum welders and such—trailing along in its wake, giving the sled a raggedy, gypsy look.

'Those explosives you got stashed,' Gerald said, staring after the sled.

'They're safe.'

'I hope so. We didn't have 'em, they might have moved on us by now. Done a hostage thing. Or maybe just blown something up. I'm pretty sure nothing else has been brought on station, so you can just keep a close watch on that shit. That's our hole card.'

'I don't like waiting for them to make the first move.'

'I know you don't. Was up to you, we'd be stiffening citizens right and left, and figuring out later if they guilty or not. That's how come you got the teeth, and I'm holding the leash.'

Though his face was hidden, I knew he was not smiling.

'Your way's not always the right of it, Gerald,' I said. 'Sometimes my way's the most effective, the most secure.'

'Yeah, maybe. But not this time. This is too bullshit, this mess. Too many upper-level people involved. We scratch the wrong number off the page, we be down the tube in a fucking flash. You don't want to be scuffling around back on Earth, do you? I sure as hell don't.'

'I'd prefer it to having my lungs sucked out through my mouth like Thirwell.'

'Would you, now? Me, I'm not so sure. I want a life that's more than just gnawing bones, John. I ain't up to that kind of hustle no more. And I don't believe you are, either.'

We stood without speaking for a minute or so. It was getting near time for a shift change, and everywhere bits of silver were lifting from the blotched surface of the station, flocking together in the brilliant beams of light shooting from the transport bays, their movements as quick and fitful as the play of dust in sunlight.

'You're thinking too much these days, man,' Gerald said. 'You're not sniffing the air, you're not feeling things here.' He made a slow, ungainly patting motion above his gut.

'That's rot!'

'Is it? Listen to this. "Life has meaning but no theme. There is no truth we can assign to it that does not in some way lessen the bright flash of being that is its essential matter. There is no lesson learned that does not signal a misapprehension of our stars. There is no moral to this darkness." That's some nice shit. Extremely profound. But the man who wrote that, he's not watching the water for sharks. He's too busy thinking.'

'I'm so pleased,' I said, 'you've been able to access my computer once again. I know the childlike joy it brings you. And I'm quite sure Ernesto is absolutely thrilled at having a peek.'

'Practice makes perfect.'

'Any further conclusions you've drawn from poking around in my personal files?'

'You got one helluva fantasy life. Or else that Arlie, man, she's about half some kind of beast. How come you write all that sex stuff down?'

'Prurience,' I said. 'Damn! I don't know why I put up with this shit from you.'

'Well, I do. I'm the luckiest Chief of Security in the system, see, 'cause I've got me a big, bad dog who's smart and loyal, and' – he lifted one finger of his gauntleted hand to signify that this was key – 'who has no ambition to take my job.'

'Don't be too sure.'

'No, man, you don't want my job. I mean, you'd accept it if it was handed to you, but you like things the way they are. You always running wild and me trying to cover your ass.'

'I hope you're not suggesting that I'm irresponsible.'

'You're responsible, all right. You just wouldn't want the kind of responsibility I've got. It'd interfere with your style. The way you move around the station, talking bullshit to the people, everything's smooth, then all of a sudden you go Bam! Bam! and take somebody down, then the next second you're talking about Degas or some shit, and then, Bam! somebody else on the floor, you say, Oops, shit, I guess I messed up, will you please forgive me, did I ever tell you 'bout Paris in the springtime when all the poets turn into cherryblossoms, Bam! It's fucking beautiful, man. You got half the people so scared they crawl under the damn rug when they see you coming, and the other half loves you to death, and most all of 'em would swear you're some kind of Robin Hood, you whip 'em 'cause you love 'em and it's your duty, and you only use your powers for goodness and truth. They don't understand you like I do. They don't see you're just a dangerous, amoral son of a bitch.'

'Is this the sort of babble that goes into your personnel reports?'

'Not hardly. I present you as a real citizen. A model of intregrity and courage and resourcefulness.'

'Thanks for that,' I said coldly.

'Just don't ever change, man. Don't ever change.'

The sleds that had lifted from the station had all disappeared, but others were materializing from the blackness, tiny points of silver and light coming home from the assembly platforms, looking no more substantial than the clouds of barnacles. Finally Gerald said, 'I got things to take care of.' He waved at the barnacles. 'Leave this shit alone, will you? After everything else gets settled, maybe then we'll look into it. Right now all you doing is wasting my fucking time.'

I watched him moving off along the curve of the module toward the airlock, feeling somewhat put off by his brusque reaction and his analysis. I respected him a great deal as a professional, and his clinical assessment of my abilities made me doubt that his respect for me was so unqualified.

There was a faint click against the side of my helmet. I reached up and plucked off a barnacle. Lying in the palm of my gauntlet, its plates closed, its olive surface threaded with gold and crimson, it seemed cryptic, magical, rare, like something one would find after a search lasting half a lifetime, a relic buried with a wizard king, lying in his ribcage in place of a heart. I had shifted my position so that the light from the port behind me cast my shadow over the surface, and, a neurological change having been triggered by the shift in light intensity, some of the barnacles in the shadow were opening their plates and probing the vacuum with stubby grey 'tongues', trying to feed. It was an uncanny sight, the way their 'tongues' moved, stiffly, jerkily, like bad animation, like creatures in a grotesque garden hallucinated by Hawthorne or Baudelaire, and standing there among them, with the technological hodgepodge of the station stretching away in every direction, I felt as if I were stranded in a pool of primitive time, looking out onto the future. It was, I realized, a feeling akin to that I'd had in London whenever I thought about the space colonies, the outposts strung across the system.

Gnawing bones.

As my old Classics professor would have said, Gerald's metaphor was 'a happy choice'.

And now I had time to consider, I realized that Gerald was right: after all the years on Solitaire, I would be ill-suited for life in London, my instincts rusty, incapable of readjusting to the city's rabid intensity. But I did not believe he was right to wait for Samuelson to move against us. Once the Magnificence set their sights on a goal, they were not inclined to use half-measures. I was too disciplined to break ranks with Gerald, but there was nothing to prevent me from preparing myself for the day of judgement. Samuelson might bring us down, I told myself, but I would see to it that he would not outlive us. I was not aware, however, that judgement day was almost at hand.

Perhaps it was the trouble of those days that brought Arlie and me closer together, that reawakened us to the sweetness of our bodies and the sharp mesh of our souls, to all those things we had come to take for granted. And perhaps Bill had something to do with it. As dismal an item as he was, it may be his presence served – as Arlie had suggested – to supply us with some missing essential of warmth or heart. But whatever the cause, it was a great good time for us, and I came once again to perceive her not merely as someone who could cure a hurt or make me stop thinking for a while, but as the embodiment of my hopes. After everything I had witnessed, all the shabby, bloody evidence I had been presented of our kind's pettiness and greed, that I could feel anything so pure for another human being . . . Christ, it astounded me! And if that much could happen, then why not the fulfilment of other, more improbable hopes? For instance, suppose a ship were to return with news of a habitable world. I pictured the two of us boarding, flying away, landing, being washed clean in the struggle of a stern and simple life. Foolishness, I told myself. Wild ignorance. Yet each time I fell into bed with Arlie, though the darkness that covered us seemed always imbued with a touch of black satin, with the sticky patina of the Strange Magnificence, I would sense in the back of my mind that in touching her I was flying away again, and in entering her I was making landfall on some perfect blue-green sphere. There came a night, however, when to entertain such thoughts seemed not mere folly but the height of indulgence.

It was close upon half-eleven, and the three of us, Bill, Arlie, and I, were sitting in the living room, the walls playing a holographic scenario of a white-capped sea and Alps of towering cumulus, with whales breeching and a three-masted schooner coasting on the wind, vanishing whenever it reached the corner, then reappearing on the adjoining wall. Bill and Arlie were on the sofa, and she was telling him stories about Earth, lies about the wonderful animals that lived there, trying to distract him from his obsessive nattering about the barnacles. I had just brought out several of the packet charges that Gerald and I had hidden away, and I was working at reshaping them into smaller units, a project that had occupied me for several nights. Bill had previously seemed frightened by them and had never mentioned them. That night, however, he pointed at the charges and said, ' 'Splosives?'

'Very good,' I said. 'The ones we found, you and I. The ones I was working with yesterday. Remember?'

'Uh-huh.' He watched me re-insert a timer into one of the charges and then asked what I was doing.

'Making some presents,' I told him.

'Birthday presents?'

'More like Guy Fawkes Day presents.'

He had no clue as to the identity of Guy Fawkes, but he nodded sagely as though he had. 'Is one for Gerald?'

'You might say they're all for Gerald.'

He watched me a while longer, then said, 'Why is it presents? Don't 'splosives hurt?'

' 'E's just havin' a joke,' Arlie said.

Bill sat quietly for a minute or so, his eyes tracking my fingers, and at last he said, 'Why won't you talk to Gerald about the barnacles? You should tell him it's important.'

'Give it a rest, Billy,' Arlie said, patting his arm.

'What do you expect Gerald to do?' I said. 'Even if he agreed with you, there's nothing to be done.'

'Leave,' he said. 'Like the barnacles.'

'What a marvellous idea! We'll just pick up and abandon the place.'

'No, no!' he shrilled. 'CPC! CPC!'

'Listen 'ere,' said Arlie. 'There's not a chance in 'ell the corporation's goin' to authorize usin' the CPC for somethin' loike that. So put it from mind, dear, won't you?'

'Don't need the corporation,' Bill said in a whiny tone.

'He's got the CPC on the brain,' I said. 'Every night I come in here and find him running the file.'

Arlie shushed me and asked, 'What's that you said, Bill?'

He clamped his lips together, leaned back against the wall, his head making a dark, ominous-looking interruption in the path of the schooner; a wave of bright water appeared to crash over him, sending up a white spray.

'You 'ave somethin' to tell us, dear?'

'Be grateful for the silence,' I said.

A few seconds later Bill began to weep, to wail that it wasn't fair, that everyone hated him.

We did our best to soothe him, but to no avail. He scrambled to his feet and went to beating his fists against his thighs, hopping up and down, shrieking at the top of his voice, his face gone as red as a squalling infant's. Then of a sudden he clutched the sides of his head. His legs stiffened, his neck cabled. He fell back on the sofa, twitching, screaming, clawing at the lump behind his ear. Mister C had intervened and was punishing him with electric shocks. It was a hideous thing to see, this enormous, babyish man jolted by internal lightnings, strings of drool braiding his chin, the animation ebbing from his face, his protests growing ever more feeble, until at last he sat staring blankly into nowhere, an ugly, outsized doll in a stained white jumpsuit.

Arlie moved close to him, mopped his face with a tissue. Her mouth thinned; the lines bracketing the corners of her lips deepened. 'God, 'e's a disgustin' object,' she said. 'I don't know what it is about 'im touches me so.'

'Perhaps he reminds you of your uncle.'

'I realize this is hard toimes for you, luv,' she said, continuing to mop Bill's face. 'But do you really find it necessary to treat me so sarcastic, loike I was one of your culprits?'

'Sorry,' I said.

She gave an almost imperceptible shrug. Something shifted in her face, as if an opaque mask had slid aside, revealing her newly vulnerable. 'What you fink's goin' to 'appen to 'im?'

'Same as'll happen to us, probably. It appears our fates have become intertwined.' I picked up another charge. 'Anyway, what's it matter, the poor droob? His best pal is a little black bean that zaps him whenever he throws a wobbler. He's universally loathed, and his idea of a happy time is to pop a crystal and flog the bishop all night long. As far as I can tell, his fate's already bottomed out.'

She clicked her tongue against her teeth. 'Maybe it's us Oi see in 'im.'

'You and me? That's a laugh.'

'Nao, I mean all of us. Don't it seem sometimes we're all 'elpless loike 'im? Just big, loopy animals without a proper sense of things.'

'I don't choose to think that way.'

Displeasure came into her face, but before she could voice it, a loud buzzer went off in the bedroom – Gerald's private alarm, a device he would only use if unable to communicate with me openly. I jumped to my feet and grabbed a hand laser from a drawer in the table beside the sofa.

'Don't let anyone in,' I told Arlie. 'Not under any circumstances.'

She nodded, gave me a brisk hug. 'You 'urry back.'

The corridors of East Louie were thronged, hundreds of people milling about the entrances of the common rooms and the commissaries. I smelled hashish, perfume, pheromone sprays. Desperate with worry, I pushed and elbowed my way through the crowds toward Gerald's quarters, which lay at the opposite end of the module. When I reached his door, I found it part way open and the concerned brown face of Ernesto Carbajal peering out at me. He pulled me into the foyer. The room beyond was dark; a slant of light fell across the carpet from the bedroom door, which was open a foot or so; but I could make out nothing within.

'Where's Gerald?' I asked.

Carbajal's hands made delicate, ineffectual gestures in the air, as if trying to find a safe hold on something with a lot of sharp edges. 'I didn't know what to do,' he said. 'I didn't know . . . I . . .'

I watched him flutter and spew. He was Gerald's man, and Gerald claimed he was trustworthy. For my part, I had never formed an opinion. Now, however, I saw nothing that made me want to turn my back on him. And so, of course, I determined that I would do exactly that as soon as a suitable opportunity presented itself.

'You gave the alarm?' I asked him.

'Yes, I didn't want anyone to hear . . . the intercom. You know, it . . . I . . .'

'Yeah, yeah, I know. Calm down!' I pushed him against the wall, kept my hand flat against his chest. 'Where's Gerald?'

His eyes flicked toward the bedroom; for an instant the flesh of his face seemed to sag away from the bone, to lose all its firmness. 'There,' he said. 'Back there. Oh God!'

It was at that moment I knew Gerald was dead, but I refused to let the knowledge affect me. No matter how terrible the scene in the bedroom, Carbajal's reactions – though nicely done – were too flighty for a professional; even considering his involvement with Gerald, he should have been able to manage a more businesslike façade.

'Let's have a look, shall we?'

'No, I don't want to go back in there!'

'All right, then,' I said. 'You wait here.'

I crossed to the bedroom, keeping an ear out for movement behind me. I swallowed, held my breath. The surface of the door seemed hot to the touch, and when I slid it open, I had the thought that the heat must be real, that all the glare off the slick red surfaces within had permeated the metal. Gerald was lying on the bed, the great crimson hollow of his stomach and chest exposed and empty, unbelievably empty, cave empty, with things like glistening, pulpy red fruit resting by his head, hands and feet; but I did not admit to the sight, I kept a distant focus. I heard a step behind me and turned, throwing up my guard as Carbajal, his face distorted by a grimace, struck at me with a knife. I caught his knife arm, bent the elbow backward against the doorframe; I heard it crack as he screamed and shoved him back into the living room. He staggered off-balance, but did not fall. He righted himself, began to move in a stealthy crouch, keeping his shattered elbow toward me, willing to accept more pain in order to protect his good left hand. Disabled or not, he was still very fast, dangerous with his kicks. But I knew I had him so long as I was careful, and I chose to play him rather than end it with the laser. The more I punished him, I thought, the less resistant he would be to interrogation. I feinted, and when he jumped back, I saw him wince. A chalky wash spread across his skin. Every move he made was going to hurt him.

'You might as well hazard it all on one throw, Ernesto,' I told him. 'If you don't, you're probably going to fall over before I knock you down.'

He continued to circle me, unwilling to waste energy on a response; his eyes looked all dark, brimming with concentrated rage. Passing through the spill of light from the bedroom, he seemed ablaze with fury, a slim little devil with a crooked arm.

'It's not your karate let you down, Ernesto. It's that ridiculous drama-queen style of acting. Absolutely vile! I thought you might start beating your breast and crying out to Jesus for succour. Of course that's the weakness all you yobbos in the Magnificence seem to have. You're so damned arrogant, you think you can fool everyone with the most rudimentary tactics. I wonder why that is. Never mind. In a moment I'm going to let you tell me all about it.'

I gave him an opening, a good angle of attack. I'm certain he knew it was a trap, but he was in so much pain, so eager to stop the pain, that his body reacted toward the opening before his mind could cancel the order. He swung his right leg in a vicious arc, I stepped inside the kick, executed a hip throw; as he flew into the air and down, I wrenched his good arm out of the socket with a quick twist. He gave a cry, but wriggled out of my reach and bridged to his feet, both arms dangling. I took him back down with a leg sweep and smashed his right kneecap with my heel. Once his screaming had subsided I sat down on the edge of a coffee table and showed him the laser.

'Now we can talk undisturbed,' I said brightly. 'I hope you feel like talking, because otherwise . . .'

He cursed in Spanish, spat toward me.

'I can see there's no fooling you, Ernesto. You obviously know you're not leaving here alive, not after what you've done. But you do have one life choice remaining that might be of some interest. Quickly' – I flourished the laser – 'or slowly. What's your pleasure?'

He lay without moving, his chest heaving, blinking from time to time, a neutral expression on his face, perhaps trying to think of something he could tell me that would raise the stakes. His breath whistled in his throat; sweat beaded his forehead. My thoughts kept pulling me back into that red room, and as I sat there the pull became irresistible. I saw it clearly this time. The heart lying on the pillow above Gerald's head, the other organs arranged neatly beside his hands and feet; the darkly crimson hollow with its pale flaps. Things written in blood on the wall. It made me weary to see it, and the most wearisome thing of all was the fact that I was numb, that I felt almost nothing. I knew I would have to rouse myself from this spiritual malaise and go after Samuelson. I could trust no one to help me wage a campaign – quick retaliation was the best chance I had. Perhaps the only chance. The Magnificence had a number of shortcomings. Their arrogance, a crudeness of tactics, an infrastructure that allowed unstable personalities to rise to power. To be truthful, the fear and ignorance of their victims was their greatest strength. But their most pertinent flaw was that they tended to give their subordinates too little autonomy. With Samuelson out of the picture, the rest might very well scatter. And then I realized there was something I could do that would leave nothing to chance.

'Ernesto,' I said, 'now I've considered it, there's really not a thing you can tell me that I want to know.'

'No,' he said. 'No, I have something. Please!'

I shrugged. 'All right. Let's hear it.'

'The bosses,' he said. 'I know where they are.'

'The Magnificence, you mean? Those bosses?'

A nod. 'Administration. They're all there.'

'They're there right this moment?'

Something must have given a twinge, for he winced and said, '*Dios!*' When he recovered he added, 'Yes. They're waiting . . .' Another pain took him away for a moment.

'Waiting for the revolution to be won?' I suggested.

'Yes.'

'And just how many bosses are we speaking about?'

'Twenty. Almost twenty, I think.'

Christ, I thought, nearly half of administration gone to black satin and nightmare.

I got to my feet, pocketed the laser.

'Wha . . .' Ernesto said, and swallowed; his pallor had increased, and I realized he was going into shock. His dark eyes searched my face.

'I'm going, Ernesto,' I said. 'I don't have the time to treat you as you did Gerald. But my fervent hope is that someone else with more time on their hands will find you. Perhaps one of your brothers in the Magnificence. Or one of Gerald's friends. Neither, I suspect, will view your situation in a favourable light. And should no one come upon you in the foreseeable future, I suppose I shall have to be satisfied with knowing you died a lingering death.' I bent to him. 'Getting cold, isn't it? You've had the sweet bit, Ernesto. There'll be no more pretending you've a pretty pair of charlies and playing sweet angelina to the hard boys. No more gobble-offs for you, dearie. It's all fucking over.'

I would have loved to hurt him some more, but I did not belive I would have been able to stop once I got started. I blew him a kiss, told him that if the pain got too bad he could always swallow his tongue, and left him to what would almost certainly be the first of his final misgivings.

When I returned to my quarters Arlie threw her arms about me and held me tight while I gave her the news about Gerald. I still felt nothing. Telling her was like hearing my own voice delivering a news summary.

'I've got work to do,' I said. 'I can't protect you here. They're liable to pay a visit while I'm away. You'll have to come with me.'

She nodded, her face buried in my shoulder.

'We have to go outside,' I said. 'We can use one of the sleds. Just a short hop over to Administration, a few minutes there, and we're done. Can you manage?'

Arlie liked having something solid underfoot; going outside was a dread prospect for her, but she made no objection.

'What are you intendin'?' she asked, watching me gather the packet charges I had left scattered about the floor.

'Nothing nice,' I said, peering under the sofa; I was, it appeared, short four charges. 'Don't worry about it.'

'Don't you get cheeky with me! Oi'm not some low-heel Sharon you've only just met. Oi've a right to know what you're about.'

'I'm going to blow up the damned place,' I said, moving the sofa away from the wall.

She stared at me, open-mouthed. 'You're plannin' to blow up Admin? 'Ave you done your crust? What you finkin' of?'

I told her about the suspicious files and what Ernesto had said, but this did little to soothe her.

'There's twenty other people livin' in there!' she said. 'What about them?'

'Maybe they won't be at home,' I pushed the sofa back against the wall. 'I'm missing four charges here. You seen 'em?'

'It's almost one o'clock. Some of 'em might be out, Oi grant you. But whether it's twenty or fifteen, you're talkin' about the murder of innocent people.'

'Look here,' I said, continuing my search, heaving chairs about to bleed off my anger. 'First of all, they're not people. They're corporation deadlegs. Using the word "innocent" to describe them makes as much sense as using the word "dainty" to describe a pig's eating habits. At one time or another they've every one put the drill to some poor Joey's backside and made it bleed. And they'd do it again in a flicker, because that's all they fucking know how to do. Secondly, if they were in my shoes, if they had a chance to rid the station of the Magnificence with only twenty lives lost, they wouldn't hesitate. Thirdly' – I flipped up the cushions on the sofa – 'and most importantly, I don't have a bloody choice! Do you understand me? There's no one I can trust to help. I don't have a loyal force with which to lay siege to them. This is the only way I can settle things. I'm not thrilled with the idea of murdering – as you say – twenty people in order to do what's necessary. And I realize it allows you to feel morally superior to think of me as a villain. But if I don't do something soon there'll be hearts and livers strewn about the station like party favours, and twenty dead is going to seem like nothing!' I hurled a cushion into the corner. 'Shit! Where are they?'

Arlie was still staring at me, but the outrage had drained from her face. 'Oi 'aven't seen 'em.'

'Bill,' I said, struck by a notion. 'Where he'd get to?'

'Bill?'

'Yeah, Bill. The fuckwit. Where is he?'

''E's away somewhere,' she said. ' 'E was in the loo for a while, then Oi went in the bedroom, and when Oi come out 'e was gone.'

I crossed to the bathroom, hoping to find the charges there. But when the door slid open, I saw only that the floor was spattered with bright, tacky blood; there was more blood in the sink, along with a kitchen knife, matted hair, handfuls of wadded, becrimsoned paper towels. And something else: a thin black disc about the size of a soy wafer. It took me a while to absorb all this, to put it together with Bill's recent obsessions, and even after I had done so, my conclusion was difficult to credit. Yet I could think of no other explanation that would satisfy the conditions.

'Arlie,' I called. 'You seen this?'

'Nao, what?' she said, coming up behind me; then: 'Holy Christ!'

'That's his implant, isn't it?' I said, pointing to the disc.

'Yeah, I s'pose it is. My God! Why'd he do that?' She put a hand to her mouth. 'You don't fink 'e took the charges . . .'

'The CPC,' I said. 'He knew he couldn't do anything with Mister C along for the ride, so he cut the bastard out. And now he's gone for the CPC. Jesus! That's just what we needed, isn't it! Another fucking maniac on the loose!'

'It must 'ave 'urt 'im somethin' fierce!' Arlie said wonderingly. 'I mean, he 'ad to 'ave done it quick and savage, or else Mister C would 'ave 'ad time to stop 'im. And I never heard a peep.'

'I wouldn't worry about Bill if I were you. You think twenty dead's a tragedy? Think what'll happen if he blows the CPC. How many do you reckon will be walking between modules when they disengage? How many others will be killed by falling things? By other sorts of accidents?'

I went back into the living room, shouldered my pack; I handed Arlie a laser. 'If you see anyone coming after us, use it. Burn them low if that's all you can bear, but burn them. All right?'

She gave a tight, anxious nod and looked down at the weapon in her hand.

'Come on,' I said. 'Once we get to the airlock we'll be fine.'

But I was none too confident of our chances. Thanks to the greed of madmen and the single-mindedness of our resident idiot, it seemed that the chances of everyone on Solitaire were growing slimmer by the second.

I suppose some of you will say at this juncture that I should have known bad things were going to happen, and further will claim that many of the things that did happen might have been forestalled had I taken a few basic precautions and shown the slightest good sense. What possessed me, you might ask, to run out of my quarters leaving explosives scattered about the floor where Bill could easily appropriate them? And couldn't I have seen that his fascination with the CPC might lead to some perilous circumstance? And why had I not perceived his potential for destructiveness? Well, what had possessed me was concern for a friend, the closest to a friend that I had ever known. And as to Bill, his dangerous potentials, he had never displayed any sign that he was capable of enduring the kind of pain he must have endured, or of employing logic sufficiently well so as to plan even such a simple act as he perpetrated. It was desperation, I'm certain, that fathered the plan, and how was I to factor in desperation with the IQ of a biscuit and come up with the sum of that event? No, I reject guilt and credit both. My part in things was simpler than demanded by that complex twist of fate. I was only there, it seems, to finish things, to stamp out a few last fires, and – in the end – to give a name to the demons of that place and time. And yet perhaps there was something in that whole fury of moments that was mine. Perhaps I saw an opportunity to take a step away from the past, albeit a violent step, and moved by a signal of some sort, one too slight to register except in my cells, I took it. I would like to think I had a higher purpose in mind, and was not merely acting out the imperatives of some fierce vanity.

We docked the sled next to an airlock in the administration module, my reasoning being that if we were forced to flee, it would take less time to run back to Administration than it would to cycle the CPC airlock; but instead of entering there, we walked along the top of the corridor that connected Administration and the CPC, working our way along moulded troughs of plastic covered with the greenish-silver substrate left by the barnacles, past an electric array, beneath a tree of radiator panels thirty times as tall as a man, and entered the emergency lock at its nether end. There was a sled docked beside it, and realizing that Bill must have used it, I thought how terrified he must have been to cross even that much of the void without Mister C to lend him guidance. Before entering, I set the timer of one of the charges in the pack to a half-second delay and stuck it in the hip pouch of my pressure suit. I would be able to trigger the switch with just the touch of my palm against the pouch. A worst-case eventuality.

The cameras inside the CPC were functioning, but since there were no security personnel in evidence, I had to assume that the automatic alarms had failed and that – as usual – no one was bothered to monitor the screens. We had not gone twenty feet into the main room when we saw Bill, dressed in a pressure suit, helmet in hand, emerge from behind a plastic partition, one of many which – as I have said – divided the cavernous white space into a maze of work stations. He looked stunned, lost, and when he noticed us he gave no sign of recognition; the side of his neck was covered with dried blood, and he held his head tipped to that side, as one might when trying to muffle pain by applying pressure to the injured spot. His mouth hung open, his posture was slack, and his eyes were bleary. Under the trays of cold light his complexion was splotchy and dappled with the angry red spots of pimples just coming up.

'The explosives,' I said. 'Where are they? Where'd you put them?'

His eyes wandered up, grazed my face, twitched toward Arlie, and then lowered to the floor. His breath made an ugly glutinous noise.

He was a pitiable sight, but I could not afford pity; I was enraged at him for having betrayed my trust. 'You miserable fucking stain!' I said. 'Tell me where they are!' I palmed the back of his head with my left hand; with my right I knuckled the ragged wound behind his ear. He tried to twist away, letting out a wail; he put his hands up to his chest and pushed feebly at me. Tears leaked from his eyes. 'Don't!' he bawled. 'Don't! It hurts!'

'Tell me where the explosives are,' I said, 'or I'll hurt you worse. I swear to Christ, I won't ever stop hurting you.'

'I don't remember!' he whined.

'I take you into my house,' I said. 'I protect you, I feed you, I wash your messes up. And what do you do? You steal from me.' I slapped him, eliciting a shriek. 'Now tell me where they are!'

Arlie was watching me, a hard light in her eyes; but she said nothing.

I nodded toward the labyrinth of partitions. 'Have a fucking look round, will you? We don't have much time!'

She went off, and I turned again to Bill.

'Tell me,' I said, and began cuffing him about the face, not hard, but hurtful, driving him back with the flurries, setting him to stagger and wail and weep. He fetched up against a partition, eyes popped, that tiny pink mouth pursed in a moue. 'Tell me,' I repeated, and then said it again, said it every time I hit him, 'Tell me, tell me, tell me . . .' until he dropped to his knees, cowering, shielding his head with his arms, and yelled. 'Over there! It's over there!'

'Where?' I said, hauling him to his feet. 'Take me to it.'

I pushed him ahead of me, keeping hold of the neck ring of his suit, yanking, jerking, not wanting to give him a second to gather himself, to make up a lie. He yelped, grunted, pleaded, saying, 'Don't!' 'Stop it!' until at last he bumped and spun round a corner, and there, resting atop a computer terminal, was one of the charges, a red light winking on the timer, signalling that it had been activated. I picked it up and punched in the deactivation code. The read-out showed that fifty-eight seconds had remained before detonation.

'Arlie!' I shouted. 'Get back here! Now!'

I grabbed Bill by the neck ring, pulled him close. 'Did you set all the timers the same?'

He gazed at me, uncomprehending.

'Answer me, damn you! How did you set the timers?'

He opened his mouth, made a scratchy noise in the back of his throat; runners of saliva bridged between his upper and lower teeth.

My interior clock was ticking down, 53, 52, 51 . . . Given the size of the room, there was no hope of locating the other three charges in less than a minute. I would have risked a goodly sum on the proposition that Bill had been inconsistent, but I was not willing to risk my life.

Arlie came trotting up and smiled. 'You found one!'

'We've got fifty seconds,' I told her. 'Or less. Run!'

I cannot be certain how long it took us to negotiate the distance between where we had stood and the hatch of the administration module; it seemed an endless time, and I kept expecting to feel the corridor shake and sway and tear loose from its fittings, and to go whirling out into the vacuum. Having to drag Bill along slowed us considerably, and I spent perhaps ten seconds longer opening the hatch with my pass key; but altogether, I would guess we came very near to the fifty-second limit. And I *am* certain that as I sealed the hatch behind us, that limit was exceeded. Bill had, indeed, proved inconsistent.

As I stepped in through the inner hatch, I found that Admin had been transformed into a holographic rendering of a beautiful starfield spread across a velvety black depth in which – an oddly charming incongruity – fifteen or twenty doors were visible, a couple of them open, slants of white light spilling out, it seemed, from God's office space behind the walls of space and time. We were walking on gas clouds, nebulae, and constellate beings. Then I noticed the body of a woman lying some thirty feet away, blood pooled wide as a table beneath her. No one else was in sight, but as we proceeded toward the airlock, the outlines of the hatch barely perceptible beneath the astronomical display, three men in black gear stepped out from a doorway farther along the passage. I fired at them, as did Arlie, but our aim was off. Strikes of ruby light smoked the starry expanse beside them as they ducked back into cover. I heard shouts, then shouted answers. The next second, as I fumbled with the hatch, laser fire needled from several doorways, pinning us down. Whoever was firing could have killed us easily, but they satisfied themselves by scoring near misses. Above Bill's frightened cries and the sizzle of burning metal, I could hear laughter. I tossed my laser aside and told Arlie to do the same. I touched the charge in my hip pouch. I believed if necessary I would be able to detonate it, but the thought made me cold.

A group of men and women, some ten or eleven strong, came along the corridor toward us, Samuelson in the lead. Like the rest, he wore black satin trousers and a blouse of the same material adorned with badges. Creatures, it appeared, wrought from the same mystic stuff as the black walls and ceiling and floor. He was smiling broadly and nodding, as if our invasion were a delightful interlude that he had been long awaiting.

'How kind of you to do your dying with us, John,' he said as we came to our feet; they gathered in a semi-circle around us, hemming us in against the hatch. 'I never expected to have this opportunity. And with your lady, too. We're going to have such fun together.'

'Bet she's a real groaner,' said a muscular, black-haired man at his shoulder.

'Well, we'll find out soon enough, won't we?' said Samuelson.

'Try it,' said Arlie, 'and Oi'll squeeze you off at the knackers!'

Samuelson beamed at her, then glanced at Bill. 'And how are you today, sir? What brings you along, I wonder, on this merry outing?'

Bill returned a look of bewilderment that after a moment, infected by Samuelson's happy countenance, turned into a perplexed smile.

'Do me a favour,' I said to Samuelson, moving my hand so that the palm was almost touching the switch of the charge at my hip. 'There's something I've been yearning to know. Does that gear of yours come with matching underwear? I'd imagine it must. Bunch of ginger-looking poofs and lizzies like you got behind you, I suppose wearing black nasties is *de rigueur*.'

'For somebody who's 'bout to major in high-pitched screams,' said a woman at the edge of the group, a heavyset blonde with a thick American accent and an indecipherable tattoo on her bicep, 'you gotta helluva mouth on you, I give ya that.'

'That's just John's unfortunate manner,' Samuelson said. 'He's not very good at defeat, you see. It should be interesting to watch him explore the boundaries of this particular defeat.'

My hand had begun to tremble on the switch; I found myself unable to control it.

'What is it with you, Samuelson?' said the blonde woman. 'Every time you chop someone, you gotta play Dracula? Let's just do 'em and get on with business.'

There was a brief argument concerning the right of the woman to speak her mind, the propriety of mentally preparing the victim, of 'tasting the experience', and other assorted drivel. Under different circumstances, I would have laughed to see how ludicrous and inept a bunch were these demons; I might have thought how their ineptitude spoke to the terminal disarray back on Earth, that such a feeble lot could have gained so much power. But I was absorbed by the trembling of my hand, the sweat trickling down my belly, and the jellied weakness of my legs. I imagined I could feel the cold mass of explosives turning, giving a kick, like a dark and fatal child striving to break free of the womb. Before long I would have to reveal the presence of the charge and force a conclusion, one way or another, and I was not sure I was up to it. My hand wanted to slap the switch, pushed against, it seemed, by all the weighty detritus of my violent life.

Finally Samuelson brought an end to the argument. 'This is my show, Amy. I'll do as I please. If you want to discuss method during Retreat, I'll be happy to satisfy. Until then, I'd appreciate your full cooperation.'

He said all this with the mild ultra-sincerity of a priest settling a squabble among the Ladies' Auxiliary concerning a jumble sale; but when he turned to me, all the anger that he must have repressed came spewing forth.

'You naff little scrote!' he shouted. 'I'm sick to death of you getting on my tits! When I've done working over your slippery and that great dozy blot beside you, I'm going to paint you red on red.'

I did not see what happened at that moment with Arlie. Somebody tried to fondle her, I believe, and there was a commotion beside me, too brief to call a struggle, and then she had a laser in her hand and was firing. A beam of crimson light no thicker than a knitting needle spat from the muzzle and punched its way through the temple of a compact, greying man, exiting through the top of his skull, dropping him in a heap. Another beam spitted the shoulder of the blonde woman. All this at close quarters, people shrieking, stumbling, pushing together, nudging me, nearly causing me to set off the charge. Then the laser was knocked from Arlie's hand, and she was thrown to the floor. Samuelson came to stand astraddle her, his laser aimed at her chest.

'Carve the bitch up!' said the blonde woman, holding her shoulder.

'Splendid idea,' Samuelson said, adjusting the setting of his laser. 'I'll just do a little writing to begin with. Start with an inspirational saying, don't you think? Or maybe' – he chuckled – 'John Loves Arlie.'

'No,' I said, my nerves steadied by this frontal assault; I pulled out the packet charge. 'No, you're not going to do that. Because unless you do the right thing, in about two seconds the best part of you is going to be sliding all greasylike down the walls. I'll give you to three to put down your weapons.' I drew a breath and tried to feel Arlie beside me. 'One.' I stared at Samuelson, coming hard at him with all the fire left in me. 'You best tell 'em how mad I am for you.' I squared my shoulders; I prayed I had the guts to press the switch on three. 'That's two.'

'Do it!' he said to his people. 'Do it now!'

They let their weapons fall.

'Back it off,' I said, feeling relief, but also a ghostly momentum as if the count had continued on in some alternate probability and I was now blowing away in fire and ruin. I picked up my pack, grabbed Samuelson by the shirtfront as the rest retreated along the corridor. 'Open the hatch,' I told Arlie, who had scrambled up from the floor.

I heard her punching out the code, and a moment later, I heard the hatch swing open. I backed around the door, slung Samuelson into the airlock, slamming him up against Bill, who had wandered in on his own. At that precise moment, the CPC exploded.

The sound of the explosion was immense, a great wallop of pressure and noise that sent me reeling into the airlock, reeling and floating up, the artificial gravity systems no longer operative; but what was truly terrifying was the vented hiss that followed the explosion, signalling disengagement from the connecting corridors, and the sickening sway of the floor, and then the roar of ignition as the module's engines transformed what had been a habitat into a ship. I pictured the whole of Solitaire coming apart piece by piece, each one igniting and moving off into the nothing, little glowing bits, like the break-up of an electric reef.

Arlie had snatched up one of the lasers and she was now training it at Samuelson, urging him into his pressure suit – a difficult chore considering the acceleration. But he was managing. I helped Bill on with his helmet and fitted mine in place just as the boost ended and we drifted free. Then I broke the seal on the outer hatch, started the lock cycling.

Once the lock had opened, I told Arlie she would have to drive the sled. I watched as she fitted herself into the harness of the rocket pack, then I lashed Samuelson to one of the metal struts, Bill to another. I set the charge I had been carrying on the surface of the station, took two more out of the pack. I set the timers for ninety seconds. I had no thoughts in my head as I was doing this; I might have been a technician stripping a wire, a welder joining a seam. Yet as I prepared to activate the charges, I realized that I was not merely ridding the station of the Strange Magnificence, but of the corporation's personnel. I had, of course, known this before, but I had not understood what it meant. Within a month, probably considerably less, the various elements of the station would be a free place, without a corporate presence to strike the fear of God and Planet Earth into the hearts and minds of the workers. Oh, it was true, some corporates might have been in other modules when the explosion occurred, but most of them were gone, and the survivors would not be able to wield much power; it would be six months at least before their replacements arrived and a new administration could be installed. A lot could happen in that time. My comprehension of this was much less linear than I am reporting; it came to me as a passion, a hope, and as I activated the timers, I had a wild sense of freedom that, though I did not fathom it then, seems now to have been premonitory and inspired.

I lashed and locked myself onto a strut close to Arlie and told her to get the hell gone, pointing out as a destination the web of a transport dock that we were passing. I did not see the explosion, but I saw the white flare of it in Arlie's faceplate as she turned to watch; I kept my eyes fixed for a time on the bits and pieces of Solitaire passing silently around us, and when I turned to her, as the reflected fire died away and her eyes were revealed, wide and lovely and dark, I saw no hatred in her, no disgust. Perhaps she had already forgiven me for being the man I was. Not kindly, and yet not without kindness. Merely someone who had learned to do the necessary and live with it. Someone whose past had burned a shadow that stretched across his future.

I told her to reverse the thrusters and stop the sled. There was one thing left to do, though I was not so eager to have done with it as once I had been. Out in the dark, in the nothing, with all those stars pointing their hot eyes at you and trying to spear your mind with their secret colours, out in that absolute desert the questions of villainy and heroism grow remote. The most terrible of sins and sweetest virtues often become compressed in the midst of all that sunless cold; compared to the terrible inhumanity of space, they both seem warmly human and comprehensible. And thus when I approached the matter of ending Samuelson's life I did so without relish, without the vindictive spirit that I might have expressed had we been back on Solitaire.

I inched my way back to where I had tied him and locked onto a strut; I trained the laser on the plastic rope that lashed him to the sled and burned it through. His legs floated up, and he held onto a strut with his gauntleted hands.

'Please, God! Don't!' he said, the panic in his voice made tinny and comical by my helmet speaker; he stared down through the struts that sectioned off the void into which he was about to travel – silver frames each enclosing a rectangle of unrelieved black, some containing a few scraps of billion-year-old light. 'Please!'

'What do you expect from me?' I asked. 'What do you expect from life? Mercy? Or the accolade? Here.' I pointed at the sweep of stars and poetry, the iron puzzle of the dock beginning to loom, to swell into a massive crosshatching of girders, each strung with white lights, with Mars a phantom crescent below and the sun a yellow coal. 'You longed for God, didn't you? Where is He if not here? Here's your strange magnificence.' I gestured with the laser. 'Push off. Hard. If you don't push hard enough, we'll come after you and give you a nudge. You can open your faceplate whenever you want it to end.'

He began to plead, to bargain. 'I can make you wealthy,' he said. 'I can get you back to Earth. Not London. Nova Sibersk. One of the towers.'

'Of course you can,' I said. 'And I would be a wise man, indeed, to trust that promise, now wouldn't I?'

'There are ways,' Samuelson said. 'Ways to guarantee it. It's not that difficult. Really. I can . . .'

'Thirwell smiled at me,' I reminded him. 'He sang. Are your beliefs so shallow you won't even favour us with a tune?'

'Do you want me to sing? Do you want me to be humiliated? If that's what it'll take to get you to listen to me, I'll do it. I'll do anything.'

'No,' I said. 'That's not what I want.'

His eyes were big with the idea of death. I knew what he was feeling: all his life was suddenly thrilling, precious, new; and he was almost made innocent by the size and intensity of his fear; almost cleansed and converted by the knowledge that all this sensey splendour was about to go on forever and ever without him. It was a hard moment, and he did not do well by it.

When he began to weep I burned a hole in his radio housing to silence him. He put a hand up to shield his face, fearing I would burn the helmet; I kicked his other hand loose from the sled, sending him spinning away slowly, head over heels toward the sun, a bulky white figure growing toylike and clever against the black ground of his future, like one of those little mechanical monkeys that spins round and round on a plastic bar. I knew he would never open his faceplate – the greater the villain, the greater their inability to accept fate. He would be a long time dying.

I checked on Bill – he was sleeping! – and returned to my place beside Arlie. We boosted again toward the dock. I thought about Gerald, about the scattered station, about Bill, but I could not concentrate on them. It was as if what I saw before me had gone inside my skull, and my mind was no longer a storm of electric impulse, but an immense black emptiness lit by tiny stars and populated by four souls, one of whom was only now beginning to know the terrible loneliness of his absent god.

We entrusted Bill to the captain of the docked transport, *Steel City*, a hideous name for a hideous vessel, pitted and grey and ungainly in form, like a sad leviathan. There was no going back to Solitaire for Bill. They had checked the recordings taken in the CPC, and they knew who had been responsible for the break-up of the station, for the nearly one hundred and thirty lives that had been lost, for the billions in credit blown away. Even under happier circumstances, without Master C to guide him, he would not be able to survive. Nor would he survive on Earth. But there he would at least have a slight chance. The corporation had no particular interest in punishing him. They were not altogether dissatisfied with the situation, being pleased to learn that their failsafe system worked, and they would, they assured us, see to it that he was given institutional care. I knew what that portended. Shunted off to some vast dark building with a Catholic statue centring a seedy garden out front, and misplaced, lost among the howling damned and terminally feeble, and eventually, for want of any reason to do otherwise, going dark himself, lying down and breathing, perhaps feeding from time to time, for a while, and then, one day, simply giving up, giving out, going away on a rattle of dishes on the dinner cart or a wild cry ghosting up from some nether region or a shiver of winter light on a cracked linoleum floor, some little piece of brightness to which he could attach himself and let go of the rest. It was horrible to contemplate, but we had no choice. Back on the station he would have been torn apart.

The *Steel City* was six hours from launching inbound when

Arlie and I last saw Bill. He was in a cell lit by a bilious yellow tray of light set in the ceiling, wearing a grey ship's jumpsuit; his wound had been dressed, and he was clean, and he was terrified. He tried to hold us, he pleaded with us to take him back home, and when we told him that was impossible, he sat cross-legged on the floor, rocking back and forth, humming a tune that I recognized as 'Barnacle Bill the Spacer'. He had apparently forgotten its context and the cruel words. Arlie kneeled beside him and told stories of the animals he would soon be seeing. There were tigers sleek as fire, she said, and elephants bigger than small towns, and birds faster than rain, and wolves with mysterious lights in their eyes. There were serpents too, she said, green ones with ruby tongues that told the most beautiful stories in the world, and cries so musical had been heard in the Mountains of the Moon that no one dared seek out the creature who had uttered them for fear of being immolated by the sight of such beauty, and the wind, she said, the wind was also an animal, and to those who listened carefully to it, it would whisper its name and give them a ride around the world in a single day. Birds as bright as the moon, great lizards who roared when it thundered as if answering questions, white bears with golden claws and magical destinies. It was a wonderland to which he was travelling, and she expected him to call and tell us all the amazing things that he would do and see.

Watching them, I had a clearer sense of him than ever before. I knew he did not believe Arlie, that he was only playing at belief, and I saw in this his courage, the stubborn, clean drive to live that had been buried under years of abuse and denial. He was not physically courageous, not in the least, but I for one knew how easy that sort of courage was to sustain, requiring only a certain careless view of life and a few tricks to inspire a red madness. And I doubted I could have withstood all he had suffered, the incessant badgering and humiliation, the sharp rejection, the sexual defeats, the monstrous loneliness. Years of it. Decades. God knows, he had committed an abysmal stupidity, but we had driven him to it, we had menaced and tormented him, and in return – an act of selfishness and desperation, I admit, yet selfishness in its most refined form, desperation in its most gentle incarnation – he had tried to save us, to make us love him.

It is little enough to know of a man or a woman, that he or she has courage. Perhaps there might have been more to know about Bill had we allowed him to flourish, had we given his strength levers against which to test itself and thus increase. But at the moment knowing what I knew seemed more than enough, and it opened me to all the feeling I had been repressing, to thoughts of Gerald in particular. I saw that my relationship with him – in fact most of my relationships – was similar to the one I'd had with Bill; I had shied away from real knowledge, real intimacy. I felt like weeping, but the pity of it was, I would only be weeping for myself.

Finally it was time for us to leave. Bill pawed us, gave us clumsy hugs, clung to us, but not so desperately as he might have; he realized, I am fairly certain, that there would be no reprieve. And, too, he may not have thought he deserved one. He was ashamed, he believed he had done wrong, and so it was with a shameful attitude, not at all demanding, that he asked me if they would give him another implant, if I would help him get one.

'Yeah, sure, Bill,' I said. 'I'll do my best.'

He sat back down on the floor, touched the wound on his neck. 'I wish he was here,' he said.

'Mister C?' said Arlie, who had been talking to a young officer; he had just come along to lead us back to our sled. 'Is that who you're talkin' about, dear?'

He nodded, eyes on the floor.

'Don't you fret, luv. You'll get another friend back 'ome. A better one than Mister C. One what won't 'urt you.'

'I don't mind he hurts me,' Bill said. 'Sometimes I do things wrong.'

'We all of us do wrong, luv. But it ain't always necessary for us to be 'urt for it.'

He stared up at her as if she were off her nut, as if he could not imagine a circumstance in which wrong was not followed by hurt.

'That's the gospel,' said the officer. 'And I promise, we'll be takin' good care of you, Bill.' He had been eyefucking Arlie, the officer had, and he was only saying this to impress her with his humanity. Chances were, as soon as we were out of sight, he would go to kicking and yelling at Bill. Arlie was not fooled by him.

'Goodbye, Bill,' she said, taking his hand, but he did not return her pressure, and his hand slipped out of her grasp, flopped onto his knee; he was already retreating from us, receding into his private misery, no longer able to manufacture a brave front. And as the door closed on him, that first of many doors, leaving him alone in that sticky yellow space, he put his hands to the sides of his head as if his skull could not contain some terrible pain, and began rocking back and forth, and saying, almost chanting the words, like a bitter monk his hopeless litany, 'Oh, no . . . oh, no . . . oh, no . . .'

Some seventy-nine hours after the destruction of the CPC and the dispersal of Solitaire, the lightship *Perseverance* came home . . . came home with such uncanny accuracy, that had the station been situated where it should have been, the energies released by the ship's re-entry from the supraluminal would have annihilated the entire facility and all on board. The barnacles, perhaps sensing some vast overload of light through their photophores . . . the barnacles and an idiot man had proved wiser than the rest of us. And this was no ordinary homecoming in yet another way, for it turned out that the voyage of the *Perseverance* had been successful. There was a new world waiting on the other side of the nothing, unspoiled, a garden of possibility, a challenge to our hearts and a beacon to our souls.

I contacted the corporation. They, of course, had heard the news, and they also recognized that had Bill not acted the *Perseverance* and all aboard her would have been destroyed along with Solitaire. He was, they were delighted to attest, a hero, and they would treat him as such. How's that? I asked. Promotions, news specials, celebrations, parades, was their answer. What he really wants, I told them, is to come back to Solitaire. Well, of course, they said, we'll see what we can do. When it's time, they said. We'll do right by him, don't you worry. How about another implant? I asked. Absolutely, no problem, anything he needs. By the time I broke contact, I understood that Bill's fate would be little different now he was a hero than it would have been when he was a mere fool and a villain. They would use him, milk his story for all the good it could do them, and then he would be discarded, misplaced, lost, dropped down to circulate among the swirling masses of the useless, the doomed and the forgotten.

Though I had already – in concert with others – formed a plan of action, it was this duplicity on the corporation's part that hardened me against them, and thereafter I threw myself into the implementation of the plan. A few weeks from now, the *Perseverance* and three other starships soon to be completed will launch for the new world. Aboard will be the population of Solitaire, minus a few unsympathetic personnel who have been rendered lifeless, and the population of other, smaller stations in the asteroid belt and orbiting Mars. Solitaire itself, and the other stations, will be destroyed. It will take the corporation decades, perhaps a century, to rebuild what has been lost, and by the time they are able to reach us, we hope to have grown strong, to have fabricated a society free of corporations and Strange Magnificences, composed of those who have learned to survive without the quotas and the dread consolations of the Earth. It is an old dream, this desire to say, No more, never again, to build a society cleansed of the old compulsions and corruptions, the ancient, vicious ways, and perhaps it is a futile one, perhaps the fact that men like myself, violent men, men who will do the necessary, who will protect against all enemies with no thought for moral fall-out, must be included on the roster, perhaps this pre-ordains that it will fail. Nevertheless, it needs to be dreamed every so often, and we are prepared to be the dreamers.

So that is the story of Barnacle Bill. My story, and Arlie's as well, yet his most of all, though his real part in it, the stuff of his thoughts and hopes, the pain he suffered and the fear he overcame, those things can never be told. Perhaps you have seen him recently on the HV, or even in person, riding in an open car at the end of a parade with men in suits, eating an ice and smiling, but in truth he is already gone into history, already part of the past, already half-forgotten, and when the final door has closed on him, it may be that his role in all this will be reduced to a mere footnote or simply a mention of his name, the slightest token of a life. But I will remember him, not in memorial grace, not as a hero, but as he was, in all his graceless ways and pitiable form. It is of absolute importance to remember him thus, because that, I have come to realize, the raw and the deformed, the ugly, the miserable miracles of our days, the unalloyed baseness of existence, that is what we must learn to love, to accept, to embrace, if we are to cease the denials that weaken us, if we are ever to admit our dismal frailty and to confront the natural terror and heartbreak weather of our lives and live like a strong light across the sky instead of retreating into darkness.

The barnacles have returned to Solitaire. Or rather, new colonies of barnacles have attached to the newly reunited station, not covering it completely, but dressing it up in patches. I have taken to walking among them, weeding them as Bill once did; I have become interested in them, curious as to how they perceived a ship coming from light years away, and I intend to carry some along with us on the voyage and make an attempt at a study. Yet what compels me to take these walks is less scientific curiosity than a kind of furious nostalgia, a desire to remember and hold the centre of those moments that have so changed the direction of our lives, to think about Bill and how it must have been for him, a frightened lump of a man with a clever voice in his ear, alone in all that daunting immensity, fixing his eyes on the bright clots of life at his feet. Just today Arlie joined me on such a walk, and it seemed we were passing along the rim of an infinite dark eye flecked with a trillion bits of colour, and that everything of our souls and of every other soul could be seen in that eye, that I could look down to Earth through the haze and scum of the ocean air and see Bill where he stood looking up and trying to find us in that mottled sky, and I felt all the eerie connections a man feels when he needs to believe in something more than what he knows is real, and I tried to tell myself he was all right, walking in his garden in Nova Sibersk, taking the air with an idiot woman so beautiful it nearly made him wise. But I could not sustain the fantasy. I could only mourn, and I had no right to mourn, having never loved him – or if I did, even in the puniest of ways, it was never his person I loved, but what I had from him, the things awakened in me by what had happened. Just the thought that I could have loved him, maybe that was all I owned of right.

We were heading back toward the East Louie airlock, when Arlie stooped and plucked up a male barnacle. Dark green as an emerald, it was, except for its stubby appendage. Glowing like magic, alive with threads of colour like a potter's glaze.

'That's a rare one,' I said. 'Never saw one that colour before.'

'Bill would 'ave fancied it,' she said.

'Fancied, hell. He would have hung the damned thing about his neck.'

She set it back down, and we watched as it began working its way across the surface of the barnacle patch, doing its slow, ungainly cartwheels, wobbling off-true, lurching in flight, nearly missing its landing, but somehow making it, somehow getting there. It landed in the shadow of some communications gear, stuck out its tongue and tried to feed. We watched it for a long, long while, with no more words spoken, but somehow there was a little truth hanging in the space between us, in the silence, a poor thing not worth naming, and maybe not even having a name, it was such an infinitesimal slice of what was, and we let it nourish us as much as it could, we took its lustre and added it to our own. We sucked it dry, we had its every flavour, and then we went back inside arm in arm, to rejoin the lie of the world.

A LITTLE NIGHT MUSIC

'Dead men can't play jazz.'

'That's the truth I learned last night at the world premiere performance of the quartet known as Afterlife at Manhattan's Village Vanguard.

'Whether or not they can play, period, that's another matter, but it wasn't jazz I heard at the Vanguard, it was something bluer and colder, something with notes made from centuries-old Arctic ice and stones that never saw the light of day, something uncoiling after a long black sleep and tasting dirt in its mouth, something that wasn't the product of creative impulse but of need. But the bottom line is, it was worth hearing.

'As to the morality involved, well, I'll leave that up to you, because that's the real bottom line, isn't it, music lovers? Do you like it enough and will you pay enough to keep the question of morality a hot topic on the talk shows and out of the courts? Those of you who listened to the simulcast over WBAI have probably already formulated an opinion. The rest of you will have to wait for the CD.

'I won't waste your time by talking about the technology. If you don't understand it by now, after all the television specials and the (ohmygodpleasenotanother) in-depth discussions between your local blow-dried news creep and their pet science-fiction hack, you must not want to understand it. Nor am I going to wax profound and speculate on just how much of a man is left after reanimation. The only ones who know that aren't able to tell us, because it seems the speech centre just doesn't thrive on narcosis. Nor does any fraction of sensibility that cares to communicate itself. In fact, very little seems to thrive on narcosis aside from the desire . . . no, like I said, the *need* to play music.

'And for reasons that God or someone only knows, the *ability* to play music where none existed before.

'That may be hard to swallow, I realize, but I'm here to tell you, no matter how weird it sounds, it appears to be true.

'For the first time in memory, there was a curtain across the Vanguard's stage. I suppose there's some awkwardness involved in bringing the musicians out. Before the curtain was opened, William Dexter, the genius behind this whole deal, a little bald man with a hearing aid in each ear and the affable, simple face of someone whom kids call by his first name, came out and said a few words about the need for drastic solutions to the problems of war and pollution, for a redefinition of our goals and values. Things could not go on as they had been. The words seemed somewhat out of context, though they're always nice to hear. Finally he introduced the quartet. As introductions go, this was a telegram.

' "The music you're about to hear," William Dexter said flatly, without the least hint of hype or hyperventilation, "is going to change your lives."

'And there they were.

'Right on the same stage where Coltrane turned a love supreme into song, where Miles singed us with the hateful beauty of needles and knives and Watts on fire, where Mingus went crazy in 7/4 time, where Ornette made Kansas City R&B into the art of noise, and a thousand lesser geniuses dreamed and almost died and were changed before our eyes from men into moments so powerful that guys like me can make a living writing about them for people like you who just want to hear that what they felt when they were listening was real.

'Two white men, one black, one Hispanic, the racial quota of an all-American TV show, marooned on a radiant island painted by a blue-white spot. Alll wearing sunglasses.

'Raybans, I think.

'Wonder if they'll get a commercial.

'The piano-player was young and skinny, just a kid, with the long brown hair of a rock star and sunglasses that held gleams as shiny and cold as the black surface of his Baldwin. The Hispanic guy on bass couldn't have been more than eighteen, and the horn player, the black man, he was about twenty-five, the oldest. The drummer, a shadow with a crew cut and a pale brow, I couldn't see him clearly but I could tell he was young, too.

'Too young, you'd think, to have much to say.

'But then maybe time goes by more slowly and wisdom accretes with every measure . . . in the afterlife.

'No apparent signal passed between them, yet as one they began to play.'

Goodrick reached for his tape recorder, thinking he should listen to the set again before getting into the music, but then he realized that another listen was unnecessary – he could still hear every blessed note. The ocean of dark clouds on the piano opening over a snaky, slithering hiss of cymbals and a cluttered rumble plucked from the double bass, and then that sinuous alto line, like snake-charmer music rising out of a storm of thunderheads and scuttling claws, all fusing into a signature as plaintive and familiar and elusive as a muezzin's call. Christ, it stuck with you like a jingle for Burger King . . . though nothing about it was simple. It seemed to have the freedom of jazz, yet at the same time it had the feel of heavy, ritual music.

Weird shit.

And it sure as hell stuck with you.

He got up from the desk, grabbed his drink and walked over to the window. The nearby buildings ordered the black sky, ranks of tombstones inscribed with a writing of rectangular stars, geometric constellations, and linear rivers of light below, flowing along consecutive chasms through the high country of Manhattan. Usually the view soothed him and turned his thoughts to pleasurable agendas, as if height itself were a form of assurance, an emblematic potency that freed you from anxiety. But tonight he remained unaffected. The sky and the city seemed to have lost their scope and grandeur, to have become merely an adjunct to his living room.

He cast about the apartment, looking for the clock. Couldn't locate it for a second among a chaos of sticks of gleaming chrome, shining black floors, framed prints, and the black plush coffins of the sofas. He'd never put it together before, but the place looked like a cross between a Nautilus gym and a goddamn mortuary. Rachel's taste could use a little modification.

Two thirty a.m. . . . Damn!

Where the hell was she?

She usually gave him time alone after a show to write his column. Went and had a drink with friends.

Three hours, though.

Maybe she'd found a special friend. Maybe that was the reason she had missed the show tonight. If that was the case, she'd been with the bastard for . . . what? Almost seven hours now. Screwing her brains out in some midtown hotel.

Bitch! He'd settle her hash when she got home.

Whoa, big fella, he said to himself. Get real. Rachel would be much cooler than that . . . make that, *had been* much cooler. Her affairs were state of the art, so quietly and elegantly handled that he had been able to perfect denial. This wasn't her style. And even if she were to throw it in his face, he wouldn't do a thing to her. Oh, he'd want to; he'd want to bash her goddamned head in. But he would just sit there and smile and buy her bullshit explanation.

Love, he guessed you'd call it, the kind of love that will accept any insult, any injury . . . though it might be more accurate to call it pussywhipped. There were times he didn't think he could take it any more, times – like now – when his head felt full of lightning, on the verge of exploding and setting everything around him on fire. But he always managed to contain his anger and swallow his pride, to grin and bear it, to settle for the specious currency of her lovemaking, the price she paid to live high and do what she wanted.

Jesus, he felt strange. Too many pops at the Vanguard, that was likely the problem. But maybe he was coming down with something.

He laughed.

Like maybe middle age? Like the married-to-a-chick-fifteen-years-younger-paranoid flu?

Still, he had felt better in his time. No real symptoms, just out of sorts, sluggish, dulled, some trouble concentrating.

Finish the column, he said to himself; just finish the damn

thing, take two aspirin, and fall out. Deal with Rachel in the morning.

Right.

Deal with her.

Bring her breakfast in bed, ask how she was feeling, and what was she doing later?

God, he loved her!

Loves her not. Loves. Loves her not.

He tore off a last mental petal and tossed the stem away. Then he returned to the desk and typed a few lines about the music onto the computer and sat considering the screen. After a moment he began to type again.

'Plenty of blind men have played the Vanguard, and plenty of men have played there who've had other reasons to hide their eyes, working behind some miracle of modern chemistry that made them sensitive to light. I've never wanted to see their eyes – the fact that they were hidden told me all I needed to know about them. But tonight I wanted to see, I wanted to know what the quartet was seeing, what lay behind those sunglasses starred from the white spot. Shadows, it's said. But what sort of shadows? Shades of grey, like dogs see? Are we shadows to them, or do they see shadows where we see none? I thought if I could look into their eyes, I'd understand what caused the alto to sound like a reedy alarm being given against a crawl of background radiation, why one moment it conjured images of static red flashes amid black mountains moving, and the next brought to mind a livid blue streak pulsing in a serene darkness, a mineral moon in a granite sky.

'Despite the compelling quality of the music, I couldn't set aside my curiosity and simply listen. What was I listening to, after all? A clever parlour trick? Sleight of hand on a metaphysical level? Were these guys really playing Death's Top-Forty, or had Mr William Dexter managed to chump the whole world and programme four stiffs to make certain muscular reactions to subliminal stimuli?'

The funny thing was, Goodrick thought, now he couldn't stop listening to the damn music. In fact, certain phrases were becoming so insistent, circling round and round inside his head, he was having difficulty thinking rationally.

He switched the radio on, wanting to hear something else, to get a perspective on the column.

No chance.

Afterlife was playing on the radio, too.

He was stunned, imagining some bizarre *Twilight Zone* circumstance, but then realized that the radio was tuned to WBAI. They must be replaying the simulcast. Pretty unusual for them to devote so much air to one story. Still, it wasn't every day the dead came back to life and played song stylings for your listening pleasure.

He recognized the passage. They must have just started the replay. Shit, the boys hadn't even gotten warmed up yet.

Heh, heh.

He followed the serpentine track of the alto cutting across the rumble and clutter of the chords and fills behind it, a bright ribbon of sound etched through thunder and power and darkness.

A moment later he looked at the clock and was startled to discover that the moment had lasted twenty minutes.

Well, so he was a little spaced; so what? He was entitled. He'd had a hard wife . . . life. Wife. The knifing word he'd wed, the dull flesh, the syrupy blood, the pouty breasts, the painted face he'd thought was pretty. The dead music woman, the woman whose voice caused cancer, whose kisses left damp mildewed stains, whose . . .

His heart beat flabbily, his hands were cramped, his fingertips were numb, and his thoughts were a whining, glowing crack opening in a smoky sky like slow lightning. Feeling a dark red emotion too contemplative to be anger, he typed a single paragraph and then stopped to read what he had written.

'The thing about this music is, it just feels right. It's not art, it's not beauty; it's a meter reading on the state of the soul, of the world. It's the bottom line of all time, a registering of creepy fundamentals, the rendering into music of the crummiest truth, the statement of some meagre final tolerance, a universal alpha wave. God's EKG, the least possible music, the absolute minimum of sound, all that's left to say, to be, for them, for us . . . maybe that's why it feels so damn right. It creates an option to suicide, a place where there is no great trouble, only a trickle of blood through stony flesh and the crackle of a base electric message across the brain.'

Well, he thought, now there's a waste of a paragraph. Put that into the column, and he'd be looking for work with a weekly shopping guide.

He essayed a laugh and produced a gulping noise. Damn, he felt lousy.

Not lousy, really, just . . . just sort of nothing. Like there was nothing in his head except the music. Music and black dead air. Dead life.

Dead love. He typed a few more lines.

'Maybe Dexter was right, maybe this music *will* change your life. It sure as hell seems to have changed mine. I feel like shit, my lady's out with some dirtball lowlife and all I can muster by way of a reaction is mild pique. I mean, maybe the effect of Afterlife's music is to reduce the emotional volatility of our kind, to diminish us to the level of the stiffs who play it. That might explain Dexter's peace-and-love rap. People who feel like I do wouldn't have the energy for war, for polluting, for much of anything. They'd probably sit around most of the time, trying to think something, hoping for food to walk in the door . . .'

Jesus, what if the music actually did buzz you like that? Tripped some chemical switch and slowly shut you down, brain cell by brain cell, until you were about three degrees below normal and as lively as a hibernating bear. What if that were true, and right this second it was being broadcast all over hell on WBAI? This is crazy, man, he told himself, this is truly whacko.

But what if Dexter's hearing aids had been ear plugs, what if the son of a bitch hadn't listened to the music himself? What if he knew how the music would affect the audience, what if he was after turning half of everybody into zombies all in the name of a better world? And what would be so wrong with that?

Not a thing. Cleaner air, less war, more food to go around . . . just stack the dim bulbs in warehouses and let them vegetate, while everyone else cleaned up the mess.

Not a thing wrong with it . . . as long as you weren't in the half that had listened to the music.

The light was beginning to hurt his eyes. He switched off the lamp and sat in the darkness, staring at the glowing screen. He glanced out the window. Since last he'd looked, it appeared that about three-quarters of the lights in the adjoining buildings had been darkened, making it appear that the remaining lights were some sort of weird code, spelling out a message of golden squares against a black page. He had a crawly feeling along his spine, imagining thousands of other Manhattan nighthawks growing slow and cold and sensitive to light, sitting in their dark rooms, while a whining alto serpent stung them in the brain.

The idea was ludicrous – Dexter had just been shooting off his mouth, firing off more white liberal bullshit. Still, Goodrick didn't feel much like laughing.

Maybe, he thought, he should call the police . . . call someone.

But then he'd have to get up, dial the phone, talk, and it was so much more pleasant just to sit here and listen to the background static of the universe, to the sad song of a next-to-nothing life.

He remembered how peaceful Afterlife had been, the piano man's pale hands flowing over the keys, like white animals gliding, making a rippling track, and the horn man's eyes rolled up, showing all white under the sunglasses, turned inward toward some pacific vision, and the bass man, fingers blurring on the strings, but his head fallen back, gaping, his eyes on the ceiling, as if keeping track of the stars.

This was really happening, he thought; he believed it, yet he couldn't rouse himself to panic. His hands flexed on the arms of the chair, and he swallowed, and he listened. More lights were switched off in the adjoining towers. This was really fucking happening . . . and he wasn't afraid. As a matter of fact, he was beginning to enjoy the feeling. Like a little vacation. Just turn down the volume and response, sit back and let the ol' brain start to mellow like ageing cheese.

Wonder what Rachel would say?

Why, she'd be delighted! She hadn't heard the music, after all, and she'd be happy as a goddamn clam to be one of the quick, to have him sit there and fester while she brought over strangers and let them pork her on the living room carpet. I mean, he wouldn't have any objection, right? Maybe dead guys liked to watch. Maybe . . . His hands started itching, smudged with city dirt. He decided that he had to wash them.

With a mighty effort, feeling like he weighed five hundred pounds, he heaved up to his feet and shuffled toward the bathroom. It took him what seemed a couple of minutes to reach it, to fumble for the wall switch and flick it on. The light almost blinded him, and he reeled back against the wall, shading his eyes. Glints and gleams shattering off porcelain, chrome fixtures, and tiles, a shrapnel of light blowing toward his retinas. 'Aw, Jesus,' he said. 'Jesus!' Then he caught sight of himself in the mirror. Pasty skin, liverish, too-red lips, bruised-looking circles around his eyes. Mr Zombie.

He managed to look away.

He turned on the faucet. Music ran out along with the bright water, and when he stuck his hands under the flow, he couldn't feel the cold water, just the gloomy notation spidering across his skin.

He jerked his hands back and stared at them, watched them dripping glittering bits of alto and drum, bass and piano. After a moment he switched off the light and stood in the cool, blessed dark, listening to the alto playing in the distance, luring his thoughts down and down into a golden crooked tunnel leading nowhere.

One thing he had to admit: having your vitality turned down to the bottom notch gave you perspective on the whole vital world. Take Rachel, now. She'd come in any minute, all bright and smiling, switching her ass, she'd toss her purse and coat somewhere, give him a perky kiss, ask how the column was going . . . and all the while her sexual engine would be cooling, ticking away the last degrees of heat like how a car engine ticks in the silence of a garage, some vile juice leaking from her. He could see it clearly, the entire spectrum of her deceit, see it without feeling either helpless rage or frustration, but rather registering it as an untenable state of affairs. Something would have to be done. That was obvious. It was surprising he'd never come to that conclusion before . . . or maybe not so surprising. He'd been too agitated, too emotional. Now . . . now change was possible. He would have to talk to Rachel, to work things out differently. Actually, he thought, a talk wouldn't be necessary. Just a little listening experience, and she'd get with the programme.

He hated to leave the soothing darkness of the bathroom, but he felt he should finish the column . . . just to tie up loose ends. He went back into the living room and sat in front of the computer. WBAI had finished replaying the simulcast. He must have been in the john a long time. He switched off the radio so he could hear the music in his head.

'I'm sitting here listening to a little night music, a reedy little whisper of melody leaking out a crack in death's door, and you know, even though I can't hear or think of much of anything except that shivery sliver of sound, it's become more a virtue than a hindrance; it's beginning to order the world in an entirely new way. I don't have to explain it to those of you who are hearing it with me, but the rest of you, let me shed some light on the experience. One sees . . . clearly, I suppose, is the word, yet that doesn't cover it. One is freed from the tangles of inhibition, volatile emotion, and thus can perceive how easy it is to change one's life, and finally, one understands that with a very few changes one can achieve a state of calm perfection. A snip here, a tuck taken there, another snip-snip, and suddenly it becomes apparent that there is nothing left to do, absolutely nothing, and one has achieved utter harmony with one's environment.'

The screen was glowing too brightly to look at. Goodrick dimmed it. Even the darkness, he realized, had its own peculiar radiance. B-zarre. He drew a deep breath . . . or rather tried to, but his chest didn't move. Cool, he thought, very cool. No moving parts. Just solid calm, white, white calm in a black, black shell, and a little bit of fixing up remaining to do. He was almost there. Wherever *there* was.

A cool alto trickle of pleasure through the rumble of nights.

'I cannot recommend the experience too highly. After all, there's almost no overhead, no troublesome desires, no ugly moods, no loathsome habits . . .'

A click – the front door opening, a sound that seemed to increase the brightness in the room. Footsteps, and then Rachel's voice.

'Wade?'

He could feel her. Hot, sticky, soft. He could feel the suety weights of her breasts, the torsion of her hips, the flexing of live sinews, like music of a kind, a lewd concerto of vitality and deceit.

'There you are!' she said brightly, a streak of hot sound, and came up behind him. She leaned down, hands on his shoulders, and kissed his cheek, a serpent of brown hair coiling across his neck and onto his chest.

'How's the column going?' she asked, moving away.

He cut his eyes toward her. That teardrop ass sheathed in silk, that mind like a sewer running with black bile, that heart like a pound of red-raw poisoned hamburger. Those cute little puppies bounding along in front.

The fevered temperature of her soiled flesh brightened everything. Even the air was shining. The shadows were black glares.

'Fine,' he said. 'Almost finished.'

'. . . only infinite slow minutes, slow thoughts like curls of smoke, only time, only a flicker of presence, only perfect music that does not exist like smoke . . .'

'So how was the Vanguard?'

He chuckled. 'Didn't you catch it on the radio?'

A pause. 'No, I was busy.'

Busy, uh-huh. Hips thrusting up from a rumpled sheet, sleek with sweat, mouth full of tongue, breasts rolling fatly, big ass flattening.

'It was good for me,' he said.

A nervous giggle.

'Very good,' he said. 'The best.'

He examined his feelings. All in order, all under control . . . what there was of them. A few splinters of despair, a fragment of anger, some shards of love. Not enough to matter, not enough to impair judgement.

'Are you okay? You sound funny.'

'I'm fine,' he said, feeling a creepy, secretive tingle of delight. 'Want to hear the Vanguard set? I taped it.'

'Sure . . . but aren't you sleepy? I can hear it tomorrow.'

'I'm fine.'

He switched on the recorder. The computer screen was blazing like a white sun.

'. . . the crackling of a black storm, the red thread of a fire on a distant ridge, the whole world irradicated by a mystic vibration, the quickened inches of the flesh becoming cool and easy, the White Nile of the calmed mind flowing everywhere . . .'

'Like it?' he asked. She had walked over to the window and was standing facing it, gazing out at the city.

'It's . . . curious,' she said. 'I don't know if I like it, but it's effective.'

Was that a hint of entranced dullness in her voice? Or was it merely distraction? Open those ears wide, baby, and let that ol' black magic take over.

'. . . just listen, just let it flow in, let it fill the empty spaces in your brain with muttering, cluttering bassy blunders and a crooked wire of brassy red snake fluid, let it cosy around and coil up inside your skull . . .'

The column just couldn't hold his interest. Who the hell was going to read it anyway? His place was with Rachel, helping her through the rough spots of the transition, the confusion, the unsettled feelings. With difficulty, he got to his feet and walked over to Rachel. Put his hands on her hips. She tensed, then relaxed against him. Then she tensed again. He looked out over the top of her head at Manhattan. Only a few lights showing. The message growing simpler. Dot, dot, dot. Stop. Dot, dot. Stop.

Stop.

'Can we talk, Wade?'

'Listen to the music, baby.'

'No . . . really. We have to talk!'

She tried to pull away from him, but he held her, his fingers hooked on her hipbones.

'It'll keep 'til morning,' he said.

'I don't think so.' She turned to face him, fixed him with her intricate green eyes. 'I've been putting this off too long already.' Her mouth opened, as if she were going to speak, but then she looked away. 'I'm so sorry,' she said after a considerable pause.

He knew what was coming, and he didn't want to hear it.

Couldn't she just wait? In a few minutes she'd begin to understand, to know what he knew. Christ, couldn't she wait?

'Listen,' he said. 'Okay? Listen to the music and then we'll talk.'

'God, Wade! What is it with you and this dumb music?'

She started to flounce off, but he caught her by the arm.

'If you give it a chance, you'll see what I mean,' he said. 'But it takes a while. You have to give it time.'

'What are you talking about?'

'The music . . . it's really something. It does something.'

'Oh, God, Wade! This is important!'

She fought against his grip.

'I know,' he said, 'I know it is. But just do this first. Do it for me.'

'All right, all right! If it'll make you happy.' She heaved a sigh, made a visible effort at focusing on the music, her head tipped to the side . . . but only for a couple of seconds.

'I can't listen,' she said. 'There's too much on my mind.'

'You're not trying.'

'Oh, Wade,' she said, her chin quivering, a catch in her voice. 'I've been trying, I really have. You don't know. Please! Let's just sit down and . . .' She let out another sigh. 'Please. I need to talk with you.'

He had to calm her, to let his calm generate and flow inside her. He put a hand on the back of her neck, forced her head down on his shoulder. She struggled, but he kept up a firm pressure.

'Let me go, damn it!' she said, her voice muffled. 'Let me go!' Then, after a moment: 'You're smothering me.'

He let her lift her head.

'What's wrong with you, Wade?'

There was confusion and fright in her face, and he wanted to soothe her, to take away all her anxieties.

'Nothing's wrong,' he said with the sedated piety of a priest. 'I just want you to listen. Tomorrow morning . . .'

'I don't want to listen. Can't you understand that? I don't. Want. To listen. Now let me go.'

'I'm doing this for you, baby.'

'For me? Are you nuts? Let me go!'

'I can't, baby. I just can't.'

She tried to twist free again, but he refused to release her.

'All right, all right! I was trying to avoid a scene, but if that's how you want it!' She tossed back her hair, glared at him defiantly. 'I'm leaving . . .'

He couldn't let her say it and spoil the evening; he couldn't let her disrupt the healing process. Without anger, without bitterness, but rather with the precision and control of someone trimming a hedge, he backhanded her, nailed her flush on the jaw with all his strength, snapping her head about. She went hard against the thick window glass, the back of her skull impacting with a sharp crack, and then she slumped to the floor, her head twisted at an improbable angle.

Snip, snip.

He stood waiting for grief and fear to flood in, but he felt only a wave of serenity as palpable as a stream of cool water, as a cool golden passage on a distant horn.

Snip.

The shape of his life was perfected.

Rachel's too.

Lying there, pale lips parted, face rapt and slack, drained of lust and emotions, she was beautiful. A trickle of blood eeled from her hairline, and Goodrick realized that the pattern it made echoed the alto line exactly, that the music was leaking from her, signalling the minimal continuance of her life. She wasn't dead; she had merely suffered a necessary reduction. He sensed the edgy crackle of her thoughts, like the intermittent popping of a fire gone to embers.

'It's okay, baby. It's okay.' He put an arm under her back and lifted her, supporting her about the waist. Then he hauled her over to the sofa. He helped her to sit, and sat beside her, an arm about her shoulders. Her head lolled heavily against his, the softness of her breast pressed into his arm. He could hear the music coming from her, along with the electric wrack and tumble of her thoughts. They had never been closer than they were right now, he thought.

He wanted to say something, to tell her how much he loved her, but found that he could no longer speak, his throat muscles slack and useless.

Well, that was okay.

Rachel knew how he felt, anyway.

But if he could speak, he'd tell her that he'd always known they could work things out, that though they'd had their problems, they were made for each other . . .

The light was growing incandescent, as if having your life ultimately simplified admitted you to a dimension of blazing whiteness. It was streaming up from everything, from the radio, the television, from Rachel's parted lips, from every surface, whitening the air, the night, whiting out hope, truth, beauty, sadness, joy, leaving room for nothing except the music, which was swelling in volume, stifling thought, becoming a kind of thirsting presence inside him. It was sort of too bad, he said to himself, that things had to be like this, that they couldn't have made it in the usual way, but then he guessed it was all for the best, that this way at least there was no chance of screwing anything up.

Jesus, the goddamn light was killing his eyes! Might have known, he thought, there'd be some fly in the ointment, that perfection didn't measure up to its rep.

He held onto Rachel tightly, whispering endearments, saying, 'Baby, it'll be okay in a minute, just lie back, just take it easy,' trying to reassure her, to help her through this part of things. He could tell the light was bothering her as well by the way she buried her face in the crook of his neck.

If this shit kept up, he thought, he was going to have to buy them both some sunglasses.

HUMAN HISTORY

Stories, I'm told by old Hay (who's told enough of them to pass for an expert), must have a beginning and middle and end that taken altogether form a shape, a movement that pleases the mind of the listener. And so in order to give my chronicle of those weeks in Edgeville and the land beyond a proper shape, I must begin before the beginning, create a false beginning that will illuminate the events of later days. I'm not sure this is the most truthful way to go about things. Sometimes I think it would be best to jump right in, to leap backward and forward in chronology like an excited man telling his story for the first time; but since I've never written anything down before, I guess I'll play it conservative and do as old Hay has advised.

This happened in the summer, then, when the apes and the tigers keep mostly to the high country, the snow peaks east of town, and strangers come from Windbroken, the next town north, and from even farther away, with goods for trade or maybe to settle, and it's more or less safe to ride out onto the flats. Edgeville, you see, is tucked into a horseshoe canyon of adobe-coloured stone, its sides smoothly dimpled as if by the pressure of enormous thumbs; the houses and shops – shingle-roofed and painted white for the most part – are set close together toward the rear of the canyon, thinning out toward the mouth, where barricades of razor wire and trenches and various concealed traps are laid. Beyond the canyon the flats begin, a hardpan waste that appears to stretch into infinity, into a line of darkness that never lifts from the horizon. Out there live the Bad Men and the beasts, and on the other side . . . well, it's said by some that the other side doesn't exist.

I'd taken a little roan out onto the flats that morning to look for

95

tiger bones, which I use for carving. I rode east toward the mountains, keeping close to the cliffs, and before I'd gone more than a couple of miles I began to hear a mechanical hooting. Curious, I followed the sound, and after another mile I caught sight of a red car with a bubble top parked at the base of a cliff. I'd seen a couple like it last time I was to market in Windbroken; some old boy had built them from plans he'd gotten from the Captains. They were the talk of the town, but I didn't see much point to them – only place level enough to drive them was on the flats. Whoever was inside the car wore a golden helmet that sparkled in the sun. As I drew closer, I realized that the driver was pressing the middle of the steering wheel with the heel of his hand, and that was causing the hooting noise. He kept it up even after I had pulled the roan to a halt beside the car, acting as if he didn't notice me. I sat watching him for half a minute, and then shouted, 'Hey!' He glanced at me, but continued beating on the steering wheel. The sound was wicked loud and made the roan skittish.

'Hey!' I shouted again. 'You don't quit doin' that, you gonna bring down the apes.'

That stopped him . . for a moment. He turned to me and said, 'You think I care 'bout apes? Shit!' Then he went back to beating on the wheel.

The helmet had a funny metal grille across the front that halfway hid his face; what I could see of it was pinched, pale, and squinty-eyed, and his body – he was wearing a red coverall that matched the car's paint – appeared to be starved-thin. 'You may not care 'bout 'em,' I said. 'But you keep up with that nonsense, they gonna start droppin' rocks down on you. Apes like their peace and quiet.'

He stopped making his racket and stared at me defiantly. 'Ain't gonna happen,' he said. 'I'm a man of destiny. My future is a thing assured.'

'Yeah?' I said with a laugh. 'And how's that?'

He popped open the bubble top and clambered out. The roan backed off a few paces. 'I'm gonna cross the flats,' he said, puffing up his chest and swaggering in place: you might have thought he was ten feet tall instead of the puny piece of work he was.

'That right?' I said, gazin' west toward nothing, toward that empty land and dark horizon. 'Got any last requests? Messages to your kinfolks?'

'I 'spect you heard that before,' he said. 'You probably get lots out here tryin' to make a crossin'.'

'Nope, never met anybody else that much of a damn fool.'

'Well, you never met nobody with a map, neither.' He reached into the car, pulled out some bedraggled-looking papers and shook them at me, causing the roan to snort and prance sideways. He glanced from side to side as if expecting eavesdroppers and said, 'This world ain't nothing like you think it is . . . not a'tall. I found these here maps up north, and believe you me, they're a revelation!'

'What you gonna do with the Bad Men? Hit 'em over the head with them papers?' I got the roan under control and slipped off him; I must have stood a head taller than the driver, even with his helmet.

'They'll never spot me. I'm goin' where they ain't got the balls to go.'

There was no point in arguing with a lunatic, so I changed the subject. 'You ain't gonna have a chance to hide out from the Bad Men, you don't quit hootin' at the apes. What for you doin' that, anyway?'

'Just gearin' up,' he said. 'Gettin' up my energy.'

'Well, I'd do it out away from the cliff if I was you.'

He glanced up at the clifftop. 'I ain't never seen them apes. What're they like?'

'They got white fur and blue eyes . . . least most of 'em. 'Bout the size of a man, but skinnier. And 'bout as smart, too.'

'Now I don't believe that,' he said. 'Not one lick.'

'I didn't neither.' I said. 'But I know someone who went up amongst 'em, and after he come back, well, I believed it then.'

He looked at me expectantly. I hadn't been meaning to get into it, but seeing that I had nothing pressing, I told him a little about Wall.

'The man was huge,' I said. 'I mean I never seen anybody close to that big. He musta stood close to seven feet . . . and he wasn't just tall. He was big all over. Chest like a barrel, thighs like a bull. Man, even his fingers were big. Bigger'n most men's dinguses, if you know what I'm talkin' 'bout.'

The driver chuckled.

'One peculiar thing. He had this real soft voice. Almost like a woman's voice, just deeper. And that just accentuated his ugliness. Shit, I seen apes better lookin'! He had these big tufted eyebrows that met up with his hairline. Hair all over him. He come from one of them ruined cities up to the north. A hard place, the way he told it. Lotta Bad Men. Cannibalism. Stuff like that. But he wasn't no savage, he was all right. Didn't say much, though. I figger he liked the apes 'bout as good as he did us.'

'He went and lived with 'em, did he?'

'Not "lived",' I said. 'Not exactly. Kinda hung around 'em, more like. He was helpin' us, y'see. The apes they steal our babies, and he thought he might be able to get 'em back.'

'And did he?'

The roan grunted and nuzzled the driver's chest; he swatted its nose.

'He said we wouldn't want 'em back, the way they was. But he told us a lot 'bout how the apes live. Said they had this cave where they . . .' I broke off, trying to remember how Wall had described it. The wind blew lonely cold notes in the hollows of the cliff; the sky seemed the visual counterpart of that music: a high mackerel sky with a pale white sun. 'They'd taken the skulls of the people they'd killed, busted 'em up and stuck 'em on the walls of this cave. Stuck 'em flat, y'know, like flattened skull faces all over the walls and ceiling. Painted 'em all over with weird designs. Our babies, our kids, were livin' in the cave, and the apes, they'd go into the cave and fuck 'em. Girls, boys. Didn't make no difference. They'd just do 'em.'

'Damn,' said the driver, sympathizing.

'Now don't that sound like they smart like men?' I said. 'Don't it?'

'Guess it does at that,' he said after a bit. 'Damn.'

'You don't wanna mess with them apes,' I told him. 'I was you, I'd be movin' my car.'

'Well, I reckon I will,' he said.

There was nothing more I could do for him. I mounted up,

swinging the roan's head so he faced toward the dark end of everything.

'What you doin' out here?' asked the driver.

'Just huntin' for tiger bones,' I said. 'I carve shit from 'em.'

'Huh,' he said as if this were a great intelligence. Now that he saw I was making to leave, he didn't want to let me go. I could tell he was scared.

'You don't think I'm gonna make it, do ya?' he said.

I didn't want to hex him but I couldn't lie. 'Not hardly. It's a long way to forever.'

'You don't understand,' he said. 'I got maps, I got secret knowledge.'

'Then maybe you'll be all right.' I wheeled the roan around and waved to him. 'Luck to you!'

'Don't need it!' he cried as I started away. 'I got more heart than that horse of yours, I got . . .'

'Take it anyway!' I shouted, and spurred the roan westward.

How did it happen, this world? Our ancestors decided they didn't care to know, so they told the Captains to take that knowledge from them. Maybe I would have done the same if I was them, but sometimes I regretted their decision. What I did know happened was that one day the Captains came down from the orbital stations and waked the survivors of a great disaster, brought them forth from the caves where they were sleeping, and told them the truth about the world. The Captains offered our ancestors a choice. Said they could live up on the stations or on the earth. A bunch of our ancestors flew to the stations to take a look-see: it must have been pretty bad, because not a one wanted to emigrate. The Captains weren't surprised; they didn't think all that highly of themselves or of their life, and our ancestors got the notion that maybe the Captains felt responsible for what had happened to the world. But no matter whether or not they were responsible, the Captains were a big help. They asked our ancestors if they wanted to remember what had happened or if they wanted to forget; they had machines, they said, that could erase memory. Our ancestors apparently couldn't live with the idea of all that death behind them, maybe because it was too close to deal with easily, and so they chose to forget. And they also chose further to reject many of the old world's advantages, which is why we have rifles and horses and hydroponics and no more . . . except for our hobbies (like the man in the gold helmet with his bubble car) and the hospitals. The hospital in Edgeville was a long silver windowless building where we went to get injections and also where we talked to the Captains. We'd punch a black stud on a silver panel and their images would fade in on a screen. It was almost never the same Captain, but they looked a lot alike and they wouldn't say their names. Ask them, and they merely said, 'I am the Captain of the Southern Watch.' They have these lean pale faces and wet-looking purplish eyes, and they are every one skinny and nervous and not very tall. The apes and the tigers? My guess is that there were animals in the sleeping caves, too. Our ancestors could have had the Captains do away with them; but maybe it was decided that enemies were needed to keep us strong. I used to hate our ancestors for that, though I suppose I understood it. They wanted a challenging life, one that would make us hardy and self-sufficient, and they got that sure enough. Gazing out from the Edge into that rotten darkness at the end of the flats, you had the idea you were looking back into that gulf of time between now and the destruction of the old world, and you'd get sick inside with the feelings that arose. That alone was almost too much to bear. And on top of that the Bad Men burned our houses and stole our women. The apes defiled our children, and the tigers haunted us with their beauty . . . Could be that was the worst thing of all.

How did this world happen?

That's the whole of what I used to know about human history, and even now I don't know a whole lot more. It wasn't enough to make a clear picture, but for seven hundred years it was all the knowing most of us wanted.

I woke one morning to the smell of snow in the air. Snow meant danger. Snow meant apes and maybe tigers. The apes used the snow for cover to infiltrate the town, and sometimes it was all we could do to beat them off. I rolled over. Kiri was still asleep, her black hair fanned out over the pillow. Moonlight streamed through the window beside her, erasing the worry lines from her brow, the faint crow's-feet from around her eyes, and she looked eighteen again. Visible on her bared shoulder was the tattoo of a raven, the mark of a duellist. Her features were sharp, but so finely made their sharpness didn't lessen her beauty: like a hawk become a woman.

I was tempted to wake her, to love her. But if it was going to be a big snow, soon she'd be up in the high passes, sniping at the apes filtering down, and she'd be needing all the sleep she could get. So I eased out of bed and pulled on my flannel shirt and denims, my leather jacket, and I tiptoed into the front room. The door to Bradley's room was open, his bed empty, but I didn't worry much. Here in Edgeville we don't baby our kids. We let them run and learn the world their own way. What little worry I did feel was over the fact that Bradley had lately been running with Clay Fornoff. There wasn't much doubt in anybody's mind that Clay would wind up a Bad Man, and I just hoped Bradley would have better sense than to follow him the whole route.

I cracked the front door, took a lungful of chill air and stepped out. Our house was at the back of the canyon, and the moonlight was so strong that I could see the shapes of separate shingles on the hundreds of roofs packed together on the slope below. I could see the ruts in the dirt streets brimful of shadow, the fleeting shapes of dogs, blazes of moonlight reflected from a thousand windows, and at the centre of it all, the silver rectangle of the hospital. Leafless trees stood sentinel on the corners, and darkness looked to be welling through the mouth of the canyon from the flats. If I strained my eyes, I thought, I might see eight thousand souls shining in their little frame shacks.

I walked at a brisk pace down through the town. The shadows were sharp, dead-black, and the stars glittered like points of ice. My boots made husking noises on the frozen dirt, and my breath steamed, turning into ice chips on my beard. From the sty in back of Fornoff's store I could hear the muffled grunt of some pig having a dream.

Fornoff's was a lantern-lit barnlike place, with sacks of meal and garden tools stored up in the rafters, the walls ranged by shelves stocked with every kind of foodstuff, most of it dried or preserved. Brooms, bolts of cloth, small tools, and just about everything else were stacked in corners or heaped in bins, and in the back was a cold box where Fornoff kept his meat. A group of men and women were sitting on nail kegs around the pot-bellied stove, drinking coffee and talking in low voices; they glanced up and gave a wave when I entered. Dust adrift in the orange light glowed like pollen. The fat black stove snapped and crackled. I wrangled up another keg and joined them.

'Where's Kiri at?' asked Marvin Blank, a tall, lean man with a horsy face that struck a bargain between ugly and distinctive; he had a sticking plaster on his chin to cover a shaving nick.

'Sleepin',' I told him, and he said that was fine, he'd pick her a mount and fetch her when it came time.

The others went back to their planning. They were Cane Reynolds, Dingy Grossman, Martha Alardyce, Hart Menckyn, and Fornoff. All in their early to mid-thirties, except for Fornoff, who was beer-bellied and vast and wrinkled, with a bushy grey beard bibbing his chest. Then Callie Dressler came in from the back with a tray of hot rolls. Callie was about twenty-five, twenty-six, with a feline cleverness to her features. She had a deep tan, blackberry eyes, chestnut hair to her shoulders, and a nice figure. You could see her nipples poking up her wool shirt, and her denims couldn't have been any tighter. She was a widow, just moved to town from Windbroken, and was helping out at the store. According to Fornoff's wife, the reason she'd moved was to kick up her heels. Windbroken is fairly strait-laced compared to Edgeville. Among the population of Windbroken we had the deserved reputation of not being too concerned over who was sleeping with whom ... maybe because having to deal with the apes and the tigers gave us a less hidebound perspective on the importance of fidelity. Anyway, I was made both pleased and nervous by Callie's presence. Kiri didn't mind if I got it wet away from home once in a while, but I knew how she'd react if I ever got involved with anyone, and Callie was a temptation in that regard: she had in her both wildness and innocence, a mixture that has always troubled my heart. And so when old Fornoff announced that he was assigning me and Callie to guard the front of the store, I was of two minds about it. Not that the assignment didn't make sense. What with Callie being new, me not being much with a rifle, and the store being hard to get at, it was probably the best place for us. Callie smiled coyly and contrived to nudge my shoulder with her breast as she handed me a roll.

I'd been intending to go back and wake Kiri myself, but the snow began falling sooner than I'd expected. Marvin Blank heaved up from his keg, said he was going to fetch her and stumped out. The others followed suit, and so it was that at first light, with snow whirling around us, I found myself sitting hip-to-hip with Callie in the recessed doorway, blankets over our knees and rifles at the ready. The sky greyed, the snow came in big flakes like bits of ragged, dirty wool, and the wind sent it spinning in every direction, howling, shaping mournful words from the eaves and gutters. All I could see of the houses across the street were intimations of walls and dark roofpeaks. It was going to be a bad one, and I didn't try to avoid Callie when she nestled close, wanting all the creature comforts I could get.

We talked a little that first hour, mostly just things such as 'You got enough blanket?' and 'Want some more coffee?' Every so often we heard gunfire over the wind. Then, just when I was starting to think that nothing much was going to happen, I heard glass breaking from the side of the store. I came to my feet and told Callie to stay put.

'I'm comin' with you,' she said, wide-eyed.

'No,' I said. 'Someone's got to watch the front. Stay here. I'll be back in a minute.'

Out in the wind, my beard and eyebrows iced up at once. Visibility wasn't more than a few feet. I kept flat against the wall until I reached the corner, then jumped out, levelling my gun. Nothing but whirling snow met my eye. I eased along the wall, my heart pumping. Suddenly the wind spun the flakes in a kind of eddy, clearing an avenue of sight, and I spotted the ape. He was standing about a dozen feet away beside a broken window, his fur almost the same dirty white colour as the snow, and he was carrying a bone club. He was a scrawny specimen, old, his fur worn down to the nub in patches, and the black mask of his face as wrinkled as a prune. Yet in the centre of his face were set two young-looking blue eyes. It's hard to think of blue eyes being savage, but these were. They blinked rapidly, seeming to semaphore rage and shock and madness, and their force stunned me for a split second. Then he came at me, swinging the club, and I fired. The bullet reddened his chest and blew him backward into a drift. I went over to him, keeping the rifle trained. He lay spread-eagled, looking up at the toiling sky. Blood was bubbling from his chest, miring his fur, and for a moment his eyes fixed on me. One hand clenched, his chest heaved. Then the eyes jellied and went dead. Snowflakes fell down to cover them. Watching them whiten, I felt a touch of regret. Not for him personally, you understand, just the sort of generalized, winnowing sadness you feel when you see death happen.

I walked back to the front of the store, calling as I went to Callie so she wouldn't think me an ape and shoot. 'What was it?' she said as I settled next to her.

'Ape,' I said. 'An old one. He probably wanted to die, that's why he was tryin' for the store. They know the odds are against them this deep into town.'

'Why'd he do that?' she said, and from the depth of her perplexity, the innocence of her question, I realized that she was so young and vital, it could never be made clear to her how apes and people will just up and grow weary of the world.

'Beats me,' I told her. 'Just crazy, I guess.'

While we kept watch, she told me some about Windbroken. I'd only visited the town twice and hadn't thought much of it. Prettier than our town, that's for sure. With nicer houses and picket fences and larger trees. But the people acted as if that prettiness made them superior: seems they don't have quite enough danger in their lives to keep them real. Callie didn't strike me that way, however, and I figured that she had found her rightful place in Edgeville.

She cuddled closer to me, and before long she slipped a hand under the blanket and rested it on my thigh, moving her fingers a bit, enough to get my dingus twitching. I told her to stop it, and she grinned. 'What for?' she asked. 'Don't you like it?'

'That ain't the point.' I lifted her hand away. 'I'm married.'

'Oh, I heard 'bout how married you are from Miz Fornoff.' She shifted away, acting huffy. 'Says you 'bout as married as a tomcat.'

'That ol' woman don't know nothin'!'

104

'Don't tell me that! She ain't the only one talks 'bout you.' Her grin came back, sexy and mischievous. 'Clare Alardyce, Martha's girl? You oughta hear what she says! And Laney Fellowes, and Andrea Simpkins – she told me 'bout the time you and her went out on the flats and . . .'

'Well, so what?' I said angrily. 'It's no business of yours what I do!'

'Not yet.'

'Not ever!'

'Why?' She asked this with the stubborn rectitude of a child denied a treat. 'Don't ya think I'm pretty?'

I couldn't say she wasn't, so I got by with 'You're all right.'

'If I'm just all right,' she said, pitching her voice husky, 'how come you try to see down my shirt every time you come in the store?'

I shrugged and stared off into the snow. 'Just 'cause a man takes a peek, don't mean he's gonna buy the goods.'

'You don't have to peek,' she said.

The odd tremor in her voice made me turn to her. She had opened her coat and was unbuttoning her shirt, exposing the plump upper slopes of her breasts: they were as brown as the rest of her and looked full of juice. She slipped loose another button, and I could see one of her nipples, erect, the dark areola pebbled from the cold. I swear to God, I think my mouth started to water. She had the shirt mostly unbuttoned now, and she took my free hand and brought it over to cup one breast. I couldn't help giving it a squeeze, and when I did, she arched into the pressure, closed her eyes and let out a hiss of pleasure. Next thing I knew, I was bending to her and putting my mouth where my hand had been, and she was saying my name over and over, saying it soft so I could just hear it above the wind and pushing my head down into a sweet warmth that smelled of harsh soap and vanilla water. And then she stiffened, froze right up, and was pushing me away, whispering my name with a different kind of urgency. 'What's the matter?' I asked, and she nodded her head toward the street, her lips parted, eyes bugged. I looked around and forgot all about Callie Dressler's breasts.

Standing in the middle of the street was a tiger . . . and not just an ordinary tiger, if any of them can be said to be ordinary. He appeared to be more than twice the length of a man, and his head would have come at least to my shoulder. His fur was pure white, and his stripes were vaguely drawn the way some lines are in a delicate charcoal sketch. In the thick eddying snow he kept vanishing and reappearing as would a dream creature or the image of a beast surfacing in a magic mirror. But he was no dream. The wind brought his heavy scent to me, and for the time he stood there, I lived in terror that the wind would shift, that he would twitch his head toward us, burn me with those yellow eyes like sad crystals.

I had seen tigers prowling the slopes of the mountains at a distance, but never had I been so close to one, and it seemed that the vast weight of his life was diminishing mine, that if he were to stand there long enough I would be crushed and transformed into some distillate of being. I had no thought for my gun, for Callie, and barely any thought for my own safety. All my thoughts were as insubstantial and flighty as the flakes whirling about his massive head. He remained motionless for several seconds, testing the wind. His tail lashed, he made a small thunder in his throat, and then he sprang off along the street, disappearing into a tornado of snow that spun up from one of the drifts.

My chest ached, and I realized I had stopped breathing. I continued staring at the spot where the tiger had been. I turned to Callie, my mouth open. She lifted her eyes to mine, and a scratchy sound came from her throat. 'I . . .' she said, and gave her head a shake.

'I know,' I said. 'God almighty damn!'

Her face seemed to have been made even more beautiful by the apparition of tiger, as if the keenness of the sight had carved away the last of her baby fat, hollowing her cheeks, bringing out the sensitivity and soulfulness of the woman she would become. In that moment she looked to have captured something of the tiger's beauty, and maybe she had, maybe we both had, because she was staring at me as intently as I at her, as if she were seeing a new element in my face. I don't remember wanting to kiss her, I just did. The kiss lasted a long, long time. Like the tiger, it was not ordinary. It was a kind of admission, that kiss, an ultimate acknowledgement, and it was far more of a threat to Kiri and me than had been my fumbling with Callie's breasts. It was an event that would be very hard to pull back from. We stood most of the remainder of the watch in silence, and we didn't get cosy again. We talked stiffly of inconsequential matters and were overly solicitous of one another's comfort. Both of us knew that what might have been a fling had gotten out of hand.

We had a tiger between us, now.

It had been bad up in the passes, Kiri said. Charlie Hatton had been bitten in the neck, Mick Rattiger's skull had been crushed. Four men dead altogether. She stripped off her clothes and stood by the bedroom window, staring out at the moonstruck snow, her tawny skin drenched in whiteness. Duelling scars on her stomach and arms. Lean and small-breasted, with long fluid muscles running from thigh to buttock, and wings of black hair pulled back from her face: she posed a polar opposite to Callie's almost teenage beauty, her butterfat breasts and berry mouth. She slipped beneath the covers, lay on her back and took my hand. 'How was it with you?' she asked.

I wanted to tell her about the tiger, but I didn't have the words yet, the words with which to tell her, anyway. My incapacity had only a little to do with Callie; I wanted to tell Kiri in a way that would open her to her own beauty. She'd never been a happy woman; too much of her was bound up by the disciplines of a duellist, by the bleakness of her youth in the northern ruins. She expected death, she believed in the lessons of pain, and she lived by a harsh code that I could never fully understand. I think she looked upon Brad and me as an aberration on her part, a sign that she had grown soft.

'Shot an ape,' I said. 'That's 'bout it.'

She made a dry, amused noise and closed her eyes.

'I saw Bradley,' I said. 'He did fine, but I think he's off with Clay again tonight.'

'He'll be all right.'

She turned on her side to face me and caressed my cheek, a sign that she wanted to make love. Directness was at odds with her nature: she lived by signs, hints, intimations. I kissed her mouth, the tiny crow tattoo on her shoulder. Pressing against me, her body felt supple, sinuous, all her muscles tensed as if for battle. There's always been a mean edge to our lovemaking, and that night was no exception. She seemed to be fighting me as I entered her, and she clawed my back so fiercely, I had to pin her wrists above her head, and when she cried out at the end, it sounded like a cry of victory, a celebration of triumph over her body's resistance to pleasure.

She went to sleep almost immediately afterward, and I sat on the edge of the bed, writing at the night table by the light of the moon. I was trying to write some words for Kiri, talking not about the tiger, but about how it had been that night with her. I had, you see, come to the realization of how much I loved her, how much I wanted to split open her hard shell and make her bloom at least for a season. Whatever I felt for Callie, I decided, was nothing by comparison, no matter if it was real.

But thinking all this made me restless and unhappy, and no words would come. So I dressed, grabbed a rifle and went for a walk, going knee-deep through the snowcrust, ploughing ahead, having no real destination in mind. The town was quiet, but there were maybe a dozen fires flickering atop the canyon walls, and from those fires came the howling of apes mourning their dead. They'd be coming back with the next storm. The rooftops were mantled with snow; snow ledged the windows and marbled the boughs of the leafless trees, and the sound of my breath seemed harsh and unnatural in all that white stillness. I turned a corner and came in sight of the hospital, its silver metal walls flashing and rippling with the moonlight. Seeing it, I realized that therein lay the only soul to whom I could speak my heart, the only one who was bound to listen and who would be sure to feel the current in my words. I walked to the door, put my hand flat against an inset silver rectangle, and after a second the door slid open with a hiss. I stepped into the anteroom. Soft light began to shine from the walls, and a whispery voice asked if I needed treatment.

'Just a little conversation,' I said.

The room was about fifteen by fifteen, and a large screen occupied most of the rear wall, fronted by three chairs of silver metal and some sort of foam. I plopped into one and punched the black button. The screen brightened, dissolving to a shot of a solitary Captain. A woman. It's difficult to tell sometimes what sex they are, because they all wear the same purple robes, almost the exact dark shade as their eyes, and their hair is uniformly close-cropped, but I knew this one for a woman, because when the picture had come into focus, she had been turned a bit sideways and I could see that her robe was pushed out a tad in front. Her skin was the colour of the winter moon, and her cheeks were so hollowed that she looked toothless (yet she was pretty in an exotic way), and her eyes were too large for her face, a face that registered a gloomy, withdrawn quality during the entire time we talked.

'What's your name?' I asked; I always hoped one of them would just say to hell with it and come clean.

'I am the Captain of the Southern Watch.' Her voice was so soft as to be toneless.

I studied her a moment, thinking where to begin, and for some reason I decided to tell her about the tiger. 'Listen,' I said. 'I want your promise that you're not goin' to go off and hurt yourself after I'm done.'

She appeared reluctant but said, 'You have my word.'

You had to get this out of them before you told them anything fraught with emotion, or else they were liable to kill themselves; at least that was what I'd heard all my life. Their guilt over what happened to the world was to blame . . . Or so I thought at the time. But sometimes I would think that we were to them like the tigers were to us: beautiful strong lives that wounded them by merely being.

'Ever see a tiger?' I asked.

'Pictures of them,' she said.

'Naw, I mean up close . . . so close you could smell it.'

The idea seemed to trouble her: she blinked, her mouth thinned and she shook her head.

'I saw one that close this morning,' I said. 'Twenty, twenty-five feet away.'

I went on to tell her of its heart-stopping beauty, its power, how I couldn't breathe on seeing it; I told her what had happened as a result between me and Callie. I could see my words were hurting her – her bony fingers curled into fists, and her face grew strained – but I couldn't stop. I wanted to hurt her, to make her feel as diminutive and worthless as the tiger had made me feel. I knew this wasn't fair. No matter if the Captains were responsible for the way things were, they weren't responsible for tigers; I was sure that either tigers or something like them must always have existed to help whomever was around to keep things in perspective.

By the time I finished, she was trembling, leaning away from me, as if my words had a physical value that was beating her back. She glanced from one side to the other, then – apparently finding no help for her condition – she turned back to me. 'Is that all?' she said.

'Why do you talk to us?' I asked after a pause. 'You obviously don't enjoy it.'

'Enjoy?' The concept seemed to perplex her. 'You are our lives.'

'How can that be? We don't know your names, we never see you in the flesh.'

'Do the important things of your life all lie close at hand?'

I thought about it. 'Yeah.'

She shrugged. 'Then in this we are different from you.'

I tipped my head, trying to see her in a new light, to read the world behind that pale mask. 'But you want us close at hand, don't you?'

'Why do you think that?'

'Just a theory of mine.'

She arched an eyebrow.

'Y'see,' I said, 'you got us livin' with a limited technology, but whenever somebody wants to know somethin' new, a hobby, you let 'em investigate whatever it is . . . less it's somethin' too big. I figure you're lettin' us work our way to you.'

Her eyes narrowed, but she said nothing.

'I've talked to a whole buncha you people in my time, and I get the idea you're ashamed of what you are, that you don't want us to see it . . . 'least not 'til we're strong enough to swallow whatever it is you're hidin'.'

'Suppose that is the truth,' she said. 'How would you feel about us?'

'Probably not much different from now.'

'And how is that?'

'Tell you the truth. I don't feel much 'bout you one way or the other. You're just faces and voices is all, and you don't have any real mystery to you like there is to stuff like God. You're like distant cousins who never come to visit, and who nobody misses at family reunions.'

The hint of a smile lifted the corner of her mouth. I had the idea my answer had pleased her, though for no reason I could fathom.

'Well,' I said, standing, picking up my rifle. 'It's been fun.'

'Goodbye, Robert Hillyard,' she said.

That irritated me, her knowing my name and the reverse not being true. 'Why the hell won't you tell us your names?' I asked her.

She almost smiled again. 'And you claim we have no mystery,' she said.

Days, I worked in the hydroponic shed, a long, low building of caulked boards and plastic foam two streets east of the hospital. The shed and its contents were my hobby, and I liked breathing its rich air, mixing chemicals, watering, strolling along the aisles and watching the green shoots that had pushed up. I would hum, make up songs and forget about everything else. Nights – at least for the next couple of weeks – I spent with Kiri. She had a duel coming up, and she was working herself up into that fierce calm in which she did her best fighting. It wasn't to be a duel to the death – she had stopped fighting those when Brad came along – but you could get hurt badly enough in a first-blood duel, and she was deadly serious. Kiri was one of the best there was. It had been years since she'd lost, but now, in her thirties, she had to work harder than ever to keep her edge. Sometimes there was just no being around her during her preparation. She would snap and snarl and dare you to say Boo. On several occasions I thought about dropping over to Fornoff's and seeing how Callie was doing; but I managed to resist the impulse. Kiri needed me, and I knew that pretty soon she would have to give up duelling, and then she'd need me even more to help her get through that time. So whenever it became necessary for her to have some solitude, I would take a rifle and climb up to the north wall of the canyon and see if I could pick off an ape or two. The north wall was higher than the south, where the apes tended to congregate, and was cut off from the ape encampments by a deep cut that we had mined with explosives and otherwise booby-trapped. Though it was a clear shot, you couldn't see the apes very well unless they started dancing around their fires; even then, the range was so extreme, you had to be lucky to score a hit. Funny thing was, they didn't seem to mind when you did; they just kept dancing.

One night Brad and I climbed up to the top of the north wall. He was a lanky kid of thirteen and favoured Kiri some, having her black hair and thin, hawkish face. We staked ourselves out behind a pile of loose rocks, rested our rifles across our knees and sat back to enjoy the night air. The weather had warmed a little; the sky was clear, and the stars were winking with such intensity they looked to be jumping from place to place. It was so quiet, the silence had a hum. There were fires on the south wall, but no apes in sight, and we got to talking about this and that. I could tell there was something weighing on his mind, but he couldn't seem to spit it out. Finally, though, he screwed up his courage and told me what was troubling him.

'Y'know Hazel Aldred?' he said.

'Big ol' girl?' I said. 'Kinda pretty, but on the heavy side?'

'Yeah.' He dug his heel into some loose gravel and set to carving out a trench.

'Well, what about her?'

'Nothin',' he said after a bit; he stared off toward the south wall.

I studied him and made a guess. 'Don't tell me you been gettin' prone and lowdown with ol' Hazel?'

'How'd you know?' He pushed hair back from his eyes and stared at me fiercely. 'Who told you?'

'It don't take no genius to figure it out.' I aimed at a distant fire and squeezed off an imaginary round. 'So what about it?'

'Well . . .' More digging with his heel.

'Didn't go so hot . . . That it?'

He ducked his eyes and mumbled. 'Uh-huh.'

I waited for him to say more, and when he kept quiet, I said, 'Am I gonna have to tell this story?'

Silence.

'Lookit, Bradley,' I said. 'I been gettin' my share for a long time now, and I'm here to tell you, it don't always work out so hot, no matter how many times you done it.'

'That ain't what Clay says.'

'Shit! Clay! You believe everything he tells you?'

'Naw, but . . .'

'You're goin' on like you do!'

On the south wall a solitary ape capered for a moment in front of a fire, looking like a spirit or a devil dancing inside the flame. To ease the pressure on Brad, I took aim and sent a round in the ape's direction.

'Dija get him?'

'Don't see him,' I said. 'But I think he just went to ground.'

Wind sprayed grit into our faces.

'Anyway,' I went on. 'I can't tell you the times it's gone bad for me with the ladies. Mostly the limps, y'know. Too much drinkin', or just a case of nerves. That what happened to you?'

'Naw.' Bradley trained his rifle on the south wall, but had no target; his mouth was set grim.

'Guess I can't think of but one other thing that coulda happened,' I said. 'Maybe you was a little too excited to begin with.'

'Yeah,' he said sharply.

'And how'd she take that?'

He worried his lower lip. 'She told me to clean off her dress,' he said finally. 'And everybody laughed.'

'Everybody?'

'Clay and the rest.'

'Damn, Bradley,' I said. 'I ain't gonna tell you not to go down with a crowd. I mean it happens that way sometimes. But it sure is a lot nicer to do it with just you and whoever.'

'I ain't never gonna do it again,' he said sullenly.

'Now I doubt that.'

'I ain't!' He fired a round into nowhere and pretended to watch it travel.

'Why you feel that way?'

'I dunno.'

'Talk to me, boy.'

'I just don't know what to do,' he said in a rush. 'I mean I seen it, I seen guys hop on and it's over real quick, and the girl she acts like ain't nothin' happened. So what's the damn point?'

He fired a couple of more rounds. Some apes were dancing around a fire near the canyon mouth, but he hadn't been aiming that way.

'Listen up, son,' I said. 'Like I said, I ain't gonna tell you not to do what you been doin'. But I am gonna give you some advice. You listenin'?'

'Yes, sir.' He rested the rifle across his knees and met my eyes in that steady, sober way of his mother's.

'All right.' I leaned my rifle against my shoulder. 'You find yourself a girl who wants to be with you, just you and nobody watchin', and then you take her somewhere nice, maybe up to that storage shack near Hobson's by the rear wall. Got a coupla boards missin', and if you look out, you can see the waterfall.'

'Yeah, I know.'

'All right. If you start gettin' too excited, you try to think 'bout somethin' else. Think 'bout your mama's duel or somethin' that don't have nothin' to do with the subject at hand. And then, when the time comes and she wants you in her, you go in slow, don't just jab it home, y'know. And when you're there, when you're in all the way, don't go crazy all at once. Just move your hips the tiniest bit, so little you barely feel you're movin', and then pull out maybe an inch and hold there, and then sink back in and pin her, grind into her, like all you want is to be right where you are or maybe more so. And y'know what that'll do?'

He was all eyes. 'Un-uh?'

'No matter what happens after that,' I told him, 'like as not, you'll have been the first one to treat that little girl like you wanted to be all through her. Most guys, y'see, once they get in the saddle they don't think about what the girl's hopin' to feel. You do what I say, chances are she's gonna think you 'bout the best thing to come along since berries and cream.'

'You swear?'

'You're hearin' the voice of experience,' I said. 'So take it to heart.'

He mulled it over. 'Y'know Sara Lee Hinton?'

'Oh, yeah!' I said. 'Now that's the kinda girl you wanna be

dealin' with, not an ol' ploughhorse like Hazel.' I mussed his hair. 'But you ain't got a chance with Sara Lee.'

'I do, too!' he said defiantly. 'She told me so.'

'Well, go to it then,' I said. 'And remember what I told you. You got it in mind?'

'Yeah,' he said, and grinned.

I gave him a shove. 'Let's do some shootin'.'

Before long, the apes came out in force and took to dancing around their fires like black paper dolls brought to life. We fired round after round with no measurable result. Then as Brad fired, one of the apes did a dive and roll, and went out of sight. I'd seen that move many times; it was a part of their normal style of dancing. But I figured the boy could use another boost in confidence, and I gave him a hug and shouted, 'Goddamn! I believe you got him!'

It was three nights later that Clay Fornoff turned Bad Man. Everyone had been expecting it since his trouble with Cindy Aldred, Hazel's big sister. Clay had been sweet-talking her, trying to persuade her to go out onto the flats with him . . . not that she needed much persuasion. Cindy's reputation was no better than her sister's. But even a girl like Cindy likes a little sweet talk, and she was playing hard to get when Clay lost his patience. He slapped her silly, dragged her into the bushes and had her rough and mean. The next day Cindy accused him, and he made no bones that he had done it. He could have suffered plenty, but Cindy must have been soft on him, or else he had something on her that stayed her anger. She asked for mercy, and so Clay was put on warning, which meant that we would all be watching him, that one more slip would buy him a one-way ticket onto the flats.

That night there was a full moon, a monstrous golden round that looked to be hovering just out of reach, and whose light made the canyon walls glow like they were made of light themselves. I was ambling along with Brad past Fornoff's, which had closed down a couple of hours earlier, taking the air, talking, when I heard something crash inside the store. In the corral a few doors down, the horses were milling, pushing against the fence. I shoved Brad behind me and eased around the corner of the store, holding my rifle at the ready. A shadow sprinted from the rear of the store and crossed the street to the corral, then ducked down so as to hide in the shadows. I aimed, held my breath, but before I could fire, Brad knocked the barrel off-line.

'It's Clay,' he whispered.

'How the hell you know?'

'I just can tell!'

'That makes it worse. Stealin' from his daddy's store.' I brought the rifle up again, but Brad caught hold of it and begged me to hold back.

The shadow was duck-walking along beside the corral, and the horses, their eyes charged with moonlight, were moving in tight circles, bunched together, like eddies in a stream.

'Let go,' I said to Brad. 'I won't hurt him.'

The shadow flattened against the wall of the dress shop next to the corral. I pushed Bradley back around the corner, aimed at the shadow and called out in a soft voice, 'Don't you move now, Clay Fornoff!'

Clay didn't make a sound.

'Get out in the light where I can see you,' I told him. 'Or I'll kill you quick!'

After a second he did as I'd said. He was a muscular blond kid some five of six years older than Brad, and he was wearing a sheepskin coat that his daddy had bought him up in Windbroken. His mouth was full and petulant, his eyes set wide apart in a handsome face, and in his hands were a shotgun and several boxes of shells. The wind lifted his long hair, drifted it across his eyes.

'What you plannin' to do with all the firepower?' I asked, walking out into the middle of the street.

He gave no reply, but stared daggers at Brad.

'I 'spect you oughta throw down the gun,' I said.

He heaved it toward me.

'Shells, too. Just drop 'em, don't throw 'em.'

When he had done what I asked, I walked over and gave him a cold eye. 'I turn you in,' I said, 'they'll have you walkin' west without boots or blankets. And if you stick around, I'm bound to turn you in.'

He wasn't afraid, I give him credit; he just stared at me.

'Lemme take a horse,' he said.

I thought about that. If I were to tell old Fornoff what had happened, I figured he'd be glad to pay the price of the horse. 'All right,' I said. 'Go ahead. And take the gun, too. Your daddy would want that. But I see you back here, I ain't gonna think twice 'bout how to handle it. Understand?'

All he did by way of thanking me was to grunt.

I kept him covered while he cut out a bay and saddled it. Brad hung back, acting like he was having no part of the matter, but saying nothing. I didn't blame him for not facing up to Clay, I would probably have done the same at his age.

Clay mounted up, pulled hard on the reins, causing the horse to rear. His head flew back, his hair whipping in the breeze, and the moon struck him full in the eyes, making it seem that wicked fires had suddenly been kindled there. For that split second I could feel how it would be to give up on the law, to turn Bad Man, to take a long ride west of anywhere and hope you come to something, and if you didn't . . . Well, for the length of the ride at least you lived as wild and strong and uncaring as a tiger. But Clay spoiled the moment by cursing Brad. He wheeled the bay around, then, and spanked it into a gallop west, and in a second he was gone, with only a few puffs of frozen dust settling on the street to show he'd ever been.

Brad's chin was trembling. God only knows what part of life he had just watched riding out of sight. I patted him on the shoulder, but most of my thoughts were arrowing toward the next morning. It wasn't going to be easy to tell old Fornoff that his son had gone to the Devil for a shotgun and a couple of boxes of shells.

The night before Kiri left for Windbroken and her duel, a couple of months after Clay Fornoff had gone Bad, I tried to talk to her about the future, about when she planned to quit fighting, but she wouldn't have any part of it, and instead of gentling her as I'd intended, I just made her mad. We went to bed strangers, and the next morning she gave me a cold peck on the cheek and a perfunctory wave, and stalked out the door. I can't say I was angry at her . . . more frustrated. Sooner or later, I knew, she was going to be in for a bad time, and that meant bad times for me as well. And perhaps it was my frustration with this sense of imminent trouble that led me to seek out trouble on my own.

That same afternoon I dropped into Fornoff's to buy some seed. Fornoff and his wife were off somewhere, and Callie was the only one on duty. There were a few other customers, and she couldn't leave the counter to go in the back where the seed was stored, so I told her to send it over to the hydroponics building when she had time. She leaned forward, resting her elbows on the counter; her shirt belled, exposing the slopes of her breasts; every little move she made caused them to sway and signal that they were sweet and easy and free for the evening.

'What time you want 'em?' she asked.

'Any ol' time's fine,' I said. 'Whenever's convenient.'

'Well, when do you need 'em?' She laid heavy emphasis on the word 'need'.

'Ain't nothin' urgent,' I said. 'But I would like 'em by tomorrow.'

'Oh, we can manage that,' said Callie, straightening. 'I don't get 'round to it 'fore evenin', I'll walk 'em over myself after work.'

'Whatever,' I said, pretending that I hadn't picked up on the none-too-subtle undertone of the conversation; even after I had left the store, I kept up the pretence and pushed the matter from mind.

The main hydroponics shed was set directly behind the hospital, a long, low building of tin and structural plastic, so low that if you were standing up by my house, the hospital and a low ridge would have blocked it from view, even though it enclosed nearly a dozen acres. Inside, there was corn and tomatoes and lettuce and at the rear, next to the office – a little room with tin walls and a couple of pictures, a desk and a cot where I slept whenever Kiri was away – I'd erected some trellises and was growing grapes. I enjoyed the peace of the place and liked to walk up and down the aisles, checking the nutrients in the tanks, squeezing the tomatoes, petting the corn, generally just feeling at home and master of it all. The greenness of the leaves coloured the air, creating a green shade under the ultraviolets, and the muted vibration of the generator created the rumour of a breeze that made all the plants whisper together. I spent a lot of time in the office reading, and that evening I was sitting at my desk with my feet up, reading a book called *The Black Garden* written by a man from Windbroken, a fantasy about the world that used to be. I'd read it before, more than once, as had most other readers in the town. Books were expensive to make, and there weren't many of them. Most pretended to be histories, recounting the innumerable slaughters and betrayals and horrors that supposedly comprised our past, but this one was a refreshing change, featuring a number of colour illustrations, several depicting a vast underground chamber floored with exotic plants and trees, threaded by canopied pathways, and the strange dark area that lay beyond it, a lightless cavern choked with black bushes and rife with secret doors that opened into little golden rooms where the inhabitants of the place explored the limits of pleasure. Their idea of pleasure, according to the author, was kind of nasty, but still it beat all to hell the stories of massacres and mass torture that you usually ran across in books. Anyway, I was leafing through the pages, wondering if what the author had written bore any relation to the truth and marvelling once again at the detail of the illustrations, when Callie poked her head in through the office door.

'Well, ain't you cosy?' she said, and came on in. 'I left the seed out front.' She glanced around the room, her eyes lingering on the cot. 'Got yourself a regular home away from home here, don'tcha?'

'S'pose I do.' I closed the book, looked at her, then, feeling antsy, I got to my feet and said, 'I gotta check on somethin'.'

I went out into the shed, fiddled with some dials on the wall, tapped them as if that were meaningful. At this point I wasn't sure I had the will or the need to get horizontal with Callie, but then she came out of the office, went strolling along an aisle, asking questions about the tanks and the pipes, touching leaves, and watching her, seeing her pretty and innocent-looking in the green darkness of my garden, I realized I didn't have a choice, that while she had not been foremost on my mind lately, I'd been thinking about her under the surface so to speak, and whenever a gap cleared in the cloudiness of my daily concerns with Kiri and Brad, there Callie would be. She walked off a ways, then turned back, face solemn, a hand toying with the top button of her shirt. I knew she was waiting for me to say or do something. I felt awkward and unsure, like I was Brad's age once again. Callie leaned against one of the tanks and sighed; the sigh seemed to drain off some of the tension.

'You look worried,' she said. 'You worryin' 'bout me?'

I couldn't deny it. I said, 'Yeah,' and by that admission I knew we would likely get past the worry. Which worried me still more. 'It's Kiri, too,' I went on. 'I don't know . . . I . . .'

'You're feelin' guilty,' she said, and ducked her head. 'So am I.' She glanced up at me. 'I don't know what's happenin'. First off, I just wanted some fun . . . That's all. And I wouldn't have felt guilty 'bout that. Then I got to wantin' more, and that made me feel bad. But the worse I feel' – she flushed and did a half-turn away from me – 'worse I feel, the more I want you.' She let out another sigh. 'Maybe we shouldn't do nothin', maybe we should just go our own ways.'

I intended to say, 'Maybe so,' but what came out was, 'I don't know 'bout you, but I don't think I could do it.'

'Oh, sure you could,' she said, downcast. 'We both could.'

I knew she meant what she was saying, but there was also a challenge in those words, a dare for me to prove what I had said, to prove that what I felt had the power of compulsion. I went over and put my hands on her waist; I could feel a pulse all through her. She looked up, holding my eyes, and I couldn't do anything else but kiss her.

There's a lot of false in everything that people do, particularly when it comes to the dealings between men and women. There's games played, lies traded, and fantasies given undue weight. But if those things are combined and cooked by the passage of time in just the right way, then a moment will arrive when everything that's false can get true in a flash, when the truest love can be made out of all that artifice, and once the games and the lies have been tempered into something solid and real, the process keeps on going, and you discover what worlds have changed, which lives have been diminished, which ones raised to glory. We can't know in advance what we make when we go to making love. If we could, maybe there would be a whole lot less of it made. But chances are, knowing in advance wouldn't change a thing, because those moments are so strong they can overwhelm most kinds of knowledge. Even knowing all I do now, I doubt I could have resisted the forces that drew Callie and me together.

We went into my office, and we lay down on the cot, and seeing her naked, I recognized that her sleek brown body was at home here among the growing things, that this was the place for us, surrounded by corn and green leaves and tomatoes bursting with juice, whereas Kiri's place was in that sad, barren little cabin up on the slope, with the apes howling above and a view of emptiness out the bedroom window. I felt that what Callie and me had was something growing and fresh, and that what I had with Kiri was dry and brittle and almost gone, and though it hurt me to think that, it pleasured me to think it, too. I liked being with a woman who was gentle, who didn't force me to take what I wanted, one whose cries were soft and full of delight, not tormented and fierce. I liked the easy way she moved with me, the joyful greed with which she drew me in deep. I knew there were going to be trials ahead, but I wasn't ready to confront them. Kiri would be gone for ten days, and I wanted to relish each and every one.

There was a good deal of little girl in Callie. One minute she could be tender, all concern and care and thoughtfulness, and the next she might become petulant, stubborn, wilful. That girlish side only came into play in good ways at the beginning – in bed, mostly – and it plumped up my ego to be able to feel paternal toward her, giving me a distant perspective on her that was as loving in its own fashion as the intimate perspective we shared when we lay tangled and sweaty on the cot in my office. And, too, she brought out the boy in me, a part of my character that I'd had to keep under wraps for the duration of my marriage. Love with Callie was a kind of golden fun, serious and committed, untainted with desperation. It wouldn't always be just fun; I was aware of that, and I was sure we would have our ups and downs. Yet I thought at the core of what we were was that tiger, that emblem of beauty and power, something that could be whirled away in the snow, but would always return to buck us up no matter how painful or difficult the circumstance.

However, I had no idea of the difficulties that would arise when Kiri returned from Windbroken.

One afternoon I came into the house whistling, direct from Callie's arms, and found Brad sitting in a straight-backed chair by the closed door of the bedroom. His sombre look cut through my cheerful mood, and I asked why he was so low.

'Mama's home,' he said.

That knocked me back a step. I covered my reaction and said, 'That ain't nothin' to be all down in the mouth about, is it?'

'She lost.' He said this in almost a questioning tone, as if he couldn't quite believe it.

There was nothing cheerful I could say to that. 'She all right?'

'Got a cut on her arm is all. But that ain't what's bad.'

'She's grievin', is she?'

He nodded.

'Well,' I said. 'Maybe we can nudge her out of it.'

'I don't know,' he said.

I ran my hands along my thighs as if pushing myself into shape, needing the feel of that solidity, because everything I had been anticipating had been thrown out of kilter. It seemed I could feel the weight of Kiri's despair through the wood of the door. I gave Bradley a distracted pat on the head and went on in. Kiri was sitting on the edge of the bed, bathed in the sunset that came russet through the shade, giving the air the colour of old blood. Except for a bandage around her bicep, she was naked. She didn't move a muscle, eyes fixed on the floor. I sat beside her as close as I dared, hesitant to touch her; there had been times she'd been so lost in herself that she had lashed out at me when I startled her.

'Kiri,' I said, and she shivered as if the sound had given her a chill.

Her face was drawn, cheeks hollowed, lips thinned. 'I should have died,' she said in a voice like ashes.

'We knew this time was coming.'

She remained silent.

'Damn, Kiri,' I said, feeling more guilt and self-recrimination than I had thought possible. 'We'll get through this.'

'I don't want that,' she said, the words coming out slow and full of effort. 'It's time.'

'Bullshit! You ain't livin' up north no more.'

Her skin was pebbled with the cold. I forced her to lie down and covered her with blankets. Then, knowing the sort of warming she most needed, I stripped and crawled in with her. I held her close and told her I didn't want to hear any more crap about it being her time, that here in Edgeville just because somebody lost a fight didn't mean they had to walk out into the Big Nothing and die. And I told her how Brad was relying on her, how we both were, feeling the bad place that the lie I'd been living made inside my chest. I doubt she heard me, or if she did, the words had no weight. Her head lolled to one side, and she stared at the wall, which grew redder and redder with the declining sun. I think she could have willed herself into dying right then, losing had made her so downhearted. I tried to love her, but she resisted that. I guess I was grateful not to have to lie in that way as well, and I just held onto her and talked until it got late, until I fell asleep talking, mumbling in her ear.

I had thought during the night that my attentions were doing Kiri some good, but if anything, her depression grew deeper. I spent day after day trying to persuade her of her worth, sparing time for little else, and achieved nothing. She would sit cross-legged by the window, staring out over the flats, and from time to time would give voice to savage-sounding chants. I feared for her. There was no way I could find to penetrate the hard shell of misery with which she had surrounded herself. Logic; pleading; anger. None of these tactics had the least effect. Her depression began to communicate to me. I felt heavy in my head, my thoughts were dulled and drooping, and I couldn't summon the energy for even the lightest work. Despite my concern for Kiri, I missed Callie – I needed her clean sweetness to counteract the despair that was poisoning me. I managed a couple of fleeting conversations with her during the second week after Kiri's return and told her I'd get out as soon as I could and asked her to take the late shift at the store, because it would be easier for me to get free after work. And finally one night after Kiri had taken to chanting, I slipped out the door and hurried down through the town to Fornoff's.

I stood outside in the cold, waiting until the last few customers and then old Fornoff had gone, leaving Callie to close up. Just as she was about to lock the door, I darted inside, giving her a start. She had her hair up and was wearing a blue dress with a small check, and she looked so damn good, with her plush hips flaring from that narrow waist, I wanted to fall down and drown inside her. I tried to give her a hug, but she pushed me away. 'Where the hell you been?' she said. 'I been going crazy!'

'I told you,' I said. 'I had to . . .'

'I thought you was gonna tell her 'bout us?' she shrilled, moving deeper into the store.

'I'm gonna tell her!' I said, beginning to get angry. 'But I can't right now. You know that.'

She turned her back on me. 'I don't mean nothin' to you. All that sweet talk was just . . . just talk.'

'Goddammit!' I spun her around, catching her by the shoulders. 'You think I been havin' a wonderful time this last week? I been livin' in hell up there! I wanna tell her, but I can't 'long as she's like she is now.' It stung me to hear myself talking with such callousness about Kiri, but strong emotion was making me stupid. I gave Callie a shake. 'You understand that, don'tcha?'

'No, I don't!' She pulled away and stalked off toward the storeroom. 'Even if everything you say's true, I don't understand how anyone could be as peculiar as you say she is!'

'She ain't peculiar, she's just different!'

'Oh, well!' She shot me a scornful look. 'I didn't know she was *different*. All I been hearin' 'til now is how she can't satisfy you no more.'

'That don't mean she ain't good-hearted. And it don't mean she's peculiar. You know damn well I never said I didn't care 'bout her. I always said she was someone I respected, someone I loved. Not like I love you, I admit that. But it's love all the same. And if I have to kill her so we can get together, then it's sure as shit gonna kill whatever I feel for you.' I came toward her. 'You just don't understand 'bout Kiri.'

'I don't wanna understand!'

'Where she comes from it's so bad, times get hard, they kill the weak ones for food, and when they feel they're worthless, they'll take a walk out into nowhere so they won't be a burden. I know it's hard to understand what that kinda life does to you. I didn't understand for a long while myself.'

Her chin quivered, and she looked away. 'I'm scared,' she said after a second. 'I seen this before up in Windbroken, this exact same thing. 'Cept it was the woman who's married. But it was the same. The man she loved, not her husband, this boy . . . When she couldn't leave her husband 'cause he was took ill, he like to gone crazy.' Tears leaked from her eyes. 'Just like I been doin'.'

I started for her, but she backed into the dimly lit storeroom, holding up a hand to fend me off. 'You keep away from me,' she said. 'I don't need no more pain than I got right now.'

'Callie,' I said, feeling helpless.

'Naw, I mean it.' She kept on backing, beginning to sob. 'I'm sorry for what I said about her, I truly am. I do feel bad for her. But I just can't keep on bein' self-sacrificin', you hear? I just can't. If it's gonna be over, I want it to be over now.'

It was funny how everything we said and did in that dusty old store, in that unsteady lantern light, with the pot-bellied stove snapping in the background, seemed both ultimately false, like a scene from a bad play, and ultimately true at the same time. How it led us toward the one truth we were, how it commanded us to make every lying thing true. The things I said were things I couldn't keep from saying, even though some of them rang like tin to my ear.

'Damn, Callie,' I said, moving after her into the storeroom. 'You just gotta give it some time. I know it looks bad now, but believe me, it's gonna work out.'

She fetched up against the wall next to a stack of bulging sacks of grain; the sacks were each stamped with fancy lettering and the picture of a rooster, and seemed to be leaking their faded colours up to stain the air the grainy brown of the burlap. A barrel full of shovels, blades up, to her right, and coils of rope on pegs above her. She let her head droop to one side as if she didn't want to see what would happen next.

'You believe me, don'tcha?' I said, coming up to her, losing the last of my reason in her smell of warmth and vanilla water, pulling her hips against mine.

'I want to,' she said. 'God knows, I want to.'

Her breasts felt like the places where my hands had been formed, her mouth stopped my thirst. Berry lips and black eyes and brown skin all full of juice. I didn't know her, but I felt she knew me, and sometimes it seems that's the most of love, believing that the other sees you clear. I hitched up her skirt, muffling her protests with my mouth, and wrangled down the scrap of a thing that covered her heat, and then I lifted her up a bit and pushed inside, pinning her against the rough boards. She was like honey melting over me. I tangled a hand in her hair, yanking back her head and baring her neck. I kissed her throat and loved the simple sounds she made. In the dimness her dazed expression looked saintly and her movements were frantic, her big rear end pounding the planking, one foot hooked behind my knee. 'Oh, God! I love you, Bob,' she said. 'I love you so much.' The shovel blades were quivering in the barrel, the coils of rope were jiggling; a trowel suspended from a nail started to clank in rhythm with us. It was a cluttered act, bone-rattling and messy. Our teeth clicked together in a kiss, and my palm picked up splinters as I groped for purchase on the wall. But it was pure and urgent and the best thing that had happened to me in a long time. Callie began saying 'love' every time I plunged into her as if I were dredging love up from the place it had been hiding. And she said other things, too — gushes of breath that might have been words in a strange windy language, a language whose passion made me feel twice the man I was and goaded me to drive harder into her. Then she was pushing at me, saying 'Oh, God,' her tone suddenly gone desperate, her expression no longer dazed, but horrorstruck, saying, 'Stop it . . . stop!' and staring past my shoulder. 'What is it?' I asked, trying to gentle her, but she shoved me hard and I slipped out of her. I turned, my cock waving stupidly in the air, and saw Kiri standing at the door in her black duelling clothes, her face stony with anger.

'Kiri,' I said, trying to stuff myself back into my pants, feeling shame and fear and sorrow all at once.

She whirled on her heel and stalked toward the door.

'Kiri!' I stumbled after her, buttoning my pants. 'Wait!'

I caught at her shoulder, spinning her half around, and before I could speak another word, she hit me three times, twice in the face, and the last – a blow delivered with the heel of her hand to the chest – taking my wind and sending me onto my back. Something black hovered over me as I lay curled on the floor, fighting to breathe, and when my vision cleared, I saw Kiri's dark face looming close.

'Can you hear me?' she asked in a voice empty as ashes.

I nodded.

'What I'm doing now,' she said, 'isn't because of this. It's because of who I am. You're not to blame yourself for what I do. Are you listening?'

Uncomprehending, I managed to gasp out, 'Yes.'

'Are you sure? What I'm going to do isn't because of you and . . . the girl.' She made 'the girl' sound like 'the worm' or 'the rat'.

'Wha . . .' I gagged, choked.

'But I will not forgive what you've done,' she said, and struck me in the jaw, sending white lights shooting back through my eyes and into my skull. When I regained consciousness, she was gone.

It took me most of that night to discover that Kiri had left Edgeville, that she'd taken one of Marvin Blank's horses and ridden out onto the flats. I knew she was gone for good. I would have ridden after her straightaway, but I didn't want to leave without telling Brad, and he was nowhere to be found. I decided I'd give him a couple of hours, and then I was going, no matter whether he had returned or not. I sat on the bed, with Callie beside me, and we waited, each minute like a glass prison that lasted too long to be measured except by its weight and its silence. Callie had put on her riding clothes, and I'd quit trying to persuade her to stay behind. Her arguments were sound: it was as much her fault as mine, we were in this together, and so forth. I didn't want to go alone, anyhow. That was the main reason I'd left off arguing with her. The honourable reason, the reason I kept telling myself was the most important one, and maybe the one that had the most chance of working out to be true, of being the kind of hopeful lie that breeds a passionate truth, was that I needed to be honest with Brad about Callie, about everything that had happened, because that was the only way that any good could come out of it for him, for Callie and me. Having her along was part of that honesty. To be considering all this at the time may appear self-absorbed, but I have always been a pragmatic soul, and though I cared about Kiri, I didn't expect to see her again; I knew that whenever she made a decision, she decided it to death, and by giving thought to Brad and Callie, I was hoping to salvage something of the mess I'd made. It might be that I didn't deserve anything good, but we were foolish people, not evil, and our lives were hard enough without demanding perfection of either ourselves or one another. Living on the Edge, you learned to make the best of things and not waste too much time in recriminations, and you left the indulgence of self-pity to those who could afford the luxury of being assholes.

Brad came home about an hour after first light, dishevelled and sleepy-looking, his hair all stuck up in back. He stared at me, at my bruises, at Callie, and asked where his mama was.

'Let's go find her,' I said. 'I'll tell you what happened on the way.'

He backed away from me, his pale face tightening just like Kiri's might have. 'Where's she gone?'

'Listen to me, son,' I said. 'There'll be time later for you to get all over my butt if you want. But right now findin' your mama's what's important. I waited for you 'cause I knew you'd want to help. So let's just go now.'

Callie eased back behind me as if Brad were hurting her with his stare.

'She's rode out,' he said. 'That it?'

I said, 'Yeah.'

'What'd you do?'

'Bradley,' I said. 'Ten seconds more, and I'm gone.'

He peered at Callie and me fiercely, trying to see the rotten thing we'd done. 'Hell, I reckon I don't need no explanation,' he said.

I could write volumes about the first days of our ride; nothing much happened during them, but their emptiness was so profound that emptiness itself became intricate and topical, and the bleakness of the land, the frozen hardpan with its patches of dead nettles and silverweed, the mesas rising in the distance like black arks, became a commentary on our own bleakness. The mountains faded into smoky blue phantoms on the horizon, the sky was alternately bleached and clouded grey. Now and then I'd glance at Callie on my left, Brad on my right. With their dark hair flying in the wind and their grave expressions, they might have been family, and yet they never spoke a word to the other, just maintained a remorseless concentration on the way ahead. By day we followed Kiri's sign, taking some hope from the fact that she wasn't trying to cover her tracks. Nights, we camped in the lee of boulders or a low hill, with wind ghosting from the dark side of forever, and our cooking fire the only light. Snow fell sometimes, and although most of it would melt by the time the sun was full up, what had collected in the hoofprints of the horses would last a while longer, and so in the mornings we would see a ghostly trail of white crescents leading back in the direction of home.

The first night out I let Brad vent his anger over what had happened, but it wasn't until the second night that I really talked with him about it. We were sitting watch together by the fire, our rifles beside us, and Callie was asleep beneath some blankets a few yards away, tucked between two boulders. Despite Kiri's parting gift of absolution, I took the blame for everything; but he told me that Kiri wouldn't have said what she had unless she'd meant it.

'She woulda gone ridin' sooner or later,' he said. 'She wanted you to know that. But that don't mean I forgive you.'

'Whatever,' I said. 'But I 'spect you're liable to forgive me 'fore I forgive myself.'

He just sniffed.

'I never told you I was perfect,' I said. ' 'Fact, ain't I always tellin' you how easy it is for men and women to screw each other up without meanin' harm to nobody? I thought you understood about all that.'

'Understandin' ain't forgivin'.'

'That's true enough,' I said.

He shifted so that the firelight shined up one side of his face, leaving the other side in inky shadow, as if his grim expression were being eclipsed. His lips parted, and I thought he was going to say something else, but he snapped his mouth shut.

'What is it?' I asked.

'Nothin',' he said.

'Might as well spit it out.'

'All right.' He glared at Callie. 'She shouldn't oughta be here. I mean if we find mama, she ain't gonna want to see her with us.'

'That may be,' I said. 'But Callie's got her own needs, and she needs to be here.' Brad made to speak, but I cut him off. 'You know damn well if your mama don't wanna be found, we ain't gonna find her. We all hope we find her, and we're gonna try hard. But if we don't, then it's important for every one of us that we did try. You may not like Callie, but you can't deny her that.'

He gave a reluctant nod, but looked to be struggling over something else.

'Don't hold back now,' I said.

'I thought . . .' He turned away, probably to hide his face; there was a catch in his voice when he spoke again. 'I don't understand why . . . Why you and mama had to . . . Why you . . .'

'I can't tell you why this happened. Shit, I never even could figure out how things got started 'tween me and your mama. The two of us together never seemed to make any damn sense. We loved each other but I think love was something that came from need, 'stead of the other way around.'

Brad jerked his thumb toward Callie. 'It make more sense with her?'

'It might have, bad as that may sound to you. But now . . . now, I don't know. This all mighta killed it. Maybe that's how it should be. Anyhow, that ain't nothin' we have to deal with this minute.'

The wind made a shivery moan down through the rocks, and the flames whipped sideways. Brad lowered his eyes, scooped up a handful of dust, let it sift through his fingers. 'Don't guess there's any more to be said.'

I let his words hang.

'I keep thinkin' 'bout Mama out there,' he said after a bit. 'I keep seein' her like . . . like this little black dot in the middle of nowhere.' He tossed dust into the fire. 'Y'figure anything lives out here?'

'Just us, now.' I spat into the fire, making the embers sizzle. 'Maybe a tiger or two what wanders out to die.'

'What 'bout Bad Men?'

'Why'd they want to be way out here? It's more likely they're livin' north of Edgeville up in the hills.'

'Clay told me he'd met somebody lived out here.'

'Well, Clay wasn't no big authority now, was he?'

'He wasn't no liar, either. He said this fella come in once in a while to buy shells. Never bought nothin' but shells. The fella told him he lived out on the flats with a buncha other men. He wouldn't say why. He told Clay if he wanted to learn why, he'd have to come lookin' for 'em.'

'He's just havin' some fun with Clay.'

'Clay didn't think so.'

'Then he was a fool.'

Brad gave me a sharp look, and I had the feeling he was seeing me new. 'He ain't a fool just 'cause you say he is.'

'Naw,' I said. 'There's a hell of a lot more reason than that, and you know it.'

He made a noise of displeasure and stared into the flames. I stared at them, too, fixing on the nest of embers, a hive of living orange jewels shifting bright to dark and back again as they were fanned by the wind. The glow from the fire carved a bright hollow between the two boulders where Callie was sleeping. I would have liked to have crawled under the blankets with her and taken whatever joy I could in the midst of that wasteland; but Kiri was too much on my mind. I wished I could have limited my vision of her to a black dot; instead, I pictured her hunkered down chanting in the darkness, making her mind get slower and slower, until it grew so slow she would just sit there and die.

I straightened and found Brad looking at me. He met my eyes, and after a long moment he slumped and let his head hang; from that exchange I knew we had been thinking pretty much the same thing. I put my hand on his arm; he tensed, but didn't shrug it off as he might have the night before. I saw how worn down and tired he was.

'Go and get some sleep,' I told him.

He didn't argue, and before long he was curled up under his blankets, breathing deep and regular.

I lay back, too, but I wasn't sleepy. My mind was thrumming with the same vibration that underscored the silence, as if all the barriers between my thoughts and the dark emptiness had been destroyed, and I felt so alive that it seemed I was floating up a fraction of an inch off the ground and trembling all over. A few stars were showing as pale white points through thin clouds. I tried to make them into a constellation, but couldn't come up with a shape that would fit them; they might have been the stars of my life, scattered from their familiar pattern, and I realized that even if we could find Kiri, I was never going to be able to put them back the way they had been. Life for me had been a kind of accommodation with questions that I'd been too cowardly or just too damn stupid to ask, and that was why it had been blown apart so easily. If Kiri hadn't been the victim of the piece, I thought, having it blown apart might have been a good result.

I made an effort to see what lay ahead for us. The way things stood, however, there was no figuring it out, and my thoughts kept drifting back to Kiri. I stared off beyond the fire, letting my mind empty, listening to the wind scattering grit across the stones. At last I grew drowsy, and just before I woke Callie to stand her watch, I could have sworn I saw one of the tiny pale stars dart off eastward and then plummet toward the horizon; but I didn't think much about it at the time.

Five days out, and no sign of Kiri. Her trail had vanished like smoke in a mirror, and I did not know what to do. Five days' ride from Edgeville was considered an unofficial border between the known and unknown, and it was generally held that you would be risking everything by continuing past that limit. Nobody I'd ever met had taken up the challenge, except maybe for the man in the bubble car. We had enough supplies to keep going for a couple more days, yet I felt we'd be wasting our time by doing so and I decided to bring the matter up that night.

We camped in a little depression among head-high boulders about fifty yards from the base of a hill that showed like a lizard's back against the stars, and as we sat around the fire, I made my speech about returning.

After I had done, Callie said with some force, 'I ain't goin' back 'til we find her.'

Brad made a noise of disgust. 'You got nothin' to say about it,' he told her. 'Wasn't for you, wouldn't none of this happened.'

'Don't you be gettin' on me!' she snapped. 'There's a lot about all this you ain't got the brains to understand.'

'I'll say whatever the hell I want,' he came back.

'Both of you shut up,' I said.

The fire popped and crackled; Brad and Callie sat scowling at the flames.

'We're not gonna argue about this,' I said. 'Everybody knows what happened, and we all got reason for being here. We started together and we're gonna finish together. Understand?'

'*I* understand,' said Callie, and Brad muttered under his breath.

'Say it now,' I told him. 'Or keep it to yourself.'

He shook his head. 'Nothin'.'

'We'll go on a couple more days,' I said after a pause. 'If we ain't found her by then, there ain't gonna be no findin' her.'

Brad's face worked, and once again he muttered something.

'What say?'

'Nothin'.'

'Don't gimme that,' I said. 'Let's hear it. I don't want you pissin' and moanin' any more. Let's get everything out in the open.'

His cheekbones looked as if they were going to punch through the skin. 'If you gave a damn about Mama, you wouldn't stop 'til we found her. But all you wanna do is to get back home and crawl in bed with your whore!' He jumped to his feet. 'Whyn't you just do that? Go on home! I don't need you, I'll find her myself.'

A hot pressure had been building in my chest, and now it exploded. I launched myself at Brad, driving him back against one of the boulders and barring my forearm under his jaw. 'You little shit!' I said. 'Talk to me like that again, I'll break your goddamn neck.'

He looked terrified, his eyes tearing, but all hell was loose in me and I couldn't stop yelling at him. Callie tried to pull me off him, but I shoved her aside.

'I'm sick'n tired of you remindin' me every damn minute 'bout what it is I done,' I said to Brad. 'I know it to the goddamn bone, y'hear? I don't need no fuckin' reminders!'

Suddenly I had a glimpse of myself bullying a thirteen-year-old. My anger drained away, replaced by shame. I let Brad go and stepped back, shaking with adrenaline. 'I'm sorry,' I said. But he was already sprinting off into the night and I doubt he heard me.

'He'll be back,' said Callie from behind me. 'It'll be all right.'

I didn't want to hear that anything was all right, and I moved away from her; but she followed and pressed against my back, her arms linking around my waist. I didn't want tenderness, either; I pried her arms loose.

'What's the matter?' she asked.

'What the hell you think?'

'I mean with us. I know you can't be lovin' to me with Bradley around. But it's more'n that.'

'Maybe,' I said. 'I don't know.'

I stepped away from the fire, moving off into the dark; the hardpan scrunched beneath my boot heels. The dark seemed to be pouring into my eyes. I felt that everything was hardening around me, locking me into a black mood, a black fate.

'You know what we need to do?' I said bitterly, not even looking at Callie. 'We need to just keep on ridin' . . . more'n a couple of days, I mean. We should just keep ridin' and ridin' 'til that's the only thing we can do, 'til we're nothin' but bones and saddles.'

I guess I figured she would object to that, promote some more optimistic viewpoint, but she said nothing, and when I looked back at her, I saw that she was sitting by the fire with her knees drawn up, holding her head in her hands.

I'd expected my mood would lift with the morning, but it did not, and the weather seconded my gloom, blowing up to near a gale, driving curtains of snow into our faces and obscuring us one from another. I rode with a scarf knotted about my face, my collar up, my eyebrows frosted. My thoughts revolved in a dismal cycle . . . less thoughts, really, than recognitions of a new thing inside me, or rather the breaking of some old thing and the new absence that had replaced it, solid and foreboding as the shadowy granite of the hills. Something had changed in me forever. I tried to deny it, to reason with myself, saying that a flash of temper and a moment's bitterness couldn't have produced a marked effect. But then I thought that maybe the change had occurred days before, and that all my fit of temper had achieved was to clear away the last wreckage of my former self. I felt disconnected from Callie and Bradley. Emotionless and cold, colder than the snowy air. My whole life, I saw, was without coherence or structure. An aimless scattering of noises and heats and moments. Recognizing this, I felt to an extent liberated, and that puzzled me more. Maybe, I thought, this was how Bad Men really felt; maybe feeling this way was a stage in the making of a Bad Man. That notion neither cheered nor alarmed me. It had no colour, no tonality. Just another icy recognition. Whenever Bradley or Callie drifted close, I saw in their faces the same hard-bitten glumness, and whenever we made eye contact, there was no flash of hatred or love or warmth. I recalled what I'd said the night before about riding until we were nothing but bones and saddles, and I wondered now if that might not have been prophetic.

Toward mid-afternoon, the wind dropped off and the snow lightened. What I'd thought were snow peaks on the horizon proved to be clouds, but rocky brown hills burst from the hardpan, leaving a narrow channel between them along which we were passing. Though there was no sign of life other than patches of silverweed, though the landscape was leached and dead, I had a sense that we were moving into a less barren part of the flats. The sky brightened to a dirty white, the sun just perceptible, a tinny glare lowering in the west. I felt tense and expectant. Once I thought I spotted something moving along the crest of a hill. A tiger, maybe. I unsheathed my rifle and kept a closer watch, but no threat materialized.

That evening we camped in a small box canyon cut about a hundred yards back into the side of the hill. I did for the horses, while Bradley and Callie made a fire, and then, with full dark still half an hour off, not wanting any conversation, I went for a walk to the end of the canyon, passing between limestone walls barely wider than my armspan and rising thirty and forty feet overhead. A few thorny shrubs sprouted from the cliffs, and there was an inordinate amount of rubble underfoot as if the place had experienced a quake. In certain sections, the limestone was bubbled and several shades darker than the surrounding rock, a type of formation I'd never seen before. I poked around in the rubble, unearthing a spider or two, some twigs; then, just as I was about to head back to the campsite, I caught sight of something half-buried under some loose rock, something with a smooth, unnatural-looking surface. I kicked the rocks aside, picked it up. It was roughly rectangular in shape, about three inches long and two wide, and weighed only a couple of ounces; it was slightly curved, covered with dust, and one edge was bubbled and dark like the limestone. I brushed away the dust, and in the ashen dusk I made out that its colour was metallic gold. I turned it over. The inner surface was covered with padding.

It wasn't until a minute or so later, as I was digging through the rubble, looking for more pieces, that I put together the fragment in my hand with the golden helmet that the driver of the bubble car had worn. Even then I figured that I was leaping to a conclusion. But the next moment I uncovered something that substantiated my conclusion beyond a doubt. At first I thought it a root of some sort. A root with five withered, clawed projections. Then I realized it was a mummified hand. I straightened, suddenly anxious, suspicious of every skittering of wind, sickened by my discovery. At length I forced myself to start digging again. Before long I had uncovered most of a body. Shreds of bleached, pale red rags wrapping the desiccated flesh. Bigger fragments of the helmet. And most pertinently, a hole the size of my fist blown in the back of the skull; the edges of the bone frothed into a lace of tiny bubbles. Gingerly, I turned the body over. The neck snapped, the head broke away. I fought back the urge to puke and turned the head. Black slits of eyes sewn together by brittle eyebrows. It was the face of a thousand-year-old man. There was no exit wound in the front of the skull, which meant – as I'd assumed – that the wound could not have been made by a rifle, nor by any weapon with which I was familiar.

It's strange how I felt at that moment. I wasn't afraid, I was angry. Part of my anger was related to memories of that pitiful little man and his red car and his foolhardiness with the apes; but there was another part I didn't understand, a part that seemed to bear upon some vast injustice done me, one I could feel in my guts but couldn't name. I held onto the anger. It was the first strong thing I'd felt all day, and I needed it to sustain me. I could understand why apes danced, why tigers howled. I wanted to dance myself, to howl, to throw some violent shape or sound at the sky and kill whatever was responsible for my confusion.

I think my mind went blank for a while; at any rate, it seemed that a long time passed before I next had a coherent thought. I didn't know what to do. My instincts told me that we should head back to Edgeville, but when I tried to settle on that course, I had the sudden suspicion that Edgeville was more dangerous than the flats, that I was well out of there. I knew I had to tell Brad and Callie, of course. Nothing would be gained by hiding this from them. I just wasn't sure what it all meant, what anything meant. My picture of the world had changed. Everything that had seemed to make sense now seemed pitiful and pointless, thrown out of kilter by the last day's ride and my discovery of the body; I couldn't see anything in my past that had been done for a reason I could understand. I was sure of one thing, however, and though knowing it was not an occasion for joy, it gave me a measure of confidence to be sure of something. The flats were not empty. Something was living out there, something worse than Bad Men. And I knew we must be close to whatever it was. We might die if we were to stay, but I doubted now that it would be by starvation.

As I've said, I intended to tell Brad and Callie about the dead man, but I wasn't eager to do it. At the end of the canyon, the stone sloped up at a gentle incline, gentle enough so I could scramble up it, and after I had done this, I walked along the rim of the canyon wall until I could see the glow of our fire. I sat down, my feet dangling, and went with my thoughts, which were none of them of the happy variety. I still didn't know what course to follow, but the more I studied on it, the more I wanted to find out what had killed the man in the bubble car. It was a fool's mission. Yet I could not let go of the idea; my hold on it seemed unnaturally tenacious, as if it were something I'd waited all my life to pursue. At last I wore out on thinking and just sat there stargazing, watching a thin smoke rise from our fire.

I'm not sure when I first noticed that some of the stars were moving; I believe I registered the fact long before I began to be alarmed by it. There were three stars involved, and instead of falling or arcing across the sky, as would have been the case with meteors, they were darting in straight lines, hovering, then darting off again. What eventually alarmed me was that I realized they were coming closer, that they were following the line of the hills. And what put the fear of God into me was when one of them began to glow a pale green and from it a beam of emerald brilliance lanced down to touch the slopes and I heard a distant rumble. At that I jumped to my feet and raced along the main rim of the canyon, fear a cold knot in my groin, shouting to Brad and Callie, who peered up at me in confusion.

'Get the horses!' I yelled. 'Bring 'em on up here! Now!'

They exchanged concerned glances.

'What's the matter?' Brad called out.

I looked out across the flats; the three stars were getting very close.

'Now!' I shouted. 'Hurry, damn it! Trouble's comin'!'

That got them moving.

By the time they reached me with the horses, I could see that the three stars weren't shaped like stars at all, but like the spearpoints the apes used: curved cylinders with the blunt tip at one end, thirty or forty feet long, with a slightly convex underside. I couldn't make out any details, but I had no desire to stick around and observe. I swung onto my horse, reined it in, and said to Bradley and Callie, ' 'Member that cave we spotted up top?'

'What are they?' asked Callie, staring at the three stars.

'We'll find out later,' I said. 'Come on! Head for the cave!'

It was a wild ride we had, plunging up the dark slope, with the horses sliding on gravel, nearly losing their footing, but at length we made it to the cave. The entrance was just wide enough for the horses, but it widened out inside and looked to extend pretty far back into the hill. We hobbled the horses deep in the cave, and then crept back to the entrance and lay flat. A couple of hundred feet below, those three glowing things were hovering over the canyon we had just vacated. It was an eerie thing to see, the way they drifted back and forth with an unsteady, vibrating motion, as if lighter than air and being trembled by an updraft. They were bigger than I'd judged, more like sixty feet long, and the white light appeared to be flowing across their surfaces – metal surfaces, I supposed – and was full of iridescent glimmers. The light was hard to look at close up; it made your eye want to slide off it. They made a high-pitched, quivering noise, something like a flute, but reedier. That sound wriggled into my spine and raised gooseflesh on my arms.

I was more frightened than I'd been in all my life. I shivered like a horse that has scented fire and stared with my eyes strained wide until I was poured so full of that strange glittering white light, all my thoughts were drowned. Then I yanked at Callie and Brad, and hauled them after me into the cave. We scuttled back deep into the darkness and sat down. The horses snorted and shifted about; their noises gave me comfort. Brad asked what we were going to do, and I said, what did he want to do? Throw rocks at the damn things? We'd just sit tight, I said, until our company had departed. I could barely see him, even though he was a couple of feet away, but talking to him stiffened my spine some. Yet with half my mind I was praying for the things outside just to go away and leave us be. I could still hear their weird fluting, and I saw a faint white glow from the cave mouth.

Callie asked again what I thought they were. I said I reckoned they must be some sort of machines.

'I can see that,' she said, exasperated. 'But who you figger's flyin' 'em?'

I hadn't really had time to think about that until then, but still, it struck me as particularly stupid on my part that I hadn't already come up with the answer to her question.

'The Captains,' I said. 'Has to be them. Couldn't nobody else make a machine like that.'

'Why'd they be chasin' us?' Brad asked.

'We don't know they are,' said Callie. 'They could just be after doin' their own business.'

'Then why'd we run?'

I realized I hadn't told them about the dead man, and I decided that now wasn't the time – it would be too much bad news all at once.

'We did right to run,' I said. 'Believe me, we did right.'

' 'Sides,' said Callie, 'we don't know for absolute sure it's the Captains. I mean what your pa says makes good sense, but we don't know for sure.'

We were silent for a bit and finally Brad said, 'You think Mama run into them things?'

I gave a sigh that in the enclosed space of the cave seemed as loud as one of the horses blowing out its breath. 'I was watchin' 'em for a long time 'fore I hollered,' I said. 'From the way they're patrollin' the hills, I figger that's possible.'

There followed another silence, and then he said, 'Maybe after they gone, maybe we should try trackin' 'em.'

I was about to say that we'd be doing good just to get shut of them, when the cave mouth was filled with an emerald flash, and I was flung back head over heels, and the next thing I knew I was lying in pitch darkness with dirt and stone chips in my mouth, and my ears ringing. Some time later I felt Brad's hands on my chest, heard him say, 'Dad?' Then I heard the horses whinnying, their hooves clattering as they tried to break free of their hobbles. I wanted to sit up but was too woozy.

'Callie,' I said.

'She's gone to see if there's a way out.'

'Wha . . .' I broke off and spat dirt.

'The entrance is blocked. Must be a ton of rock come down over it.'

'Shit!' I said, touching the back of my head; there was a lump coming. Patches of shiny blackness swam before my eyes. 'The horses awright?'

'Just scared.'

'Yeah,' I said. 'Me too.'

I sat up cautiously, groped for Brad, found his shoulder and gave it a squeeze. I couldn't think; I was so numb that I only felt the first trickles of fear. It was as if the explosion was still taking place in my skull, a dark cloud of smoke and splintered rock boiling up and whirling away the last of my good sense.

Seconds later Callie's voice called from a distance, telling us to come ahead, she'd found something.

Still dizzy, I let Brad take the lead, going in a crouch deeper into the hill, and after a minute I saw stars and a ragged oval of blue-dark sky.

Callie's voice came again, issuing from beyond the opening. 'See it?'

'Almost there!' I told her.

The opening was set about six feet up in the wall, not too high and easily wide enough for a man to pass through, but no horse was ever going to leave the cave that way. Without the horses, I thought, we might as well have died in the explosion. However, when I pulled myself out into the chill air beside Callie and saw what she had found, I forgot all about our plight.

On this side of the hill, too, the hardpan flowed off toward the horizon. But there was one distinct difference. Below us, its rim no more than a few hundred yards from the base of the hill, lay a large crater, roughly circular and perhaps a mile in diameter, like a bowl brimful of golden light. Light so brilliant it obscured all but the deepest cuts and bulges in the crater's rock walls. It resembled a glowing golden sore on a cracked, stretched-tight hide. The three flying machines were flitting back and forth above it with the agitation of mites swarming above a dead squirrel, and as we watched they descended into the crater, vanishing beneath the rim. After they had gone out of view, none of us moved or said a thing. I can't speak for Brad or Callie, but for my part, though I'd already had my basic notion of how the world worked shaken considerably, the sight of the crater completely shattered all my old conceptions. Maybe it was simply the size of the thing that affected me . . . The size and the upward pour of light. Maybe all the little wrong bits that had come before had had the irritating effect of putting a few sand grains in my boots, and now this, this immense wrongness, had scraped the skin off my soles and left me unable to walk or do anything other than reckon with shock and bewilderment. Even a half-hour earlier, I might – if asked – have given a fair approximation of where I stood. With my son and my lover, six days out on the Flats from Edgeville, I would have said. In the heart of the wasteland where once the old world flourished, countless centuries after the disaster that ended it. I would have thought this a fine answer, and I would have been certain of my place and purpose. Now I felt I was in the company of strangers, in the midst of a great darkness with light below, a barren place of unrelieved abstraction that offered no clue as to its nature. Perhaps the depth of my reaction seems unreasonable. After all, we had long supposed that the Captains must have flying machines, and though I had never seen one, I shouldn't have been so thoroughly disconcerted by the sight. And I had seen craters before, albeit never one this big. But it was as if all the tidy structures of my life had been abolished, all rules of logic broken, and I could not come up with a new picture of the world that would fit inside my head. I realize now that this breakdown had been a long time coming, that what had provoked it had been working on me for days; but at the time it seemed sudden, catastrophic, totally disorienting.

It was Callie who broke the silence, saying we had to go down to the crater, we had no other choice. I am not clear how I responded; I recall saying something about the horses, about how even if we went down, we'd have to come back and shoot them, we couldn't leave them to die of thirst. There was a little more conversation, but I cannot recall it. Eventually we began picking our way down the slope, glancing up now and again to see that the crater had swelled and grown brighter, a vast golden pit into which we were preparing to descend.

We were, I'd estimate, about fifty feet from the base of the hill when a woman's voice hailed us from the darkness and ordered us to drop our rifles. I was so bewildered and startled, I obeyed without hesitation. I guess it seemed right given the circumstance that voices should issue from the dark and command us. I heard footsteps crunching nearby, caught sight of shadowy figures moving toward us through the rocks. Lots of them. Maybe thirty, maybe more. They assembled about us, some gaining detail against the nimbus of light shining up from the crater behind them, yet most of them remaining shadows, looking evil as crows in their slouch hats and long coats.

'Just who are you people?' asked another voice, this one a man's, deeper than the woman's, but softer and oddly familiar.

We gave our names, said we were from Edgeville.

'Bob Hillyard,' said the voice musingly. 'I'll be damned.'

'That's his boy with him,' said someone else. 'And that girl there works for ol' Fornoff.'

'Just who in creation are you?' I asked, not wanting to let on how intimidated I was – I knew we had fallen in with Bad Men. I should have felt more afraid than I did, but I was still so confused, so daunted by the overall situation, the threat these men presented did not seem of moment.

'You know some of us,' said still another voice. 'Leastways, I bet you know me.'

A match flared, caught on a twist of something in one of the figure's hands, and as he moved nearer, holding a torch so that it shone up onto his face, making ghoulish shadows under the eyes, I saw it was Clay Fornoff. Heavier; chin covered with pale stubble; wearier-looking. But still with that petulant sneer stamped onto his face.

'Wasn't for this man here, I'd never have taken the ride,' he said.

"'Spect you owe him one, don'tcha, Clay?' said somebody.

'You know I didn't have no choice,' I told him.

'Don't matter,' he said. 'Turns out you did me a favour. But you didn't have that in mind, didja now? You was just runnin' me off to die.'

A huge shadow moved up beside Clay and nudged him aside.

'You got a score to settle,' he said to Clay in that soft voice, 'deal with it later.' He moved full into the light of the torch, and I saw what I'd begun to suspect seconds before: it was Wall. A monstrous slab of a man with owl-tufted brows, a shaggy greying beard, thick lips and a bulging forehead, his face as expressionless as an idol's. A waterfall of dark hair spilled from under his hat to his shoulders.

'Goddamn, Bob,' he said to me. 'Man shoots as poorly as you got no business this far out on the flats.'

I'd always admired Wall, and that his most salient memory of me was my poor shooting eye made me feel stupid and childlike. Kind of like being dressed down by your boyhood hero.

'Ain't like I wanna be here,' I said. 'Just had somethin' needed doin'.'

Wall studied Callie and Brad, who were gawping at him, apparently overwhelmed by the sight of this enormous man.

'Feelin' confused, are ye?' he said with mild good humour, as if he were talking to children. 'Seem like even simple things like right and left ain't what they used to be?'

That struck me as odd, that he would offer such an accurate analysis of my mental condition and do it so casually, as if how I felt was something usual, something any fool could have predicted.

'What the hell you know about it?' I asked him.

'Hits ever'body the same,' he said. 'The conditionin' starts breakin' down 'bout five days out. Time a man gets this far, he's usually got more questions in him than answers. Y'see' – he coughed, spat up a hocker and aimed it off to his right – 'it ain't only doctorin' you get at the hospitals. The Captains condition you to be happy with your lot. It's sorta like hypnotizin' ye. Takes a mighty strong reason for a man to break down the conditionin'. Seems powerful emotion's 'bout the only cure.' He cocked his head, gave me a searching look. 'What brings ye here?'

'My wife Kiri,' I said, still trying to absorb what he had told us. 'She lost a duel and come out here to die.'

'Kiri,' said Wall. 'I remember her. She was a good fighter.'

Bradley piped up. 'We figger she's down in that hole.'

Wall's eyes flicked toward him. 'She might be at that.'

From the cautious flatness of his tone, I had the impression that if Kiri was down in the crater, it wasn't likely we were going to see her again.

'I don't get it,' I said, and began talking fast to blot out the pictures I was conjuring of Kiri's fate. 'What the hell's goin' on? What're the Captains doin' by givin' us this here conditionin'?' How come . . .'

'Slow down there, man,' Wall said, and put a hand on my shoulder; I was shocked into silence by the weight and solidity of it. 'I ain't got time just now to be givin' a history lesson. Truth is, I don't know if I got much to teach ye, anyway. Far as we can prove, things're 'bout the way the Captains say they was. Though I got a suspicion that the folks who survived the bad time wasn't given a choice 'bout how they wanted to live, they was just put where the Captains wanted 'em and conditioned to accept it. But there's a coupla things different for certain sure. One is, they ain't our friends, they just playin' with us, tormentin' us. Hell, might be they could kill us all in a flash, they had a mind. But even if that's so, it'd ruin their game. So our job is to be dangerous for 'em, kill a few here and there, give 'em trouble. They enjoy that kinda trouble. Our aim is to get strong without 'em realizin' it, so the day'll come when we're strong enough to finish 'em. And that day ain't far off. But you got time to learn all 'bout that. What you need to unnerstan' is' – he spat again – 'you're Bad Men now. You may not unnerstan' it this minute, but ye can't go back now your conditionin's broke. Ain't nothin' for ye back there. Your life is here now, and you gotta make the best of it. That means you're with us in ever'thing we do. We make a raid for supplies on Edgeville, you're part of it. There ain't no middle ground.'

'If things is like you say,' Callie asked, 'whyn't you just tell it to the people back in Edgeville or Windbroken . . . Or wherever?'

'Someday maybe we will. But the way things is now, buncha Bad Men waltz into town and start goin' on 'bout how the Captains is enemies of mankind . . . Shit! How do you think that'd set? Think they'd believe us? Naw, you gotta ride out way past gone onto the flats 'fore you can hear the truth when it's told ye. But after you take that ride, you don't need to hear it more'n once.' He sucked on a tooth, making a smacking noise. 'Anyways, there's plenty of Bad Men ain't been brought into the fold. That's somepin' we need to take care of first, 'fore we go bringin' the word to Edgeville.'

We stood there wrapped in the weighty stuff of all he had said. The desolation his words implied had slotted into a ready-made place inside my brain – it seemed something I had always known. But the fact that I was now a Bad Man, that was almost impossible to believe. The longer I had to digest what Wall had told us, the less like a Bad Man I felt. I had the sense we were stranded at the bottom of an empty well, and far above, invisible against the black circle of sky, strange, cruel faces were peering down at us, deciding which ones to pluck up and gut. I felt more abandoned than afraid: I could not have felt more so had I woken up to find myself naked and alone in the middle of nowhere. If it had been left to me I would have sat down there on a rock and stayed sitting until I had gotten a better handle on how things were, but Bradley grabbed my arm and said, 'We gotta go down there. We gotta find Mama.'

'Not tonight, boy,' Wall said. 'You try goin' down there tonight, you'd last 'bout as long as spit on a griddle. We'll be goin' down tomorrow night. We'll have a look 'round for her.'

'I'm goin' with you,' said Bradley.

'Listen, little man,' Wall told him; despite its softness, his voice was so resonant, it might have issued from a cave. 'You do what you told from now on. This ain't no fine time we're havin' here. This is desperate business. I admire you stickin' by your mama, I swear I do. And maybe we can help her. But ain't nobody gettin' in the way of what's gotta be done tomorrow night, so you might as well get used to it.'

Bradley stood his ground but said nothing. After a second Clay Fornoff handed his torch to another man and came up beside Brad and slung an arm around his shoulder. 'C'mon, kid,' he said. 'We'll getcha somethin' to eat.'

I didn't much like Clay taking him under his wing, but I knew Brad didn't want to be with me, so I let them go off into the darkness without a squawk.

Wall moved a couple of steps closer; despite the cold, I smelled his gamey odour. Beneath those owlish brows, his eyes were aglow with fierce red light from the torch. Generally I've found that people you haven't seen in a while shrink some from the image you hold of them in your mind. But not Wall. With that golden glare streaming up from the crater behind him, he still looked more monument than man. 'Where'd you stake your horses at?' he asked.

I told him.

'Shitfire!' He slapped his hand against his thigh. Then he spoke to another man, instructing him to take a party up to the cave and see what could be done. When he turned back to me he let out a chuckle; he was missing a front tooth, and the gap was about the same size as the first joint of my thumb. 'Perk up there, Bob,' he said. 'You look like you 'spectin' the devil to fly down your chimney. Believe me, you a damn sight better off'n you was 'fore you run into us.'

I had no doubt this was the truth, but it didn't much gladden me to hear it.

'This your woman?' Wall asked me, jerking a thumb toward Callie.

Callie's eyes met mine, then ducked away, locking on the ground. I got something more than fear from that exchange, but I was too weary to want to understand what.

'Yeah,' she said, beating me to it by a hair.

'We'll fix ya up with some blankets directly.' Wall heaved a sigh and stared off toward the crater. 'I'm mighty glad to see you out here, Bob. We been needin' more people to work in the gardens.'

'Gardens?' I said dully.

'That's right. As I recall you had yourself some fine-looking tomatoes back in Edgeville.'

'You growin' things out here?' I asked. 'Where?'

'Somebody'll fill you in 'bout all that. Maybe in the mornin'.' Wall took off his hat and did some reshaping of the brim, then jammed it back on. 'Meantime you get some food in ye and try to sleep. Gonna be a big night tomorrow. Big night for ever'body in the whole damn world.'

After we had been fed on jerky and dried fruit, Callie and I settled down in a nest made by three boulders a ways apart from the others. We spread a couple of blankets and pulled the rest up to our chins, sitting with our backs against one of the boulders, our hips and legs touching. Once I glanced over at her. Light from the crater outlined her profile and showed something of her grave expression. I had the idea she felt my eyes on her, but she gave no sign of noticing, so I tried to do as Wall suggested and sleep. Sleep would not come, however. I couldn't stop wondering what we had fallen into. Seeing so many Bad Men this far out, Wall's talk of gardens, the fact they planned a raid or something like against the Captains – all that spoke to a complexity of life out here on the flats that I couldn't fathom. And I thought, too, about what Wall had told us about 'conditioning'. Strange as the idea seemed, it made sense. How else could you explain why people would be so stupid and docile as to swallow such swill as we had about our ancestors choosing a pitiful, hard-scrabble existence over a life of ease?

There was no use in studying on any of this, I realized; sooner or later I'd learn whatever there was to learn. But my mind kept on worrying at this or that item, and I knew I wasn't going to get any sleep.

Then Callie said, 'I thought it had all gone, y'know. I thought all the bad times had wiped it away. But that ain't so. Everything's still there.'

Her face was turned toward me, too shadowed to read.

When she had spoken I hadn't understood what she meant, but now I knew she had been talking about the two of us.

'I guess I wanna hear how it is with you,' she said.

'I ain't been thinkin' about it,' I told her. 'I ain't had the time.'

'Well, you got the time right now.'

I didn't feel much like exercising my brain, but when I tried to think how I felt, it all came clear with hardly an effort. It was as if I were looking down a tunnel that ran through time from the crater to Edgeville, and I saw Kiri riding the flats alone, I saw the hurt on Brad's face, I saw myself, and I saw Callie with rime on her hat brim and a stony expression, and then those images faded, and what I was looking at, it seemed, wasn't memory but truth, not the truth I believed, because that was just like everything else in my life, a kind of accommodation. No, this truth I was seeing was the truth behind that, the underpinnings of my existence, and I realized that the things I'd thought I felt for Callie were only things I'd wanted to feel, things I'd talked myself into feeling, but that was the way the brain worked, you bought into something and more often than not it came true without your noticing, and so, while I hadn't loved Callie – not like I thought I had, anyhow – sometime between all the trouble with Kiri and the end of our ride I had come to love her exactly like that, and I was always going to be ahead of myself in that fashion, I was always going to be wanting and hoping for and believing in things because they were what I thought I should want or hope for or believe . . . except now, because some trick of conditioning the Captains had played on me had worn off, and right this minute, maybe for the first time ever, I had caught up with myself and could see exactly what I had become and what I believed in and what I loved. And there was Brad. And there was Callie. Beneath the flirty, pretty package, she was strong and flawed and sweet and needy, just like us all. But strong was most important. Strong was what I hadn't known about her. The strength it had taken for her, a girl from Windbroken who would dread the flats worse by far than any Edger, who had grown up fat and sassy in a softer world. The strength she'd had to summon to ride out into that world of less-than-death, and the reasons she had done it, for honour, for love of me and for the thing she didn't understand that made strength possible.

And Kiri was there, too, but different.

Like a picture hung in an old cobwebby room both of us had vacated years ago. Whatever lie we had believed into truth had been dead a long time, and Kiri had done what she had because of how she was, not because of how I was or how she was to me. Recognizing that didn't make me feel any better, but at least all that old fire and smoke didn't prevent me from seeing what was of consequence now. I had known all this for months, but I felt stupid for not having been able to accept any of it before, and I couldn't think of what to say, and all I managed was to repeat what Callie had said, telling her that everything was still there for me, too.

She moved into me a bit, and I put an arm around her, and then she let her head rest on my shoulder, and we sat that way for a few minutes – we were both, I suspect, feeling a little awkward, a little new to one another. Callie stretched herself and snuggled into me. Despite everything, despite fear and hard riding and all that had happened, having her there under my blanket gave me some confidence.

'You all right?' I asked her.

She said, 'Just fine,' then let out a dusty laugh.

'What's so funny?' I asked.

'I was goin' to say I wished we was home, but then I thought twice about it. Edgeville don't seem like home no more.'

'Just a little of it would be all right,' I said. 'Maybe a wood stove and some kindling.'

She made a noise of agreement and then fell silent. Big cold stars were dancing in the faraway black wild of the sky, so bright they looked to be shifting around like the ships the Captains flew, but I saw no fearful thing in them, only their glitter and the great identities they sketched in fire, the lady on the throne, the old hunter with his gemmy belt. What was it like, I wondered, to live among them, to be small and secretive with purple eyes. To be daunted by life and play with men and women as if they were dolls full of blood. Wall would probably understand them, I thought. For all his homespun ways, I had the notion he was as different from me as any Captain.

'And a bed,' Callie said out of the blue.

'Huh?'

'I was thinkin' a bed would be nice, too.'

'Oh, yeah,' I said. 'Yeah, that'd be good.' Then thinking she might have been hinting at something, I added, 'I gotta tell ya, I ain't feelin' much like doin' anything tonight.'

She picked herself up, gave me a look and laughed. 'I swear you must think you're the greatest damn thing since vanilla ice cream. I'm so wore down, I doubt I could sit up straight let alone' – she sniffed – 'do anything.'

'I was only saying it in case you were . . .'

'Just shut up, Bob!'

She settled back down next to me. I couldn't tell for certain, but I didn't believe she was really angry. After a couple of minutes she laid her head on my shoulder again, and a few seconds after that she took my hand beneath the blankets and put it up under her shirt. The warmth of her breast seemed to spread from my palm all through me, and its softness nearly caused me to faint. The feeling that held in my mind then had just a shade of lustfulness; most of what I felt was tender, trusted, loved. A feeling like that couldn't last for too long, not in that place, not at that moment, but for the time it did, it made the golden light spilling upward from the crater a fine place to rest my eyes, and pulled the starry void close around me like a good blanket, and spoke to me of something I could catch on my tongue and cradle in my hand and crush against my skin, but that I could have never put a name to.

Mornings, Kiri told me once, were lies. It was only the nights that were true. She meant a sad, desolate thing by this, she meant that the brightness of things is illusion, and the blackness of them is where the truth would fit if we had courage enough to admit it. Yet when I thought of those words now, they meant something completely opposite, because the virtues she applied to night and morning had been all switched around for me.

At any rate, in the grey, blustery morning following that brilliant night, with big flakes falling from the sky, Wall sent his second-in-command, a man named Coley, to fill us in. Coley was a tense sort, a little yappy dog to Wall's big placid one, scrawny and worried-looking, with a grizzled beard and sunken cheeks and a startling bit of colour to his outfit, a bright red ribbon for a hat band. Though his anxious manner unnerved me – he was always fidgeting, glancing around as if concerned he might be caught at something – I related to him a damn sight better than I did Wall, mostly because Coley did not seem so all-fired sure of himself.

He told us they'd been planning this raid for years, and that the purpose of it was to steal a flying machine. A few years back one of the machines had crashed out on the flats; they had captured the sole survivor, whom they called Junior, and forced him to supply information about all manner of things; he was to be the pilot of the stolen machine once Wall's people succeeded in breaking into it. Problem was, the minute they started messing with it, there was a chance that an alarm would be sounded, and we might have to fight off the Captains for as long as it took to finish the job. Maybe an hour, maybe more. There were, according to Coley, nearly five hundred men and women scattered about in the rocks, laying low, and he wasn't sure that many would be enough to keep the Captains off, though Wall was of the opinion that our casualties would be light. Coley did not agree.

'It ain't the Captains worry me,' he said. 'It's who they got doin' their fightin' for 'em. Chances are there'll be apes. Might even be some of our own people. They got ways of makin' a man do things against his will.'

'What I don't get,' Brad said, 'is how you make this here Captain do what you want. Every time I talk to 'em, I get the feelin' things don't go how they like 'em, they're liable to keel over and die.'

'That ain't quite the way of it,' Coley told him. 'They just don't think they can die is all. 'Cordin' to Junior, they make copies of themselves. Clones, he calls 'em. One dies, there's another waitin' to take his place who's got the same memories, same everything.' He shook his head in wonderment. 'Damnedest thing I ever heard of. Anyhow, they got these collars. Metal collars that fit back of the neck and the head. I don't know how it works. But slap one on somebody, and they get downright suggestible. We picked some up from the crash, and we used one on Junior.'

We all three nodded and said, 'Huh' or something similar, as if we understood, but I doubt Brad or Callie understood Coley any better than I did.

A shout came from a man downslope, and Coley turned to it; but the shout must have been directed at someone else. The crater walls looked ashen, and the whole thing seemed more fearsome now than it had with light streaming up from it. Under the clouded sky the hardpan was a dirty yellow, like old bones.

'What is this place?' I asked. 'What the hell are they doin' down there?'

'The Captains call it the Garden,' Coley said. 'Sometimes they use it for fightin'. Junior says they're all divided into clans up on the stations, and this here's where they settle clan disputes. Other times they use it for parties, and that's probably what's goin' on now. If it was a fight there'd be more ships. They like to watch fightin'.' He worked up a good spit and let it fly. 'That's how come they treasure us so much. They enjoy the way we fight.'

I let that sink in for a few seconds, thinking about Kiri fitted with a collar. A break appeared in the clouds, and Coley peered up into the sky, looking more worried than over. When I asked him what was wrong, he said, 'I'm just hopin' the weather holds. We usually don't put so many people at risk. Then if the Captains drop a net, we don't get hurt so bad.' He let out a long unsteady breath. ' 'Course even if the weather does clear, chances are they ain't lookin' this way. They're pretty careless as regards security, and they ain't very well armed. Not like you

152

might expect, anyway. They didn't have many personal weapons up in the orbitals, and we don't believe they've collected any weapons from the shelters. Why would they bother? They don't think we can hurt them. All they've got are their ships, which are armed with mining lasers. And even if they did collect weapons from the shelters, they probably wouldn't know how to use 'em. They used to be technical, but they've forgotten most of what they know. Eventually I figger their ships'll break down, and they'll be stranded up there.'

Callie asked what he meant by 'shelters', and he told us that they were underground places where people had slept away the centuries, waiting for the Captains to wake them once things on the surface were back to something approaching normal. It was in those places that the Bad Men lived. Places fortified now against attack from the sky. But it was clear to me that neither Coley's faith in those fortifications nor in the raid was absolute. Though I didn't know him, I had the impression that his anxiety was abnormal, at least in its intensity, and when I tried to talk with him about Wall, I detected disapproval.

'He's brought people together,' he said. 'He's done a lot of good things.' But I could tell his heart wasn't in the words.

Sleet began coming down, just spits of it, but enough so I could hear it hissing against the rocks.

'What's all this about?' I asked Coley; I gestured at the crater. 'All this business here. I know you said it was to get a ship. But why bother if . . .'

'It's about killin',' said Wall's voice behind me; he was leaning up against a boulder, looking down at us in that glum, challenging way of his; his long hair lifted in the wind. ' 'Bout them killin' us all these years,' he went on. 'And now us evenin' things up a touch. 'Bout finding some new thing that'll let us kill even more of 'em.'

'I realize that,' I said. 'But why not let well enough alone? Accordin' to what Coley says, we leave 'em be, sooner or later they ain't gonna be a problem.'

'Is that what Mister Coley says?' Wall pinned him with a cold glare, but Coley didn't flinch from it; he made a gruff noise in his throat and turned back to me. 'Y'see Coley's out here with us, don't ye? Don't that tell ye somethin'? He may believe what he told ye, but he ain't countin' on it to be true. He'd be crazy to count on it. S'pose they got more weapons than he figgers? Even if they don't, who knows what's in their minds? They might up and decide they're tired of games and kill us all. Nosir! Killin's the only way to deal with 'em.'

'Ain't you worried they gonna strike back at you?' Callie asked him.

'Let 'em try! They might pick off a few of us when we're out on the flats, but we're dug in too deep for them to do any real damage.'

'That's what you believe,' I said. 'But then you'd be crazy to count on it bein' true, wouldn't you?'

He tried the same stare on me that he'd tried on Coley, but for some reason I wasn't cowed by either it or his faulty logic. Coley, I noticed, seemed pleased by what I'd said.

'S'pose they got more weapons than what you figger?' I went on. 'S'pose they got some'll dig you outta your holes? They might decide to kill us all. Who knows what they got in their minds?'

Wall gave a laugh. 'You a clever talker, Bob, I'll hand you that. But ain't no point you goin' on like this. It's all been talked through and decided.'

'How 'bout everyone back on the Edge?' Callie asked. 'And Windbroken? And everywhere else? You talked it through with them, have you?'

'They ain't involved with us. Anyhow, the Captains got no reason to go hurtin' them for somethin' we done.'

'No reason you know of, maybe,' Callie said.

'Well,' said Wall after a bit, looking off into the distance, 'this is a real nice chat we're havin', but like I told ye, it comes a little late in the game. We'll be going down into the Garden at dusk.' He cut his eyes toward me. 'You come along with me if you want, Bob, and have a look for Kiri. But keep in mind she's not the main reason you're goin' to be there. Keepin' the Captains back from the ship is. That clear?'

Brad started to speak, but Wall cut him short.

'The boy and the woman can stay with the ship. We can use another coupla rifles case any of 'em break through.'

I thought Brad was going to say something, but he just

lowered his head; I guess he was wise enough to realize that Wall couldn't be swayed by argument.

'Keep your chin up,' Wall told him. 'Time'll come soon enough for ye to do some real killin'.'

The three of us spent the remainder of the afternoon huddled among the rocks. We talked some, more than we had recently at any rate, but it was for the most part anxious talk designed to stop us from fretting over what lay ahead, and never touched on the things we needed to talk about. Snow fell steadily, capping the boulders in white, and as the sky darkened, golden light began to stream up from the crater once again. Then, as dusk began to accumulate, I caught sight of Coley and a couple of others leading a diminutive pale figure down the slope. It was a Captain, all right, but like none I'd seen before. Dressed in rags; emaciated; scarred. As they drew near, I got to my feet – we all did – fascinated by the proximity of this creature whom I had previously thought of in almost godlike terms. There was nothing godlike about him now. His nose was broken, squashed nearly flat, and his scalp was crisscrossed by ridged scars; one of his eyes was covered by a patch, and his other had a listless cast. The only qualities he retained similar to those curious entities I had spoken to in Edgeville were his pallor and his size. About his neck and cupping the back of his skull was a metal apparatus worked with intricate designs resembling those I'd seen on antique silver; its richness was incongruous in contrast to his sorry state. I had expected I might feel hatred on seeing him, or something allied, but I felt nothing apart from a dry curiosity; yet after he had passed I realized that my hands were shaking and my legs weak, as if strong emotion had occupied me without my knowing and left only these symptoms, and I stood there, as did Brad and Callie, watching until the Captain – Junior – had been reduced by distance to a tiny shadow crossing the hardpan toward the crater.

It was not long afterward that Wall came to collect me. Callie and Brad went off with a big, broad-beamed woman who reminded me some of Hazel Aldred, and Wall led me over to a group of men and women who were sitting and squatting at the edge of the hardpan, and gave me over to the care of a woman named Maddy, who fitted me out with a hunting knife and a pistol and an ammunition belt. She was on the stringy side, was Maddy, with dirty blonde hair tied back in a ponytail; but she had a pretty face made interesting and more than a little sexy by the lines left by hard weather and hard living, and she had a directness and good humour that put me somewhat at ease.

'I know a red-blooded sort like you's all bucked up and rarin' to go,' she said, flashing a quick grin, 'but you keep it holstered till I give you the word, y'hear?'

'I'll do my level best,' I told her.

'We'll be goin' down soon,' she said. 'If there's an attack and things get confused, stick with me and chances are you'll be fine. We believe there's gonna be some of our own people down there. They'll be collared, and like as not they'll be comin' after us. If you gotta kill 'em, nobody's goin' to blame you for it. But if you can, aim at their legs. Maybe we can save one or two.'

I nodded, looked out between boulders across the hardpan. A handful of Bad Men were visible as silhouettes at the rim of the crater, black stick figures blurred against the pour of golden light; I couldn't make out what they were doing. The thought of descending into that infernal light turned my nerves a notch higher; I couldn't have worked up a spit even if the price of spit had suddenly gone sky-high.

'Ain't no point my tellin' you not to be afraid,' Maddy said. 'I 'spect we're all afraid. But once we get down to business, you'll be all right.'

'You sure 'bout that?' I said, trying to make it sound light; but I heard a quaver in my voice.

'You come all this way from the Edge, I guess I ain't worried 'bout you seizin' up on me.'

'How bout Wall? You reckon he's afraid?'

She made a non-committal noise and glanced down at her hands; with her head lowered, a wisp of hair dangling down over her forehead, her expression contemplative, the crater light glowing on her face, eroding some of the lines there, I could see the girl she once had been.

'Probably not,' she said. 'He likes this kind of thing.'

There was disapproval in her voice. This was the second time I'd detected a less than favourable feeling toward Wall, and I was about to see if I could learn where it came from, when Clay Fornoff hunkered down beside us.

'He all set?' he asked Maddy.

She said, 'Yes.' Then, following a pause, she asked how much longer before we started.

'Any minute now,' Fornoff said.

I didn't really have anything to say, but I thought talking might ease my anxiety, and I asked him what sort of opposition we'd be facing aside from people wearing collars.

'What's the matter, Bob?' He made a sneering noise of my name. ' 'Fraid you gonna wet yourself?'

'I was just makin' conversation.'

'You wanna be friends, is that it?'

'I don't much care about that one way or another,' I said.

His face tightened. 'Just shut the hell up! I don't wanna hear another damn word from ya.'

'Sure thing. I understand. I s'pose you don't want to hear nothin' 'bout your folks either, do ya?'

He let a a few beats go by then said, 'How they doin'?' But he kept his eyes trained on the crater.

I told him about his folks, his father's rheumatism, about the store and some of his old friends. When I had done he gave no sign that he had been in any way affected by the news from home. Maddy rolled her eyes and shot me an afflicted smile, as if to suggest that I wasn't the only one who considered Fornoff a pain in the ass. I'd been coming around 180 degrees in my attitude towards Bad Men, thinking of them more as heroes, rebels, and so forth; but now I told myself that some Bad Men were likely every bit as rotten as what I'd once supposed. Or maybe it was just that I was part of a time with which Fornoff would never be able to reach an accommodation; he would never be able to see me without recalling the night when he had gone Bad, and thus he would always react to me with loathing that might have better been directed at himself.

Not long afterward I heard a shout, and before I could prepare myself, I was jogging alongside Maddy and Fornoff toward the crater, watching the chute of golden light jolt sideways with every step; a couple of minutes later I found myself in the company of several hundred others descending the crater wall on ropes. The three ships rested at the bottom of the crater on a smooth plastic floor, from beneath which arose the golden light. We paused beside one of them as Wall, with the help of two other men, worked feverishly at the smallest of the mining lasers that protruded from the prow. I saw that it was a modular unit that could be snapped into place. Once they had removed it, Wall shrugged out of his coat and lashed the unit to his right arm with a complex arrangement of leather straps; the way it fitted, his fingers could reach a panel of studs set into the bottom, and I realized it must have been designed to be portable. Wall pressed a stud and a beam of ruby light scored a deep gouge in the rock face. On seeing this he laughed uproariously, and swung the thing, which must have weighed 70 or 80 pounds, in a celebratory circle above his head.

Beyond the ships, at the bottom of a gently declining ramp, lay the entrance to a vast circular chamber – I guessed it to be about a half-mile across – floored with exotic vegetation, some of the plants having striped stalks and huge rubbery leaves, unlike anything I'd ever seen; the domed ceiling was aglow with ultraviolet panels, the same sort of light I used to grow my peas and beans and tomatoes back in Edgeville, and the foliage was so dense that the four narrow paths leading away into it were entirely overgrown. Mists curled above the treetops, rising in wraithlike coils to the top of the ceiling, lending the space a primitive aspect like some long-ago jungle, daunting in its silence and strangeness.

And yet the place was familiar.

I couldn't quite figure why at first; then I recalled that Wall had said the Captains called the crater the Garden, and I thought of the book I'd read and reread back in the hydroponics building, *The Black Garden*, and the illustrations it contained – this chamber was either the model for one of those illustrations or the exact copy of the model. Confused and frightened already, I can't begin to tell you the alarm this caused me. Added to everything that I previously had not understood but had managed to arrange in a makeshift frame of reference, this last incomprehensible thing, with its disturbing echoes of decadence, now succeeded in toppling that shaky structure, and I felt as unsteady in my knowledge of what was as I had during our ride from Edgeville. I had an urge to tell someone about my sudden recognition, but then I realized that thanks to Junior, they must know far more than I did about the Garden, and of course damn near everybody knew about the book. But none of these rationalizations served to calm me, and I got to thinking what it meant that the Captains would give us these clues about their existence, what it said about their natures.

Approximately a hundred of us headed down each of the avenues, moving quietly, but at a good pace. Maddy, Clay Fornoff, and I were attached to a party led by Wall. Once beneath the canopy we were immersed in a green twilight; sweetish scents reminiscent of decay, but spicier, issued from the foliage and a humming sound rose from the polished stones beneath our feet – that sound, apart from the soft fall of our footsteps – was the only break in the silence. No rustlings or slitherings, no leaves sliding together. Every now and then we came to a section of the path where the stones had been replaced by a sheet of transparent panelling through which we could see down into a black space picked out here and there by golden lights, and once again I was reminded of *The Black Garden*, of what the book had related about a region of black foliage and secret rooms. Once we walked beneath a crystalline bubble the size of a small room suspended in the branches, furnished with cushions, and with a broad smear of what appeared to be dried blood marring its interior surface. Far too much blood to be the sign of anything other than a death. The sight harrowed me, and Maddy, after a quick glance at the bubble, fixed her eyes on the path and did not lift them again until it was well behind us.

No more than fifty yards after we had passed beneath the bubble, we encountered the first of two side paths – the second lay barely another twenty-five yards farther along – and at each of these junctions we left a quarter of our number, who hid among the ferns that lined the way. I expected to be left with them, but I imagine Wall wanted to give me the best possible chance of locating Kiri, and though uneasy with the fact that I was moving deeper and deeper into this oppressive place, I was at the same time grateful for the opportunity. After about fifteen minutes we reached the far side of the chamber, a place where the path planed away into a well-lit tunnel that led downward at a precipitous angle. We proceeded along it until we came to another chamber, smaller than the first yet still quite large, perhaps a hundred yards in diameter, its walls covered with white shiny tiles, each bearing a red hieroglyph, and dominated by a grotesque fountain ringed by benches and banks of tree ferns, whose centrepiece, the life-sized statue of a naked crouching woman with her mouth stretched open in anguish, bled red water from a dozen gashes carved in the greyish-white stone of her flesh. The statue was so real-looking, I could have sworn it was an actual person who had been magicked into stone. Vines with serrated leaves climbed the walls and intertwined across the white tray of ultraviolet light that occupied the ceiling, casting spindly shadows.

On first glance I'd assumed the chamber to be untouched by age, but then I began to notice worn edges on the benches, corners missing from tiles, a chipped knuckle on the statue, and other such imperfections. The idea that the place was old made it seem even more horrid, speaking to a tradition of the perverse, and the longer I looked at the statue, the more certain I became that it had been rendered from life; there was too much detail to the face and the body, details such as scars and lines and the like, to make me think otherwise. I imagined the woman posing for some pallid little monster, growing weaker and weaker from her wounds, yet forced by some terrifying presence, some binding torment, to maintain her pose, and the anger that I had not been able to feel on seeing Junior now surfaced in me and swept away my fear. I grew cold and resolved, and I imagined myself joyfully blowing holes in the pulpy bodies of the Captains.

We crossed the chamber, progressing with more caution than before. Judging by the way Wall turned this way and that, searching for a means of egress – none was apparent – I had the notion that the existence of the chamber came as a surprise to him, that Junior must not have informed him of it. Unnerved by what this might mean, whether it was that the collars were not totally controlling and Junior had lied, or else that he had been so stupefied he had forgotten to mention the place, I put my hand on my pistol and turned to Maddy to see what her reaction might be to this turn of events; but as I did, a section of the wall opposite us slid back to reveal a wedge of darkness beyond, a void that the next moment was choked with emaciated men and women wearing metal collars like the one Junior had worn, dozens of them, all armed with knives and clubs, driven forward by white-furred apes that differed from the Edgeville apes by virtue of their barbaric clothing – leather harnesses and genital pouches. The most horrifying thing about their approach was that they – the men and women, not the apes – made no sound as they came; they might have been corpses reanimated by a spell.

I glanced back to the tunnel and saw that it was blocked with an equally savage-looking force; then the attackers were on us, chopping and slashing. There was no hope of aiming discriminately as Maddy had suggested. Everything became a chaos of gunshots and screams and snarling mouths, and we would have all died if it hadn't been for Wall. He swung his laser in sweeping arcs, cutting a swath in the ranks of our adversaries, and headed straight for the opening on the far side of the chamber and the darkness beyond it.

It was a matter of sheer luck that I was standing close to Wall when he made his charge. During the first thirty seconds of the attack I had emptied my pistol; I'm sure I hit something with every shot – it would have been nearly impossible not to do so – yet I have no clear memory of what I hit. Faces, ape and human, reeled into view, visible for split seconds between other faces, between bodies, and blood was everywhere, streaking flesh, matting fur, spraying into the air. I simply poked the barrel of my pistol forward and fired until the hammer clicked. Then as I went to reload, a club glanced off the point of my left shoulder, momentarily numbing my hand, and I dropped the pistol. Even with the ape stink thickening the air, I could smell my own fear, a yellow, sour reek, and while I didn't have the time to indulge that fear, I felt it weakening me, felt it urging me to flee. And I might have if I had seen a safe harbour. I drew my knife and slashed at an ape's hand that was grabbing for me, going off-balance and falling backward into Wall. He shoved me away, and inadvertently I went in a staggering run toward the opening from which the apes and their collared army had emerged, so that in effect I wound up guarding his flank, though it was Maddy, beside me, who did the lion's share of the guarding. She had managed to reload, and in the brief time it took to cross the remaining distance she shot four apes and two collared men, while Wall burned down countless others, the laser severing limbs and torsos.

When we reached the darkness beyond the doorway, Wall turned back, continuing to fire into the mêlée, and shouted to us to search for a switch, a button, something that would close off the chamber. As I followed his order, my hands trembling, fumbling, groping at the wall, I saw that seven or eight of our group were pinned against the fountain, and before the wall slid shut to obscure my view, sealing us into the dark, I saw three fall, each killed by collared men and women. Many lay dead already, and many others, wounded, were trying to crawl away; but the apes were on them before they could get far, slicing with long-bladed knives at their necks. It appeared that the red water from the fountain had been splashed and puddled everywhere, and that the open-mouthed woman at the centre of the fountain was screaming in a dozen voices, lamenting the carnage taking place around her.

The instant the chamber vanished from sight, isolating us in the dark, Wall demanded to know who had found the control, and when a woman's voice answered, he had her lead him to it and burned it with the laser so that the door could not be opened again. He then asked us to speak our names so that he could determine how many had survived. Sixteen names were sounded. Clay Fornoff's was not among them. I tried to remember if I had seen him fall, but could not. The darkness seemed to deepen with this recognition. I could see nothing; even though I knew that the door to the chamber was within arm's reach, I felt as if I were standing at the centre of a limitless void. It seemed strange that only now, now that I could not see it, did I have a powerful apprehension of the size of the place.

'All right,' Wall said. 'We're in the shit, and we can't just stand around. Only way we're going to get home is to find one of the little bastards and make him show us a safe passage. We know they're in here somewhere. So let's go find 'em.'

He said this with such relish, such apparent delight, as if what had occurred was exactly what he'd been hoping for, that – dismayed and frightened as I was – I found it kind of off-putting. Maybe his words affected others the same, because he didn't get much of a response.

'Do you wanna die?' he asked us. 'Or is it just you're scared of the dark? Well, I can fix that!'

I felt him push past me, saw the ruby stalk of the laser swing out into the blackness. In an instant several fires sprouted in the dark. Bushes turned to torches by the laser, their light revealing an uneven terrain of moss or fungus or maybe even some sort of black grass, like a rug thrown over a roomful of lumpy furniture. Bushes and hollows and low rises. Here and there, barely visible in the flickering light, thin seams of gold were laid in against the black ground, and once again recalling *The Black Garden*, I realized that these likely signalled the location of doorways into secret rooms. There were no signs of walls or a ceiling. Even with the light, we had no way to judge the actual size of the place; but the fires gave us heart, and without further discussion, we headed for the nearest of those gold seams. When we reached it Wall burned down the door and we poured inside. By chance more than by dint of courage, I was beside him as we entered, and I had a clear view of the opulent interior. A cavelike space of irregular dimensions, considerably higher than it was long or wide, with a terraced floor and slanted ceiling, a golden grotto draped in crimson silks, stalks of crystal sprouting from the floor and a miniature waterfall splashing down upon boulders that looked to be pure gold. Silk cushions were strewn everywhere. An aquarium was set into the wall, teeming with brightly coloured fish as different from the drab brown trout and bottom feeders with which I was familiar as gems from common rocks; the ornament of the aquarium through which the fish swam was a human spine and rib cage.

But what held my attention was the presence of three Captains lying on the cushions: two men and a woman, their pale, naked, hairless bodies almost childlike in appearance. There were also three collared women, who had apparently been sexually engaged with the Captains, and showed bruises and other marks of ill use, and a collared man who was obviously dead; his chest and limbs were deeply gashed, and he was lying arms akimbo by a wall, as if he had been tossed aside. When we entered, one of the Captains, the larger of the two men, put a knife to the throat of a collared woman; the other two reached for what I assumed to be weapons – short metal tubes resting on the floor at arm's reach; yet their movements were languid, casual, as if they were not really afraid of us. Or perhaps they were drugged. Whatever the case, they were overwhelmed before they could pick up the tubes and dragged from the room. The Captain holding the knife looked at me – directly at me, I'm sure of it – and smiling, slashed the woman's throat. She began to thrash about, clutching at the wound, and the Captain pushed her off to the side. He was still smiling. At me. The daft little shit was amused by my reaction. His androgynous features twisted with amusement. Something gave way inside me, some elemental restraint – I felt it as tangibly as I might have felt the parting of my tissues from a knife stroke – and I rushed at him, ignoring Wall's order to hold back. The Captain kind of waved the knife at me, but again he did not seem overly concerned with any threat I might pose. Even after I kicked the knife aside and yanked him to his feet, even after I grabbed him by the throat and shoved him back against the wall, he continued to regard me with that mild, dissipated smile and those wet purplish eyes that gave no hint of what might lie behind, as empty as the eyes of a fish. I had the notion that I was doing exactly as he expected, and that my predictable behaviour was something that reinforced his feelings of superiority.

'Let him go,' said Wall from behind me.

'In a minute,' I said, tightening my grip on the Captain's throat. I was still full of loathing, but it was a colder emotion now, albeit no less manageable. I fixed my gaze on those inhuman eyes, wanting to learn if anything would surface in them at the end, and I plunged my knife hilt-deep into the top of his skull. His mouth popped open, the eyes bulged, and thick blood flowed down over his head like syrup over a scoop of vanilla. Spasms shook him, and a stream of his piss wetted my legs. Then it was over, and I let him fall. It looked for all the world as though his head had grown a bone handle. In some part of me that had been obscured by anger, I could feel a trivial current of revulsion, but most of what I felt at first was satisfaction, though not long afterward I began to shake with the aftershocks of my violent act.

I turned to Wall, who stood regarding me with a thoughtful expression. 'You got two of 'em,' I said. 'Two's enough.'

Behind him, they were trying to remove the collars from the surviving women. Neither was doing well; blood was leaking from their ears.

'There's more,' Wall said. 'You gonna kill 'em all?'

The question did not seem in the least rhetorical, and I did not take it as such.

'Long as we're here,' I said.

But I did no further killing that night. The vengeful, outraged spirit that had moved me gradually eroded as we passed through the Black Garden, led by the two collared Captains, our path lit by burning shrubs and doorways into golden light left open to reveal scenes of luxury and carnage, like a score of tiny stages mounted on the dark upon whose boards the same terrible play had been performed, and I only watched the others do the bloody work. The violence I'd committed had worked a change in me, or else had exposed some central weakness, and I grew disinterested in the outcome of our expedition. Maddy had to urge me along, or else I might have just stood there and waited for my end, displaying no more concern for my fate than the Captain that I'd killed; and I wondered if the fact that they had done so much violence was at the heart of their dismissive attitude toward life and death – but I don't believe that. To imbue them with human qualities would be assuming too much. They were no more human than the apes, and the apes, despite what I'd said long before to the man in the bubble car, which had been something I'd said mostly to impress him, were in no way human.

Apes came at us now and again as we went, singly sometimes and sometimes in small groups, flying at us from dark crannies, their knives flashing with reflected fire, and they succeeded in killing three of our people; but they were disorganized, without slaves to support them, and this gave us hope that the other three parties had done well, that the battle, if not yet finished, was on the verge of being won. We killed them all, and we also killed every Captain whom we came across.

Wall was in his element. He burned and burned, and when the laser gave out or broke or whatever it is that lasers do when they go wrong, he killed with his hands, in several instances literally tearing the heads off scrawny white necks. There was a joyful flair in the way he went about it, and I was not the only one who noticed this; I saw others staring at him with a confused mixture of awe and distaste as he carried out the business of slaughter. It was not that the Captains deserved any less, nor was it that vengeance was inappropriate to the moment. No, it was instead that Wall did not appear to be carrying out a vengeful process. Watching him was like watching a farmer scything wheat – here was a man engaged in his proper work and enjoying it immensely. The minor wounds he accumulated, the red stains that flowered on his rough shirt, his arms and face, gave him the look of an embattled hero, but the sort of hero, perhaps, whom we – who were ourselves the pitiful result of laws that heroes had written thousands of years before – no longer cared to exalt; and we moved ever more slowly in his wake, letting him run ahead of us, separating ourselves from him, as if this would lessen our complicity and devalue our support.

Still, we made no move to keep him from his pleasure. The things we found inside those golden rooms, the flayed bodies, bits of men and women used for ornament or more perverted purposes yet, the collared dead, the few that survived, shaking and delirious, all this legislated against our reining Wall in, and we might have let him go on forever had there been a sufficient number of Captains and if there had been nothing else to capture our attention. But then there came two explosions, distant, the one following hard upon the other, and a ragged cheer went up.

'We got it!' Maddy said; she sounded happy yet bewildered, as if she couldn't quite accept some great good news, and when I asked what the explosions signified, she said, 'The ship. They must have blown up the other two. They weren't supposed to do that until we had the ship.'

'You mean they flew it away and all?' I said.

'I think so!' She gave my hand a squeeze. In the garish orange light of the burning, she looked like she was about to hop up and down from excitement. 'I can't be sure 'til we see for ourselves, but I think so.'

Wall was prevailed upon to break off his hunt, so we could determine what had happened, and with the two collared Captains still in the lead, we began to make our way back toward the crater.

But Wall was not yet finished with death.

As we came out from yet another hidden door into the chamber where we had been ambushed, we spotted an ape squatting by one of its fallen companions, rocking back and forth on its heels in an attitude that seemed to signal grief, though – again – I can't say for certain what the thing was doing there. Just as likely it had gone crazy over something I could never understand. Someone fired at it, and with a fierce scream, it scuttled off into the tunnel that angled up toward the crater.

Wall sprinted after it.

A handful of people, Maddy included, followed him at a good clip, but the rest of us, governed by a weary unanimity, kept plodding along, stepping between the bodies, friend and foe, that lay everywhere. I'd seen so much dying that night, you would have thought that the scene in the chamber would not have affected me, but it took me by storm. That red fountain and the woman of stone and the bloody hieroglyphs figuring the tiles, and now the bodies, more than a hundred of them, I reckoned, scattered about under benches, in the ferns, their pallor and the brightness of their blood accentuated by the glaring light – it was such a unity of awful place and terrible event, it struck deep, and I knew it would hurt me forever, like a work of art whose lines and colours match up perfectly with some circuit in your brain or some heretofore unmapped country in your soul, all the graceless attitudes of the dead's arms and legs and the humped bodies like archipelagoes in the sea of red.

I found Clay Fornoff lying under the lip of the fountain, his chest pierced innumerable times, eyes open, blond hair slick with blood. Something, an ape probably, had chewed away part of his cheek. Tears started from my eyes – I don't know why. Maybe because I couldn't disassociate Clay from Bradley, or maybe it was just death working its old sentimental trick on me, or maybe I'd hoped to reconcile with Clay and now that hope was gone I felt the loss. I don't know. It was no matter any more, whatever the reason. Feeling as tired as I'd ever been, I kneeled beside him and collected his personals, his gun, a silver ring of Windbroken design, a leather wallet, and a whistle whittled out of some hard yellowish wood. I intended to give them to his folks if I ever saw them again, but I ended up keeping the whistle. I'd never figured Clay to be one for making whistles, and I suppose I wanted to keep that fact about him in mind.

I couldn't think of anything much to say over him, so I just bowed my head and let whatever I was feeling run out of me. I recall thinking I was glad I hadn't seen him die, and then wishing I had, and then wondering whether he had been brave or a fool or both. Then there was nothing left but silence. I closed his eyes and walked on up the tunnel.

Wall had caught up with the ape – or the ape had let him catch it – at the end of the tunnel, right where the canopy of foliage began, and he was fighting it hand to hand when I straggled up, while the remainder of those who had survived the ambush and the Garden stood in a semi-circle and watched. Without much enthusiasm, I thought. Their faces slack and exhausted-looking.

Wall had killed apes with his bare hands before; he was one of the few men alive strong enough to accomplish this, and under different circumstances it might have been incredible to see, like a scene out of a storybook, this giant locked up hard with a six-foot white-furred ape in a leather harness. But as things stood, realizing that this was just more of Wall's . . . I'm not sure what to call it, because it was more than him showing off. His folly, I guess. His making certain that the world stayed as violent and disgraceful as he needed it to be. Anyway, recognizing this, the sight of the two of them rolling about, tearing and biting, screaming, grunting, it did not seem vital or heroic to me, merely sad and depressing. To tell the truth, despite everything that had happened, I had a fleeting moment during which I found myself rooting for the ape; at least, I thought, it had displayed something akin to human emotion back in the chamber.

There came a point when, still grappling, they came to their feet and reeled off along the canopied pathway; mired in that green dimness they seemed even more creatures out of legend, the ape's small head with its bared fangs pressed close to the great shaggy bulk of Wall's head. Like insane lovers. Wall's arms locked behind the ape's back, his muscles bunched like coiled snakes, and the ape clawing at Wall's neck. Then Wall heaved with all his might, at the same time twisting his upper body, a wrestler's quick move, lifting the ape and slinging him up and out higher than his head, its limbs flailing, to fetch up hard against a tree trunk. The ape was hurt bad. It came up into a crouch, but fell onto its side and made a mewling sound; it clawed frantically at its own back, as if trying to reach some unreachable wound. Finally it got to its feet, but it was an unsteady, feeble movement, like that of an old man who's mislaid his cane. It snarled at Wall, a grating noise that reminded me of a crotchety generator starting up. I could tell it wanted to charge him, that its ferocity was unimpaired, but it was out of juice, and so was waiting for Wall to come to it. And Wall would have done just that if Maddy, who was standing about ten feet away from me, hadn't taken her pistol and shot the ape twice in the chest.

Wall stared incredulously at the ape for a second, his chest heaving, watching it twitch and bleed among the ferns lining the path; then he spun about, and asked Maddy what the fuck she'd had in mind.

'We got better to do than watch you prove what a man you are.' She looked drawn and on edge, and her pistol was still in hand, trained a little to the left of Wall.

'Who the hell put ye in charge?' he said.

'You want to argue 'bout it,' she said, 'we'll argue later. Right now we got to get movin'.'

'Goddamn it!' Wall took a step toward her. With his hair falling wild about his shoulders and his coarse features stamped with sullen anger, he looked every inch an ogre, and he towered over Maddy. 'I'm sick right down to the bone of your bullshit. There ain't a single damn thing we done, you ain't stood in the way of.' He started toward her again, and Maddy let the pistol swing a few degrees to the right. Wall stopped his advance.

'You don't care who you kill, do you?' she said. 'Can't be the ape, might as well be one of us.'

Wall put his hands on his hips and glared at her. 'Go on and shoot, if that's your pleasure.'

'Nothin' 'bout this here is my pleasure,' she said. 'You know that. Just leave it alone, Wall. You've had your victory, you've got your ship. Let's go home.'

'You hear this?' Wall said to the others, none of whom had changed their listless expressions and attitudes. 'I mean have you been listenin' to her?'

'They're too damn tired to listen,' Maddy told him. 'Death and killin' makes people tired. That's somethin' you ain't figured out yet.'

Wall kept staring at her for a few beats, then let out a forceful breath. 'All right,' he said. 'All right for now. But we're gonna settle this later.'

And with that he strode off along the path, ripping away a big rubbery leaf that hung down in his face with a furious gesture; he quickly rounded a turn and went out of sight, like he didn't much care if any of us were to follow.

'Son of a bitch ain't gonna be happy till he gets every one of us dead,' Maddy said, holstering her pistol; the lines around her mouth were etched sharp, and she looked years older than she had earlier in the evening. But then maybe we all did.

It wasn't my place to say anything, I suppose, but since Wall had been part of Edgeville for a time, I felt an old loyalty to him.

'He mighta got carried away some,' I said. 'But you can't deny he's done us all a world of good down there today.'

Maddy dropped a little thong over the hammer of her pistol to keep it from bouncing out of the holster; she gave me a sharp look.

'You don't know nothin' 'bout Wall like you think you do,' she told me in a weary tone. 'But you stick around, you gonna find out way more'n you can stand.'

When at last we reached the surface and took shelter among the rocks, we discovered that only about hundred and thirty of us had survived the Garden. Brad and Callie were fine, as were most of those who had stayed with the flying machines; there had been scant fighting in the crater. But of the nearly four hundred who had gone deep into the Garden, fewer than seventy had returned, along with a handful of men and women who'd been saved from the collars, and five Captains. Wall wanted to ride out immediately, to return to wherever it was they'd set out from; but Coley, Maddy, and others told him, Fine, go ahead, but we're going to wait a while and see if anyone else comes out. More than three hundred dead had shaken people's faith in Wall – that was a sight more than what you would call 'light casualties', and resentment against him appeared to be running high, even though we'd managed to steal the flying machine. I had thought the argument between him and Maddy was personal, but it was now obvious that politics was involved.

After heated discussion, it was decided that Wall would take a group on ahead, and the rest of us would follow within the hour. But then they got to arguing about how many were to go with Wall and how many were to stay, and whether or not all the prisoners, who were sitting against boulders at the edge of the hardpan, should go with Wall's party. It was hard to credit that people who had so recently fought together could now be all snarled up in these petty matters, and after a few minutes of hanging about the fringes of the argument, I gave up on them and went off and sat with Brad and Callie higher up among the boulders.

From the way everything looked, with that golden light still streaming up from the crater, and the moonstruck hardpan running flat and fissured to the mountains on the horizon, and cold stars glinting through thin scudding clouds, it appeared that nothing much could have happened down below the world; I would have expected some sign of what had transpired, coloured smokes curling up, strange flickering radiances, a steam of dead souls rising from the deep, and there should have been scents of rot and corruption on the wind, not merely the cool, dry smell of desolation; but all was as peaceful and empty as before, and for some reason this lack of evidence that anything had occurred afflicted me and I began to remember the things I had witnessed and the things I had done. As each of them passed before my mind's eye, a new weight settled in my chest, making a pressure that hurt my heart and caused the flow of my thoughts to stick and swell in my head as if something had damned them up. Brad asked me about Kiri, about Clay, and all I could do was shake my head and say I'd tell him later. Of course he must have known Clay was done for, seeing I had the man's possessions. But I didn't realize this at the time, because all my mind was turned inside.

I have no idea how much time had passed, but Wall, Maddy and the rest were still arguing down on the edge of the hardpan when the last survivors crawled up over the rim of the crater and came toward us at a sluggish pace, black and tiny and featureless against the golden light, like sick ants wandering away from a poisoned hole. They were strung out over about a dozen yards or so. Twenty, twenty-five of them. And as they drew near, the group who'd been arguing broke up and some went out to meet them. A couple looked to be wounded and were being supported by their companions. Brad got to his feet and moved a little way downslope, staring out at them. I was so worn out, I couldn't think what might have caught his interest, and even when he started out across the hardpan all I said to Callie was, 'Where the hell's he goin'?' But Callie, too, had gotten to her feet by then and was peering hard in the direction of the stragglers.

'Damn,' she said. 'I think . . .' She broke off and moved closer to the edge of the hardpan. I saw her Adam's apple working. 'Bob, it's her,' she said.

I stood and had a look for myself and saw a lean, dark woman stepping toward us; she was too far away for me to make out her features, but her quick stride and stiff posture, things I'd always taken for telltales of Kiri's rage, were thoroughly familiar.

What was passing through my mind as I walked out onto the hardpan toward Kiri was almost every emotion I've ever had, up to love and down to fear and all their lesser permutations. I'd like to believe that the main thing I felt was relief and happiness, and I'm pretty sure that's the case, but I know that it was mixed in with a sizeable portion of worry about what would happen to all of us now. I had already given up on Kiri, you see; I had buried her and the past along with her, and it wasn't easy to recalibrate my heart and mind to her presence.

She had one of the Bad Men's coats draped over her shoulders and was naked underneath it; she hardly seemed to see Brad, who was hanging on her when I came up; her eyes were fixed on some point beyond us both, and though her gaze wavered and cut toward me, the only other sign of acknowledgement she gave was to tousle Brad's hair absently and say something in a croaky voice that might have been my name, but might also have been an involuntary noise. An old bruise was going yellow on one of her cheekbones, and when the wind feathered her hair, I saw the marks on her neck made by a collar; but otherwise she seemed fine, albeit distant . . . Though as it turned out, I mistook single-mindedness for abstraction.

As we reached the group of Bad Men waiting at the bottom of the slope, Kiri gave me a hard shove, sending me staggering, and although I hadn't felt her hand on my sheath, I saw my knife in her hand. Quick as a witch, before anybody could move, she was in among the Bad Men and had grabbed one of the seated Captains and dragged him upslope behind a boulder. Some made to go after her, but Wall blocked their way and said, 'I were you, I wouldn't try to stop her.'

Coley – I recognized him by the red ribbon on his hat – said something by way of disagreement, but there was not much point in arguing about this particular trouble. A high-pitched scream issued from back of the boulder; it faltered, but then kept on going higher and higher, lasting an unreasonable length of time. It broke off suddenly, as if the voice had been permanently stilled; but soon it started up again. And so it went for a goodly while. Starting and stopping, growing weaker but no less agonized. It was plain Kiri had found a way of engaging the Captain's interest in the matter of life and death.

When at last she stood up from behind the boulder, she was wild-eyed, covered with blood, her face so strained it appeared her cheekbones might punch through the skin. I caught sight of Brad standing off to the side near Callie. He looked like he was about to cry, and I understood that he must understand what I had known for a while – that though we had found Kiri, she would never find us again. Whether it had been the lost duel or her troubles with me or everything since or a combination of all those things, she was gone into a distance where we could never travel, into the world that had bred her, a world whose laws would never again permit the enfeebling consolations of home and hearth.

We all watched her, standing in ragged ranks like a congregation stunned and disoriented by some terrible revelation from the pulpit, waiting for her to give some sign of what she might do next, but she remained motionless – she might have been a machine that had been switched off. The silence was so deep, I could hear the wind skittering gravel across the hardpan, and I had the notion that the night was hardening around us, sealing us inside the moment – it felt more like resolution than anything that had happened down in the crater. Like a violent signature in the corner of a painting of blood and degradation and loss. Finally Wall moved up beside her. He outweighed her by a couple of hundred pounds, but even so he was extremely cautious in his approach. He was talking to her, but I couldn't make out the words; from the sound of the fragments I was able to distinguish, however, I figured he was speaking in a northern tongue, one they shared. After a bit he took the knife from her hand and wiped it clean on his coat.

'Well then,' he said to us, without a trace of sarcasm and maybe with just a touch of regret. 'I guess we can go now.'

In the end it happened that Wall was proved both right and wrong. As he'd predicted, the Captains weren't able to root us out of the deep places where we hid, but they came damn close and many lives were lost. Eventually that time passed, and things returned to normal . . . at least as normal as normal gets out here in the Big Nothing. We live in a strange subterranean labyrinth beneath a black mesa, a place of tunnels and storage chambers containing all manner of marvels, and machines whose purpose we may never determine, where once our ancestors slept and dreamed of a sweet untroubled world that would be born upon their waking. Bradley attends school, and though the subjects he studies are far removed from the rudimentary ones he studied back on the Edge, he remains nonetheless a schoolboy. I grow vegetables and fruits and wheat and such on the subsurface farms; Callie helps to administer stocks of food and weapons and so forth; Kiri trains our people in combat. So it would seem that very little has changed for us, but of course almost everything has.

When I finished the main body of this story, I showed it to Callie and after she had read it she asked why I'd called it 'Human History', because it dealt with such a brief period of time and ignored what we had learned of the world of our ancestors. And that's the truth, it does ignore all that. I've seen the paintings our ancestors created, I've read their books and listened to their music, I've experienced no end of their lofty thoughts and glorious expressions, and I admire them for the most part. But they don't counterbalance the mass slaughters, the barbarities, the unending tortures and torments, the vilenesses, the sicknesses, the tribal idiocies, the trillion rapes and humiliations that comprise the history of that world up until its mysterious ending (I doubt we'll ever learn what happened, unless the Captains decide to tell us). What the Captains did to us in the Black Garden pales by comparison to the nature of those ancient atrocities, even if you figure in seven hundred years of evil duplicity. And at any rate, to my mind the Captains are relics of that old world, and soon they'll be gone, relegated to that distant past. As will, I believe, men and women such as Wall and Kiri. And there we'll be, the whole human race freed from that tired old history, maybe not completely, but with a chance of doing something new, if we've got the heart to take it.

Back when I was living in Edgeville, I never thought much about God or religion. The Captains, I suppose, took the place of God, and having God available to talk with any hour of the day or night caused me to think less than perhaps I should have about the system of life. But maybe that was a blessing in disguise, because when I look back at all the trouble caused by religion in the old world, I have to think that I'm better off the way I am. Once I found an ageworn Bible, and in the front was a picture of the God known as Jehovah, an old man with fierce eyes and cruel lips and a beard and tufted eyebrows. He looked a lot like Wall, and sometimes when I go outside and glance up into the stormy sky – the skies out here are rarely clear – I imagine I see that angry old bearded Jehovah face come boiling out of the snow clouds, and I wonder if Wall wasn't standing in for him, if he wasn't the kind of leader man once made in the image of their god – strong, blustery, bloody-minded men who knew only one way of achieving their goals. We need Wall and Kiri now, we need their violent hearts, their death-driven need to dominate; but it's clear – at least so it seems – that there'll soon come a time when we don't need them any longer, and maybe that's all we can hope for, that we'll learn to choose our leaders differently, that we won't end up apes or Captains.

Old Hay forgot to tell me how to wind down a story, and I'm sure I'm going about it all wrong, trying to explain what I mean by 'Human History', and how limiting the definition of that term to a period of a few weeks of happiness and a betrayal and a ride out onto the flats and a battle still seems to incorporate all the essentials of the process, as well as to voice some faint hope that we can change. But it's my story, the only one I've got worth telling, so I'll just go ahead and do my worst and hope that having it finish wrong or awkwardly will suit the ungainly nature of the tale, its half-formed resolution, and the frayed endings and uncompleted gestures that make up most of the substance of our lives.

In the days and weeks that followed the battle, Callie and I drifted apart. This was chiefly due to Kiri's presence – we could not feel easy with her around, even though she did not display the least interest in either one of us. I had an affair with Maddy, more of a healing than a passion. No hearts were broken, no souls transformed, but it was a fine place to be for the time it lasted. Even in the midst of it I half hoped that Callie and I might get back together but after Maddy and I went our separate ways, Callie remained aloof from me and I could not find it in myself to go to her. As had happened that night when Kiri had caught us at it in the store, I came to have a sense that the love we'd made back then had been childish, that the people we'd been were characters, part of a dramatis personæ, our desire a consummate fakery, emblematic of a need to be the centre of attention of those around us, like actors in a pleasurable yet somehow despicable farce. And so we continued to deny what now seems inevitable.

I won't try to make any great dramatic presentation of how we did get back together, because it wasn't dramatic in the least. One night she walked into the little room I'd made for myself on one of the farms to sleep in when I didn't want to return to my regular quarters, and after some dodging around and a bit of inconsequential talk, we became lovers again. But the grave tenderness we expressed, touching each other carefully, treasuringly, like a blind man would touch the face of a statue, it was a far cry from the way it had been back in Edgeville, from our sweaty, joyful, self-deluding first time, and I recognized that whatever good had existed in our beginning had grown and flourished, and that's the wonder of it, that's the amazing thing, that despite the betrayals and failures and all the confused principles that contend in us, seed will sprout in this barren soil we call the human spirit and sometimes grow into something straight and green and true. As I lay with Callie that night, maybe it was wrong of me, but I couldn't feel sorry for anything that had happened, for any of us, not even for Kiri in the black wish of her sleep shaping herself into an arrow that one day would find an enemy's heart. It occurred to me that we were all becoming what we needed to be, what our beginnings had charged us to become: Kiri a death; Brad a man; Callie and I ordinary lovers, something we might once have taken for granted, but that now we both understood was more than we'd ever had the right to hope that we could come to be. It was a pure and powerful feeling to tear away the shreds and tatters of our old compulsions, and steep ourselves in the peace that we gave to one another, and know who we were and why, that Bad Men were mostly only good men gone over the edge to freedom, and that the past was just about done with dying, and the future was at hand.

SPORTS IN AMERICA

While they waited for Milchuk to show, Carnes leafed through *Sports Illustrated*, the NFL Preview issue, and Penner checked out the baseball scores in *The Globe*. They were parked on Main Street in Hyannis, across from the Copper Kitchen, where Milchuk – so they had been told – liked to have his breakfast. It was a quarter to seven of a bitter September morning, a few raindrops spitting down and ridges of leaden cloud shouldering in off the harbour. Carnes, pinch-faced and wiry, with sprays of straw-coloured hair sticking out from beneath his Red Sox cap, betrayed no sign of anxiety. But Penner, who had never done this sort of work before, shifted restlessly about, flexing his neck muscles, reshaping the folds of his newspaper, and glancing this way and that.

Christ, he thought, I don't want this. He had been insane to go along with it. His mind had not been right. Too much pressure. Too much drink, too many sleepless nights. He would run, he decided, lose himself among the houses down by the ferry dock. His hand inched toward the door handle.

Carnes coughed, noisily turned the pages of his magazine, and Penner, stiffening, gave up any idea of running. He touched the pistol stuck in his belt, the envelope stuffed with bills in his windbreaker, as if acknowledging the correspondence between his salvation and another man's extinction.

To strengthen his resolve, he pictured himself returning home, with Barbara warm and sweet in their bed, hair fanned out across the pillow, her cheekbone perfection evident even in sleep. Fifty grand, he'd say to her, tossing the money onto the sheet as if it were nothing. Fifty fucking grand. And that's just for starters. Then he would show her the gun, tell her what he had done for her and how much he intended to do, maybe frighten her a little, make her understand that she might be at risk here, that the next affair might not be so readily forgiven, and that perhaps she had not chosen wrongly after all, perhaps this newly desperate, bloody-handed Penner was just the man to guarantee her summers in Newport and winters in Bermuda.

He gazed out the window, searching for favourable signs, something to restore his sense of purpose. Overhead, a pair of laced-together sneakers looped over a telephone line heeled and kicked in a stiff breeze, bringing to mind a gallows dance. The deserted sidewalks and glass storefronts with their opaque wintry reflections had the look of a stage set waiting for lights, camera, action.

'Y'see this article here 'bout the guy owns the 'Niners,' Carnes said with sudden animation. 'Y'know, that guy DiBartalo.'

'Fuck the son of a bitch,' said Penner glumly.

Carnes folded his magazine into a tube and stared at him deadpan.

'Lighten up, willya?' he said. 'Ain't no reason you gettin' nervous. The man shows . . . *bing!* We're outta here.'

'I'm not nervous,' Penner said. 'I just don't feel like bullshitting seven o'clock in the morning 'bout some dumb-ass owns a football team.'

'The guy's okay, man! He ain't nothin' like the other schmucks own teams.' And he explained how DiBartalo was in the habit of lavishing gifts upon his players. Ten-thousand-dollar rings, trips to Hawaii. How he sent their wives on shopping sprees at Neimann Marcus.

'Just 'cause he treats 'em like prize poodles, that makes him into Albert Schweitzer?' Penner said. 'Get real!'

'I'm tellin' ya, man! Y'should read the article!'

'I don't hafta read the article, I know all 'bout the bastard. He's a short little fucker, right? 'Bout five-five or something.'

'So?' Carnes said stiffly; he stood about five-eight himself.

'So he's got a Napoleonic complex, man. His dick's on the line with the goddamn team. He could give a shit about 'em really, but 'long as they win, sure, he's gonna throw 'em a bone now and then.'

Carnes muttered something and went back to reading. The

silence oppressed Penner. Carnes' conversation had stopped him from thinking about Barbara. It struck him as an irony that Carnes could in any way be a comfort to him. In high school fifteen years before they had taken an instant dislike to one another. Since that time they had maintained the scantiest of relationships, this only due to the fact of their having roots in the same neighbourhood, the same gang. Both men had been in the process of being groomed for positions in the Irish mob. Providing cheap muscle, running drugs. After high school Carnes had continued on this track, whereas Penner, dismayed by the bloody requisites of the life, had attended Boston College and then gotten into real estate. Yet here they were. Partnered once again by hard times and a common heritage.

'You still root for the 'Niners, huh?' he asked, and Carnes said, 'Yeah,' without glancing up.

'How come you root for a team like that, man? Fucking team's gotta quarterback named for a state, for Chrissakes! Joe Montana! Sounds like some kinda New York art faggot. Some guy takes pictures of dudes with umbrellas stuck up their ass.'

Carnes blinked at him, more confused than angry. 'Fuck you talkin'?'

'Man was named for another state, I could relate,' Penner went on. 'Like New Jersey. I could support him maybe, he was named Joe New Jersey. Maybe he'd play a little tougher, too.'

'You're fuckin' crazy!' Carnes looked alarmed, as if what Penner had said was so extreme, it might be symptomatic of dangerous behaviour. 'Joe Montana's the greatest quarterback in the history of the NFL.'

Penner gave an amused sniff. 'Yeah, he's history, all right. Sorta like the Red Sox, huh? What's it they lost now? Six in a row? Seven? The tradition continues.'

Carnes glared at him. 'Don't start with that shit, okay?'

Penner fingered out a pack of Camels. In school, he had delighted in mind-fucking Carnes, pushing him to the brink of rage, making the creepy little mad boy twitch, then easing up. Pushing and easing up, over and over, until Carnes was punchy from surges of adrenaline. The Red Sox, to whom he was irrationally, almost mystically devoted, had been a particular sore point.

LUCIUS SHEPARD

"Course,' Penner went on in a lighthearted tone, 'soon as Clemens comes back, he'll make it all better. Isn't that right, man? Ol' Rocket Roger! This redneck with the IQ of a doughnut, guy doesn't have the brains to lift himself from the game when his shoulder blows up the size of a watermelon, he's gonna walk on water and win three in the Series.' He shook his head in mock sympathy and lit up a Camel. 'Don'tcha ever get sick of it, man?'

'I'm fuckin' sick of you, that's for sure.'

'Naw, I mean doesn't it ever sink in that the guys own the Sox, they're never gonna put out the money y'need to have a winner. Alls they care 'bout is the stadium's full. Else why'd they pass up grabbin' Willie McGee off the waiver wire. See that fat fuck Gorman on TV the other night? "Where would we play McGee?" he's saying. Right! Like where we gonna play a guy steals you fifty bases and leads the National League in hitting?'

'It's easy for you talkin' this shit!' Carnes said angrily. 'You're just a frontrunner, man. You don't know how it is, you grow up with a team, you follow 'em your whole life.'

'Bullshit, I'm a frontrunner!'

'Hell you ain't! Every team gets goin' good, you jump on the goddamn bandwagon. First you're a Lakers' fan. Then the A's start winnin', and . . .'

'I told you, man, I lived four years in Oakland.'

'Big fuckin' deal! I lived in Houston, and I ain't no Astros fan.'

'What'd be the point? They're even more pathetic than the Sox.'

'Goddamn it! I don't hafta take this crap!' Carnes pounded a fist against the dash. 'I told McDonough I couldn't work with you, man! You ain't professional! Fuckin' guy's gotta be crazy thinkin' I can spend a coupla hours in a fuckin' car with you!'

This broke Penner's mood. 'Yeah, maybe,' he said, remembering McDonough in the lamplit gloom of his study, his white hair agleam, patrician features seamed with anguish, noble head bowed under the weight of a daughter's dishonour. His pain, or rather Penner's sympathy with it, had glossed over the illogic of McDonough's proposal that he and Carnes become partners in a proxy vengeance. And yet afterward he'd had the thought that

182

the scene seemed posed. Too perfect a setting, too splendid a grief. A cinematic version of Celtic woe.

' "Maybe", what?' said Carnes fiercely.

'I just can't figure it.'

'What? What can't you figure?'

'Everything, man. Like why'd the man pay us so much? And in advance. He coulda hired somebody half the price. Less, even.'

'He's always doin' shit like that. Remember when Bobby Doyle's kid needed a new liver. Fuckin' McDonough, he don't ask for no collection. He just digs down in his pocket. Like the man said. We help him, he helps us. We whack out the guy did his daughter, he takes care of us. That's how he's always been.'

'Sure, he's a fucking saint.'

'Hey, man! He's a mick's got some power in the state house and ain't forgotten where he comes from. In Southie that amounts to the same thing. You spent more time in the neighbourhood steada hangin' out with those guido fucks in Back Bay, maybe you start thinkin' like an Irishman again.'

'That still doesn't explain why he'd put the two of us together.'

It appeared that Carnes was about to speak, but he remained silent.

'What were you gonna say?' asked Penner.

'Nothin', man!'

Penner, edging toward paranoia, could have sworn he detected the beginnings of a smirk.

A Grey Lincoln Town Car came quiet as a shadow past them; it pulled into a parking space thirty feet farther along. Carnes' hand went inside his jacket. A cold, crawly trickle inched down between Penner's shoulder blades. He stubbed out his cigarette in the ash tray. His fingers looked oddly white and unreal the way they pushed and worked at the butt, like the segmented parts of some weird animal. Please God, he said to himself, unsure whether he was praying for strength or permission to chicken out.

'Just you get in back of him.' Carnes' voice was tight. 'I'll handle the talkin'.'

They waited until Milchuk started to climb out of the Lincoln. Then they walked rapidly toward him, their breath steaming white. Milchuk was bending down into the car, fussing with papers in a briefcase. He straightened, looked puzzled. He was younger and bigger than Penner had figured. Early thirties. Six-three, six-four, maybe two-twenty. His handsome, squarish face had a rosy-cheeked pallor. His black hair and moustache were neatly trimmed, but his jaw was dirtied with stubble. He had on a very nice herringbone tweed overcoat, the kind with velvet on the lapels. Penner himself owned a similar coat, though it was several years older and far more worn. He felt a measure of resentment toward Milchuk for inadvertently showing him up.

"Scuse me, Mister Milchuk. We have a minute of your time?' Carnes took a stand that forced Milchuk to turn his back on Penner.

Milchuk made an impatient noise and said, 'I got an appointment.'

When Penner poked him with his automatic, he stiffened but did not turn his head to try and see the gun as someone might who had never been that route before. Penner could feel Milchuk's pulse in his gun hand, he could feel the whole breathing mass of nerves, bones, and meat. In the chill air the man's cologne had a stinging, astringent scent.

'Awright, be cool, guys,' Milchuk said. 'I got a coupla hundred in my wallet. Inside pocket of the overcoat.'

'How 'bout you takin' a stroll over to the car,' Carnes said. 'The blue Caddy back there.'

'What?' said Milchuk. He snuck a peek at the car, and Penner, in a sympathetic reaction, had a peek along with him. With its vanity plates that read SOX FAN 1 and the Red Sox logo painted on the hood, the Caddy had an absurdly innocent look.

Carnes let out an exasperated sigh. 'Hope you ain't gonna give us no trouble, Mister Milchuk, 'cause this is a very simple deal, what's happenin' here. Now I wantcha to get in the back seat of the Caddy with my associate there, okay? We're gonna drive you down the Cape a ways to where a man's waitin' for us. He's gonna talk to ya, tell ya a few things. Then we'll drive you back to Hyannis so's you can have your breakfast.'

Milchuk darted his eyes from side to side. Searching for police cars, brave strangers. 'You guys workin' for Masacola?'

'Masacola?' Carnes said. 'Who's that?'

'Listen,' said Milchuk, talking fast. 'I dunno what this is alla 'bout, but we can work somethin' out, you guys and me.'

'Either get in the fuckin' car,' Carnes said flatly, 'or swear to God I'm gonna knock you cold and throw ya in it. Now I'm very sincere about this, Mister Milchuk. Nothin' bad's gonna happen 'long as you don't give us no shit. Little drive in the country, little conversation. But dick us around, man, I'm gonna put lumps on your lumps. Okay?'

Milchuk drew a deep breath, blew it out. 'Okay,' he said, and took a step toward the Caddy.

'Hey!' Carnes pulled him back. 'You gonna leave your car wide open! Your briefcase just lyin' there?' He seemed appalled by the prospect.

Milchuk glanced at Penner, as if seeking a form of validation. Penner tried to keep his face empty.

'Lock the bitch, willya?' Carnes said. 'If you want, take the case with ya. You leave a fuckin' car like that unlocked, man, some nigger's gonna be ridin' it around Roxbury.'

This solicitude was a beautiful touch, Penner thought. Extremely professional. He could not help admiring Carnes for it. Milchuk collected his papers, locked up the Lincoln. And as they walked to the Caddy, Penner could tell by the firmness of his step that the dead man felt much better about his future.

Ten minutes out of Hyannis, heading toward Cotuit, and the overcast started to break. There was the merest line of blue above the islands, and directly ahead, a blare of silvery sunlight in roughly the shape of a cross seamed the division between mountains of black clouds, making a dark and mysterious glory of the eastern sky. Now and then Penner saw flashes of sun-spattered water between the sparsely needled pines along the roadside. Despite the tackle shops, the clam shacks, motels and souvenir stores, there was something eerie and desolate about the Cape, a fundamental emptiness. It was a flat, scoured jumble of a land, flat rocks and flat fields, thickets and stunted trees, moors punctuated by the blue dots of glacial ponds, sloping shingles figured with capsized scallop boats, cork floats, torn fishing nets, all surrounded by the dreary flatness of the sea. Penner found it more than usually depressing.

Static burst from the radio as Carnes spun the tuning dial, settling on a talk show – some asshole with a sardonic baritone goading housewives into bleating out idiot opinions on the economy. Penner kept his gun pressed against Milchuk's side and watched him out of the corner of his eye. He halfway hoped Milchuk would try for the gun. But Milchuk sat like a man in a trance, holding the briefcase to his chest, staring straight ahead. Once he asked how far they had left to go, and Carnes, with folksy amiability, said damn if he knew, he'd never been out on the Cape before, but it couldn't be much farther.

The talk show host began discussing the Red Sox, their recent decline, and Carnes said over his shoulder, 'Ever play any ball, Mister Milchuk? You look like a ballplayer to me.'

Milchuk was startled. 'I played in college,' he said after a second.

'I thought so. What's your position? First base? Outfield?'

'Rightfield.'

'So I guess you a Sox fan, huh?'

'Yeah, sure.'

'Follow 'em your whole life, didja?'

Milchuk said yes, yes he had.

'Then maybe you can explain to my pal there what it's like to be a true fan.' Carnes filled him in on the argument they had been having about the Red Sox and their alleged penury.

Penner did not think Milchuk would respond, but it may have been that Milchuk, like Penner, was using the argument to escape the turmoil of his thoughts.

'Seems to me he's gotta point.' He spoke dully, as if it were a litany in which he no longer believed. 'Lookit how they let Bruce Hurst get away. You gotta lefthander wins nineteen in Fenway, you don't just let him walk.'

'Hurst was gone no matter what they offered,' Carnes said. 'Guy's a religious fanatic. He didn't go for all the shit about Boggs porkin' that cunt what's-her-name.'

'That's just the excuse Gorman used.' Milchuk shifted forward, warming to the subject. 'Truth is, they just didn't wanta pay him. Same shit they pulled when they let Fisk jump. They claimed it was a fuck-up, they sent him his contract late. But they just didn't wanta pay the man. They couldn't say that 'cause they didn't wanta look bad, but that's how it was.'

The tension in the car had dissipated to a small degree. Penner maintained vigilance, but with part of his mind he slipped beneath the moment into a warm, nurturing place. It seemed he had been liberated, that the extreme nature of what he was about had freed him of the past. His life was a transparency. It could take on any colour, any condition, No longer was he required to be hopeless Penner, bankrupt Penner, pitiful, pussy-whipped Penner. He was blank, empty, a hollow shell fitted with a few basic drives. He could be anything he chose. He could escape the noose of circumstance and drive to Florida, catch a plane to Rio, grow grey-haired and eccentric on some isolated beach, companioned by canny parrots and foolish women. He could divorce not only his wife, but also his feelings for her; he could spit them out like a mouthful of tepid beer. Yet as they drew closer to the turn-off, to the place where they were to kill Milchuk, his daydream began to fray and he became less and less capable of avoiding the issue at hand. Panic grew large in him. He considered murder charges, the plight of his immortal soul, and he threw himself into the baseball argument with uncharacteristic vehemence.

'You take Burks, now,' he said. 'He's gotta be one of the fastest guys in the league, right?'

'That's right,' said Milchuk, nodding vigorously. 'You're absolutely right.'

'So what is it with him? He gets on first, he looks lost. What's he got now? Seven or eight stolen bases? You figure they'd hire somebody to teach him how to steal, wouldn'tcha? But naw!' He tapped Carnes on the shoulder. 'What's that all 'bout, man? They just too damn cheap? Or is it 'cause they're fuckin' prejudiced? Maybe they're trying to make Burks look so bad they'll hafta trade him, then they can have the only all-white team in the league.'

'Sox ain't prejudiced against niggers,' Carnes said; from the hunched set of his neck and shoulders, Penner knew that he was fuming.

'Hear that, man?' said Penner, giving Milchuk a nudge. 'They ain't prejudiced against *niggers*.'

187

Milchuk grinned, shook his head in amusement.

'I didn't say *I* wasn't prejudiced, motherfucker!' said Carnes. 'I said the Sox wasn't.'

'That's garbage!' said Milchuk. 'Check out the fuckin' record. If Jim Rice played his career in New York, they'd make a fuckin' statue to him. Here they just tell the guy, "See ya later." And even before that, the sportswriters are on his case day in, day out. I admit the guy wasn't hittin'. But Yaz, man, whenever Yaz didn't hit, the fuckin' writers acted like all they wanna do is hold the guy's prick and make him feel better.'

'Damn straight,' said Penner. 'Fuckin' town's built on prejudice. Take what happened to Dee Brown the other day. He's the Celtics' number one pick, right? So he's sitting out front the post office in Wellesley with his fiancée. He's in his car, reading his mail. He just picked it up, see. He's got an apartment not too far away. Next thing some broad in the bank across the street spots him and says, Holy shit, a Nee-gro! Why that must be the same Nee-gro robbed us a few weeks back. Makes sense, right? I mean what would a Nee-gro be doing in Wellesley he wasn't there to rob a bank? So here come the cops. Eight of 'em. They roust Brown and his girlfriend, and force 'em to lie face down on the sidewalk for twenty fucking minutes. At gunpoint, man! Twenty fucking minutes! You believe that?'

'No shit!' said Milchuk. 'That's what happened, no shit?'

'It don't matter,' said Carnes. 'If you're a true fan, none of that crap matters.'

'True fan!' said Penner disparagingly. 'What the hell's that mean? The Red Sox front office screws everybody over. Fans, players. They're no different from the government, man. They do just enough to get by, just enough to confuse people into thinking it's all gonna be okay, when the fact is the storm's coming and ain't no roof on the barn. They're not gonna be able to re-sign half their fucking players, their best pitcher probably needs psychiatric help. Their manager looks like an old alcoholic and talks about his freaking vegetable garden whenever you ask him 'bout his problem at shortstop. You hafta go back to prehistory to find when's the last time they won the Series. Nineteen-fucking-eighteen! And the Celtics, man, they're just watching their players grow old. Fucking Larry Bird's starting to look like Freddy Krueger with a limp. And the Patriots . . . Jesus Christ! Only thing they're good at's waggling their dicks at female reporters.'

They were almost at the turn-off, and a terrifying hilarity was mounting inside Penner. He heard the reediness of fear in his voice, yet he had the idea that if he kept on ranting he might accidentally work a spell that would abolish the need to kill Milchuk.

'And still you people keep going to the goddamn games,' he went on, his voice shrilling. 'You support this crapola. I mean nothing stops you. The fact that these assholes in three-piece suits are selling your dreams down the fucking river, it just doesn't sink in. Here they go gettin' rid of your best reliever 'cause he's black, pickin' up white guys with bad backs and dead arms, and you think it's wonderful. They lose your best pitching prospect 'cause they forget to put his name on the protected list. And whaddaya do? You boycott? You try and change anything? Fuck, no! You go on buying your dumb hats and your T-shirts, your shamrock jackets. You make stupid into a religion. Stand around chanting, Ooh, ooh, ooh whenever the team wins, like those pathetic rejects on Arsenio Hall. You don't even notice the whole thing's going down the toilet. You just sit there and babble about next year, while everything turns to shit around you. True fans, my ass! Fans appreciate the game, they can argue the finer points, y'know. They wanta win, but they don't act like lobotomy cases when they lose. They understand when they're getting jerked around. But you guys . . . Jesus Christ! All you guys are is a buncha fucking lemmings!'

Carnes made no sound or movement, but his anger was as palpable as heat from an open furnace. The silence grew long and prickly. The humming of the Caddy's tyres seemed to register the increase of tension.

'That Lisa Olson deal,' said Milchuk tentatively. 'Those assholes flashin' her in the Pats locker room, that was the worst, man.' He glanced at Penner, his face stamped with an expression of concern. 'I ain't sayin' I don't have problems with women in the locker room, y'know, but geez!'

'Now that's terrific, that is,' said Carnes. 'It's really great gettin' an education on how to treat broads from the guy cornholed Lori McDonough.'

A look of bewilderment washed over Milchuk's stolid face. 'What're you talkin', man?'

Carnes slammed his hand against the steering wheel and shouted, 'You raped her, you fuckin' Polack sleaze! You raped her, then you fucked her up the ass!'

Milchuk sat stunned for a few beats. Then he said, 'Fuck I did! Hey!' He turned to Penner. 'That what this is alla 'bout, man? I didn't do nothin' to Lori. I been goin' out with her six months. This is fuckin' nuts! We been talkin' 'bout gettin' married, even!'

Penner said, with unconvincing sternness, 'Take it easy,' and poked him with the muzzle of the gun as a reminder. He felt queasy, nauseated.

'It was Lori's old man hired you guys, wasn't it?' said Milchuk. 'It hadda be. Look, I swear to fucking Christ, I didn't do nothin'! It's her old man. He's against me from the start, he told me he didn't want me sniffin' around her.'

'Guess you shoulda listened, huh?' said Carnes brightly.

'I didn't do nothin', man. Swear to God! All ya gotta do is to give Lori a call.'

'Maybe we should,' said Penner, trying to hide a certain eagerness.

'Yeah!' said Milchuk. 'Call her, for Christ's sake.'

'You musta done somethin',' Carnes said to Milchuk. 'Maybe all you are's a pain in the ass to McDonough. But a guy like you, you musta done somethin'.'

Milchuk put both hands to his face. 'This is crazy,' he said into his palms. 'Crazy!'

'How you figure?' Penner asked of Carnes. 'You don't even know the guy!'

'Oh, I know him,' Carnes said. 'He pals around with the Vitarellis down in Providence. He's a wise guy. You better believe the son of a bitch got blood on his hands. Whackin' him out ain't no worse than steppin' on a cockroach.'

'He's with the Mob?' Penner said, incredulous. 'We're supposed to hit a Mob guy?'

Without reducing his speed, Carnes swung onto a gravel road that wound away through low thickets, the leaves mostly gone to brown. The Caddy soared over bumps and ruts, landing heavily, its rear end slewing. Black branches slapped at the windows.

'Nobody said anythin 'bout hitting a Mob guy!' Penner yelled.

Milchuk gripped the front seat with both hands and began talking, half-sobbing the words, offering a string of temptations and threats of Vitarelli vengeance, like a strange, primitive prayer. Carnes' only response was to increase their speed. The Caddy seemed to be trying to lift off, to go sailing up into the sky of broken silver light and black clouds. The world beyond the side windows was a chaos of tearing leaves and clawing twigs.

'So whaddaya wanna do, man?' Carnes shouted. 'Wanna let him go?'

'Yes!' said Penner. 'Fuckin' A, I wanna let him go!'

'Okay, say we do it, say we let him go. Know what happens next? The son of a bitch goes to the Vitarellis, he says, Chuckie, man, Chuckie, he says, that fucker McDonough tried to put a hit on me, and Chuckie says, we can't have that shit, now can we, and he sends his people up to Southie. And you know who gets it? Not McDonough. Nosir! It's you and me, buddy! We wind up on a beach somewheres with our dicks hangin' out our mouths.' He swerved the Caddy around a tight bend. 'We're fuckin' committed, man!'

The thickets gave way abruptly to a grassy clearing centred by the grey-shingled ruin of a one-storey house, nearly roofless, with a shattered door and glassless windows; it looked out over the Atlantic toward a spit that rose at its seaward end into a pine-fringed pinnacle standing up some sixty feet above the water, the highest point of land in sight. Carnes brought the Caddy to a shuddering halt and switched off the engine. The rush of silence hurt Penner's head. Carnes turned to them, resting his elbow on the seat. A silver-plated gun dangled from his hand. He grinned at Milchuk.

'Party time,' he said.

Milchuk met his eyes for a second, then hung his head. All thought of resistance seemed to have left him.

'Outside,' Carnes told him, and without hesitation or objection, he opened the door and climbed out. He still clung to his briefcase, still held it against his chest. His face slack, eyes empty, he stared off over the water.

Penner slid out after him. After so many hours in the car, standing in the open disoriented him. The world was too wide, too full of light and colour; the soughing sounds of the waves and the seething wind; he could not gather it all inside him. He kept his gun trained on Milchuk.

'Drop the gun,' said Carnes, coming up behind him.

Startled, Penner made to turn but stopped when the muzzle of Carnes' automatic jabbed into the side of his neck. He let the gun fall, and Carnes kicked him in the back of the legs, driving him to his knees in the tall grass. Another kick, this directly on the tailbone, sent him onto his stomach.

'Still curious 'bout why McDonough paid so much, are ya?' said Carnes. 'Want me to fill ya in on the programme, motherfucker?'

Penner rolled onto his back. Carnes straddled him, his feet planted on either side of Penner's thighs, automatic aimed at his chest. Milchuk, whom he could not see, was somewhere behind him.

'This here's gonna be a doubleheader, pal,' said Carnes gloatingly. 'Man's payin' me to whack you out, too. Betcha can't guess why.'

Penner was afraid, but the fear was dim. Looking up at the muzzle of the gun, feeling the stony shoulder of earth beneath him, seeing the dark clouds wheeling like great slow wings above Carnes, he felt oddly peaceful, even sleepy. It would be all right, he thought, to close his eyes.

'It's your fuckin' old lady,' said Carnes. 'Her and McDonough been bumpin' bellies for a year now. Whaddaya think about that, shithead?'

The news surprised Penner. And hurt him. Yet because of the numb drowsiness that had stolen over him, the hurt was slight, as if a heavy stone had been placed on his chest, making him sink deeper into the cold grass, closer to sleep. Carnes seemed disappointed in his reaction. His eyes darted elsewhere – toward Milchuk, probably – then he looked down again at Penner, a nerve jumping in his cheek.

'McDonough tells me she can't get enough of his dick,'

Carnes said. 'Says her pussy's like twitchin' alla time. Says he's gonna marry the bitch.'

Penner did not believe that McDonough would have confided in Carnes, but the words opened him to visions of Barbara and McDonough in bed, to the bitter comprehension that this was everything she had wanted, a man of wealth and power. He should have anticipated her choice, he should have known that McDonough would never have concocted such a simple scheme as the one he had laid out. McDonough had seen a way to kill two birds with one stone and had orchestrated it beautifully, and Penner's sadness was a reaction not only to the betrayal, but to how easily he had been taken in.

'Man, I can't tell ya how good this feels. I fuckin' cannot tell ya!' Carnes let out a lilting, girlish laugh. 'I been wantin' to do you since I was fifteen fuckin' years old. Just goes to show, man. Don't never give up on your dreams.' He took a shooter's grip on the automatic. 'Wanna gimme some more bullshit 'bout the Sox? C'mon, man! Let's hear it! Y'ain't gonna have no chances after this.'

Penner was unable to speak, and Carnes said, 'What's your problem, fuckhead! This is your big moment. Talk to me!' And kicked him again.

The kick dislodged something in Penner, tipped over a little reservoir of loathing that for the moment washed away fear.

'You're fucking ridiculous!' he said. 'Both you and the fuckin' Sox!'

Muscles twitched in Carnes' jaw, that weaselly face jittering with hate. 'I am gonna kill you a piece at a time,' he said.

Something black and flat and angular – Milchuk's briefcase, Penner later realized – smacked into Carnes' gun hand and knocked it aside. The automatic discharged, the round burrowed into the earth close to Penner's cheek, spraying him with dirt. Carnes remained straddling him, and Penner was not sure if he had actually thought of kicking Carnes or if the movement of his leg had been a startled reaction to the gunshot; whatever the case, his foot drove hard into Carnes' balls. He screamed and dropped to his knees, then pitched onto his side, curling up around the pain. When Penner threw a wild punch that glanced off his shoulder, Carnes rolled away and tried to bring his gun to bear; but he was still in too much pain to function. Sucking for air, his hand trembling violently. His eyes were weepy and narrowed to slits. With his Red Sox cap and the tears, he looked like a savage, terrified little boy. Then he puked, heaving up a geyser of coffee and bad fluids.

Penner saw his own gun gleaming in the grass. Luminous with fright, he made a dive for it and came up firing. The first shot half-deafened him, ranging off somewhere into the sky, but the second hammered a red nailhead into Carnes' jacket just below the collar. The third blew bloody fragments from his lower jaw. There was no need for another.

Penner came unsteadily to his feet. His ears were ringing, his legs shaking. He gazed out over the thickets, the dry, turned leaves rippling with the same agitated motion as the chop on the water. The emptiness of the place assaulted him, and after a second, moved by a perverse need to connect with something, he staggered over to the body. The sight of the jellied eyes and ruined jaw sickened him at first and hurt his heart; but then, thinking of the man, he was furious. Carnes' Red Sox cap had fallen off, and Penner gave it a vicious kick.

Then he remembered Milchuk. He went quickly along the edge of the clearing, peering into the thickets. It was doubtful Milchuk would contact the police, but he would certainly have a talk with the Vitarellis.

After a moment he spotted him. Surfacing among the camouflage colours of the bushes. Running fast. Hurdling a fallen log. Zig-zagging around some obstacle. Moving like a halfback in the broken field. Penner might have admired his athleticism had it not been so futile – Milchuk was headed not for the highway but toward the spit of land. He must not be able to see it because of the low ground over which he was running, the bushes and a few trees obscuring his view; any moment now, however, he would realize he was trapped, that he would have to make his way along the shore. Because the spit formed the eastern enclosure of a bay, because the bay was cut back behind the clearing, the shore line lay close to where Penner was standing. He should be able to catch up to Milchuk without much difficulty.

He started toward the shore line west of the spit. He ran

easily, confidently, with what seemed to him astonishing grace, turning sideways to avoid the clutches of twigs and branches. Not a misstep, not a stumble. He felt charged by this simple physical competence. It was as if the pure necessity of the moment had invoked a corresponding purity in him, eliminating all clumsiness, fear and hesitancy. But on reaching the shore he saw no sign of Milchuk, and once again he became confused.

Where the hell was he?

The sun broke through again, turning the water a steely blue, and Penner, scanning the shore line, had to shade his eyes. Milchuk had outsmarted him, he thought, he had doubled back to the clearing. But then he saw him among the pines that sprouted from the rocky point at the seaward end of the spit. Apparently, he had not seen Penner. He was just standing there, looking back toward the clearing.

Penner was baffled. What could he have in mind? Did he intend to swim for it? If so, because of Penner's position and the cut-back curve of the shoreline, he would have to swim about a mile in freezing, choppy water to the opposite side of the bay – where there was a motel and some houses – in order to ensure his safety. A mile. That would take . . . what? At least an hour. Hypothermia would set in before then. And yet the man was obviously in excellent shape. Maybe he could make it.

But if that was the plan, why didn't he just dive in?

It took a minute's consideration before Penner understood Milchuk's tactic. From his vantage, Milchuk could see not only the clearing and the house, but also the dirt road. Perhaps even the highway itself. It would be impossible for Penner to pretend to leave; in order to persuade Milchuk to abandon his position, he would have to drive a considerable distance away, far enough to allow Milchuk to escape along the shore. If he were to try and take Milchuk on the spit, Milchuk would risk the swim; he would likely have decided how closely he would let Penner approach, and once that line was crossed, he would swim for the far side, never permitting his pursuer within pistol range. Very smooth, very economical.

The spiritual vacuum that the shooting had created in Penner was losing its integrity, filling in with vengeful thoughts concerning McDonough and Barbara, fearful thoughts of the

Mafia, the police, God's justice. The idea of lying down somewhere and yielding up his fate to the operations of chance was more than a little inviting. The inside of his head felt hot and agitated, as if his thoughts were whirling like dust, like excited atoms. But this was no time, he told himself, for his usual collapse, his usual fuck-up, and he forced himself to focus on the matter at hand.

He would not be able to kill Milchuk – he admitted to that – and eventually the Vitarellis would learn what had happened. That being the case, he could not risk returning to Southie. Well, that was okay. He had his fifty grand. And he would have Carnes' share as well. It would be a bloody business, tugging off Carne's money belt. Have to look at those eyes again, that marbled cross-section of gore and splintered bone. But he could manage it. A hundred grand would buy a lot of future in the right country. The thing to do now would be to neutralize Milchuk as much as possible so as to secure a chance at freedom. He'd ditch the Caddy in Hyannis, catch a bus into Boston. Fly out of Logan, maybe. Or buy a junker and drive south. Whatever. He could work the details out later. In the meantime, there was a flaw in Milchuk's plan . . . or if not a flaw, an inherent softness that he might be able to exploit. He pulled out his handkerchief, wiped off the gun with meticulous care, then wadding the handkerchief in his palm to prevent further contact with his skin, he gripped the gun by the muzzle and set out walking toward the spit. He called to Milchuk as he went, not wanting to startle him into a hasty dive. 'Hey!' he shouted. 'Don't be afraid, man! It's over! It's okay!'

Milchuk started down the slope of the point toward the water; he was shrugging off his overcoat.

Penner paused at the landward end of the spit; the opposite end was thirty, maybe forty yards distant.

'It's okay, man,' he yelled. 'Here! Look!' He waved the gun back and forth above his head. 'I'm leaving this for ya! Leaving it right here!'

Milchuk stopped his descent and rested in a crouch halfway down the slope, peering at him.

Penner tossed the gun out onto the spit, surreptitiously

pocketed his handkerchief. 'I'm outta here, okay? No more shooting! No more bullshit!'

Being unarmed made him feel exposed, but he knew that Milchuk would wait until he had retreated more than a pistol shot away before going after the gun. More likely he'd wait until he watched the Caddy pull down the highway. There would be plenty of time for Penner to make it back to the clearing and collect Carnes' money and his gun.

'You hear me?' Penner called.

A beam of sunlight fingered Milchuk among the stones, accentuating his isolation and the furtiveness of his pose. The sight caught at Penner. He could not help but sympathize with the man.

'If you hear me,' he called, 'gimme a sign! Okay?'

Milchuk remained motionless for a bit, then – reluctantly, it seemed – lifted his right arm as if in salute; after a second he let it fall back heavily. The sun withdrew behind the clouds, and he was reduced to a dark primitive form hunkered among the rocks. Behind him, toiling masses of black and silver muscled towards the top of the sky, and the sea, dark as iron, moved in a vast, uneasy swell, as if the entire world had been nudged sideways.

'Okay, I'm outta here!' Penner half-turned away, and then, moved by a fleeting morality, a vestigial remnant of innocence, he shouted, 'Hey! Good luck!' It amazed him, the sincerity he had felt while saying it.

Penner was more than satisfied with his performance during the phone call to the police. He had exhibited, he thought, just the right mix of paranoia and breathless excitement.

'The little guy knew the shooter,' he'd said. 'I heard him say the bastard's name, anyway. Millbuck, Mil ... something. I don't know. He might still be around there, man, you hurry.'

After hanging up, he decided to get some coffee before hitting the highway, but as he stepped around the corner from the pay phone into the dining area of the roadside McDonald's, through the window he saw a green Buick pull up behind the Caddy, blocking it in. Two men climbed out of the Buick. Beefy, florid men, one – the taller – balding, with a fringe of dark hair curling low on his neck, and the other with straight red hair falling over his collar. Irish-looking men. Cops, was Penner's first thought; they must have traced the call. But then he realized that their hair was too long, their suits too expensive. They peered in the windows of the Caddy, at the hood, exchanged a few words; then the red-haired man slid back into the Buick and drove it into a parking space. The other made for the front door.

A weight shifted loosely in Penner's bowels. Christ, he should have figured! McDonough could not allow a loose cannon like Carnes to jeopardize his position. Carnes had likely been instructed to drive somewhere after the job, to follow some specific course; these men had been set to meet him, and – no doubt – to dispatch him and reclaim the money. The advance payment made perfect sense now.

Wrong again, Carnes.

We're talking a tripleheader here.

Beautiful, thought Penner. This was McDonough functioning at the peak of his political acumen. Minimal involvement of his people. Minimal risk to himself. A neat system of checks and balances. Snick, snick, snick. Three problems solved, all's right with the world, and the great man could look forward to a lubricious future with the former Mrs Penner. After an appropriate period of mourning, of course. What a player he was! What a master of the fucking game!

Penner retreated around the corner. The primary colours of the walls were making his skin hot, and the merry babble of the diners generated a fuming commotion inside his head. Hostages, he thought. Grab somebody off line, drag them into the parking lot. The idea had an outlaw charm that appealed to the absurdist witness who seemed to be sharing the experience with him. Mad Dog Penner. But instead, he ducked into the bathroom. The windows were high and narrow. A skinny dwarf might have managed an escape. He flattened against the wall behind the door, holding Carnes' gun muzzle-up beside his cheek. The white tiles were vibrating. The stainless-steel fixtures glowed like treasure. Every living gleam was a splinter in his eye. His thoughts were singing. Oh, Jesus Jesus Jesus please! What if some cute little tyke comes in to take his first solo piss, and you splatter the wee fuck's brains all over the hand drier? God, let me live, I'll say a billion Hail Marys, I swear it, right here in this holy nowhere of a bathroom I'm opening myself up to You, this is one of Your chosen speaking, an Irishman, a former acolyte, as sorry a lamb as ever strayed, and I'm begging, no, I'm fucking demanding a religious experience!

The big, balding man pushed into the bathroom, his entrance accompanied by a venting of happy chatter from the restaurant, and said, 'Shit' under his breath. He bent with hands on knees to peak beneath the doors of the stalls, exposing the back of his head. Joy surged in Penner's heart on seeing that tonsured bull's-eye, and as the man straightened, he stepped forward and smashed the gun butt against his scalp. The blow made a plush, heavy sound that alarmed him. But he struck again as the man toppled, rills of blood webbing the patch of mottled skin, and then dropped to his knees beside the man and struck a third time. He remained kneeling there with gun held high, like a child who has hit a spider with a shoe and is watching to see if its legs wiggle. More blood was pooling inside the man's ear. Penner's mind went skittering, unable to seize upon a thought. The white tiles seemed to be exuding a thick silence.

The red-haired man, he said to himself at last; he would exercise extreme caution when his friend failed to reappear. Nothing to be gained by waiting for him. He, Penner, would have to balls it out. Take a stroll off into Ronald McDonaldland and see what we can see. Tra la. He laughed, and the hollowness of the sound sobered him a touch, heightened his alertness. He caught the handle of a stall door and pulled himself up.

'Stay right there,' he told the balding man, and gave him a wink. 'One false move, and I'll hafta plug ya.'

He squared his shoulders, took a deep breath. Maybe they were still looking for Carnes, maybe the red-haired man wouldn't recognize him. Who could say on a day like today? He stuffed the gun into the pocket of his windbreaker. He felt giddy, but the giddiness acted as a restorative, a nervy drug that encouraged him.

'Yoicks,' he said. 'Tally ho!'

It was a fabulous day in Ronald McDonaldland. The sun had come out, the restaurant was thronged with golden light and pleasant smells, young secretaries and construction workers were stuffing Egg McMuffins into their mouths, and the red-haired man was just turning from the line of waiting customers when Penner stepped up and let him feel the gun in his side.

'Why don't we take a walk outside?' Penner said. 'I mean that's what *I'd* like to do. But I don't really care what happens, so you choose, okay?'

The man scarcely hesitated before obeying. The act of a professional, thought Penner, submitting by course to the rule of might. Beautiful.

They pushed through the glass doors out into the sun. The freshness and brightness of the air infected Penner, making him incredibly light and easy on his feet. Life was everywhere in him, plumping out all his hollows. The poor dead, he said to himself, not to have this, not to know. He felt like weeping, like singing.

'What's the story here?' he asked, screwing the muzzle of Carnes' gun deeper into the man's side. 'How'd you find me?'

'You kiddin'?' said the man. 'You drivin' a Cadillac with vanity plates and a pair of red socks painted on the hood, you think you're hard to find?'

His disdainful attitude unnerved Penner.

'Where's Carnes?' the man asked.

'Ah, well, now,' Penner said blithely. 'That's one for the philosophers, that is.'

He forced the man to deposit his gun in the dumpster at the side of the building. The man's doughy face registered an almost comical degree of worry, and Penner considered telling him everything was going to work out, but realized that the man would not believe him. Instead, he asked for the keys to the Buick.

'Beautiful,' he said, accepting the keys, and pushed the man forward, moving through the asphalt dimension of the parking lot, the humming of traffic, like the dark general noise of life itself.

He had the man sit on the floor of the front seat with his back to the engine, his head wedged under the dash, legs stuck between the seat and the side panel. A tight fit, but the man managed it. It pleased Penner to have devised this clever prison.

'Comfy?' he asked.

The man gave no reply.

Driving also pleased Penner. In the golden light the cars shone with the lustre of gemstones under water, and he cut in and out of traffic with the flash of a Petty, a Yarborough. Lapping the field in the Penner 500.

What to do, what to do, he thought.

South on I-93 to New York, Washington, Miami and points beyond?

Brazil?

Just the place, so they said, for a man with a gun on the run.

He let the rhyme sing inside his head for a minute or so, liking the erratic spin it lent to all his thoughts. He switched on the radio. He heard the amplified crack of a bat and brash music. Then a man's voice blatted from the speaker, saying that his guest was Mike Greenwell of the Boston Red Sox. Penner had to laugh.

'What the fuck's goin' on?' asked the red-haired man; he crooked his head to the side so he could get a look at Penner.

'You gotta name?' Penner asked.

'Yeah . . . Tom,' said the man with bad grace.

'You a Sox fan, Tom?'

The man said, 'What?'

'I said you a Sox fan? It's not a trick question.'

Silence.

'Know what I think about the Sox, Tom? They're God's baseball joke. A metaphor for man's futility. The Sisyphus of the American League East.'

The man's face showed no sign of comprehension. His eyes were flat and regarding. A serpent, Penner thought. There is a serpent in my garden.

'Where's McDonough?' Penner asked him.

More silence.

'Now you don't *have* to answer.' Penner jabbed the muzzle of the gun into the man's belly. 'But I just bet he's waiting for a call from you.'

'Home,' said the man. 'He's at home.'

'Anyone with him? A woman, maybe?'

'How the fuck should I know?'

'Right,' said Penner, pulling back the gun. 'How, indeed?'

But Penner knew his Barbara. She would be with McDonough. She was part of this. And she would be able to live with it, to make that kind of moral trade-off. He experienced a hiccup of emotion and pictured pale limbs asprawl, a gory tunnel burrowed into a shock of white hair. Could he really waste them? he wondered. How would it feel? Amazingly enough, it had felt pretty damn good so far. Since blood from the ears was not considered a healthy sign, he figured his score for the day was two. Four would not be a problem.

But, after all, it would be nice to survive this. As Barbara herself was wont to say, the best revenge was living well.

He had not, he realized, been considering the prospect of survival until this moment. Not really. Not with the calculation you needed to weigh the possibilities, nor with the calmness necessary to believe in them.

On the radio Mike Greenwell was saying there was no reason to panic, they just had to take 'em one at a time.

Sound philosophy, Mike. Words to live by.

A pick-up truck roared past, somebody screamed a curse at Penner. He noticed that he had let the speed of the car drop to thirty.

Brazil.

Take the money and run. What could be the problem with that?

He caught movement out of the corner of his eye. Ol' Tom shifting about ever so slightly, preparing to try and kick the gun. Penner couldn't much blame him for trying – unless he were a cockeyed optimist, he could not like his chances very much. He had proved a surly bastard, had Tom, and Penner elected not to extend him a warning.

The problem, he decided, making an effort to concentrate, the problem was in himself. In the Penner he always ended up being, no matter how promising the circumstance. Sad, sorrowful Penner. Christ the Penner inevitably borne toward some unimportant Passion.

But that, he thought, was the old Penner, the bumbling, good-hearted villain, the con man with a conscience.

Who was he now? he wondered. Was this Penner any better off?

Hot, he thought. Excessive heating of the face and palms seemed the primary characteristic of this particular Penner. A few aches and pains, a desire for an end to all this. Otherwise, very little to report. Pared down to almost nothing.

'You can't do better than your best,' Mike Greenwell was saying. 'You give a hundred and fifty per cent, you got no reason to hang your head.'

Amen to that, Mike.

The red-haired man had worked a leg up onto the seat, and Penner thought a confrontation might be just the way to decide such a momentous issue as one's future or the lack thereof. Let him make his play. If Penner won, he would do . . . something. He'd figure out exactly what later.

Despite the indecisiveness of this resolution, Penner felt there was a fine weight to it, an Irish logic that defied interpretation. To make things interesting, he boosted their speed to 50. Then to 60. He kept pressing his foot harder on the gas, watching the needle climb, feeling that the speed was the result of him being pulled toward something. There was a curve coming up about a mile ahead, and he wondered how it would be just to keep going straight when he reached it. To go arcing up into stormlight over the water, into the golden glare and big-muscled clouds. And then down.

Do I hear any objections? he asked himself.

Fucking A, I object, he anwered. Fuck all that remorseful Catholic bullshit! This is your goddamn life, Penner. This is the Hundred-Thousand-Dollar Challenge! Are you man enough to accept it?

'You play a hunnerd and sixty-two games,' Mike Greenwell said, 'you gotta expect a few bad days. But we'll be there in the end.'

Dead on, Mike me boyo!

Penner could tell that the red-haired man was waiting for him to look away, to do something that would give him an advantage; but that was no longer a problem. The game was in hand, and all the signs were auspicious. Light was flowing around the car, fountaining up behind in an incandescent wake, and the green world was blurring with their momentum, and the corners of Penner's mind were sharp and bright as never before.

Life hot as a magnesium flare, as Brazil, as freedom and the future, all the love in him sizzling high. He boosted their speed to 65 as they approached the curve, enjoying the feeling of being on the edge.

'Hey!' said the red-haired man; he had curled his fingers about the door handle, his eyes were round with fright. 'Hey, you're going too fast!'

The old Penner might have lied, made a gentle promise, offered hope or perhaps spoken persuasively of the afterlife. But this was not the old Penner.

Far from it.

'Not me,' said the Wild Blue-Eyed Penner, lifting his gun. As the Caddy swung into the sweet gravity of the curve, he trained the gun at his enemy's heart, seeing only an interruption of the light, a dark keyhole set in a golden door. The thunderous report and the kick made it seem that the man's life had travelled up his arm, charging him with a fierce new spirit. He took in the sight without flinching. Blood as red as paper roses. The body with its slack, twisted limbs looked larger than before, more solid, as if death were in essence a kind of important stillness. He stared at it until he was completely at ease. A smile sliced his face, the sort of intent expression that comes from peering into strong sunlight or hard weather. He thought about the disposal problem, a passport, opportunities for tropical investment. He spun the tuning dial, found an easy listening station. Paul Simon was going to Graceland, and he was going with him.

'Not me,' said Penner the Implacable, the Conscienceless, the Almost Nothing Man. 'I'm just hitting my stride.'

THE SUN SPIDER

. . . In Africa's Namib Desert, one of the most hostile environments on the face of the earth, lives a creature known as the sun spider. Its body is furred pale gold, the exact colour of the sand beneath which it burrows in search of its prey, disturbing scarcely a grain in its passage. It emerges from hiding only to snatch its prey, and were you to look directly at it from an inch away, you might never notice its presence. Nature is an efficient process, tending to repeat elegant solutions to the problem of survival in such terrible places. Thus, if – as I posit – particulate life exists upon the Sun, I would not be startled to learn it has adopted a similar form.

Reynolds Dulambre, *Alchemical Diaries*

1
Carolyn

My husband Reynolds and I arrived on Helios Station following four years in the Namib, where he had delivered himself of the *Diaries*, including the controversial Solar Equations, and where I had become adept in the uses of boredom. We were met at the docking arm by the administrator of the Physics Section, Dr Davis Brent, who escorted us to a reception given in Reynolds' honour, held in one of the pleasure domes that blistered the skin of the station. Even had I been unaware that Brent was one of Reynolds' chief detractors, I would have known the two of them for adversaries: in manner and physicality, they were total opposites, like cobra and mongoose. Brent was pudgy, of medium stature, with a receding hairline, and dressed in a drab standard-issue jumpsuit. Reynolds – at thirty-seven, only two years younger – might have been ten years his junior. He was tall and lean, with chestnut hair that fell to the shoulders of his cape, and possessed of that craggy nobility of feature one associates with a Shakespearian lead. Both were on their best behaviour, but they could barely manage civility, and so it was quite a relief when we reached the dome and were swept away into a crowd of admiring techs and scientists.

Helios Station orbited the south pole of the Sun, and through the ports I had a view of a docking arm to which several of the boxy ships that journeyed into the coronosphere were moored. Leaving Reynolds to be lionized, I lounged beside one of the ports and gazed toward Earth, pretending I was celebrating Nation Day in Abidjan rather than enduring this gathering of particle-pushers and inductive reasoners, most of whom were gawking at Reynolds, perhaps hoping he would live up to his reputation and perform a drugged collapse or start a fight. I watched him and Brent talking. Brent's body language was toadying, subservient, like that of a dog trying to curry favour; he would clasp his hands and tip his head to the side when making some point, as if begging his master not to strike him. Reynolds stood motionless, arms folded across his chest.

At one point Brent said, 'I can't see what purpose you hope to achieve in beaming protons into coronal holes,' and Reynolds, in his most supercilious tone, responded by saying that he was merely poking about in the weeds with a long stick.

I was unable to hear the next exchange, but then I did hear Brent say, 'That may be, but I don't think you understand the openness of our community. The barriers you've erected around your research go against the spirit, the . . .'

'All my goddamned life,' Reynolds cut in, broadcasting in a stagey baritone, 'I've been harassed by little men. Men who've carved out some cosy academic niche by footnoting my work and then decrying it. Mousy little bastards like you. And that's why I maintain my privacy . . . to keep the mice from nesting in my papers.'

He strode off toward the refreshment table, leaving Brent smiling at everyone, trying to show that he had not been affected by the insult. A slim brunette attached herself to Reynolds, engaging him in conversation. He illustrated his points with florid gestures, leaning over her, looking as if he were about to enfold her in his cape, and not long afterward they made a discreet exit.

Compared to Reynolds' usual public behaviour, this was a fairly restrained display, but sufficient to make the gathering forget my presence. I sipped a drink, listening to the chatter, feeling no sense of betrayal. I was used to Reynolds' infidelities, and, indeed, I had come to thrive on them. I was grateful he had found his brunette. Though our marriage was not devoid of the sensual, most of our encounters were ritual in nature, and after four years of isolation in the desert, I needed the emotional sustenance of a lover. Helios would, I believed, provide an ample supply.

Shortly after Reynolds had gone, Brent came over to the port, and to my amazement, he attempted to pick me up. It was one of the most inept seductions to which I have ever been subject. He contrived to touch me time and again as if by accident, and complimented me several times on the largeness of my eyes. I managed to turn the conversation into harmless channels, and he got off into politics, a topic on which he considered himself expert.

'My essential political philosophy,' he said, 'derives from a story by one of the masters of twentieth-century speculative fiction. In the story, a man sends his mind into the future and finds himself in a utopian setting, a greensward surrounded by white buildings, with handsome men and beautiful women strolling everywhere . . .'

I cannot recall how long I listened to him, to what soon became apparent as a ludicrous Libertarian fantasy, before bursting into laughter. Brent looked confused by my reaction, but then masked confusion by joining in my laughter. 'Ah, Carolyn,' he said. 'I had you going there, didn't I? You thought I was serious!'

I took pity on him. He was only a sad little man with an inflated self-opinion; and, too, I had been told that he was in danger of losing his administrative post. I spent the best part of an hour in making him feel important; then, scraping him off, I went in search of a more suitable companion.

My first lover on Helios Station, a young particle physicist named Thom, proved overweening in his affections. The sound of my name seemed to transport him; often he would lift his head and say, 'Carolyn, Carolyn,' as if by doing this he might capture my essence. I found him absurd, but I was starved for attention, and though I could not reciprocate in kind, I was delighted in being the object of his single-mindedness. We would meet each day in one of the pleasure domes, dance to drift, and drink paradisiacs – I developed quite a fondness for Amouristes – and then retire to a private chamber, there to make love and watch the sunships return from their fiery journeys. It was Thom's dream to be assigned someday to a sunship, and he would rhapsodize on the glories attendant upon swooping down through layers of burning gases. His fixation with the scientific adventure eventually caused me to break off the affair. Years of exposure to Reynolds' work had armoured me against any good opinion of science, and further I did not want to be reminded of my proximity to the Sun: sometimes I imagined I could hear it hissing, roaring, and feel its flames tonguing the metal walls, preparing to do us to a crisp with a single lick.

By detailing my infidelity, I am not trying to characterize my marriage as loveless. I loved Reynolds, though my affections had waned somewhat. And he loved me in his own way. Prior to our wedding, he had announced that he intended our union to be 'a marriage of souls'. But this was no passionate outcry, rather a statement of scientific intent. He believed in souls, believed they were the absolute expression of a life, a quality that pervaded every particle of matter and gave rise to the lesser expressions of personality and physicality. His search for particulate life upon the Sun was essentially an attempt to isolate and communicate with the anima, and the 'marriage of souls' was for him the logical goal of twenty-first-century physics. It occurs to me now that this search may have been his sole means of voicing his deepest emotions, and it was our core problem that I thought he would someday love me in a way that would satisfy me, whereas he felt my satisfaction could be guaranteed by the application of scientific method.

To further define our relationship, I should mention that he once wrote me that the 'impassive, vaguely oriental beauty' of my face reminded him of 'those serene countenances used to depict the solar disc on ancient sailing charts'. Again, this was not the imagery of passion: he considered this likeness a talisman, a lucky charm. He was a magical thinker, perceiving himself as more akin to the alchemists than to his peers, and like the alchemists, he gave credence to the power of similarities. Whenever he made love to me, he was therefore making love to the Sun. To the great detriment of our marriage, every beautiful woman became for him the Sun, and thus a potential tool for use in his rituals. Given his enormous ego, it would have been out of character for him to have been faithful, and had he not utilized sex as a concentrative ritual, I am certain he would have invented another excuse for infidelity. And, I suppose, I would have had to contrive some other justification for my own.

During those first months I was indiscriminate in my choice of lovers, entering into affairs with both techs and a number of Reynolds' colleagues. Reynolds himself was no more discriminating, and our lives took separate paths. Rarely did I spend a night in our apartment, and I paid no attention whatsoever to Reynolds' work. But then one afternoon as I lay with my latest lover in the private chamber of a pleasure dome, the door slid open and in walked Reynolds. My lover – a tech whose name eludes me – leaped up and began struggling into his clothes, apologizing all the while. I shouted at Reynolds, railed at him. What right did he have to humiliate me this way? I had never burst in on him and his whores, had I? Imperturbable, he stared at me, and after the tech had scurried out, he continued to stare, letting me exhaust my anger. At last, breathless, I sat glaring at him, still angry, yet also feeling a measure of guilt ... not relating to my affair, but to the fact that I had become pregnant as a result of my last encounter with Reynolds. We had tried for years to have a child, and despite knowing how important a child would be to him, I had put off the announcement. I was no longer confident of his capacity for fatherhood.

'I'm sorry about this.' He waved at the bed. 'It was urgent I see you, and I didn't think.'

The apology was uncharacteristic, and my surprise at it drained away the dregs of anger. 'What is it?' I asked.

Contrary emotions played over his face. 'I've got him,' he said.

I knew what he was referring to: he always personified the object of his search, although before too long he began calling it 'the Spider'. I was happy for his success, but for some reason it had made me a little afraid, and I was at a loss for words.

'Do you want to see him?' He sat beside me. 'He's imaged in one of the tanks.'

I nodded.

I was sure he was going to embrace me. I could see in his face the desire to break down the barriers we had erected, and I imagined now his work was done, we would be as close as we had once hoped, that honesty and love would finally have their day. But the moment passed, and his face hardened. He stood and paced the length of the chamber. Then he whirled around, hammered a fist into his palm, and with all the passion he had been unable to direct toward me, he said, 'I've got him!'

I had been watching him for over a week without knowing it: a large low-temperature area shifting about in a coronal hole. It was only by chance that I recognized him; I inadvertently nudged the colour controls of a holo tank, and brought part of the low-temperature area into focus, revealing a many-armed ovoid of constantly changing primary hues, the arms attenuating and vanishing: I have observed some of these arms reach ten thousand miles in length, and I have no idea what limits apply to their size. He consists essentially of an inner complex of ultracold neutrons enclosed by an intense magnetic field. Lately it has occurred to me that certain of the coronal holes may be no more than the attitude of his movements. Aside from these few facts and guesses, he remains a mystery, and I have begun to suspect that no matter how many elements of his nature are disclosed, he will always remain so.

Reynolds Dulambre, *Collected Notes*

2
Reynolds

Brent's face faded in on the screen, his features composed into one of those fawning smiles. 'Ah, Reynolds,' he said. 'Glad I caught you.'

'I'm busy,' I snapped, reaching for the off switch.

'Reynolds!'

His desperate tone caught my attention.

'I need to talk to you,' he said. 'A matter of some importance.'

I gave an amused sniff. 'I doubt that.'

'Oh, but it is . . . to both of us.'

An oily note had crept into his voice, and I lost patience. 'I'm going to switch off, Brent. Do you want to say goodbye, or should I just cut you off in mid-sentence?'

'I'm warning you, Reynolds!'

'Warning me? I'm all aflutter, Brent. Are you planning to assault me?'

His face grew flushed. 'I'm sick of your arrogance!' he shouted. 'Who the hell are you to talk down to me? At least I'm productive . . . you haven't done any work for weeks!'

I started to ask how he knew that, but then realized he could have monitored my energy usage via the station computers.

'You think . . .' he began, but at that point I did cut him off and turned back to the image of the Spider floating in the holo tank, its arms weaving a slow dance. I had never believed he was more than dreams, vague magical images, the grandfather wizard trapped in flame, in golden light, in the heart of power. I'd hoped, I'd wanted to believe. But I hadn't been able to accept his reality until I came to Helios, and the dreams grew stronger. Even now I wondered if belief was merely an extension of madness. I have never doubted the efficacy of madness: it is my constant, my reference in chaos.

The first dream had come when I was . . . what? Eleven, twelve? No older. My father had been chasing me, and I had sought refuge in a cave of golden light, a mist of pulsing, shifting light that contained a voice I could not quite hear: it was too vast to hear. I was merely a word upon its tongue, and there had been other words aligned around me, words I needed to understand or else I would be cast out from the light. The Solar Equations – which seemed to have been visited upon me rather than a product of reason – embodied the shiftings, the mysterious principles I had sensed in the golden light, hinted at the arcane processes, the potential for union and dissolution that I had apprehended in every dream. Each time I looked at them, I felt tremors in my flesh, my spirit, as if signalling the onset of a profound change, and . . .

The beeper sounded again, doubtless another call from Brent, and I ignored it. I turned to the readout from the particle traps monitored by the station computers. When I had discovered that the proton bursts being emitted from the Spider's coronal hole were patterned – coded, I'm tempted to say – I had been elated, especially considering that a study of these bursts inspired me to create several addenda to the Equations. They had still been fragmentary, however, and I'd had the notion that I would have to get closer to the Spider in order to complete them . . . perhaps join one of the flights into the coronosphere. My next reaction had been fear. I had realized it was possible the Spider's control was such that these bursts were living artefacts, structural components that maintained a tenuous connection with the rest of his body. If so, then the computers, the entire station, might be under his scrutiny . . . if not his control. Efforts to prove the truth of this had been inconclusive, but this inconclusiveness was in itself an affirmative answer: the computers were not capable of evasion, and it had been obvious that evasiveness was at work here.

The beeper broke off, and I began to ask myself questions. I had been labouring under the assumption that the Spider had in some way summoned me, but now an alternate scenario presented itself. Could I have stirred him to life? I had beamed protons into the coronal holes, hadn't I? Could I have educated some dumb thing . . . or perhaps brought him to life? Were all my dreams a delusionary system of unparalleled complexity and influence, or was I merely a madman who happened to be right?

These considerations might have seemed irrelevant to my colleagues, but when I related them to my urge to approach the Spider more closely, they took on extreme personal importance. How could I trust such an urge? I stared at the Spider, at its arms waving in their thousand-mile-long dance, their slow changes in configuration redolent of Kali's dance, of myths even more obscure. There were no remedies left for my fear. I had stopped work, drugged myself to prevent dreams, and yet I could do nothing to remove my chief concern: that the Spider would use its control over the computers (if, indeed, it did control them) to manipulate me.

I turned off the holo tank and headed out into the corridor, thinking I would have a few drinks. I hadn't gone fifty feet when Brent accosted me; I brushed past him, but he fell into step beside me. He exuded a false heartiness that was even more grating than his usual obsequiousness.

'Production,' he said. 'That's our keynote here, Reynolds.'

I glowered at him.

'We can't afford to have dead wood lying around,' he went on. 'Now if you're having a problem, perhaps you need a fresh eye. I'd be glad to take a look . . .'

I gave him a push, sending him wobbling, but it didn't dent his mood.

'Even the best of us run up against stone walls,' he said. 'And in your case, well, how long has it been since your last major work. Eight years? Ten? You can only ride the wind of your youthful successes for so . . .'

My anxiety flared into rage. I drove my fist into his stomach, and he dropped, gasping like a fish out of water. I was about to kick him, when I was grabbed from behind by the black-clad arms of a security guard. Two more guards intervened as I wrenched free, cursing at Brent. One of the guards helped Brent up and asked what should be done with me.

'Let him go,' he said, rubbing his gut. 'The man's not responsible.'

I lunged at him, but was shoved back. 'Bastard!' I shouted. 'You smarmy little shit, I'll swear I'll kill you if . . .'

A guard gave me another above.

'Please, Reynolds,' Brent said in a placating tone. 'Don't worry . . . I'll make sure you receive due credit.'

I had no idea what he meant, and was too angry to wonder at it. I launched more insults as the guards escorted him away.

No longer in the mood for a public place, I returned to the

apartment and sat scribbling meaningless notes, gazing at an image of the Spider that played across one entire wall. I was so distracted that I didn't notice Carolyn had entered until she was standing close beside me. The Spider's colours flickered across her, making her into an incandescent silhouette.

'What are you doing?' she asked, sitting on the floor.

'Nothing.' I tossed my notepad side.

'Something's wrong.'

'Not at all . . . I'm just tired.'

She regarded me expressionlessly. 'It's the Spider, isn't it?'

I told her that, Yes, the work was giving me trouble, but it wasn't serious. I'm not sure if I wanted her as much as it seemed I did, or if I was using sex to ward off more questions. Whatever the case, I lowered myself beside her, kissed her, touched her breasts, and soon we were in that heated secret place where – I thought – not even the Spider's eyes could pry. I told her I loved her in that rushed breathless way that is less an intimate disclosure than a form of gasping, of shaping breath to accommodate movement. That was the only way I have ever been able to tell her the best of my feeling, and it was because I was shamed by this that we did not make love more often.

Afterward I could see she wanted to say something important: it was working in her face. But I didn't want to hear it, to be trapped into some new level of intimacy. I turned from her, marshalling words that would signal my need for privacy, and my eyes fell on the wall where the image of the Spider still danced . . . danced in a way I had never before witnessed. His colours were shifting through a spectrum of reds and violets, and his arms writhed in a rhythm that brought to mind the rhythms of sex, the slow beginning, the furious rush to completion, as if he had been watching us and was now mimicking the act.

Carolyn spoke my name, but I was transfixed by the sight and could not answer. She drew in a sharp breath, and seconds later I heard her cross the room and make her exit. The Spider ceased his dance, lapsing into one of his normal patterns. I scrambled up, went to the controls and flicked the display switch to off. But the image did not fade. Instead, the Spider's colours grew brighter, washing from fiery red to gold and at last to a white so brilliant, I had to shield my eyes. I could almost feel his heat on my skin, hear the sibilant kiss of his molten voice. I was certain he was in the room, I knew I was going to burn, to be swallowed in that singeing heat, and I cried out for Carolyn, not wanting to leave unsaid all those things I had withheld from her. Then my fear reached such proportions that I collapsed and sank into a dream, not a nightmare as one might expect, but a dream of an immense city, where I experienced a multitude of adventures and met with a serene fate.

> . . . To understand Dulambre, his relationship with his father must be examined closely. Alex Dulambre was a musician and poet, regarded to be one of the progenitors of drift: a popular dance form involving the use of improvised lyrics. He was flamboyant, handsome, amoral, and these qualities, allied with a talent for seduction, led him on a twenty-five-year fling through the boudoirs of the powerful, from the corporate towers of Abidjan to the Gardens of Novo Sibersk, and lastly to a beach on Mozambique, where at the age of forty-four he died horribly, a victim of a neural poison that purportedly had been designed for him by the noted chemist Virginia Holland. It was Virginia who was reputed to be Reynolds' mother, but no tests were ever conducted to substantiate the rumour. All we know for certain is that one morning Alex received a crate containing an artificial womb and the embryo of his son. An attached folder provided proof of his paternity and a note stating that the mother wanted no keepsake to remind her of an error in judgement.
>
> Alex felt no responsibility for the child, but liked having a relative to add to his coterie. Thus it was that Reynolds spent his first fourteen years globe-trotting, sleeping on floors, breakfasting off the remains of the previous night's party, and generally being ignored, if not rejected. As a defence against both this rejection and his father's charisma, Reynolds learned to mimic Alex's flamboyance and developed similar verbal skills. By the age of eleven he was performing regularly with his father's band, creating a popular sequence of drifts that detailed the feats of an all-powerful wizard and the trials of those who warred against him. Alex took pride in these performances; he saw himself as less father than elder

brother, and he insisted on teaching Reynolds a brother's portion of the world. To this end he had one of his lovers seduce the boy on his twelfth birthday, and from then on Reynolds also mimicked his father's omnivorous sexuality. They did, indeed, seem brothers, and to watch Alex drape an arm over the boy's shoulders, the casual observer might have supposed them to be even closer. But there was no strong bond between them, only a history of abuse. This is not to say that Reynolds was unaffected by his father's death, an event to which he was witness. The sight of Alex's agony left him severely traumatized and with a fear of death bordering on the morbid. When we consider this fear in alliance with his difficulty in expressing love – a legacy of his father's rejections – we have gone far in comprehending both his marital problems and his obsession with immortality, with immortality in any form, even that of a child . . .

Russell E. Barrett, *The Last Alchemist*

3
Carolyn

Six months after the implantation of Reynolds' daughter in an artificial womb, I ran into Davis Brent at a pleasure dome where I had taken to spending my afternoons, enjoying the music, writing a memoir of my days with Reynolds, but refraining from infidelity. The child and my concern for Reynolds' mental state had acted to make me conservative: there were important decisions to be made, disturbing events afoot, and I wanted no distractions.

This particular dome was quite small, its walls Maxfield Parrish holographs – alabaster columns and scrolled archways that opened onto rugged mountains drenched in the colours of a pastel sunset; the patrons sat at marble tables, their drab jumpsuits at odds with the decadence of the décor. Sitting there, writing, I felt like some sad and damaged lady of a forgotten age, brought to the sorry pass of autobiography by a disappointment at love.

Without announcing himself, Brent dropped onto the bench opposite me and stared. A smile nicked the corners of his mouth. I waited for him to speak, and finally asked what he wanted.

'Merely to offer my congratulations,' he said.

'On what occasion?' I asked.

'The occasion of your daughter.'

The implantation had been done under a seal of privacy, and I was outraged that he had discovered my secret.

Before I could speak, he favoured me with an unctuous smile and said, 'As administrator, little that goes on here escapes me.' From the pocket of his jumpsuit he pulled a leather case of the sort used to carry holographs. 'I have a daughter myself, a lovely child. I sent her back to Earth some months back.' He opened the case, studied the contents, and continued, his words freighted with an odd tension. 'I had the computer do a portrait of how she'll look in a few years. Care to see it?'

I took the case and was struck numb. The girl depicted was seven or eight, and was the spitting image of myself at her age.

'I never should have sent her back,' said Brent. 'It appears the womb has been misshipped, and I may not be able to find her. Even the records have been misplaced. And the tech who performed the implantation, he returned on the ship with the womb and has dropped out of sight.'

I came to my feet, but he grabbed my arm and sat me back down. 'Check on it if you wish,' he said. 'But it's the truth. If you want to help find her, you'd be best served by listening.'

'Where is she?' A sick chill spread through me, and my heart felt as if it were not beating but trembling.

'Who knows? São Paolo, Paris. Perhaps one of the Urban Reserves.'

'Please,' I said, a catch in my voice. 'Bring her back.'

'If we work together, I'm certain we can find her.'

'What do you want, what could you possibly want from me?'

He smiled again. 'To begin with, I want copies of your husband's deep files. I need to know what he's working on.'

I had no compunction against telling him; all my concern was for the child. 'He's been investigating the possibility of life on the Sun.'

The answer dismayed him. 'That's ridiculous.'

'It's true, he's found it!'

He gaped at me.

'He calls it the Sun Spider. It's huge . . . and made of some kind of plasma.'

Brent smacked his forehead as if to punish himself for an oversight. 'Of course! That section in the *Diaries*.' He shook his head in wonderment. 'All that metaphysical gabble about particulate life . . . I can't believe that has any basis in fact.'

'I'll help you,' I said. 'But please bring her back!'

He reached across the table and caressed my cheek. I stiffened but did not draw away. 'The last thing I want to do is hurt you, Carolyn. Take my word, it's all under control.'

Under control.

Now it seems to me that he was right, and that the controlling agency was no man or creature, but a coincidence of possibility and wish such as may have been responsible for the spark that first set fire to the stars.

Over the next two weeks I met several times with Brent, on each occasion delivering various of Reynolds' files; only one remained to be secured, and I assured Brent I would soon have it. How I hated him! And yet we were complicitors. Each time we met in his lab, a place of bare metal walls and computer banks, we would discuss means of distracting Reynolds in order to perform my thefts, and during one occasion I asked why he had chosen Reynolds' work to pirate, since he had never been an admirer.

'Oh, but I am an admirer,' he said. 'Naturally I despise his personal style, the passing off of drugs and satyrism as scientific method. But I've never doubted his genius. Why, I was the one who approved his residency grant.'

Disbelief must have showed on my face, for he went on to say, 'It's true. Many of the board were inclined to reject him, thinking he was no longer capable of important work. But when I saw the Solar Equations, I knew he was still a force to reckon with. Have you looked at them?'

'I don't understand the mathematics.'

'Fragmentary as they are, they're astounding, elegant. There's something almost mystical about their structure. You get the idea there's no need to study them, that if you keep staring at them they'll crawl into your brain to work some change.' He made a church-and-steeple of his fingers. 'I hoped he'd finish them here but . . . well, maybe that last file.'

We went back to planning Reynolds' distraction. He rarely left the apartment any more, and Brent and I decided that the time to act would be during his birthday party the next week. He would doubtless be heavily drugged, and I would be able to slip into the back room and access his computer. The discussion concluded, Brent stepped to the door that led to his apartment, keyed it open and invited me for a drink. I declined, but he insisted and I preceded him inside.

The apartment was decorated in appallingly bad taste. His furniture was of a translucent material that glowed a sickly bluish-green, providing the only illumination. Matted under glass on one wall was a twentieth-century poster of a poem entitled 'Desiderata', whose verses were the height of mawkish romanticism. The other walls were hung with what appeared to be ancient tapestries, but which on close inspection proved to be pornographic counterfeits, depicting subjects such as women mating with stags. Considering these appointments, I found hypocritical Brent's condemnation of Reynolds' private life. He poured wine from a decanter and made banal small talk, touching me now and then as he had during our first meeting. I forced an occasional smile, and at last, thinking I had humoured him long enough, I told him I had to leave.

'Oh, no,' he said, encircling my waist with an arm. 'We're not through.'

I pried his arm loose: he was not very strong.

'Very well.' He touched a wall control, and a door to the corridor slid open. 'Go.'

The harsh white light shining through the door transformed him into a shadowy figure and made his pronouncement seem a threat.

'Go on.' He drained his wine. 'I've got no hold on you.'

God, he thought he was clever! And he was . . . more clever than I, perhaps more so than Reynolds. And though he was to learn that cleverness has its limits, particularly when confronted by the genius of fate, it was sufficient to the moment.

'I'll stay,' I said.

. . . In the dance of the Spider, in his patterned changes in colour, the rhythmic waving of his fiery arms, was a kind of language, the language that the Equations sought to clarify, the language of my dreams. I sat for hours watching him; I recorded several sequences on pocket holographs and carried them about in hopes that this propinquity would illuminate the missing portions of the Equations. I made some progress, but I had concluded that a journey sunwards was the sort of propinquity I needed – I doubted I had the courage to achieve it. However, legislating against my lack of courage was the beauty I had begun to perceive in the Spider's dance, the hypnotic grace: like that of a Balinese dancer, possessing a similar allure. I came to believe that those movements were signalling all knowledge, infinite possibility. My dreams began to be figured with creatures that I would have previously considered impossible – dragons, imps, men with glowing hands or whose entire forms were glowing, all a ghostly, grainy white; now these creatures came to seem not only possible but likely inhabitants of a world that was coming more and more into focus, a world to which I was greatly attracted. Sometimes I would lie in bed all day, hoping for more dreams of that world, of the wizard who controlled it. It may be that I was using the dreams to escape confronting a difficult and frightening choice. But in truth I have lately doubted that it is even mine to make.

Reynolds Dulambre, *Collected Notes*

4

Reynolds

I remember little of the party, mostly dazed glimpses of breasts and thighs, sweaty bodies, lidded eyes. I remember the drift, which was performed by a group of techs. They played Alex's music as an *hommage*, and I was taken back to my years with the old bastard-maker, to memories of beatings, of walking in on him and his lovers, of listening to him pontificate. And, of course, I recalled that night in Mozambique when I watched him claw at his eyes, his face. Spitting missiles of blood, unable to scream, having bitten off his tongue. Sobered, I got to my feet and staggered into the bedroom, where it was less crowded, but still too crowded for my mood. I grabbed a robe, belted it on and keyed my study door.

As I entered, Carolyn leaped up from my computer. On the screen was displayed what looked to be a page from my deep files. She tried to switch off the screen, but I caught her arm and checked the page: I had not been mistaken. 'What are you doing?' I shouted, yanking her away from the computer.

'I was just curious.' She tried to jerk free.

Then I spotted the microcube barnacled to the computer: she had been recording. 'What's that?' I asked, forcing her to look at it. 'What's that? Who the hell are you working for?'

She began to cry, but I wasn't moved. We had betrayed each other a thousand times, but never to this degree.

'Damn you!' I slapped her. 'Who is it?'

She poured out the story of Brent's plan, his demands on her. 'I'm sorry,' she said, sobbing. 'I'm sorry.'

I felt so much then, I couldn't characterize it as fear or anger or any specific emotion. In my mind's eye I saw the child, that scrap of my soul, disappearing down some earthly sewer. I threw off my robe, stepped into a jumpsuit.

'Where are you going?' Carolyn asked, wiping away tears.

I zipped up the jumpsuit.

'Don't!' Carolyn tried to haul me back from the door. 'You don't understand!'

I shoved her down, locked the door behind me, and went storming out through the party and into the corridor. Rage flooded me. I needed to hurt Brent. My reason was so obscured that when I reached his apartment, I saw nothing suspicious in the fact that the door was open . . . though I later realized he must have had a spy at the party to warn him of anything untoward. Inside, Brent was lounging in one of those ridiculous glowing chairs, a self-satisfied look on his face, and it was that look more than anything, more than the faint scraping at my rear, that alerted me to danger. I spun around to see a security guard bringing his laser to bear on me. I dived at him, feeling a discharge of heat next to my ear, and we went down together. He tried to gouge my eyes, but I twisted away, latched both hands in his hair and smashed his head against the wall. The third time his head impacted, it made a sofer sound than it had the previous two, and I could feel the skull shifting beneath the skin like pieces of broken tile in a sack. I rolled off the guard, horrified, yet no less enraged. And when I saw that Brent's chair was empty, when I heard him shouting in the corridor, even though I knew his shouts would bring more guards, my anger grew so great that I cared nothing for myself, I only wanted him dead.

By the time I emerged from the apartment, he was sprinting around a curve in the corridor. My laser scored the metal wall behind him the instant before he went out of sight. I ran after him. Several of the doorways along the corridor slid open, heads popped out, and on seeing me, ducked back in. I rounded the curve, spotted Brent, and fired again . . . too high by inches. Before I could correct my aim, half a dozen guards boiled out of a side corridor and dragged him into cover. Their beams drew smouldering lines in the metal by my hip, at my feet, and I retreated, firing as I did, pounding on the doors, thinking that I would barricade myself in one of the rooms and try to debunk Brent's lies, to reveal his deceit over the intercom. But none of the doors opened, their occupants having apparently been frightened by my weapon.

Two guards poked their heads around the curve, fired, and one of the beams came so near that it torched the fabric of my jumpsuit at the knee. I beat out the flames and ran full tilt. Shouts behind me, beams of ruby light skewering the air above my head. Ahead, I made out a red door that led to a docking arm, and having no choice, I keyed it open and raced along the narrow passageway. The first three moorings were empty, but the fourth had a blue light glowing beside the entrance hatch, signalling the presence of a ship. I slipped inside, latched it, and moved along the tunnel into the airlock; I bolted that shut, then went quickly along the mesh-walled catwalk toward the control room, toward the radio. I was on the point of entering the room, when I felt a shudder go all through the ship and knew it had cast loose, that it was headed sunward.

Panicked, I burst into the control room. The chairs fronting the instrument panel were empty, the panel itself aflicker with lights; the ship was being run by computer. I sat at the board, trying to override, but no tactic had any effect. Then Brent's voice came over the speakers. 'You've bought yourself a little time, Reynolds,' he said. 'That's all. When the ship returns, we'll have you.'

I laughed.

It had been my hope that he had initiated the ship's flight, but his comments made clear that I was now headed toward the confrontation I had for so long sought to avoid, brought to this pass by a computer under the control of the creature for whom I had searched my entire life, a creature of fire and dreams, the stuff of souls. I knew I would not survive it. But though I had always dreaded the thought of death, now that death was hard upon me, I was possessed of a strange confidence and calm . . . calm enough to send this transmission, to explore the confines of this my coffin, even to read the manuals that explain its operation. I had never attempted to understand the workings of the sunships, and I was interested to read of the principles that underlie each flight. As the ship approaches the Sun, it will monitor the magnetic field direction and determine if the Archimedean spiral of the solar wind is oriented outward.

If all is as it should be, the ship will continue to descend and eventually will skip off the open-diverging magnetic field of a coronal hole. It will be travelling at such a tremendous speed, its actions will be rather like those of a charged particle caught in a magnetic field, and as the field opens out, it will be flung upward, back toward Helios . . . that is, it will be flung up and out if a creature who survives by stripping particles of their charge does not inhabit the coronal hole in question. But there is little chance of that.

I wonder how it will feel to have my charge stripped. I would not care to suffer the agonies of my father.

The closer I come to the Sun, the more calm I become. My mortal imperfections seem to be flaking away. I feel clean and minimal, and I have the notion that I will soon be even simpler, the essential splinter of a man. I have so little desire left that only one further thing occurs to me to say.

Carolyn, I . . .

*. . . A man walking in a field of golden grass under a bright
sky, walking steadfastly, though with no apparent destination,
for the grasslands spread to the horizon, and his thoughts are
crystal-clear, and his heart, too, is clear, for his past has
become an element of his present, and his future – visible as a
sweep of golden grass carpeting the distant hills, beyond
which lies a city sparkling like a glint of possibility – is as
fluent and clear as his thought, and he knows his future will
be shaped by his walking, by his thought and the power in his
hands, especially by that power, and of all this he wishes now
to speak to a woman whose love he denied, whose flesh had
the purity of the clear bright sky and the golden grasses who
was always the heart of his life even in the country of lies, and
here in the heartland of the country of truth is truly loved at
last . . .*
        The Resolute Lover, part of The White Dragon Cycle

5
Carolyn

After Reynolds had stolen the sunship – this, I was informed, had
been the case – Brent confined me to my apartment and accused
me of conspiring with Reynolds to kill him. I learned of
Reynolds' death from the security guard who brought me supper
that first night; he told me that a prominence (I pictured it to be a
fiery fishing lure) had flung itself out from the Sun and
incinerated the ship. I wept uncontrollably. Even after the
computers began to translate the coded particle bursts emanat-
ing from the Spider's coronal hole, even when these proved to
be the completed Solar Equations, embodied not only in
mathematics but in forms comprehensible to a layman, still I
wept. I was too overwhelmed by grief to realize what they might
portend.

I was able to view the translations on Reynolds' computer,
and when the stories of the White Dragon Cycle came into view,
I understood that whoever or whatever had produced them had

something in particular to say to me. It was *The Resolute Lover*, the first of the cycle, with its numerous references to a wronged beautiful woman, that convinced me of this. I read the story over and over, and in so doing I recalled Brent's description of the feelings he had had while studying the Equations. I felt in the focus of some magical lens, I felt a shimmering in my flesh, confusion in my thoughts . . . not a confusion of motive but of thoughts running in new patterns, colliding with each other like atoms bred by a runaway reactor. I lost track of time, I lived in a sweep of golden grasses, in an exotic city where the concepts of unity and the divisible were not opposed, where villains and heroes and beasts enacted ritual passions, where love was the ordering pulse of existence.

One day Brent paid me a visit. He was plumped with self-importance, with triumph. But though I hated him, emotion seemed incidental to my goal – a goal his visit helped to solidify – and I reacted to him mildly, watching as he moved about the room, watching me and smiling.

'You're calmer than I expected,' he said.

I had no words for him, only calm. In my head the Resolute Lover gazed into a crystal of Knowledge, awaiting the advent of Power. I believe that I, too, smiled.

'Well,' he said. 'Things don't always work out as we plan. But I'm pleased with the result. The Spider will be Reynolds' great victory . . . no way around that. Still, I've managed to land the role of Sancho Panza to his Don Quixote, the rationalist who guided the madman on his course.'

My smile was a razor, a knife, a flame.

'Quite sufficient,' he went on, 'to secure my post . . . and perhaps even my immortality.'

I spoke to him in an inaudible voice that said Death.

His manner grew more agitated; he twitched about the room, touching things. 'What will I do with you?' he said. 'I'd hate to send you to your judgement. Our nights together . . . well, suffice it to say I would be most happy if you'd stay with me. What do you think? Shall I testify on your behalf, or would you prefer a term on the Urban Reserves?'

Brent, Brent, Brent. His name was a kind of choice.

'Perhaps you'd like time to consider?' he said.

I wished my breath was poison.

He edged toward the door. 'When you reach a decision, just tell the guard outside. You've two months 'til the next ship. I'm betting you'll choose survival.'

My eyes sent him a black kiss.

'Really, Carolyn,' he said. 'You were never a faithful wife. Don't you think this pose of mourning somewhat out of character?'

Then he was gone, and I returned to my reading.

Love.

What part did it play in my desire for vengeance, my furious calm? Sorrow may have had more a part, but love was certainly a factor. Love as practised by the Resolute Lover. This story communicated this rigorous emotion, and my heartsickness translated it to vengeful form. My sense of unreality, of tremulous being, increased day by day, and I barely touched my meals.

I am not sure when the Equations embodied by the story began to take hold, when the seeded knowledge became power. I believe it was nearly two weeks after Brent's visit. But though I felt my potential, my strength, I did not act immediately. In truth, I was not certain I could act or that action was to be my course. I was mad in the same way Reynolds had been: a madness of self-absorption, a concentration of such intensity that nothing less intense had the least relevance.

One night I left off reading, went into my bedroom and put on a sheer robe, then wrapped myself in a cowled cloak. I had no idea why I was doing this. The seductive rhythms of the story were coiling through my head and preventing thought. I walked into the front room and stood facing the door. Violent tremors shook my body. I felt frail, insubstantial, yet at the same time possessed of fantastic power: I knew that nothing could resist me . . . not steel or flesh or fire. Inspired by this confidence, I reached out my right hand to the door. The hand was glowing a pale white, its form flickering, the fingers lengthening and attenuating, appearing to ripple as in a graceful dance. I did not wonder at this. Everything was as it should be. And when my hand slid into the door, into the metal, neither did I consider that remarkable. I could feel the mechanisms of the lock, I – or rather my ghostly fingers – seemed to know the exact function of every metal bit, and after a moment the door hissed open.

The guard peered in, startled, and I hid the hand behind me. I backed away, letting the halves of my cloak fall apart. He stared, glanced left and right in the corridor, and entered. 'How'd you do the lock?' he asked.

I said nothing.

He keyed the door, testing it, and slid it shut, leaving the two of us alone in the room. 'Huh,' he said. 'Must have been a computer foul-up.'

I came close beside him, my head tipped back as if to receive a kiss, and he smiled, he held me around the waist. His lips mashed against mine, and my right hand, seeming almost to be acting on its own, slipped into his side and touched something that beat wildly for a few seconds, and then spasmed. He pushed me away, clutching his chest, his face purpling, and fell to the floor. Emotionless, I stepped over him and went out into the corridor, walking at an unhurried pace, hiding my hand beneath the cloak.

On reaching Brent's apartment, I pressed the bell, and a moment later the door opened and he peered forth, looking sleepy and surprised. 'Carolyn!' he said. 'How did you get out?'

'I told the guard I planned to stay with you,' I said, and as I had done with the guard, I parted the halves of my cloak.

His eyes dropped to my breasts. 'Come in,' he said, his voice burred.

Once inside, I shed the cloak, concealing my hand behind me. I was so full of hate, my mind was heavy and blank like a stone. Brent poured some wine, but I refused the glass. My voice sounded dead, and he shot me a searching look and asked if I felt well. 'I'm fine,' I told him.

He set down the wine and came toward me, but I moved away.

'First,' I said, 'I want to know about my daughter.'

That brought him up short. 'You have no daughter,' he said after a pause. 'It was all a hoax.'

'I don't believe you.'

'I swear it's true,' he said. 'When you went for an exam, I had the tech inform you of a pregnancy. But you weren't pregnant. And when you came for the implantation procedure, he anaesthetized you and simply stood by until you woke up.'

It would have been in character, I realized, for him to have done this. Yet he also might have been clever enough to make up the story, and thus keep a hold on me, one he could inform me of should I prove recalcitrant.

'But you can have a child,' he said, sidling toward me. 'Our child, Carolyn. I'd like that, I'd like it very much.' He seemed to be having some difficulty in getting the next words out, but finally they came: 'I love you.'

What twisted shape, I wondered, did love take in his brain?

'Do you?' I said.

'I know it must be hard to believe,' he said. 'You can't possibly understand the pressure I've been under, the demands that forced my actions. But I swear to you, Carolyn, I've always cared for you. I knew how oppressed you were by Reynolds. Don't you see? To an extent I was acting on your behalf. I wanted to free you.'

He said all this in a whining tone, edging close, so close I could smell his bitter breath. He put a hand on my breast, lifted it . . . Perhaps he did love me in his way, for it seemed a treasuring touch. But mine was not. I laid my palely glowing hand on the back of his neck. He screamed, went rigid, and oh, how that scream made me feel! It was like music, his pain. He stumbled backward, toppled over one of the luminous chairs, and lay writhing, clawing his neck.

'Where is she?' I asked, kneeling beside him.

Spittle leaked between his gritted teeth. 'I'll . . . find her, bring her . . . oh!'

I saw I could never trust him. Desperate, he would say anything. He might bring me someone else's child. I touched his stomach, penetrating the flesh to the first joint of my fingers, then wiggling them. Again he screamed. Blood mapped the front of his jumpsuit.

'Where is she?' I no longer was thinking about the child: she was lost, and I was only tormenting him.

His speech was incoherent, he tried to hump away. I showed him my hand, how it glowed, and his eyes bugged.

'Do you still love me?' I asked, touching his groin, hooking my fingers and pulling at some fibre.

Agony bubbled in his throat, and he curled up around his pain, clutching himself.

I could not stop touching him. I orchestrated his screams, producing short ones, long ones, ones that held a strained hoarse chord. My hatred was a distant emotion. I felt no fury, no glee. I was merely a craftsman, working to prolong his death. Pink films occluded the whites of his eyes, his teeth were stained to crimson, and at last he lay still.

I sat beside him for what seemed a long time. Then I donned my cloak and walked back to my apartment. After making sure no one was in the corridor, I dragged the dead guard out of the front room and propped him against the corridor wall. I reset the lock, stepped inside, and the door slid shut behind me. I felt nothing. I took up *The Resolute Lover*, but even my interest in it had waned. I gazed at the walls, growing thoughtless, remembering only that I had been somewhere, done some violence; I was perplexed by my glowing hand. But soon I fell asleep, and when I was waked by the guards unlocking the door, I found that the hand had returned to normal.

'Did you hear anything outside?' asked one of the guards.

'No,' I said. 'What happened?'

He told me the gory details, about the dead guard and Brent. Like everyone else on Helios Station, he seemed more confounded by these incomprehensible deaths than by the fantastic birth that had preceded them.

The walls of the station have been plated with gold, the corridors are thronged with tourists, with students come to study the disciplines implicit in the Equations, disciplines that go far beyond the miraculous transformation of my hand. Souvenir shops sell holos of the Spider, recordings of The White Dragon Cycle (now used to acclimatize children to the basics of the Equations), and authorized histories of the sad events surrounding the Spider's emergence. The pleasure domes reverberate with Alex Dulambre's drifts, and in an auditorium constructed for this purpose, Reynolds' clone delivers daily lectures on the convoluted circumstances of his death and triumph. The place is half amusement park, half shrine. Yet the greatest memorial to Reynolds' work is not here; it lies beyond the orbit of Pluto and consists of a vast shifting structure of golden light wherein dwell those students who have mastered the disciplines and overcome the bonds of corporeality. They are engaged, it is said, in an unfathomable work that may have taken its inspiration from Reynolds' metaphysical flights of fancy, or – and many hold to this opinion – may reflect the Spider's design, his desire to rid himself of the human nuisance by setting us upon a new evolutionary course. After Brent's death I thought to join in this work. But my mind was not suited to the disciplines; I had displayed all the mastery of which I was capable in dispensing with Brent.

I have determined to continue the search for my daughter. It may be – as Brent claimed – that she does not exist, but it is all that is left to me, and I have made my resolve accordingly. Still, I have not managed to leave the station, because I am drawn to Reynolds' clone. Again and again I find myself in the rear of the auditorium, where I watch him pace the dais, declaiming in the most excited manner. I yearn to approach him, to learn how like Reynolds he truly is. I am certain he has spotted me on several occasions, and I wonder what he is thinking, how it would be to speak to him, touch him. Perhaps this is perverse of me, but I cannot help wondering . . .

Carolyn Dulambre, *Days In The Sun*

6
Carolyn/Reynolds

I had been wanting to talk with her since . . . well, since this peculiar life began. Why? I loved her, for one thing. But there seemed to be a far more compelling reason, one I could not verbalize. I suppressed the urge for a time, not wanting to hurt her; but seeing that she had begun to appear at the lectures, I finally decided to make an approach.

She had taken to frequenting a pleasure dome named Spider's. Its walls were holographic representations of the Spider, and these were strung together with golden webs that looked molten against the black backdrop, like seams of unearthly fire. In this golden dimness the faces of the patrons glowed like spirits, and the glow seemed to be accentuated by the violence of the music. It was not a place to my taste, nor – I suspect – to hers. Perhaps her patronage was a form of courage, of facing down the creature who had caused her so much pain.

I found her seated in a rear corner, drinking an Amouriste, and when I moved up beside her table, she paid me no mind. No one ever approached her; she was as much a memorial as the station itself, and though she was still a beautiful woman, she was treated like the wife of a saint. Doubtless she thought I was merely pausing by the table, looking for someone. But when I sat opposite her, she glanced up and her jaw dropped.

'Don't be afraid,' I said.

'Why should I be afraid?'

'I thought my presence might . . . discomfort you.'

She met my eyes unflinchingly. 'I suppose I thought that, too.'

'But . . . ?'

'It doesn't matter.'

A silence built between us.

She wore a robe of golden silk, cut to expose the upper swells of her breasts, and her hair was pulled back from her face, laying bare the smooth, serene lines of her beauty, a beauty that had once fired me, that did so even now.

'Look,' I said. 'For some reason I was drawn to talk to you, I feel I have . . .'

'I feel the same.' She said this with a strong degree of urgency, but then tried to disguise the fact. 'What shall we talk about?'

'I'm not sure.'

She tapped a finger on her glass. 'Why don't we walk?'

Everyone watched as we left, and several people followed us into the corridor, a circumstance that led me to suggest that we talk in my apartment. She hesitated, then signalled agreement with the briefest of nods. We moved quickly through the crowds, managing to elude our pursuers, and settled into a leisurely pace. Now and again I caught her staring at me, and asked if anything was wrong.

'Wrong?' She seemed to be tasting the word, trying it out. 'No,' she said. 'No more than usual.'

I had thought that when I did talk to him I would find he was merely a counterfeit, that he would be nothing like Reynolds, except in the most superficial way. But this was not the case. Walking along that golden corridor, mixing with the revellers who poured between the shops and bars, I felt toward him as I had on the day we had met in the streets of Abidjan: powerfully attracted, vulnerable, and excited. And yet I did perceive a difference in him. Whereas Reynolds' presence had been commanding and intense, there had been a brittleness to that intensity, a sense that his diamond glitter might easily be fractured. With this Reynolds, however, there was no such inconstancy. His presence – while potent – was smooth, natural, and unflawed.

Everywhere we walked we encountered the fruits of the Equations: matter transmitters; rebirth parlours, where one could experience a transformation of both body and soul; and the omnipresent students, some of them half-gone into a transcorporeal state, cloaked to hide this fact, but their condition evident by their inward-looking eyes. With Reynolds beside me, all this seemed comprehensible, not – as before – a carnival of meaningless improbabilities. I asked what he felt on seeing the results of his work, and he said, 'I'm really not concerned with it.'

'What are you concerned with?'

'With you, Carolyn,' he said.

The answer both pleased me and made me wary. 'Surely you must have more pressing concerns,' I said.

'Everything I've done was for you.' A puzzled expression crossed his face.

'Don't pretend with me!' I snapped, growing angry. 'This isn't a show, this isn't the auditorium.'

He opened his mouth, but bit back whatever he had been intending to say, and we walked on.

'Forgive me,' I said, realizing the confusion that must be his. 'I . . .'

'No need for forgiveness,' he said. 'All our failures are behind us now.'

I didn't know from where these words were coming. They were my words, yet they also seemed spoken from a place deep inside myself, one whose existence had been hidden until now, and it was all I could do to hold them back. We passed into the upper levels of the station, where the permanent staff was quartered, and as we rounded a curve, we nearly ran into a student standing motionless, gazing at the wall: a pale young man with black hair, a thin mouth, and a grey cape. His eyes were dead-looking, and his voice sepulchral. 'It awaits,' he said.

They are so lost in self-contemplation, these students, that they are likely to say anything. Some fancy them oracles, but not I: their words struck me as being random, sparks from a frayed wire.

'What awaits?' I asked, amused.

'Life . . . the city.'

'Ah,' I said. 'And how do I get there?'

'You . . .' He lapsed into an open-mouthed stare.

Carolyn pulled at me, and we set off again. I started to make a joke about the encounter, but seeing her troubled expression, I restrained myself.

When we entered my apartment, she stopped in the centre of the living room, transfixed by the walls. I had set them to display the environment of the beginning of *The Resolute Lover*: an endless sweep of golden grasses, with a sparkling on the horizon that might have been the winking of some bright tower.

'Does this bother you?' I asked, gesturing at the walls.

'No, they startled me, that's all.' She strolled along, peering at the grasses, as if hoping to catch sight of someone. Then she turned, and I spoke again from that deep hidden place; a place that now – responding to the sight of her against those golden fields – was spreading all through me.

'Carolyn, I love you,' I said . . . and this time I knew who it was that spoke.

He had removed his cloak, and his body was shimmering, embedded in that pale glow that once had made a weapon of my right hand. I backed away, terrified. Yet even in the midst of fear, it struck me that I was not as terrified as I should have been, that I was not at the point of screaming, of fleeing.

'It's me, Carolyn,' he said.

'No,' I said, backing further away.

'I don't know why you should believe me.' He looked at his flickering hand. 'I didn't understand it myself until now.'

'Who are you?' I asked, gauging the distance to the door.

'You know,' he said. 'The Spider ... he's all through the station. In the computer, the labs, even in the tanks from which my cells were grown. He's brought us together again.'

He tried to touch me, and I darted to the side.

'I won't hurt you,' he said.

'I've seen what a touch can do.'

'Not my touch, Carolyn.'

I doubted I could make it to the door, but readied myself for a try.

'Listen to me, Carolyn,' he said. 'Everything we wanted in the beginning, all the dreams and fictions of love, they can be ours.'

'I never wanted that,' I said. 'You did! I only wanted normality, not some . . .'

'All lovers want the same thing,' he said. 'Disillusionment leads them to pretend they want less.' He stretched out his hands to me. 'Everything awaits us, everything is prepared. How this came to be, I can't explain. Except that it makes a funny kind of sense for the ultimate result of science to be an incomprehensible magic.'

I was still afraid, but my fear was dwindling, lulled by the rhythms of his words, and though I perceived him to be death, I also saw clearly that he was Reynolds, Reynolds made whole.

'This was inevitable,' he said. 'We both knew something miraculous could happen ... that's why we stayed together, despite everything. Don't be afraid. I could never hurt you more than I have.'

'What's inevitable?' I asked. He was too close for me to think of running, and I thought I could delay him, put him off with questions.

'Can't you feel it?' He was so close, now, I could feel his heat. 'I can't tell you what it is, Carolyn, only that it is, that it's life . . . a new life.'

'The Spider,' I said. 'I don't understand, I . . .'

'No more questions,' he said, and slipped the robes from my shoulders.

His touch was warmer than natural, making my eyelids droop, but causing no pain. He pulled me down to the floor, and in a moment he was inside me, we were heart to heart, moving together, enveloped in that pale flickering glow, and amidst the pleasure I felt, there was pain, but so little it did not matter . . .

. . . and I, too, was afraid, afraid I was not who I thought, that flames and nothingness would obliterate us, but in having her once again, in the consummation of my long wish, my doubts lessened . . .

. . . and I could no longer tell whether my eyes were open or closed, because sometimes when I thought them closed, I could see him, his face slack with pleasure, head flung back . . .

. . . and when I thought they were open I would have a glimpse of another place wherein she stood beside me, glimpses at first too brief for me to fix them in mind . . .

. . . and everything was whirling, changing, my body, my spirit, all in flux, and death – if this was death – was a long decline, a sweep of golden radiance, and behind me I could see the past reduced to a plain and hills carpeted with golden grasses . . .

. . . and around me golden towers, shimmering, growing more stable and settling into form moment by moment, and people shrouded in golden mist who were also becoming more real, acquiring scars and rags and fine robes, carrying baskets and sacks . . .

. . . and this was no heaven, no peaceful heaven, for as we moved beneath those crumbling towers of yellow stone, I saw soldiers with oddly shaped spears on the battlements, and the crowds around us were made up of hard-bitten men and women wearing belted daggers, and old crones bent double under the weight of sacks of produce, and younger women with the look of ill-usage about them, who leaned from the doors and windows of smoke-darkened houses and cried out their price . . .

. . . and the sun overhead seemed to shift, putting forth prominences that rippled and undulated as in a dance, and shone down a ray of light to illuminate the tallest tower, the one we had sought for all these years, the one whose mystery we must unravel . . .

. . . and the opaque image of an old man in a yellow robe was floating above the crowd, his pupils appearing to shift, to put forth fiery threads as did the sun, and he was haranguing us, daring us all to penetrate his tower, to negotiate his webs and steal the secrets of time . . .

. . . and after wandering all day, we found a room in an inn not half a mile from the wizard's tower, a mean place with grimy walls and scuttlings in the corners and a straw mattress that crackled when we lay on it. But it was so much more than we'd had in a long, long time, we were delighted, and when night had fallen, with moonlight streaming in and the wizard's tower visible through a window against the deep blue of the sky, the room seemed palatial. We made love until well past midnight, love as we had never practised it: trusting, unfettered by inhibition. And afterward, still joined, listening to the cries and music of the city, I suddenly remembered my life in that other world, the Spider, Helios Station, everything, and from the tense look on Carolyn's face, from her next words, I knew that she, too, had remembered.

'Back at Helios,' she said, 'we were making love, lying exactly like this, and . . .' She broke off, a worry line creasing her brow. 'What if this is all a dream, a moment between dying and death?'

'Why should you think that?'

'The Spider . . . I don't know. I just felt it was true.'

'It's more reasonable to assume that everything is a form of transition between the apartment and this room. Besides, why would the Spider want you to die?'

'Why has he done any of this? We don't even know what he is . . . a demon, a god.'

'Or something of mine,' I said.

'Yes, that . . . or death.'

I stroked her hair, and her eyelids fluttered down.

'I'm afraid to go to sleep,' she said.

'Don't worry,' I said. 'I think there's more to this than death.'

'How do you know?'

'Because of how we are.'

'That's why I think it *is* death,' she said. 'Because it's too good to last.'

'Even if it is death,' I told her, 'in this place death might last longer than our old lives.'

Of course I was certain of very little myself, but I managed to soothe her, and soon she was asleep. Out the window, the wizard's tower – if, indeed, that's what it was – glowed and rippled, alive with power, menacing in its brilliance. But I was past being afraid. Even in the face of something as unfathomable as a creature who has appropriated the dream of a man who may have dreamed it into existence and fashioned thereof either a life or a death, even in a world of unanswerable questions, when love is certain – love, the only question that is its own answer – everything becomes quite simple, and, in the end, a matter of acceptance.

We live in an old chaos of the sun
Wallace Stevens

ALL THE PERFUMES OF ARABY

For nearly two years after my arrival in Egypt, I put off visiting the Pyramids. I had seen them once, briefly at sunset, while *en route* by car from Alexandria to Cairo. Looming up from the lion-coloured sands, their sunstruck sides ignited to a shimmering orange, as if the original limestone veneer had been magically restored, and the shadows in their lee showed a deep mysterious blue, almost purple, like the blood of Caesar's Rome. They diminished me, those ancient tombs. Too much beauty for my deracinated spirit, too much grandeur and immensity. They made me think of history, death, and folly. I had no wish to endure the bout of self-examination a longer visit might provoke. It would be best, I thought, to live a hard, modern life in that city of monuments, free of ponderous considerations and intellectual witness. But eventually curiosity got the best of me, and one afternoon I travelled out to Giza. This time, swarmed by tourists, displayed beneath an oppressive grey sky, it was the Pyramids that looked diminished: dull brown heaps like the spoor of a huge, strangely regular beast.

I wandered about for more than an hour. I regarded the faceless mystery of the Sphinx and managed to avoid having a video taken atop a camel by a ragged teenager with an old camcorder and the raw scar of an AIDS inoculation on his bicep. At length I leaned up against my Land Rover and smoked a hand-rolled cigarette salted with hashish and opium flakes. I thought in pictures, my eyes closed, imagining ibis gods and golden sun boats. When a woman's voice with more than a touch of Southern accent spoke from nearby, saying, 'You can smell that shit fifty feet away,' I was so distanced I felt only mild resentment for this interference in the plotlessness of my life, and said, because it required little energy, 'Thanks.'

She was tall and slender and brown, with a slightly horsey face and generous features and a pronounced overbite, the sort of tomboyish look I'd always found attractive, though overall she was a bit sinewy for my tastes. Late twenties, I'd say. About my age. Her skin, roughened by the sun, was just starting to crack into crow's-feet, her cheekbones were sharply whittled, and her honey-brown hair, tied back with a bandanna, was streaked blonde and brittle at the ends. She had on chino shorts and a white T-shirt and was carrying a net bag that held a canteen, a passport wallet, and some oranges.

'Aren't you goin' to put it out?' She gestured at my cigarette.

'Guess I better,' I said, and grinned at her as I ground out the butt, expecting her to leave now that her prim mission had been accomplished; but she remained standing there, squinting at me.

'You're that smuggler guy, right?' she said. 'Shears.'

'Shields. Danny Shields.' I was not alarmed that she knew my business – many did – but I was annoyed at not being able to recall her. She had nice eyes, dark brown, almost oriental-shaped. Her legs were long, lean and well defined, but very feminine. 'Sorry,' I said. 'I don't remember your name.'

'Kate Corsaro,' she said after a moment's hesitation. 'We've never met. Just somebody pointed you out to me in a night club. They told me you were a smuggler.' She left a pause. 'I thought you looked interestin'.'

'First impressions,' I said. 'You can never trust 'em.'

'Oh, I don't know 'bout that.' She gazed off toward the Great Pyramid; then, after a second or two: 'So what do you smuggle? Drugs?'

'Too dangerous. You run drugs, you're looking at the death penalty. I have something of a moral problem with it, too.'

'Is that right?' She glanced down at the remains of my cigarette.

'Just because I use doesn't mean I approve of the business.'

'Seems to me that's tacit approval.'

'Maybe so, but I see a distinction. Whatever else pays, I'll deal with it. Diamonds, exotic software, hacksaw blades . . . what-ever. But no drugs.'

'Hacksaw blades?' She laughed. 'Can't be much profit in that.'

'You might be surprised.'

'Been a while since anything's surprised me,' she said.

A silence stretched between us, vibrant as a plucked wire. I wanted to touch the soft packs of muscle that bunched at the corners of her mouth. 'You've come to the right place,' I said. 'I'm surprised all the time here.'

'Is that so?'

'Like now,' I said. 'Like this very minute, I'm surprised.'

'This here?' she said. 'This is just doin' what comes naturally.'

Despite her flirtatious tone, I had an idea she was getting bored. To hold her interest I told stories about my Arab partner in the old bazaar, about moving robotic elements and tractor parts. It's odd, how when you come on to someone, even with the sort of half-assed move I was making, you invest the proceedings with unwarranted emotion, you imbue every action and thought with luminous possibility, until suddenly all the playful motives you had for making the move begin to grow legitimate and powerful. It is as if a little engine has been switched on in your heart due to some critical level of heat having been reached. It seems that random and impersonal, that careless. Not that I was falling in love with her. It was just that everything was becoming urgent, edgy. But soon I began to bore myself with my own glibness, and I asked Kate how she had ended up in Egypt.

'I was in the Middle East nine years ago. I had an itch to see it again.'

'In Egypt?'

'Naw, I was in Saudi. But I didn't want to go back. I couldn't walk around free like here.'

I was just putting those two facts together, 1990 and Saudi Arabia, when the sun came out full, and something glinted on the back of her right hand: three triangular diamond chips embedded in the flesh. I noticed a slight difference in colouration between the wrist and forearm, and realized it was a prosthesis. I had seen similar ones, the same pattern of diamond chips, all embedded in artificial limbs belonging to veterans of Desert Storm. Kate caught me staring at the hand, shifted it behind her hip; but a second later she moved it back into plain view.

'Somethin' botherin' you?' she asked flatly.

'Not at all,' I said.

She held my eyes for a few beats. The tension in her face dissolved. 'It bothers some,' she said, flexing the fingers of the hand, watching them work. She glanced up at me again. 'I flew a chopper, case you're wonderin'.'

I made a noncommittal noise. 'Must have been tough.'

'Yeah, maybe, I don't know. Basically what happened was just plain stupid.' She lapsed into another silence, and I grew concerned again that I might be losing her interest.

'Would you like to go somewhere?' I asked. 'Maybe have a drink?'

She worried her lower lip. 'A drink's not all we're talkin' about here, is it?'

I was pleased by her frankness, her desire to move things along. Like her ungilded exterior, I took this to indicate inner strength. 'I suppose not.'

She let out a breath slowly. 'Know why I came back to this part of the world? I want somethin' from this place. I don't even know what exactly. Sometimes I think it's just to feel somethin' strong again, 'cause I've been so insulated against feelin' the past nine years. But whatever, I don't wanna be hangin' around anybody who's goin' to hold me back.' Another sigh. 'It's probably weird, me sayin' all this, but I don't want any misunderstandin's.'

'No, it's not weird. I can relate.' Sad for her, I was careful not to let the words sound too facile, because though I *did* understand her, I no longer believed in what she thought was out there. I felt I should make a stab at honesty. 'Me, I'm not looking for anything,' I told her. 'I just try to accept what comes.'

'That's more than most,' she said glumly.

Overhead the contrail of a fighter became visible, arrowing east toward Syria and the latest headlines. Seeing it appeared to brighten Kate.

'Well,' she said, shouldering her bag. 'I reckon I'll take you up on that drink.'

Around midnight I got up from my bed and went into the living room, to a telephone table by French doors that stood open onto a balcony, where I dialled the Belgian girl whom I had been fucking for the past year. When she answered I said, 'Hey, Claire.'

'Danny? Where are you?'

'Out and about.' I tried to think of something else to say. She was helping to install an advanced computer in one of the mosques, one of those projects cloaked in secrecy. I found the whole thing immensely boring, but now I thought talking about it might be distracting. 'How's work?' I asked.

'The usual. The mullahs are upset, the technicians are incompetent.'

I imagined I could hear her displeasure in the bursts of static on the line. It was a cool night, and I shivered in the breeze. Sweat was drying on my chest, my thighs. Faint wailing music and a chaos of traffic noises from the street below. A slant of moonlight fell over the tile floor, a thin tide that sliced across my ankles and bleached my feet bone white. Beyond the light, two chairs and a sofa made shadowy puzzles in a blue darkness.

'You're with somebody, aren't you?' Claire said.

'You know me,' I said.

'Perhaps I should come over. Make it a threesome.'

'Not this time.' But I could not help picturing them together. Claire, soft and white, black hair and large, startling indigo eyes, the submissive voluptuary, the intellectual with a doctorate in artificial intelligence. Kate, all brown and lithe, passionate and violently alive.

'Who is she?'

'An American. She just got a divorce, she's doing some travelling.'

A prickly silence. 'Why did you call?'

'I wanted to hear your voice.'

'That's bullshit,' she said. 'You're worried about something. I always get these calls when something's not going the way you planned.'

I hung my head, listening to the little fizzing storms on the line.

'Is she getting to you, Danny? Is that it?'

Through the French doors I could see a corner of the building that housed police headquarters on Tewfik Square, and facing it, reddish-brown under the arc lights, the colossal statue of Rameses II, marooned on a traffic island, ruler now of a tiny country of parched grass and chipped cement, a steady stream of traffic coursing around it.

'That's why you called,' Claire said. 'Maybe you're falling in love a little bit, and you wanted . . . what do you say? A reality check. Well, don't worry, Danny. The world's still just like it was this morning. The big ones still eat the little ones, and you and I, we have our arrangement. We still' – she let rancour creep into her voice – 'we still are there for each other.'

'It must be the drugs that make you so wise,' I said, both irritated and comforted that she knew me so well.

'That's it! That's it, exactly. And you, lover. It's been an education with you.'

I heard a noise behind me. Kate was standing in the bedroom door, a sheet wrapped around her body, her face in shadow.

'I've got to go,' I said to Claire.

'Duty calls, eh? All right, Danny. I know you'll be busy for a while, but give me a call when you get tired of it. Okay?'

'Okay.'

'Who was that?' Kate asked as I hung up.

'I was breaking a date,' I said.

'For tomorrow?' She came toward me, holding the sheet closed at her breasts. The cloth was dazzlingly white in contrast to her tan. With her hair tumbled about her shoulders, she had acquired an animal energy that had not been noticeable earlier. There was a sullen wariness in her face.

'For tonight,' I said.

'That wasn't very thoughtful.' She put her right hand on my chest; I could feel my heart beating against it.

'I'm not a very nice guy,' I said.

She frowned at that. 'I'm s'posed to believe 'cause you say you're not a nice guy, you really are? I'm s'posed to overlook the fact that after rollin' around with me, you hop outta the sack and call another woman?'

'I think,' I said, 'you should probably take it to heart.'

Saying this affected me like a confession, the blurting out of a truth that until then I had only dimly perceived, and I felt heavy with the baggage of my trivial past, my deceits and delusions, the confidence game I had made of ordinary days and nights.

Kate studied me for a second or two. Her eyes looked all dark. Then she moved her hand lower, her fingers trailing across my stomach. 'Hell, I'm fed up with nice guys,' she said, and curled her fingers around my cock.

This made me a little nervous. That right hand of hers was a marvel. Earlier that evening she had crushed an ice cube into powder between her forefinger and thumb to win a bet, and had flicked off the top of a beer bottle as easily as I would have flicked a piece of lint from my jacket. She might, I thought, want to punish me because of the phone call. But she only caressed me, bringing my erection to life. The sheet slid to the floor, and I touched her breasts. They were small, with puffy coral-coloured areolae. I let their soft weights cosy in my hands. 'Ah, baby,' she said, a catch in her voice. 'Baby.' I could feel her trembling. She drew me to the sofa, perched on the back of it, and hooked her legs about my waist. My cock scored the crease of her, nuzzled the seep of juices. She guided me inside, worked me partway in. Her head came forward to rest on my shoulder, and her mouth pressed against my throat, breathing a moist, warm circle on my skin. She held me motionless, hands clamped to my buttocks. I pushed against her, trying to seat myself more deeply.

'No!' She pricked me with her nails. 'Stay like this a minute.'

'I want to be all the way in you,' I said. She laughed happily, said, 'Oh, I thought I had it all,' and angled herself to accommodate me. I went in deeper with that silky glide that makes you think you are going to flow along with it forever, like the entry of a diver or the dismount of a gymnast, so perfect and gravityless, it should mark the first stage of a journey and not merely an abrupt transition into a clumsier state. I needed to feel it again, and I fucked her heavily, supporting her with both hands. She quit trying to hold me and thrust with her hips, losing her balance and putting a strain on my arms. We wobbled, nearly tumbled off the sofa. It was clear we were not going to make a success of things in this position.

'Let's go back in the bedroom,' I said.

'Stay inside me,' she said, and threw her arms around my neck. 'I need you there. Carry me.'

I lifted her and went weaving toward the bedroom, into the thick darkness, lurching sideways but managing to keep the tip of my cock lodged inside her; then I lowered her carefully, awkwardly, onto the cool, rumpled sheet. We wriggled about until we were centred on the bed, and I sank into her again. She bridged up on her elbows. I thought she would kiss me, but she only put her lips to my ear and whispered, 'Do everything to me.'

Those words seemed so innocent, as if she were new to all this sweet struggle, they made me feel splendid and blessed and full of love. But as I moved in her again, caution ruled me, and though I told her I loved her, I spoke in the softest of voices, a windy phrase almost indistinguishable from a sigh, and not so she could hear.

Two days later as we explored the old bazaar, the Khan al Khalili, idling along the packed, dusty streets among beggars, acrobats, men selling holograms of the Sphinx and plastic cartouches, ox-carts laden with bricks, hooting taxis, more beggars, travelling through zones of garbage stink, spicy cooking odours, perfumes, incense, hashish, walking through a thousand radio musics in the elaborate shade of mosques and roof warrens, past bamboo stalls and old slave markets with tawny arched façades and painted doors in whitewashed walls that might lead into a courtyard populated by doves and orange trees and houris or the virtual reality of a wealthy businessman with violet skies and flames bursting from black rock and djinns in iron armour, it occurred to me that while I had come to know a great deal about Kate during the past forty-eight hours, incidents from her armed service, sundry drab episodes from her marriage, her family in Virginia, she knew next to nothing about me. Having identified me as 'that smuggler guy' appeared to have satisfied her curiosity. Not that there was anything more salient to know – my life had gone unchanged for almost a decade, and the colours of my youth had no real bearing on the man I had become, aimless and pleasure-seeking and competent in unimportant ways. I recognized that Kate was hoping to recapture the intensity she had experienced during her war, the talent for intensity that had been shrouded by marriage, and I realized now it was my occupation, not my winning personality, that had attracted her. I was to be the centrepiece of her furious nostalgia, a sinister element of the design. This comprised an irony I did not believe she would appreciate, for I was far from the adventurous soul she assumed me to be. My success in business was due to an attention to detail and the exercise of caution. The urge to play Indiana Jones was not in my canon. On the other hand, a large portion of what had attracted me to her was more or less the same quality she thought to perceive in me: her drive toward the edge, her consuming desire to put herself in harm's way on both emotional and physical levels. Because of the imbalance of our involvements, I knew that by allowing myself to become obsessed – and I had already developed a pounding fascination with her – I was opening myself up to a world of hurt; but that, too, the possibility of emotional risk, was part of her appeal. In ways I did not understand, I was committed to whatever course she cared to choose. It was as if when I first looked at her and saw the glitter of that impersonal desire in her eyes, that lust for whatever would excite her, I'd heard the future roaring in my ears and said to myself, Now, old son, now you can throw your life away for no reason at all.

The interior of the shop belonging to Abdel Affifi, my partner in crime, was a nondescript clutter: glass display counters ranked with bottles of various essences, shelves laden with toy camels and cotton shirts, cheap luggage, gilt bathrobes, fly whisks, bearded plastic heads with tiny fibreoptic memories that recited verses from the Koran, trays heaped with fraudulent antiquities. A beggar peered in through the window, his wizened face visible between two camel saddles, an artefact of the culture more authentic than any the shop had for sale. Abdel himself was a hook-nosed old man clad in a fez and a shabby suit coat worn over a gallibeya. He made a fuss over Kate, who had on a summery print dress and looked very pretty; he served her mint tea and insisted she try his most expensive essence. He failed to notice her prosthesis and seized her right hand; before she could object, he applied a drop of the oily stuff to the inside of her wrist. The perfume, designed to react with the skin to form a unique fragrance, gave off scarcely any odour at all. She pretended to be delighted, but moments later I caught her staring grimly at the wrist, and when I tried to console her, she shook me off.

Not long afterward a plump, animated middle-aged Arab entered the shop, a man whom I knew as Rollo. Sleek black hair; flourishing moustache; western-style suit. He and Abdel struck up a conversation by the door. This did not please me. Rollo had been trying to involve us in drug-trafficking in the Sinai. I wanted nothing to do with him, but Abdel, who was under some heavy financial pressure, had showed signs of weakening. I must admit I was also tempted by the money, but I had refused to give in to temptation. My policy of not dealing drugs was one of the few fixed points remaining on my moral compass; I needed to maintain it, I thought, in order to maintain my separateness from the chaotic amorality of my environment . . . though it may be that a form of superstitious fear, perhaps an apprehension that I would expose myself to karmic peril if I breached the policy, had supplanted any true moral feeling.

'Who's that?' Kate asked, and when I told her, she said, 'Rollo? That's hilarious!'

'His father was a guide for the Brits in World War II. He taught Rollo the King's English, or at least some fishwife's version of it. The name'll make sense when you hear him talk.'

After a minute or so Rollo came toward us, beaming like an uncle who had just spied his favourite nephew – this despite the fact he knew I detested him. 'Danny!' he said joyfully, giving me a hug, enveloping me in an aura of flowery cologne. Then, turning his white smile on Kate, he said in the ripest of Cockney accent, "Oo's the bird?'

Kate managed to keep a straight face during the introductions and the exchange of pleasantries that followed, but after Rollo had drawn me aside I saw her over his shoulder, laughing silently.

'Look 'ere, mate,' Rollo was saying. 'My friend Abdel and Oi 'ave made us an agreement, but we can't do nuffin' 'less you're part of it. Oi need you to settle things with the Israelis. They've 'eard of you, and they'll be 'appier finkin' a Yank's in charge.'

'Fuck off,' I said.

'Listen to this offer, my friend,' Abdel said, making a plaintive face.

With an air of vast self-importance, Rollo took a notepad from the pocket of his suit coat, scribbled on it and then showed me the percentages he had written. I tried to look blasé and told him I wasn't interested.

'Nao, you're not interested!' said Rollo. 'Your eyes 'alf bugged out, they did!'

'He's only asking for you to make some arrangements,' said Abdel in a wheedling tone. 'You won't be carrying drugs.'

'Damn right I won't.' Abdel started to say something more, but I cut him off. 'There's worse than Israeli troops out in the Sinai. With or without drugs, what he's asking is risky as hell. I don't know shit about these people. They might take a dislike to me and blow my fucking head off.'

Abdel continued trying to persuade me, and this put me in a thorny position. I could have made my own way in Cairo without much difficulty, but Abdel had taken me under his wing, treated me more like a son than a partner, and as a result I was doing very well indeed. He was no saint, God knows; but compared to Rollo he was an innocent. I did not want him to get in over his head. Yet it was hard to deny him, knowing he was in trouble. I'd had dealings in the Sinai before, and I believed I could deal with Rollo's people. Crossing the border was no problem – though detection systems should have made such crossing impossible, there were many Israelis these days willing to look the other way for a price. It was the Palestinians who concerned me. Since the Intifada had failed, all manner of eccentric fundamentalism, some of it arcane in nature, had come to flourish in the camps and villages of the Sinai, and I had heard stories that gave me pause.

'I'll think it over,' I said at last, figuring that if I could put him off, some wiser business opportunity might arise.

He spread his hands in a gesture of acquiescence, but Rollo, tactful as ever, brayed at me, saying, 'Yeah, g'wan, fink it over! We'll just await your pleasure, shall we?'

After we had left Abdel's I explained to Kate what had happened. We were walking along a narrow street of open-front shops, ignoring the pleas of the beggars. The sun had lowered behind a mosque on our left, and the golden light had the mineral richness of the light you often get in the tropics when the sun is shining through rain clouds. As we neared the edge of the bazaar Kate leaned into me, pressed her breasts against my arm, and said coyly, 'Can't we go? I'd like to watch you in action!'

'You want to go with me?' I chuckled. 'Not a chance!'

She pulled back from me, angry. 'What's so funny? I've been in the desert before. And I know how to handle myself. Maybe better than you!'

'Maybe,' I said, trying to mollify her. 'But you've never dealt with people like this. I wouldn't want to be responsible for what could happen.'

That stirred her up even more. 'Let's get this straight,' she said. 'I'm nobody's responsibility but my own, okay? Just 'cause we're screwin', that doesn't mean . . .'

'Kate,' I said, uncomfortable with the crowd that was gathering, the taxi honking at us to clear the way. We were standing beside a store that sold baskets, and the owner and customers had come out to watch. A trolley so clotted with humanity, people stuffed inside, hanging all over the outside, that you could scarcely see the green enamel finish of the car, passed on the street adjoining the entrance to the bazaar, and it seemed all those brown arms were waving at me.

'That doesn't mean,' she went on, 'you got any papers on me. Do you understand? I don't want you to be confused!'

I was startled by the intensity of her anger. She was enraged, her face flushed, standing with hands on hips, continuing her harangue. Some of the onlookers had begun to make jokes about me; the taxi driver was leaning out his window and laughing. Even the beggars were grinning.

I caught her by the arm. She tried to wrench away, but I hauled her along, pushed her into an alley, pinned her against the wall. 'You can get all over me back at my place if you want,' I said. 'But not here. I work down here. People see me humiliated in public by a woman, word gets around, and I lose respect. That may sound sexist, but that's how it is in this culture. Respect's the main currency in my business. I can't afford to lose it.'

She grew instantly contrite, telling me she understood, apologizing, not backing away from her statement of independence, but saying that she should have known better than to cause a scene, she was just a real bitch on that particular subject.

I had expected her anger to abate, yet not so quickly, and it was not until later I realized that her sudden shift in mood was due less to my logic than to the fact that I had acted like the character she fancied me instead of like the man I was. And perhaps I *had* been putting on an act. If Claire had done to me what Kate had, I would have simply walked away from her. But of course Claire would never have acted that way.

At the time I understood little of this. I believe now that I did not want to understand, that I knew I would have to play a role in order to keep the affair on course, to satisfy Kate's demands, and I am certain that this talent for self-deception was partly responsible for all that came to happen.

All that next week I tried to distract Kate from what had become a preoccupation with illegal adventure by showing her Cairo, a city that, with its minarets and roof warrens, its modern bridges and timeless river, ubiquitous flies, computerized calls to prayer, crushing poverty and secret pleasures, seemed to embody all the toxins and exaltations of life. But Kate, though exhilarated, was not distracted. One evening as we sat surrounded by old men smoking waterpipes in a back alley club – Claire's favourite, as it happened – a place constructed of ornate carpets draped over a bamboo frame, with folding chairs and little metal tables, all centred about a makeshift stage upon which a drugged young girl wearing street clothes, her cheeks pierced by silver needles, sang a song that prophesied glory for Islam, Kate grew surly and silent, and as she often did when depressed, bent coins between the thumb and forefinger of her right hand. There was a great deal I loved about her, but this fixation on her prosthesis disturbed me no end. Once she had slit open a seam that ran across the palm, peeled back folds of plastic skin, laying bare a packed complexity of microcircuits, and demonstrated how, by stripping a wire that ran to the power pack, she could short out an electrical system. I was not happy to think that the woman with whom I was sleeping could electrocute me on a whim.

I understood her fixation – at least I sympathized with it – but there was much I did not understand about her reaction to war. I had known men of my father's generation, veterans of Vietnam, who had exhibited a similar yearning for the terrible pleasures of the battlefield; yet they had been brutally used and discarded by their country, whereas the veterans of Kate's war had been celebrated as American saints. Even if I accepted the idea that all combat veterans longed for such intensity, that did not explain the feverish quality of Kate's longing, and I thought my inability to understand her might stem from my failure to understand Desert Storm, a fabulous victory that had achieved next to nothing in terms of *realpolitik*, unless you considered the deaths of a hundred thousand Iraqis, the restoration of a cruel oligarchy in Kuwait, and the drastic upgrading of Syria's missile capacity to be achievements. Could the inconclusiveness of the action be responsible for the sickness that preyed upon Kate? Or could it be in that delirious sky over Baghdad, with white streaks and flares whirling in the electric blue of the nightscope like a kind of strange cellular activity, the darting of sperm in an inky womb, the mysterious associations of organelles, that some magic had been at work, infecting those who fought beneath it with unending dissatisfaction? I had asked Kate questions that addressed these and other notions, but she would only talk about the war in terms of anecdote, mostly humorous, mostly undermining the popular conception that Desert Storm had been an exercise of phenomenal precision, telling of crates of missiles left untended in the middle of nowhere, tank commands roaming aimlessly, misdirected platoons. Watching her that night, unable to comprehend her motives – or my own, for that matter – I acknowledged that my relationship with her was intrinsically concerned with the exploration of those motives, and so I told her that I was going into the Sinai, that she could go with me.

She glanced up from her pile of bent piastres; for an instant something glowed and shifted in her face, as if she were in the grip of an emotion that had the fierce mutability of a fire burning out of control.

'All right!' she said, and took my hand.

I had expected more of a reaction, but perhaps she too had known it was inevitable.

The young girl's song was ending. She swayed under the necklace of light bulbs that illuminated the stage, her hands describing delicate passages in the air, not a drop of blood spilling from her pierced cheeks, singing of how Muhammed returned to reign in Mecca and the blessing of Islam spread throughout the infidel world and flowers bloomed in the desert. All around me, wreathed in hashish smoke, old men were nodding, weeping, speaking the name of God. That was what I most loved about the Arabs of the bazaar, their capacity to cast aside the duplicitous context of their lives and find within themselves some holy fibre that allowed them to reduce the pain of the world to an article of faith. I shed no tears, yet I felt as one of them, wholly embracing a glorious futility, given over to the thunderous joy of belief, though I realized that the truth to which I had surrendered myself was meagre and blighted and could not long sustain me.

Two nights later as we approached our rendezvous point, which lay less than a kilometre from the abandoned Palestinian village of El Malik, I began to smell perfume. I pulled Abdel's jeep onto the shoulder, in among some thorn bushes. Kate asked what was wrong, and I told her, Nothing. But perfume was often used by smugglers to disguise the scent of opium, and I was afraid that we had been set up. The cushion of the back seat was drenched with attar of roses. I sliced the upholstery with my pocket knife, groped inside the cushion, and along with wet stuffing and perfume vials and broken glass – apparently the last pothole had done the damage – I felt thin, hard cakes wrapped in paper. Opium. And not a little of it.

Somewhere out in the darkness, among the barren hills that bulked up against the stars, an engine kicked over; I had to assume that the Israelis had spotted us, were puzzled by our having stopped, and were coming for their goods. A chill bloomed between my shoulder blades, and my legs grew feeble. I could feel the great emptiness of the Sinai solidifying around us, as malefic as a black tower in whose keep we stood. That no one had told me about the drugs made it clear that my survival was not a *fait accompli*. Rollo had viewed me as an impediment to his association with Abdel; alone, he would be able to manipulate Abdel, and he might have arranged to have me eliminated by the Israelis. An overly imaginative scenario, perhaps. But I had no desire to test its inaccuracy.

I listened to the approaching engine. Judging by its sound, the Israelis were driving something far more powerful than the jeep. We would not be able to outrun them.

'Get the guns,' I said to Kate; I dug out some of the opium and stashed it in my pack, along with several dozen of the vials, thinking I could use them for currency. Once again she asked me what was wrong. I shoved her aside and fished the guns – Belgian SMGs – out from beneath the front seat. I tossed one to her, said, 'Let's go,' and set off at a jog into the hills.

She caught up to me, grabbed my arm. 'You goin' to tell me what the hell's goin' on?'

Until that moment I had controlled my fear, but her touch broke my control, and I was galvanized with terror, furious at her for having led me into this mess, at myself for having followed, for letting her so distract me that I had neglected to take basic precautions. 'You stupid fucking bitch!' I shouted. 'You're so hot to die, stay here. Otherwise get your ass moving.' Her face was pale and stunned in the starlight. I felt a flicker of remorse, but only a flicker. 'You wanted this,' I said. 'Now deal with it.'

We had climbed about a third of a mile, I'd guess, when small arms fire sounded from the road. But no bullets struck close to us. After a few more bursts, there was a loud explosion and a fireball at the base of the hill. The jeep. Shortly thereafter I heard the Israelis' engine roar away. As I had hoped, they were satisfied with the opium and not sufficiently zealous to fulfil their part of what I assumed to have been a contract. Nevertheless I continued climbing toward El Malik, which offered decent cover and where I planned to spend the night. The next morning I intended to hook up with my own Israeli contacts and negotiate our passage back to Cairo.

The moon was rising as we came into the village, descending a slope strewn with boulders, and in that milky light, the whitewashed houses with their vacant black windows and walls gapped by Israeli artillery looked like the shards of enormous skulls. From the eastern edge of the place we gazed out across a valley figured by the lights of Israeli settlements, the formless constellations of a lesser sky. There was a heady air of desolation, a sense of lives violently interrupted yet still, in some frail, exhausted way, trying to complete their ordinary tasks, souls perceptible as a faint disturbance that underscored the silence, a vibration unaffected by the gusting of a cold wind.

We sheltered in a house with a packed dirt floor that offered a view of a public square and a ruined fountain. Kate, who had spoken little during the climb, sat against a wall and stared at me despondently.

'I'm sorry,' she said after a while. 'This is all my fault.'

'Not all of it,' I said, dropping beside her. 'Anyway, the worst is over. Tomorrow, if we're careful, we should be able to get in touch with friends of mine. They'll help us.'

She said nothing for almost a minute, then: 'I've got to be crazy. To want this, I mean.'

I chose not to absolve her of insanity, but I put an arm about her. I believe I felt then what she wanted to feel. To be in that gutted doom of a place, lent a memorial beauty by the moonlight, all its ruin seeming to turn white and bulge with living shadow; to have survived folly and betrayal — and I was not concerned that what had happened would hurt my business, I was simply interested in paying the betrayers back in kind; to be in the company of a woman who, though I did not love her, had put a lover's charge in me, a woman with whom I could practise a perfect counterfeit of passion; it was as if the events of that night had exposed a romantic core in me, and I was now entirely in the world, alive as I had not been for years.

She glanced up at me and said, 'You look happy.'

I laughed and kissed her. The kiss deepened. I touched her breasts, startled to find that anything could feel so soft and luxurious in this harsh, empty place.

Kate pulled back and gave me a searching stare. The vitality had returned to her face. After a second she jumped to her feet, backed away until she was standing in the chute of light spilling through the door.

·I came to one knee, intending to go after her, but she held up a hand to ward me off and began unbuttoning her shirt. She smiled as she shrugged out of the shirt, and watching her work her jeans down past her hips, eyes focused on the dark tangle between her thighs, visible through the opaque material of her panties, I felt heavy in my head, thick and slow, full of a red urge, like a dog restrained from feeding by its mistress's command.

I saw the man behind her a moment before he reached the doorway, but I was so stupefied, I was unable to react, only registering him as a slight figure holding an automatic rifle, wearing jeans and a windbreaker. And a mask. He shoved Kate toward me, sending her toppling, and we fell together onto the floor. By the time I managed to disengage from her, he had been joined by four others, all masked. They were evil-looking things, the masks: curved sheets of white plastic with mouth slits and eyeholes, adorned with painted symbols and religious slogans.

'Tell the whore to clothe herself,' one said in Arabic.

They watched without comment as Kate dressed; she stared back at them, not defiant, but cold, measuring. An admirable pose, but I had no urge to hand her a medal. We had, I believed, come to the end of it. The men who held us captive had lost everything, and their sole remaining ambition was to go down in flames while exacting a terrible vengeance. Oddly enough, at that moment I thought of Claire.

They collected our packs and guns and escorted us to the ruin of a small mosque, where another seven or eight masked men were assembled. Moonlight streamed through rents in the domed roof, applying a design of sharp shadows and blazing light to the floor tiles; the same fierce slogans decorating the masks had here been painted on the walls. A cooking fire burned in a shell crater. The men stationed themselves along the wall; then another man, unmasked, a sharply featured individual dressed in a striped robe, stepped out from a door at the rear of the building. He had a bronzed complexion and a neat beard salted with grey and one blind eye, white as marble. He was carrying a long, gracefully curved sword. He took a position at the centre of the room, directly beneath a gap in the roof, so that a beam of moonlight, separate and distinct, shone like a benediction upon him, and stared at us with disdain. I could feel the fanatical weight of his judgement as surely as if it were a form of radiation.

One of the others handed him my pack, whispered in his ear. He inspected the contents, removed a vial of perfume. He moved close to me, smiling, his blind eye glowing like a tiny moon. 'Thief,' he said in a voice like iron, 'my name is Mahmoud Ibrahim, and I am he who prepares the way. Thou hast stolen from me and given nothing in return. Yet because thou hast been touched by the city of Saladin, I will spare thee everything but pain.' He opened the vial and poured the contents over my head. He took out a second vial, a third, and repeated the process. I shut my eyes. The oily stuff ran into my mouth, thick and bitter, trickling cold down my cheeks, drowning the stink of my fear in a reek of flowers and humiliation.

Mahmoud took one of the cakes of opium, pinched off a substantial fragment. 'Eat,' he said, holding it out. I let him place it on my tongue like a communion wafer.

When he was satisfied that I had swallowed, he smiled, nodded. Then he gestured at Kate and handed his sword to the man who had brought him my pack. 'The woman first,' he said.

Kate shrieked as three men threw her onto the floor and positioned her right wrist atop a block. Another stood by with a torch, while the man wielding the sword laid the edge of it on her wrist, then lifted it high. The traditional Arab punishment for stealing, the lopping off of the right hand – I imagined it sheared away, blood spurting, and perhaps in her fright, Kate had also forgotten the prosthesis, for she twisted her head about, trying to find me, screaming, 'Danny! Help me!' But I was targeted by seven rifles, and I could only stand and watch, the scene burning into my brain – the stark shadows of the ruin, the men in their strange white masks, the calm prophet with his glowing eye, and Kate writhing, her face distorted by panic.

Then, with a windy noise, the sword flashed down.

As the blade bit into Kate's prosthesis, slicing through plastic and microcircuitry, there was a sizzling noise, and a rippling blue-white charge flowed up the steel, outlining blade and hilt in miniature lightnings. Sparks showered around the man holding it, and there was so much confusion and shouting I am not sure whether or not he screamed. He stood for a second or two, shivering with the voltage passing through him; smoke trickled between his fingers. Then he fell. The sword flew from his grasp and went spinning across the floor to my feet.

It was reflex that moved me to pick up the sword, and it was dumb luck that Mahmoud had recoiled from the electrocution and wound up beside me. But I did not waste the opportunity. I slid the blade under his neck, making a yoke of it, and dragged him toward the rear door. Kate was sitting up, dazed, her prosthesis dangling horribly from a spaghetti of charred wires; but when I called to her, she got to her feet and came weaving toward me. More than half the men had fled, terrified by the witchery of her hand, but the remainder were closing on me. I pulled the blade tight against Mahmoud's Adam's apple, making him stiffen and gasp.

'*Emshi!*' I shouted, and his men backed away.

With Kate at my side, I guided Mahmoud through the rear door into a small room whose back wall had been obliterated. Three cars were parked outside. Kate leaned against the wall beside me; her face was empty, slack.

'Keys,' I said to Mahmoud.

He groped in the pocket of his robe, fingered them out. 'The Peugeot,' he said, gritting out the words.

'Can you drive?' I asked Kate.

She did not answer.

I kicked her hard in the calf. She blinked; her head wobbled.

'Drive!' I told her. 'Take the keys and drive.'

Though the men harassed us, aiming their rifles, threatening us, we made it to the car. Mahmoud and I taking the back seat. I sat turned toward him, barring his throat with the blade. Then we were bumping along the cratered streets, jouncing over potholes, past the last houses and out onto a rocky, precipitous road that wound down into the moonstruck valley. No headlights showed behind us. Once the land began to flatten out, I removed the blade from Mahmoud's throat. His men would not risk confronting the Israeli patrols. I was shaking, rattled with adrenaline, yet at the same time I felt woozy, drifty, as if a cloud were building in the centre of my brain. I remembered the opium.

'Shit!' I said.

Mahmoud seemed as calm and content as a hawk with a dead mouse. Kate was staring straight ahead, her good hand clenching the wheel; her skin was pasty, and when she glanced back I had the impression that she looked like she might be going into shock.

'You okay?' I asked.

She muttered something; the car swerved wildly onto the shoulder.

It was definitely the opium coming on. I was having trouble feeling the tips of my fingers, and my head was turning into a balloon. Everything I thought left a vague colour in the air. Smoking opium was a fairly smooth sail, albeit a long ocean voyage; eating it, however, was a rocket to the moon. I was still lifting slowly from the launch pad, but in a minute or two I was going to have all the physical capacity of a cantaloupe. Or maybe a honeydew. I couldn't decide. Something round and gleaming and very, very still. I had intended to turn Mahmoud over to the Israelis; I was sure they wanted him, and I hoped that his capture would help them overlook our illegal entry. But now, with the opium taking control and Kate on the wobbly side, I could not chance having him along.

'Stop the car,' I said.

I had to repeat myself twice before she complied, and by the time she did, I had almost forgotten why I wanted her to stop.

'Get out,' I said to Mahmoud. That blind eye of his had acquired the nacreous depth of pearl, and I was beginning to see things in it. Beautiful things, amazing things. I told him again to get out. Or maybe I didn't. It was difficult to distinguish between speech and thought. Everything was so absorbing. The dark, the distant lights of a kibbutz. The attar of roses smell that clung to me. I could lose myself in any of it. Then something touched me on the brow, leaving a cool spot that went deep inside my head.

'From thy poison I have made thee a vision of the time to come,' Mahmoud said. 'What thou will have of it, I know not. But it is a gift of the Prophet, may His name be praised, and he planteth no seed that doth not bear fruit.'

In the interval between these words and when next he spoke, I heard a symphony compounded of breath and night sounds and metallic creaks that implied an entire secret history hitherto unknown to man. Then there was a whisper, as sinister as a violin tremolo in a minor key: 'Thou will not evade my punishment this night.'

I thought I heard the car door slam shut.

'Kate,' I said. 'Can you get us somewhere? A town. Some place . . .'

I never heard her reply, for I was walking along the crest of a green hill shaped like a dune. A verdant plain spread in every direction, picked out here and there by white stone houses formed into elaborate shapes, and by deep blue lakes along whose edges flamingos stalked and lions with men's voices took their ease, and by white cities where no one cried for meat and in whose highest tower lofty questions were put to a wonderful machine that had summoned and now embodied the soul of the Prophet. White clouds the size of small kingdoms floated overhead, and flying among them were golden shining things that whirled and darted like swallows, yet were made of metal not flesh. At long last I came to a pool shaped like a deep blue eye, almost purple, that lay in the midst of a bamboo thicket, with the ancient statue of an enthroned pharaoh at one end, worn faceless by the wind and the sand. I made to drink from the pool, but when I dipped my hand into the water, it began to stir and to ripple, and strange lights glowed beneath the surface illuminating an intricate thing of silver fibres and rods and other structures whose natures were not clearly revealed, and I heard a voice in the air, the voice of this silver thing, saying, 'I am the Oracle of the Past. Ask and I will tell thee where thou hast been.'

And I said to her, for it was the voice of a woman, 'Of what use is this? I wish to know the Future.'

'Truly,' she said, 'the Future is already known. This is the time of Paradise long prophesied, the time without end when all men live as brothers. Only the Past remains a mystery, and indeed, it has always been thus, for no man can know himself by knowing his future. It is from the Past that the greatest wisdom derives.'

'Then tell me who I am,' I said.

There was a silence, and finally the voice said, 'Thou art

Daniel, the infidel who is known as The Arm of Ibrahim, and thou hast struck down many enemies of Allah and also many enemies of the sons of Abraham. Thou hast faced peril and known terrible strife, yet thou hast survived to wield great power in the service of peace and righteousness, though thy life is as secret to the world as a stone at the bottom of the Nile.' The voice paused, then said, 'I do not understand thee, for it seems thy past and thy future are the same.'

(At this point I heard a scream, a tremendous noise, and felt a tearing pain in my right arm; but I was overwhelmed by the opium and it was as if these things had happened to someone else to whom I was somehow remotely physically connected.)

I, of course, understood the Oracle's confusion. Was not her past my future, and vice versa? 'What must I now do?' I asked.

'Thou must return to the city of Saladin, and there thou will build a city within the city, and all I have told you will come to pass.'

'And who will sustain me against the peril and strife that you have prophesied?'

'I will,' said the voice. 'I will sustain thee.'

'Tell me who you are,' I said.

'I am the Oracle, the soul of the machine,' the voice said. 'Yet I am also, and this I do not understand, the love of thy life come across the centuries to find thee.'

And from the pool there emerged a woman all of white metal save only her right hand which was bone and blood and milky flesh, and her eyes had the shape of the pond and were of a like colour, indigo, and it seemed I had known her for many years, though I could not call her to mind. I took her hand, and as I did, the flesh of her hand began to spread, devouring the metal, until she stood before me, a woman in all ways, complete and mortal.

(I heard anxious voices, 'Where's the driver?' 'She was thrown out.' 'Have you got him?' 'Oh, God! I can't stop the bleeding!' and felt even more intense pain. The vision had begun to fade, and I saw flashes of red light, of concerned faces, the interior of a van.)

And I lay down with the woman among the bamboo stalks, and we touched and whispered, and when I entered her she gave a soft cry that went out and out into the world, winding over the green plain and into the dark valley like the wail of a siren or a call to prayer, and in our lovemaking it seemed we were moving at great speed past strange bodies of light and towers, heading for a destination beyond that of pleasure and release, a place where all my wounds would be healed and all my deepest questions answered.

The doctors in Haifa tried to save my right arm, but in the end they were forced to amputate. It took me six months to adapt to a prosthesis, six months in which I considered what had happened and what I should do next. Kate had also been in the hospital, but she had returned to America by the time I was well enough to ask for her. She left a note in which she apologized for the accident and for involving me in her 'misguided attempt to recapture what I never really lost'. I felt no bitterness toward her. She had failed herself far more than she had failed me. My fascination with her, the psychological structure that supported strong emotion, had died that night in the ruined mosque, its charge expended.

Neither did I feel bitter toward Mahmoud Ibrahim. In retrospect, it seemed he had been no ordinary fanatic, that his poise had been the emblem of a profound internal gravity, of peacefulness and wisdom. Perhaps I manufactured this characterization in order to justify my folly in terms of predestination or some other quasi-religious precept. Yet I could not wholly disbelieve that something of the sort may have been involved. How else could Mahmoud have known that I came from Cairo, the city of Saladin? Then there was his prophecy of my 'punishment', the vision with its curiously formal frame and futuristic detail, so distinct from the random lucidity of the usual opium dream.

A gift from the Prophet?

I wondered. I doubted, yet still I wondered.

Claire came to Haifa, distraught, horrified at my injuries. She slept in the hospital room with me, she washed me, she tended me in every human way. The similarity between her and the woman of my vision was not lost upon me, nor was the fact that her studies in artificial intelligence and her secret project with the mosque gave rise to some interesting possibilities and paradoxes concerning the Oracle; yet I was reluctant to buy into something so preposterous. As the months passed, however, I could not ignore the way that things were changing between us, the tendrils of feeling that we had tried to kill with drugs and cynicism now beginning to creep forth and bud. If this much of the vision had a correspondence with reality, how then could I ignore the rest of it? The life of power and strife, the building of a city within a city: my business? It occurred to me that I had only played at business all these years, that now I was being tempted to get serious. There was much one could effect on an international level through the agency of the black market. But if I were to get serious, it would call for an increased ruthlessness on my part, a ruthlessness informed by a sense of morality and history, something I was not sure I had in me.

I did not know what I would do on my return to Cairo, but on my second night back I went for a walk alone through a secluded quarter of the Khan al Khalili, heading – I thought – in no particular direction, idling along; yet I was not altogether surprised when I came to a certain door in a certain white-washed wall, the retreat of a wealthy businessman. I hesitated. All the particulars of Mahmoud's vision came before my eyes, and I began to understand that, true or not, it offered me a design for life far superior to any I had contrived. At length I opened the door, which was locked, with no great difficulty, and stepped into a courtyard with a tiled fountain and lemon trees. I moved quietly into the house beyond, into a long study lined with books, furnished with a mahogany desk and leather chairs. I waited in the shadows for the man, idly playing with the coins in my pocket, a habit I had picked up during my rehabilitation. I left one of the coins on the desk for him to find. I knew he was a poor sleeper, that soon he would wake and come into the study. When at last he did appear, yawning and stretching, a plump fellow with a furious moustache and sleek black hair, I did not hate him as much as I had presumed; I saw him mainly as an impediment to my new goals.

He sat at the desk, switched on a lamp that cast a pool of light onto the writing surface, shuffled some papers, then spotted the ten-piastre coin that I had left for him. He picked it up and held it to the light. The coin was bent double, the image on its face erased by the pressure of my right thumb and forefinger. It seemed an article of wonder to him, and I felt a little sad for what I must do. He was, after all, much the same as I, a ruthless man with goals, except my ruthlessness was a matter of future record and my goals the stuff of prophecy.

There was no point, I realized, in delaying things. I moved forward, and he peered into the darkness, trying to make me out, his face beginning to register the first of his final misgivings. I felt ordered and serene, not in the least anxious, and I understood that this must be the feeling one attains when one takes a difficult step one has balked at for years and finds that it is not so difficult at all, but a sweet inevitability, a confident emergence rather than an escalation of fear.

'Hello, Rollo,' I said. 'I just need a few seconds of your time.'

BEAST OF THE HEARTLAND

Mears has a dream the night after he fought the Alligator Man. The dream begins with words: 'In the beginning was a dark little god with glowing red eyes . . .' And then, there it stands, hovering in the blackness of Mears' hotel room, a twisted mandrake root of a god, evil and African, with ember eyes and limbs like twists of leaf tobacco. Even after it vanishes, waking Mears, he can feel those eyes burning inside his head, merged into a single red pain that seems as if it will go on throbbing forever. He wonders if he should tell Leon about the pain – maybe he could give Mears something to ease it – but he figures this might be a bad idea. Leon might cut and run, not wanting to be held responsible should Mears keel over, and there Mears would be: without a trainer, without anyone to coach him for the eye exams, without an accomplice in his blindness. It's not a priority, he decides.

To distract himself, he lies back and thinks about the fight. He'd been doing pretty well until the ninth. Staying right on the Cuban's chest, mauling him in the corners, working the body. The Cuban didn't like it to the body. He was a honey-coloured kid a couple of shades lighter than Mears and he punched like a kid, punches that stung but that didn't take your heart like the punches of a man. Fast, though. Jesus, he was fast! As the fight passed into the middle rounds, as Mears tired, the Cuban began to slip away, to circle out of the haze of ring light and vanish into the darkness at the corners of Mears' eyes, so that Mears saw the punches coming only at the last second, the wet-looking red blobs of the gloves looping in over his guard. Then, in the ninth, a left he never saw drove him into the turnbuckle, a flurry of shots under the ribs popped his mouthpiece halfway out and another left to the temple made him clinch, pinning the Cuban's gloves against his sides.

In the clinch, that's when he caught sight of the Alligator Man. The Cuban pulled back his head, trying to wrench his right glove free, and the blurred oval of his face sharpened, resolved into features: blazing yellow eyes and pebbly skin, and slit nostrils at the end of a long snout. Although used to such visions, hallucinations, whatever this was, Mears reacted in terror. He jolted the Alligator Man with an uppercut, he spun him, landed a clubbing right high on the head, another right, and as if those punches were magic, as if their force and number were removing a curse, breaking a spell, the Alligator Man's face melted away, becoming a blurred brown oval once again. Mears' terror also grew blurred, his attack less furious, and the Cuban came back at him, throwing shots from every angle. Mears tried to slide off along the ropes but his legs were gone, so he ducked his head and put his gloves up to block the shots. But they got through, anyway.

Somebody's arms went around him, hemming him in against the ropes, and he smelled flowery cologne and heard a smooth baritone saying, 'Take it easy, man! It's over.' Mears wanted to tell the ref he could have stood up through ten, the Cuban couldn't punch for shit. But he was too weak to say anything and he just rested his head on the ref's shoulder, strings of drool hanging off his mouthpiece, cooling on his chin. And for the first time in a long while, he heard the crowd screaming for the Cuban, the women's voices bright and crazy, piercing up from the male roar. Then Leon was there, Leon's astringent smell of Avitene and Vaseline and Gelfoam, and somebody shoved Mears down onto a stool and Leon pressed the ice-cold bar of the Enswell against the lump over his eye, and the Cuban elbowed his way through the commission officials and nobodies in the corner and said, 'Man, you one tough motherfucker. You almos' kill me with them right hands.' And Mears had the urge to tell him, 'You think I'm tough, wait'll you see what's coming,' but instead, moved by the sudden, heady love that possesses you after you have pounded on a man for nine rounds and he has not fallen, Mears told him that one day soon he would be champion of the world.

Mears wonders if the bestial faces that materialize in the midst of his fights are related to the pain in his head. In his heart he believes they are something else. It could be that he has been granted the magical power to see beneath the surface of things. Or they may be something his mind has created to compensate for his blindness, a kind of spiritual adrenaline that inspires him to fiercer effort, often to victory. Since his retinas became detached, he has slipped from the status of fringe contender to trial horse for young fighters on the way up, and his style has changed from one of grace and elusiveness to that of a brawler, of someone who must keep in constant physical contact with his opponent. Nevertheless, he has won twelve of seventeen fights with his handicap, and he owes much of his success to this symptom or gift or delusion.

He knows most people would consider him a fool for continuing to fight, and he accepts this. But he does not consider himself a greater fool than most people; his is only a more dramatic kind of foolishness than the foolishness of loving a bad woman or stealing a car or speculating on gold futures or smoking cigarettes or taking steroids or eating wrong or involving yourself with the trillion other things that lead to damage and death.

As he lies in that darkened room, in the pall of his own darkness, he imagines attending a benefit held to raise his medical expenses after his secret has been disclosed. All the legends are there. Ali, Frazier and Foreman are there, men who walk with the pride of a nation. Duran is there, Duran of the demonic fury, who TKO'd him in 1979, back when Mears was a welterweight. The Hit Man is there, Thomas Hearns, sinister and rangy, with a cobra-like jab that had once cut him so badly the flesh hung down into his eyes. Sugar Ray Leonard is there, talking about his own detached retina and how he could have gone the same way as Mears. And Hagler, who knocked Mears out in his only title shot, Hagler the tigerish southpaw, he is there, too. Mears ascends to the podium to offer thanks, and a reporter catches his arm and asks him, 'What the hell went wrong, Bobby? What happened to you?' He thinks of all the things he could say in response. Bad managers, crooked promoters. Alimony. I forgot to duck. The classic answers. But there is one answer they've never heard, one that he's nourished for almost two years.

'I travelled into the heartland,' he tells the reporter, 'and when I got done fighting the animals there, I came out blind.'

The reporter looks puzzled, but Ali and Foreman, Frazier and Hagler, Duran and Hearns, they nod sagely, they understand. They realize Mears' answer is partly a pride thing, partly intuitive, a summation of punches absorbed, hands lifted in victory, months of painful healing, hours of punishment in the gym. But mainly it is the recasting into a vow of a decision made years before. They would not argue that their sport is brutally stupid, run by uncaring bastards to whom it is a business of dollars and blood, and that tragedies occur, that fighters are swindled and outright robbed. Yet there is something about it they have needed, something they have chosen, and so in the end, unlike the asbestos worker who bitterly decries the management that has lied to him and led him down a fatal path, the fighter feels no core bitterness, not even at himself for being a fool, for making such a choice in the folly of youth, because he has forsworn the illusion of wisdom.

Mears is not without regrets. Sometimes, indeed, he regrets almost everything. He regrets his blindness, his taste in women, his rotten luck at having been a middleweight during the age of Marvin Hagler. But he has never regretted boxing. He loves what he does, loves the gym rats, the old dozers with their half-remembered tales of Beau Jack and Henry Armstrong, the crafty trainers, the quiet cut men with their satchels full of swabs and chemicals. He loves how he has been in the ring, honourable and determined and brave. And now, nodding off in a cheap hotel room, he feels love from the legends of the game returned in applause that has the sound of rushing water, a pure stream of affirmation that bears him away into the company of heroes and a restless sleep.

Three mornings later, as Mears waits for Leon in the gym, he listens happily to the slapping of jump ropes, the grunt and thud of someone working the heavy bag, the jabber and pop of speed bags, fighters shouting encouragement, the sandpapery whisk of shoes on canvas, the meaty thump of fourteen-ounce sparring gloves. Pale winter light chutes through the high windows like a Bethlehem star to Mears' eyes. The smell is a harsh perfume of antiseptic, resin and sweat. Now and then somebody passes by, says, 'Yo, Bobby, what's happenin'?' or 'Look good the other night, man!' and he will hold out his hand to be slapped without glancing up, pretending that his diffidence is an expression of cool, not a pose designed to disguise his impaired vision. His body still aches from the Cuban's fast hands, but in a few weeks, a few days if necessary, he'll be ready to fight again.

He hears Leon rasping at someone, smells his cigar, then spots a dark interruption in the light. Not having to see Leon, he thinks, is one of the few virtues of being legally blind. He is unsightly, a chocolate-coloured blob of a man with jowls and yellow teeth and a belly that hangs over his belt. The waist of Mears' boxing trunks would not fit over one of Leon's thighs. He is especially unsightly when he lies, which is often – weakness comes into his face, his popped eyes dart, the pink tip of the tongue slimes the gristly upper lip. He looks much better as a blur in an onion-coloured shirt and dark trousers.

'Got a fight for us, my man.' Leon drops onto a folding chair beside him, and the chair yields a metallic creak. 'Mexican name Nazario. We gon' kick his fuckin' ass!'

This is the same thing Leon said about the Cuban, the same thing he said about every opponent. But this time he may actually be sincere. 'Guy's made for us,' he continues. 'Comes straight ahead. Good hook, but a nothin' right. No fancy bullshit.' He claps Bobby on the leg. 'We need a W bad, man. We whup this guy in style, I can get us a main event on ESPN next month in Wichita.'

Mears is dubious. 'Fighting who?'

'Vederotta,' says Leon, hurrying past the name to say the Nazario fight is in two weeks. 'We can be ready by then, can't we, sure, we be ready, we gon' kill that motherfucker.'

'That guy calls himself the Heat? Guy everybody's been duckin'?'

'Wasn't for everybody duckin' him, I couldn't get us the fight. He's tough, I ain't gon' tell you no lie. He busts people up. But check it out, man. Our end's twenty grand. Like that, Bobby? Tuh-wenty thousand dollars.'

'You shittin' me?'

'They fuckin' desperate. They can't get nobody to fight the son of a bitch. They need a tune-up for a title shot.' Leon sucks on his cigar, trying to puff it alight. 'It's your ass out there, man. I'll do what you tell me. But we get past Nazario, we show good against Vederotta – I mean give him a few strong rounds, don't just fold in one – guy swears he'll book us three more fights on ESPN cards. Maybe not the main event, but TV bouts. That'd make our year, man. Your end could work out to forty, forty-five.'

'You get that in writin' 'bout the three more fights?'

'Pretty sure. Man's so damn desperate for somebody with a decent chin, he'll throw in a weekend with his wife.'

'I don't want his damn wife, I want it in writin' 'bout the fights.'

'You ain't seen his wife! That bitch got a wiggle take the kinks outta a couch spring.' Delighted by his wit, Leon laughs; the laugh turns into a wet, racking cough.

'I'm gon' need you on this one,' says Mears after the coughing has subsided. 'None of this bullshit 'bout you runnin' round all over after dope and pussy while I'm bustin' my balls in the gym, and then showin' up when the bell rings. I'm gon' need you really working. You hear that, Leon?'

Leon's breath comes hard. 'I hear you.'

'Square business, man. You gotta write me a book on that Vederotta dude.'

'I'll do my thing,' says Leon, wheezing. 'You just take care of old Señor Nazario.'

The deal concluded, Mears feels exposed, as if a vast, luminous eye – God's, perhaps – is shining on him, revealing all his frailties. He sits up straight, holds his head very still, rubs his palms along the tops of his thighs, certain that everyone is watching. Leon's breathing is hoarse and laboured, like last breaths. The light is beginning to tighten up around that sound, to congeal into something cold and grey, like a piece of dirty ice in which they are all embedded.

Mears thinks of Vederotta, the things he's heard. The one-round knockouts, the vicious beatings. He knows he's just booked himself a world of hurt. As if in resonance with that thought, his vision ripples and there is a twinge inside his head, a little flash of red. He grips the seat of the chair, prepares for worse. But worse does not come, and after a minute or so, he begins to relax, thinking about the money, slipping back into the peace of morning in the gym, with the starred light shining from on high and the enthusiastic shouts of the young fighters and the slap of leather making a rhythm like a river slapping against a bank and the fat man who is not his friend beginning to breathe easier now beside him.

When Mears phones his ex-wife, Amandla, the next night, he sits on the edge of the bed and closes his eyes so he can see her clearly. She's wearing her blue robe, slim-hipped and light-skinned, almost like a Latin girl, but her features are fine and eloquently African and her hair is kept short in the way of a girl from Brazzaville or Conakry. He remembers how good she looks in big gold hoop earrings. He remembers so much sweetness, so much consolation and love. She simply had not been able to bear his pain, coming home with butterfly patches over his stitched eyes, pissing blood at midnight, having to heave himself up from a chair like an old man. It was a weakness in her, he thinks, yet he knows it was an equivalent weakness in him, that fighting is his crack, his heroin – he would not give it up for her.

She picks up on the fourth ring, and he says, 'How you been, baby?'

She hesitates a moment before saying, 'Aw, Bobby, what you want?' But she says it softly, plaintively, so he'll know that though it's not a good thing to call, she's glad to hear his voice, anyway.

'Nothin', baby,' he says. 'I don't want nothin'. I just called to tell you I'll be sendin' money soon. Few weeks, maybe.'

'You don't have to. I'm makin' it all right.'

'Don't tell me you can't use a little extra. You got responsibilities.'

A faded laugh. 'I hear that.'

There is silence for a few beats, then Mears says, 'How's your mama holdin' up?'

'Not so good. Half the time I don't think she knows who I am. She goes to wanderin' off sometimes, and I got to—' She breaks off, lets air hiss out between her teeth. 'I'm sorry, Bobby. This ain't your trouble.'

That stings him, but he does not respond directly to it. 'Well, maybe I send you a little somethin', you can ease back from it.'

'I don't want to short you.'

'You ain't gon' be shortin' me, baby.' He tells her about Nazario, the twenty thousand dollars, but not about Vederotta.

'Twenty thousand!' she says. 'They givin' you twenty thousand for fightin' a man you say's easy? That don't make any sense.'

'Ain't like I'm just off the farm. I still got a name.'

'Yeah, but you—'

'Don't worry about it,' he says angrily, knowing that she's about to remind him he's on the downside. 'I got it under control.'

Another silence. He imagines that he can hear her irritation in the static on the line.

'But I do worry,' she says. 'God help me, I still worry about you after all this time.'

'Ain't been that long. Three years.'

She does not seem to have heard. 'I still think about you under them lights gettin' pounded on. And now you offerin' me money you gon' earn for gettin' pounded on some more.'

'Look here—' he begins.

'Blood money. That's what it is. It's blood money.'

'Stop it,' he says. 'You stop that shit. It ain't no more blood money than any other wage. Money gets paid out, somebody always gettin' fucked over at the end of it. That's just what money is. But this here money, it ain't comin' 'cause of nothin' like that, not even 'cause some damn judge said I got to give it. It's coming from me to you 'cause you need it and I got it.'

He steers the conversation away from the topic of fighting, gets her talking about some of their old friends, even manages to get her laughing when he tells her how the cops caught Sidney Bodden and some woman doing the creature in Sidney's car in the parking lot of the A&P. The way she laughs, she tips her head and tucks her chin down onto her shoulder and never opens her mouth, just makes these pleased, musical noises like a shy little girl, and when she lifts her head, she looks so innocent and pretty he wants to kiss her, grazes the receiver with his lips, wishes it would open and let him pour through to her end of the line. The power behind the wish hits his heart like a mainlined drug, and he knows she still loves him, he still loves her, this is all wrong, this long-distance shit, and he can't stop himself from saying, 'Baby, I want to see you again.'

'No,' she says.

It is such a terminal, door-slamming no, he can't come back with anything. His face is hot and numb, his arms and chest heavy as concrete, he feels the same bewildered, mule-stupid helplessness as he did when she told him she was leaving. He wonders if she's seeing somebody, but he promises himself he won't ask.

'I just can't, Bobby,' she says.

'It's all right, baby,' he says, his voice reduced to a whisper. 'It's all right. I got to be goin'.'

'I'm sorry, I really am sorry. But I just can't.'

'I'll be sending you somethin' real soon. You take care now.'

'Bobby?'

He hangs up, an effort, and sits there turning to stone. Brooding thoughts glide through his head like slow black sails. After a while he lifts his arms as if in an embrace. He feels Amandla begin to take on shape and solidity within the circle of his arms. He puts his left hand between her shoulder blades and smooths the other along her flanks, following the arch of her back, the tight rounds of her ass, the columned thighs, and he presses his face against her belly, smelling her warmth, letting all the trouble and ache of the fight with the Cuban go out of him. All the weight of loss and sadness. His chest seems to fill with something clear and buoyant. Peace, he thinks, we are at peace.

But then some sly, peripheral sense alerts him to the fact that he is a fool to rely on this sentimental illusion, and he drops his arms, feeling her fading away like steam. He sits straight, hands on knees, and turns his head to the side, his expression rigid and contemptuous as it might be during a stare-down at the centre of a boxing ring. Since the onset of his blindness, he has never been able to escape the fear that people are spying on him, but lately he has begun to worry that they are not.

*

For once Leon has not lied. The fight with Nazario is a simple contest of wills and left hooks, and though the two men's hooks are comparable, Mears' will is by far the stronger. Only in the fourth round does he feel his control slipping, and then the face of a hooded serpent materializes where Nazario's face should be, and he pounds the serpent image with right leads until it vanishes. Early in the fifth round, he bulls Nazario into a corner and following a sequence of twelve unanswered punches, the ref steps in and stops it.

Two hours after the fight, Mears is sitting in the dimly lit bar on the bottom floor of his hotel, having a draft beer and a shot of Gentleman Jack, listening to Mariah Carey on the jukebox. The mirror is a black, rippling distance flocked by points of actinic light, a mysterious lake full of stars and no sign of his reflection. The hooker beside him is wearing a dark something sewn all over with spangles that move over breasts and hips and thighs like the scattering of moonlight on choppy water. The bartender, when he's visible at all, is a cryptic shadow. Mears is banged up some, a small but nasty cut at his hairline from a head butt and a knot on his left cheekbone, which the hooker is making much of, touching it, saying, 'That's terrible-lookin', honey. Just terrible. You inna accident or somepin'?' Mears tells her to mind her own damn business, and she says, 'Who you think you is, you ain't my business? You better quit yo' dissin' 'cause I ain't takin' that kinda shit from nobody!'

He buys her another drink to mollify her and goes back to his interior concerns. Although the pain from the fight is minimal, his eyes are acting up and there is a feeling of dread imminence inside his head, an apprehension of a slight wrongness that can bloom into a fiery red presence. He is trying, by maintaining a certain poise, to resist it.

The hooker leans against him. Her breasts are big and sloppy soft and her perfume smells cheap like flowered Listerine, but her waist is slender and firm, and despite her apparent toughness, he senses that she is very young, new to the life. This barely hardened innocence makes him think of Amandla.

'Don't you wan' go upstairs, baby?' she says as her hand traces loops and circles along the inside of his thigh.

'We be there soon enough,' he says gruffly. 'We got all night.'

'Whoo!' She pulls back from him. 'I never seen a young man act so stern! 'Mind me of my daddy!' From her stagey tone, he realizes she is playing to the other patrons of the place, whom he cannot see, invisible as gods on their bar stools. Then she is rubbing against him again, saying, 'You gon' treat me like my daddy, honey? You gon' be hard on me?'

'Listen up,' he says quietly, putting a hand on her arm. 'Don't you be playin' these games. I'm payin' you good, so you just sit still and we'll have a couple drinks and talk a little bit. When the time comes, we'll go upstairs. Can you deal with that?'

He feels resentment in the tension of her arm. 'OK, baby,' she says with casual falsity. 'What you wan' talk about?'

Mariah Carey is having a vision of love, her sinewy falsetto going high into a gospel frequency, and Mears asks the hooker if she likes the song.

She shrugs. 'It's all right.'

'You know the words?'

'Uh-huh.'

'Sing it with me?'

'Say what?'

He starts to sing, and after a couple of seconds the hooker joins in. Her voice is slight and sugary but blends well with Mears' tenor. As they sing, her enthusiasm grows and Mears feels a frail connection forming between them. When the record ends, she giggles, embarrassed, and says, 'That was def, baby. You sing real good. You a musician?'

'Naw, just church stuff, you know.'

'Bobby Mears!' A man's voice brays out behind him, a hand falls heavily onto his shoulder. 'Goddamn, it is you! My fren', he saying, "Ain't that Bobby Mears over there?" and I said, "Shit, what he be doin' in here?"'

The man is huge, dark as a coal sack against the lesser darkness, and Mears has no clue to his identity.

'Yes, sir! Bobby "the Magician" Mears! I'm your biggest fan, no shit! I seen you fight a dozen times. And I ain't talkin' TV. I mean in person. Man, this is great! Can I get you a drink? Lemme buy you one. Hey, buddy! Give us another round over here, OK?'

''Nother draft, 'nother shot of the Gentleman,' says the

bartender in a singsong delivery as he pours. He picks up the hooker's glass and says with less flair, 'Vodka and coke.'

'Sister,' the man says to the hooker, 'I don't know what Bobby's been tellin' you, but you settin' next to one of the greatest fighters ever lived.'

The hooker says, 'You a fighter, baby?' and Mears, who has been seething at this interruption, starts to say it's time to leave, but the man talks through him.

'The boy was slick! I'm tellin' you. Slickest thing you ever seen with that jab of his. Like to kill Marvin Hagler. That old baldhead was one lucky nigger that night. Ain't it the truth, man?'

'Bullshit,' Mears says.

'Man's jus' bein' modest.'

'I ain't bein' modest. Hagler was hurtin' me from round one, and all I's doin' was tryin' to survive.' Mears digs a roll of bills from his pocket, peels a twenty from the top – the twenties are always on top; then the tens, then the fives. 'Anybody saw that fight and thinks Hagler was lucky don't know jack shit. Hagler was the best, and it don't make me feel no better 'bout not bein' the best, you comin' round and bullshittin' me.'

'Be cool, Bobby! All right, man? Be cool.'

The hooker caresses Mears' shoulders, his neck, and he feels the knots of muscle, like hard tumours. It would take a thousand left hooks to work out that tension, a thousand solid impacts to drain off the poisons of fear lodged there, and he experiences a powerful welling up of despair that seems connected to no memory or incident, no stimulus whatsoever, a kind of bottom emotion, one you would never notice unless the light and the temperature and the noise level, all the conditions, were just right. But it's there all the time, the tarry stuff that floors your soul. He tells the man he's sorry for having lashed out at him. He's tired, he says, got shit on his mind.

'Hey,' says the man, 'hey, it's not a problem, OK?'

There follows a prickly silence that ends when Aaron Neville comes on the jukebox. Mears goes away with the tune, with the singer's liquid shifts and drops, like the voice of a saxophone, and is annoyed once again when the man says, 'Who you fightin' next, Bobby? You got somethin' lined up?'

'Vederotta,' Mears says.

'The Heat, man? You fightin' the Heat? No shit! Hey, you better watch your ass with that white boy! I seen him fight Reggie Williams couple months back. Hit that man so hard, two his teeth come away stuck in the mouthpiece.'

Mears slides the twenty across the bar and says, 'Keep it' to the bartender.

'That's right,' says the man with apparent relish. 'That white boy ain't normal, you ax me. He jus' be livin' to fuck you up, know what I mean? He got somethin' wrong in his head.'

'Thanks for the drink,' Mears says, standing.

'Any time, Bobby, any time,' the man says as Mears lets the hooker lead him toward the stairs. 'You take my advice, man. Watch yourself with that Vederotta. That boy he gon' come hard, and you ain't no way slick as you used to be.'

Cold blue neon winks on and off in the window of Mears' room, a vague nebular shine that might be radiating from a polar beacon or a ghostly police car, and as the hooker undresses, he lies on the bed in his shorts and watches the light. It's the only thing he sees, just that chilly blue in a black field, spreading across the surface of the glass like some undersea thing, shrinking and expanding like the contractions of an icy blue heart. He has always been afraid before a fight, yet now he's afraid in a different way. Or maybe it's not the fear that's different, maybe it's his resistance to it that has changed. Maybe he's weaker, wearier. He is so accustomed to suppressing fear, however, that when he tries to examine it, it slithers away into the cracks of his soul and hides there, lurking, eyes aglow, waiting for its time. Vederotta. The man's name even sounds strong, like a foreign sin, an age-old curse.

'Ain't you wan' the lights on, honey?' asks the hooker. 'I wan' you be able see what you doin'.'

'I see you just fine,' he says. 'You come on lie down.'

A siren curls into the distance; two car horns start to blow in an impatient rhythm like brass animals angry at each other; smells of barbecue and gasoline drift in to overwhelm the odour of industrial cleaner.

Training, he thinks. Once he starts to train, he'll handle the fear. He'll pave it over with thousands of sit-ups, miles of running, countless combinations, and by fight night there'll be just enough left to motivate him.

The hooker settles onto the bed, lies on her side, leaning over him, her breasts spilling onto his chest and arm. He lifts one in his palm, squeezing its heft, and she makes a soft, pleased noise.

'Why you didn't tell me you famous?' she asks.

'I ain't famous.'

'Yeah, but you was.'

'What difference it make? Bein' famous ain't about nothin'.'

She moves her shoulders, making her breasts roll against him, and her hot, sweet scent seems to thicken. 'Jus' nice to know is all.' She runs a hand along his chest, his corded belly. 'Ain't you somepin',' she says, and then, 'How old're you, baby?'

'Thirty-two.'

He expects her to say, 'Thirty-two! Damn, baby. I thought you was twenty-five, you lookin' good.' But all she does is give a little *mmm* sound as if she's filing the fact away and goes on caressing him. By this he knows that the connection they were starting to make in the bar has held and she's going to be herself with him, which is what he wants, not some play-acting bitch who will let him turn her into Amandla, because he is sick and tired of having that happen.

She helps him off with his shorts and brings him all the way hard with her hand, then touches his cock to her breasts, lets it butt and slide against her cheek, takes it in her mouth for just seconds, like into warm syrup, her tongue swirling, getting his hips to bridge up from the mattress, wise and playful in her moves, and finally she comes astride him and says, 'I believe I'm ready for some of this, baby,' her voice burred, and she reaches for him, puts him where she needs it, and then her whole dark, sweet weight swings down slick and hot around him, and his neck arches, his mouth strains open and his head pushes back into the pillow, feeling as if he's dipped the back of his brain into a dark green pool, this ancient place with mossy-stone temples beneath the water and strange carvings and spirits gliding in and out the columns. When that moment passes, he finds she's riding him slow and deep and easy, not talking hooker trash, but fucking him like a young girl, her breath shaky and musical, hands braced on the pillow by his head, and he slides his hands around to cup her ass, to her back, pressing down so that her breasts graze and nudge his chest, and it's all going so right he forgets to think how good it is and gives himself over to the arc of his feelings and the steady, sinuous beat of her heart-filled body.

Afterward there is something shy and delicate between them, something he knows won't survive for long, maybe not even until morning, and maybe it's all false, maybe they have only played a deeper game, but if so, it's deep enough that the truth doesn't matter, and they are for now in that small room somewhere dark and green, the edge of that pool he dipped into for a second, a wood, sacred, with the calls of those strange metal beasts sounding in the distance from the desolate town. A shadow is circling beneath the surface of the pool, it's old, wrinkled, hard with evil, like a pale crocodile that's never been up into the light, but it's not an animal, not even a thought, it's just a name: Vederotta. He holds her tight, keeps two fingers pushed between her legs touching the heated damp of her, feeling her pulse there, still rapid and trilling, and he wants to know a little more about her, anything, just one thing, and when he whispers the only question he can think to ask, she wriggles around, holding his two fingers in place, turns her face to his chest and says her name is Arlene.

Training is like religion to Mears, the litanies of sparring, the penances of one-arm push-ups, the long retreats of his morning runs, the monastic breakfasts at four a.m., the vigils in the steam room during which he visualizes with the intensity of prayer what will happen in the ring, and as with a religion, he feels it simplifying him, paring him down, reducing his focus to a single consuming pursuit. On this occasion, however, he allows himself to be distracted and twice sleeps with Arlene. At first she tries to act flighty and brittle as she did in the bar, but when they go upstairs, that mask falls away and it is good for them again. The next night she displays no pretence whatsoever. They fuck wildly like lovers who have been long separated, and just before dawn they wind up lying on their sides, still joined, hips still moving sporadically. Mears' head is jangled and full of anxious incoherencies. He's worried about how he will suffer for this later in the gym and concerned by what is happening with Arlene. It seems he is being given a last sweetness, a young girl not yet hardened beyond repair, a girl who has some honest affection for him, who perhaps sees him as a means of salvation. This makes him think he is being prepared for something bad by God or whomever. Although he's been prepared for the worst for quite a while, now he wonders if the Vederotta fight will somehow prove to be worse than the worst, and frightened by this, he tells Arlene he can't see her again until after the fight. Being with her, he says, saps his strength and he needs all his strength for Vederotta. If she is the kind of woman who has hurt him in the past, he knows she will react badly, she will accuse him of trying to dump her, she will rave and screech and demand his attentions. And she does become angry, but when he explains that he is risking serious injury by losing his focus, her defensiveness – that's what has provoked her anger – subsides, and she pulls him atop her, draws up her knees and takes him deep, gluing him to her sticky thighs, and as the sky turns the colour of tin and delivery traffic grumbles in the streets, and a great clanking and screech of metal comes from the docks, and garbage trucks groan and whine as they tip Dumpsters into their maws like iron gods draining their goblets, she and Mears rock and thrust and grind, tightening their hold on each other as the city seems to tighten around them, winching up its loose ends, notch by notch, in order to withstand the fierce pressures of the waking world.

That afternoon at the gym, Leon takes Mears into the locker room and sits him on a bench. He paces back and forth, emitting an exhaust of cigar smoke, and tells Mears that the boxing commission will be no problem, the physical exam – like most commission physicals – is going to be a joke, no eye charts, nothing, just blood pressure and heart and basic shit like that. He paces some more, then says he's finished watching films of Vederotta's last four fights.

'Ain't but one way to fight him,' he says. 'Smother his punches, grab him, hold him, frustrate the son of a bitch. Then when he get wild and come bullin' in, we start to throw uppercuts. Uppercuts all night long. That's our only shot. Understand?'

'I hear you.'

'Man's strong.' Leon sighs as he takes a seat on the bench opposite Mears. 'Heavyweight strong. He gon' come at us from the bell and try to hurt us. He use his head, his elbows, whatever he gots. We can't let him back us up. We back up on this motherfucker, we goin' to sleep.'

There is more, Mears can feel it, and he waits patiently, picking at the wrappings on his hands while he listens to the slap and babble from the gym.

''Member that kid Tony Ayala?' Leon asks. 'Junior middle-weight 'bout ten years ago. Mean fuckin' kid, wound up rapin' some schoolteacher in Jersey. Big puncher. This Vederotta 'mind me of him. He knock Jeff Toney down and then he kick him. He hold up Reggie Williams 'gainst the ropes when the man out on his feet so he kin hit him five, six times more.' Leon pauses. 'Maybe he's too strong. Maybe we should pull out of this deal. What you think?'

Mears realizes that Leon is mainly afraid Vederotta will knock him into retirement, that his cut of the twenty thousand dollars will not compensate for a permanent loss of income. But the fact that Leon has asked what he thinks, that's new, that's a real surprise. He suspects that deep within that gross bulk, the pilot light of Leon's moral self, long extinguished, has been relit and he is experiencing a flicker of concern for Mears' well-being. Recognizing this, Mears is, for reasons he cannot fathom, less afraid.

'Ain't you listenin', man? I axed what you think.'

'Got to have that money,' Mears says.

Leon sucks on his cigar, spits. 'I don't know 'bout this,' he says, real doubt in his voice, real worry. 'I just don't know.'

Mears thinks about Leon, all the years, the lies, the petty betrayals and pragmatic loyalty, the confusion that Leon must be experiencing to be troubled by emotion at this stage of the relationship. He tries to picture who Leon is and conjures the image of something bloated and mottled washed up on a beach – something that would have been content to float and dream in the deep blue-green light, chewing on kelp, but would now have to heave itself erect and lumber unsightly through the bright, terrible days without solace or satisfaction. He puts a hand on the man's soft, sweaty back, feels the sick throb of his heart. 'I know you don't,' he says. 'But it's all right.'

The first time he meets Vederotta, it's the morning of the fight, at the weigh-in. Just as he's stepping off the scale, he is startled to spot him standing a few feet away, a pale, vaguely human shape cut in the middle by a wide band of black, the trunks. And a face. That's the startling thing, the thing that causes Mears to shift quickly away. It's the sort of face that appears when a fight is going badly, when he needs more fear in order to keep going, but it's never happened so early, before the fight even begins. And this one is different from the rest. Not a comic-book image slapped onto a human mould, it seems fitted just below the surface of the skin, below the false human face, rippling like something seen through a thin film of water. It's coal black, with sculpted cheeks and a flattened bump of a nose and a slit mouth and hooded eyes, an inner mask of black lustreless metal. From its eyes and mouth leaks a crumbling red glow so radiant it blurs the definition of the features. Mears recognizes it for the face of his secret pain, and he can only stare at it. Then Vederotta smiles, the slit opening wider to show the furnace glow within, and says in a dull, stuporous voice, a voice like ashes, 'You don't look so hot, man. Try and stay alive till tonight, will ya?' His handlers laugh and Leon curses them, but Mears, suddenly spiked with terror, can find no words, no solidity within himself on which to base a casual response. He lashes out at that evil, glowing face with a right hand, which Vederotta slips, and then everyone – handlers, officials, the press – is surging back and forth, pulling the two fighters apart, and as Leon hustles Mears away, saying, 'Fuck's wrong with you, man? You crazy?' he hears Vederotta shouting at him, more bellowing than shouting, no words, nothing intelligible, just the raving of the black beast.

Half an hour before the fight is scheduled to start, Mears is lying on a training table in the dressing room, alone, his wrapped hands folded on his belly. From the arena come intermittent announcements over the PA, the crowd booing one of the preliminary bouts, and some men are talking loudly outside his door. Mears scarcely registers any of this. He's trying to purge himself of fear but is not having much success. He believes his peculiar visual trick has revealed one of God's great killers, and that tonight the red seed of pain in his head will bloom and he will die, and nothing – no determined avowal, no life-affirming hope – will diminish that belief. He could back out of the fight, he could fake an injury of some sort, and he considers this possibility, but something – and it's not just pride – is pulling him onward. No matter whether or not that face he saw is real, there's something inhuman about Vederotta. Something evil and implacable. And stupid. Some slowness natural to sharks and demons. Maybe he's not a fate, a supernatural creature; maybe he's only malformed, twisted in spirit. Whatever, Mears senses his wrongness the way he would a change in the weather, not merely because of the mask but from a wealth of subtle yet undeniable clues. All these months of imagining beasts in the ring and now he's finally come up against a real one. Maybe the only real one there is. The one he always knew was waiting. Could be, he thinks, it's just his time. It's his time and he has to confront it. Then it strikes him that there may be another reason. It's as if he's been in training, sparring with the lesser beasts, Alligator Man, the Fang, Snakeman and the rest, in order to prepare for this bout. And what if there's some purpose to his sacrifice? What if he's supposed to do something out there tonight aside from dying?

Lying there, he realizes he's already positioned for the coffin, posed for eternity, and that recognition makes him roll up to his feet and begin his shadowboxing, working up a sweat. His sweat stinks of anxiety, but the effort tempers the morbidity of his thoughts.

A tremendous billow of applause issues from the arena, and not long thereafter, Leon pops in the door and says, 'Quick knockout, man. We on in five.' Then it goes very fast. The shuffling, bobbing walk along the aisle through the Wichita crowd, hearing shouted curses, focusing on that vast, dim tent of white light that hangs down over the ring. Climbing through the ropes, stepping into the resin box, getting his gloves checked a final time. It's all happening too quickly. He's being torn away from important details. Strands of tactics, sustaining memories, are being burned off him. He does not feel prepared. His belly knots and he wants to puke. He needs to see where he is, exactly where, not just this stretch of blue canvas that ripples like shallow water and the warped circles of lights suspended in blackness like an oddly geometric grouping of suns seen from outer space. The heat of those lights, along with the violent, murmurous heat of the crowd, it's sapping – it should be as bright as day in the ring, like noon on a tropic beach, and not this murky twilight reeking of Vaseline and concession food and fear. He keeps working, shaking his shoulders, testing the canvas with gliding footwork, jabbing and hooking. Yet all the while he's hoping the ring will collapse or Vederotta will sprain something, a power failure, anything to spare him. But when the announcer brays his weight, his record and name over the mike, he grows calm as if by reflex and submits to fate and listens to the boos and desultory clapping that follows.

'His opponent,' the announcer continues, 'in the black trunks with a red stripe, weighs in tonight at a lean and mean one hundred fifty-nine and one half pounds. He's undefeated and is currently ranked number one by both the WBC and WBA, with twenty-four wins, twenty-three by knockout! Let's have a great big prairie welcome for Wichita's favourite son, Toneee! The Heat! Ve-de-rot-taaaaa! Vederotta!'

Vederotta dances forward into the roar that celebrates him, arms lifted above his head, his back to Mears; then he turns, and as Leon and the cut man escort Mears to the centre of the ring for the instructions, Mears sees that menacing face again. Those glowing eyes.

'When I say "break",' the ref is saying, 'I want you to break clean. Case of a knockdown, go to a neutral corner and stay there till I tell ya to come out. Any questions?'

One of Vederotta's handlers puts in his mouthpiece, a piece of opaque plastic that mutes the fiery glow, makes it look liquid and obscene; gassy red light steams from beneath the black metal hulls that shade his eyes.

'OK,' says the ref. 'Let's get it on.'

Vederotta holds out his gloves and says something through his mouthpiece. Mears won't touch gloves with him, frightened of what this acquiescence might imply. Instead, he shoves him hard, and once again the handlers have to intervene. Screams from the crowd lacerate the air, and the ref admonishes him, saying, 'Gimme a clean fight, Bobby, or I'll disqualify ya.' But Mears is listening to Vederotta shouting fierce, garbled noises such as a lion might make with its mouth full of meat.

Leon hustles him back to the corner, puts in his mouthpiece and slips out through the ropes, saying, 'Uppercuts, man! Keep throwin' them uppercuts!' Then he's alone, that strangely attenuated moment between the instructions and the bell, longer than usual tonight because the TV camerman standing on the ring apron is having problems. Mears rolls his head, working out the kinks, shaking his arms to get them loose, and pictures himself as he must look from the cheap seats, a tiny dark figure buried inside a white pyramid. The image of Amandla comes into his head. She, too, is tiny. A doll in a blue robe, like a Madonna, she has that kind of power, a sweet, gentle idea, nothing more. And there's Arlene, whom he has never seen, of whom he knows next to nothing, African and voluptuous and mysterious like those big-breasted ebony statues they sell in the import stores. And Leon hunkered down at the corner of the ring, sweaty already, breath thick and quavery, peering with his pop eyes. Mears feels steadier and less afraid, triangulated by them: the only three people who have any force in his life. When he glances across the ring and finds that black death's head glaring at him, he is struck by something – he can see Vederotta. Since his eyes went bad, he's been unable to see his opponent until the man closes on him, and for that reason he circles tentatively at the beginning of each round, waiting for the figure to materialize from the murk, backing, letting his opponent come to him. Vederotta must know this, must have seen that tendency on film, and Mears thinks it may be possible to trick him, to start out circling and then surprise him with a quick attack. He turns, wanting to consult Leon, not sure this would be wise, but the bell sounds, clear and shocking, sending him forward as inexorably as a toy set in motion by a spark.

Less than ten seconds into the fight, goaded in equal measure by fear and hope, Mears feints a sidestep, plants his back foot and lunges forward behind a right that catches Vederotta solidly above the left eye, driving him into the ropes. Mears follows with a jab and two more rights before Vederotta backs him up with a wild flurry, and he sees that Vederotta has been cut. The cut is on the top of the eyelid, not big but in a bad place, difficult to treat. It shows as a fuming red slit in that black mask, like molten lava cracking open the side of a scorched hill. Vederotta rubs at the eye, holds up his glove to check for blood, then hurls himself at Mears, taking another right on the way in but managing to land two stunning shots under the ribs that nearly cave him in. From then on it's all downhill for Mears. Nobody, not Hagler or Hearns or Duran, has ever hit him with such terrible punches. His face is numb from Vederotta's battering jab and he thinks one of his back teeth may have been cracked. But the body shots are the worst. Their impact is the sort you receive in a car crash when the steering wheel or the dash slams into you. They sound like football tackles, they dredge up harsh groans as they sink deep into his sides, and he thinks he can feel Vederotta's fingers, his talons, groping inside the gloves, probing for his organs. With less than a minute to go in the round, a right hand to the heart drops him onto one knee. It takes him until the count of five to regain his breath, and he's up at seven, wobbly, dazed by the ache spreading across his chest. As Vederotta comes in, Mears wraps his arms about his waist and they go lurching about the ring, faces inches apart, Vederotta's arm barred under his throat, trying to push him off. Vederotta spews words in a goblin language, wet, gnashing sounds. He sprays fiery brimstone breath into Mears' face, acid spittle, the crack on his eyelid leaking a thin track of red phosphorus down a black cheek. When the ref finally manages to separate them, he tells Mears he's going to deduct a point if he keeps holding. Mears nods, grateful for the extra few seconds' rest, more grateful when he hears the bell.

Leon squirts water into Mears' mouth, tells him to rinse and spit. 'You cut him,' he says excitedly. 'You cut the motherfuck-er!'

'I know,' Mears says. 'I can see him.'

Leon, busy with the Enswell, refrains from comment, restrained by the presence of the cut man. 'Left eye,' he says, ignoring what Mears has told him. 'Throw that right. Rights and uppercuts. All night long. That's a bad cut, huh, Eddie?'

'Could be a winner,' the cut man says, 'we keep chippin' on it.'

Leon smears Vaseline on Mears' face. 'How you holdin' up?'

'He's hurtin' me. Everything he throws, he's hurtin' me.'

Leon tells him to go ahead and grab, let the ref deduct the fucking points, just hang in there and work the right. The crowd is buzzing, rumorous, and from this, Mears suspects that he may really have Vederotta in some trouble, but he's still afraid, more afraid than ever now that he has felt Vederotta's power. And as the second round begins, he realizes he's the one in trouble. The cut has turned Vederotta cautious. Instead of brawling, he circles Mears, keeping his distance, popping his jab, throwing an occasional combination, wearing down his opponent inch by inch, a pale, indefinite monster, his face sheathed in black metal, eyes burning like red suns at midnight. Each time Mears gets inside to throw his shots or grab, the price is high – hooks to the liver and heart, rights to the side of the neck, the hinge of the jaw. His face is lumping up. Near the end of the round, a ferocious straight right to the temple blinds him utterly in the left eye for several seconds. When the bell rings, he sinks onto the stool, legs trembling, heartbeat ragged. Exotic eye trash floats in front of him. His head's full of hot poison, aching and unclear. But oddly enough, that little special pain of his has dissipated, chased away by the same straight right that caused his temporary blackout.

The doctor pokes his head into the desperate bustle of the corner and asked him where he is, how he's doing. Mears says, 'Wichita' and 'OK.' When the ref asks him if he wants to continue, he's surprised to hear himself say, 'Yeah,' because he's been doing little other than wondering if it would be all right to quit. Must be some good reason, he thinks, or else you're one dumb son of a bitch. That makes him laugh.

'Fuck you doin' laughin'?' Leon says. 'We ain't havin' that much fun out there. Work on that cut! You ain't done diddly to that cut!'

Mears just shakes his head, too drained to respond.

The first minute of the third round is one of the most agonizing times of Mears' life. Vederotta continues his cautious approach, but he's throwing heavier shots now, head-hunting, and Mears can do nothing other than walk forward and absorb them. He is rocked a dozen times, sent reeling. An uppercut jams the mouthpiece edge-on into his gums and his mouth fills with blood. A hook to the ear leaves him rubber-legged. Two rights send spears of white light into his left eye and the tissue around the eye swells, reducing his vision to a slit. A low blow smashes the edge of his cup, drives it sideways against his testicles, causing a pain that brings bile into his throat. But Vederotta does not follow up. After each assault he steps back to admire his work. It's clear he's prolonging things, trying to inflict maximum damage before the finish. Mears peers between his gloves at the beast stalking him and wonders when that other little red-eyed beast inside his head will start to twitch and burn. He's surprised it hasn't already, he's taken so many shots.

When the ref steps in after a series of jabs, Mears thinks he's stopping the fight, but it's only a matter of tape unravelling from his left glove. The ref leads him into the corner to let Leon retape it. He's so unsteady, he has to grip the ropes for balance, and glancing over his shoulder, he sees Vederotta spit his mouthpiece into his glove, which he holds up like a huge red paw. He expects Vederotta to say something, but all Vederotta does is let out a maniacal shout. Then he reinserts the mouthpiece into that glowing red maw and stares at Mears, shaking his black and crimson head the way a bear does before it charges, telling him – Mears realizes – that this is it, there's not going to be a fourth round. But Mears is too wasted to be further intimidated, his fear has bottomed out, and as Leon fumbles with the tape, giving him a little more rest, his pride is called forth, and he senses again just how stupid Vederotta is, bone stupid, dog stupid, maybe just stupid and overconfident enough to fall into the simplest of traps. No matter what happens to him, Mears thinks, maybe he can do something to make Vederotta remember this night.

The ref waves them together, and Mears sucks it up, banishes his pain into a place where he can forget about it for a while and shuffles forward, presenting a picture of reluctance and tentativeness. When Vederotta connects with a jab, then a right that Mears halfway picks off with his glove, Mears pretends to be sorely afflicted and staggers back against the ropes. Vederotta's in no hurry. He ambles toward him, dipping his left shoulder, so sure of himself he's not even trying to disguise his punches, he's going to come with the left hook under, he's going to hurt Mears some more before he whacks him out. Mears peeks between his gloves, elbows tight to his sides, knowing he's got this one moment, waiting, the crowd's roar like a jet engine around him, the vicious, smirking beast planting himself, his shoulder dipping lower yet, his head dropping down and forward as he cocks the left, and it's then, right at that precise instant, when Vederotta is completely exposed, that Mears explodes from his defensive posture and throws the uppercut, aiming not at the chin or the nose, but at that red slit on the black eyelid. He lands the shot clean, feels the impact, and above the crowd noise he hears Vederotta shriek like a woman, sees him stumble into the corner, his head lowered, glove held to the damaged eye. Mears follows, spins him about and throws another shot that knocks Vederotta's glove aside, rips at the eye. The slit, it's torn open now, has become an inch-long gash, and that steaming, luminous red shit is flowing into the eye, over the dull black cheek and jaw, dripping onto his belly and trunks. Mears pops a jab, a right, then another jab, not hard punches – they don't have to be hard, just accurate – splitting Vederotta's guard, each landing on the gash, slicing the eyelid almost its entire length. Then the ref's arms wrap around him from behind and haul him back, throwing him into ring centre, where he stands, confused by this sudden cessation of violence, by this solitude imposed on him after all that brutal intimacy, as the doctor is called in to look at Vederotta's eye. He feels light and unreal, as if he's been shunted into a place where gravity is weaker and thought has no emotional value. The crowd has gone quiet and he hears the voice of Vederotta's manager above the babbling in the corner. Then a second voice shouting the manager down, saying, 'I can see the bone, Mick! I can see the goddamn bone!' And then – this is the most confusing thing of all – the ref is lifting his arm and the announcer is declaring, without enthusiasm, to a response of mostly silence and some scattered boos, that 'the referee stops the contest at a minute fifty-six seconds of the third round. Your winner by TKO: Bobby! The Magician! Mears!'

Mears' pain has returned, the TV people want to drag him off for an interview, Leon is there hugging him, saying, 'We kicked his ass, man! We fuckin' kicked his ass!' and there are others, the promoter, the nobodies, trying to congratulate him, but he pushes them aside, shoulders his way to Vederotta's corner. He has to see him, because this is not how things were supposed to play. Vederotta is sitting on his stool, someone smearing his cut with Avitene. His face is still visible, still that of the beast. Those glowing red eyes stare up at Mears, connect with the eye of pain in his head, and he wants there to be a transfer of knowledge, to learn that one day soon that pain will open wide and he will fall the way a fighter falls after one punch too many, disjointed, graceless, gone from the body. But no such transfer occurs, and he begins to suspect that something is not wrong, or rather that what's wrong is not what he suspected.

There's one thing he thinks he knows, however, looking at Vederotta, and while the handlers stand respectfully by, acknowledging his place in this ritual, Mears says, 'I was lucky, man. You a hell of a fighter. But that eye's never gon' be the same. Every fight they gon' be whacking at it, splittin' it open. You ain't gon' be fuckin' over nobody no more. You might as well hang 'em up now.'

As he walks away, as the TV people surround him, saying, 'Here's the winner, Bobby Mears' – and he wonders what exactly it is he's won – it's at that instant he hears a sound behind him, a gush of raw noise in which frustration and rage are commingled, both dirge and challenge, denial and lament, the final roar of the beast.

Two weeks after the fight he's sitting in the hotel bar with Arlene, staring into that infinite dark mirror, feeling lost, undefined, sickly, like there's a cloud between him and the light that shines him into being, because he's not sure when he's going to fight again, maybe never, he's so busted up from Vederotta. His eyes especially seem worse, prone to dazzling white spots and blackouts, though the pain deep in his head has subsided, and he thinks that the pain may have had something to do only with his eyes, and now that they're fading, it's fading, too, and what will he do if that's the case? Leon has been working with this new lightweight, a real prospect, and he hasn't been returning Mears' calls, and when the bartender switches on the TV and a rapper's voice begins blurting out his simple, aggressive rhymes, Mears gets angry, thoughts like gnats swarming around that old reeking nightmare shape in his head, that thing that may never have existed, and he pictures a talking skull on the TV shelf, with a stuffed raven and a coiled snake beside it. He drops a twenty on the counter and tells Arlene he wants to take a walk, a disruption of their usual routine of a few drinks, then upstairs. It bewilders her, but she says, 'OK, baby,' and off they go into the streets, where the Christmas lights are gleaming against the black velour illusion of night like green and red galaxies, as if he's just stepped into an incredible distance hung here and there with plastic angels filled with radiance. And people, lots of people brushing past, dark and shiny as beetles, scuttling along in this holy immensity, chattering their bright gibberish, all hustling toward mysterious crossroads where they stop and freeze into silhouettes against the streams of light, and Mears, who is walking very fast because walking is dragging something out of him, some old weight of emotion, is dismayed by their stopping, it goes contrary to the flow he wants to become part of, and he bursts through a group of shadows assembled like pilgrims by a burning river, and steps out, out and down – he's forgotten the kerb – and staggers forward into the traffic, into squealing brakes and shouts, where he waits for a collision he envisions as swift and ultimately stunning, luscious in its finality, like the fatal punch Vederotta should have known. Yet it never comes. Then Arlene, who has clattered up, unsteady in her high heels, hauls him back onto the sidewalk, saying, 'You tryin' to kill yo'self, fool?' And Mears, truly lost now, truly bereft of understanding, either of what he has done or why he's done it, stands mute and tries to find her face, wishes he could put a face on her, not a mask, just a face that would be her, but she's nowhere to be found, she's only perfume, a sense of presence. He knows she's looking at him, though.

'You sick, Bobby?' she asks. 'Ain't you gon' tell me what's wrong?'

How can he tell her that what's wrong is he's afraid he's not dying, that he'll live and go blind? How can that make sense?

And what does it say about how great a fool he's been? He's clear on nothing apart from that, the size of his folly.

'C'mon,' Arlene says with exasperation, taking his arm. 'I'm gon' cook you some dinner. Then you can tell me what's been bitin' yo' ass.'

He lets her steer him along. He's too dazed to make decisions. Too worried. It's funny, he thinks, or maybe funny's not the word, maybe it's sad that what's beginning to worry him is exactly the opposite of what was troubling him a few seconds before. What if she proves to be someone who'll stand by him no matter how bad things get, what if the pain in his head hasn't gone away, it's just dormant, and instead of viewing death as a solution, one he feared but came to rely on, he now comes to view it as something miserable and dread? The darkness ahead will be tricky to negotiate, and the simple trials of what he's already starting to characterize as his old life seem, despite blood and attrition, unattainably desirable. But no good thing can arise from such futile longing, he realizes. Loving Amandla has taught him that.

Between two department stores, two great, diffuse masses of white light, there's an alley, a doorway, a dark interval of some sort, and as they pass, Mears draws Arlene into it and pulls her tightly to him, needing a moment to get his bearings. The blackness of street and sky is so uniform, it looks as if you could walk a black curve up among the blinking red and green lights, and as Arlene's breasts flatten against him, he feels like he is going high, like it feels when the man in the tuxedo tells you that you've won and the pain is washed away by perfect exhilaration and sweet relief. Then, as if jolted forward by the sound of a bell, he steps out into the crowds, becoming part of them, just another fool with short money and bad health and God knows what kind of woman trouble, who in another time might have been champion of the world.